文評集粹讀本
Selected Readings in Literary Reviews
漢英對照（Chinese-English）

ⓒ 著者—林明理（Dr. Lin Ming-Li）
ⓒ 譯者—張智中（Prof. Zhang Zhizhong）

天空數位圖書出版

著者簡介
- About the Author & Poet -

　　學者詩人林明理博士（1961-　），臺灣雲林縣人，法學碩士、榮譽文學博士。她曾任教於大學，是位詩人評論家，擅長繪畫及攝影，著有詩集，散文、詩歌評論等文學專著 39 本書，包括在義大利合著的譯詩集 4 本。其詩作被翻譯成法語、西班牙語、義大利語、俄語及英文等多種,作品發表於報刊及學術期刊等已達 2400 篇。中國學刊物包括《南京師範大學文學院學報》等多篇。

　　Dr. Lin Mingli (1961-　)，poet and scholar, born in Yunlin County, Taiwan, master of law, honorary Ph. D. in literature. She once taught at a university and is a poetry critic, and she is good at painting and photography. She is the author of 39 literary books, including poetry collections, prose, and poetry reviews, as well as a collection of translated poems co-authored and published in Italy. Her poems have been translated into French, Spanish, Italian, Russian and English, etc., and over 2,400 poems and articles have been published in newspapers and academic journals.

文評集粹讀本
-Selected Readings in Literary Reviews-

©林明理專書 monograph、義大利出版的中英譯詩合著
Chinese-English Poetry Co-author published in Italy
© Lin Ming-Li's monographs and co-authored Chinese-English Poetry collections published in Italy

1. 《秋收的黃昏》*The evening of autumn*。高雄市：春暉出版社，2008。ISBN 978-986-695-045-2
2. 《夜櫻－林明理詩畫集》*Cherry Blossoms at Night*。高雄市：春暉出版社，2009。ISBN 978-986-695-068-9
3. 《新詩的意象與內涵－當代詩家作品賞析》*The Imagery and Connetation of New Poetry－A Collection of Critical Poetry Analysis*。臺北市：文津出版社，2010。ISBN 978-957-688-913-0
4. 《藝術與自然的融合－當代詩文評論集》*The Fusion Of Art and Nature*。臺北市：文史哲出版社，2011。ISBN 978-957-549-966-2
5. 《山楂樹》*Hawthorn Poems* by Lin Mingli（林明理詩集）。臺北市：文史哲出版社，2011。ISBN 978-957-549-975-4
6. 《回憶的沙漏》*Sandglass Of Memory*（中英對照譯詩集）英譯：吳鈞。臺北市：秀威出版社，2012。ISBN 978-986-221-900-3
7. 《湧動著一泓清泉－現代詩文評論》*A Gushing Spring-A Collection Of Comments On Modern Literary Works*。臺北市：文史哲出版社，2012。ISBN 978-986-314-024-5
8. 《清雨塘》*Clear Rain Pond*（中英對照譯詩集）英譯：吳鈞。臺北市：文史哲出版社，2012。ISBN 978-986-314-076-4
9. 《用詩藝開拓美－林明理讀詩》*Developing Beauty Though The Art Of Poetry－Lin Mingli On Poetry*。臺北市：秀威出版社，2013。ISBN 978-986-326-059-2
10. 《海頌－林明理詩文集》*Hymn To the Ocean*（poems and Essays）。臺北市：文史哲出版社，2013。ISBN 978-986-314-119-8
11. 《林明理報刊評論 1990-2000》*Published Commentaries 1990-2000*。文史哲出版社，2013。ISBN 978-986-314-155-6
12. 《行走中的歌者－林明理談詩》*The Walking singer－Ming-Li Lin On Poetry*。臺北市：文史哲出版社，2013。ISBN 978-986-314-156-3

13. 《山居歲月》Days in the Mountains（中英對照譯詩集）英譯：吳鈞。臺北市：文史哲出版社，2015。ISBN 978-986-314-252-2
14. 《夏之吟》Summer Songs（中英法譯詩集）。英譯：馬為義（筆名：非馬）（Dr. William Marr）。法譯：阿薩納斯·薩拉西（Athanase Vantchev de Thracy）。法國巴黎：索倫紫拉文化學院（The Cultural Institute of Solenzara），2015。ISBN 978-2-37356-020-6
15. 《默喚》Silent Call（中英法譯詩集）。英譯：諾頓·霍奇斯（Norton Hodges）。法譯：阿薩納斯·薩拉西（Athanase Vantchev de Thracy）。法國巴黎：索倫紫拉文化學院（The Cultural Institute of Solenzara），2016。ISBN 978-2-37356-022-0
16. 《林明理散文集》Lin Ming Li's Collected essays。臺北市：文史哲出版社，2016。ISBN 978-986-314-291-1
17. 《名家現代詩賞析》Appreciation of the work of Famous Modern Poets。臺北市：文史哲出版社，2016。ISBN 978-986-314-302-4
18. 《我的歌 My Song》，法譯：Athanase Vantchev de Thracy 中法譯詩集。臺北市：文史哲出版社，2017。ISBN 978-986-314-359-8
19. 《諦聽 Listen》，中英對照詩集，英譯：馬為義（筆名：非馬）(Dr. William Marr)，臺北市：文史哲出版社，2018。ISBN 978-986-314-401-4
20. 《現代詩賞析》，Appreciation of the work of Modern Poets，臺北市：文史哲出版社，2018。ISBN 978-986-314-412-0
21. 《原野之聲》Voice of the Wilderness，英譯：馬為義（筆名：非馬）(Dr. William Marr)，臺北市：文史哲出版社，2019。ISBN 978-986-314-453-3
22. 《思念在彼方　散文暨新詩》，Longing over the other side（prose and poetry），臺北市：文史哲出版社，2020。ISBN 978-986-314-505-9
23. 《甜蜜的記憶（散文暨新詩）》，Sweet memories（prose and poetry），臺北市：文史哲出版社，2021。ISBN 978-986-314-555-4
24. 《詩河（詩評、散文暨新詩）》，The Poetic River（Poetry review, prose and poetry），臺北市：文史哲出版社，2022。ISBN 978-986-314-603-2
25. 《庫爾特·F·斯瓦泰克，林明理，喬凡尼·坎皮西詩選》（中英對照）Carmina Selecta (Selected Poems) by Kurt F. Svatek, Lin Mingli, Giovanni Campisi，義大利：Edizioni Universum（埃迪采恩尼大學），宇宙出版社，2023.01。

26. 《紀念達夫尼斯和克洛伊》(中英對照)詩選 In memory of Daphnis and Chloe，作者：Renza Agnelli，Sara Ciampi，Lin Mingli 林明理，義大利：Edizioni Universum（埃迪采恩尼大學），宇宙出版社，書封面，林明理畫作（聖母大殿），2023.02。
27. 《詩林明理古今抒情詩一六〇首》(漢英對照) Parallel Reading of 160 Classical and New Chinese Lyrical Poems (Chinese-English)，英譯：張智中，臺北市：文史哲出版社，2023.04。ISBN 978-986-314-637-7
28. 《愛的讚歌》(詩評、散文暨新詩) Hymn Of Love (Poetry review, prose and poetry)，臺北市：文史哲出版社，2023.05。ISBN 978-986-314-638-4
29. 《埃內斯托・卡漢，薩拉・錢皮，林明理和平詩選》(義英對照)(Italian-English)，Carmina Selecta (Selected Poems) by Ernesto Kahan, Sara Ciampi , Lin Mingli Peace-Pace，義大利：Edizioni Universum（埃迪采恩尼大學），宇宙出版社，2023.11。ISBN 978-889-980-379-7
30. 《祈禱與工作》，中英義詩集，"Ora Et Labora" Trilogia di Autori Trilingue: Italiano, Cinese, Inglese 作者的三語三部曲：義大利語、中文、英語 Trilingual Trilogy of Authors: Italian, Chinese, English，作者：奧內拉・卡布奇尼 Ornella Cappuccini，非馬 William Marr，林明理 Lin Mingli，義大利，宇宙出版社，2024.06。
31. 《名家抒情詩評賞》(漢英對照) Appraisal of Lyric Poems by Famous Artists，張智中教授英譯，臺北市：文史哲出版社，2024.06。ISBN 978-986-314-675-9
32. 《山的沉默》Silence of the Mountains，散文集，臺北市：文史哲出版社，2024.09。ISBN 978-986-314-685-8
33. 《宋詩明理接千載──古今抒情詩三百首》(漢英對照) Parallel Reading of 300 Ancient and Modern Chinese Lyrical Poems (Chinese-English)，臺中市：天空數位圖書出版，2024.10，ISBN 978-626-7576-00-7
34. 《元詩明理接千載──古今抒情詩三百首》(漢英對照) Parallel Reading of 300 Ancient and Modern Chinese Lyrical Poems (Chinese-English) :Jin, Yuan, and Ming Dynasties，臺中市：天空數位圖書出版，2024.11，ISBN 978-626-7576-02-1，ISBN 978-626-7576-03-8（彩圖版）

35. 《清詩明理思千載——古今抒情詩三百首》（漢英對照）*Parallel Reading of 300 Ancient and Modern Chinese Lyrical Poems: Qing Dynasty (Chinese-English)*，臺中市：天空數位圖書出版，2025.01，ISBN 978-626-7576-08-3，ISBN 978-626-7576-09-0（彩圖版）
36. 《唐詩明理接千載——古今抒情詩三百首》（漢英對照）*Parallel Reading of 300 Ancient and Modern Chinese Lyrical Poems: Tang Dynasty (Chinese-English)*，臺中市：天空數位圖書出版，2025.02，ISBN 978-626-7576-10-6
37. 《漢魏六朝接明理——古今抒情詩三百首》（漢英對照）*Parallel Reading of 300 Ancient and Modern Chinese Lyrical Poems: Han, Wei and Six Dynasties (Chinese-English)*，臺中市：天空數位圖書出版，2025.03，ISBN 978-626-7576-12-0，ISBN 978-626-7576-11-3（彩圖版）
38. 《星野（新詩、散文和評論）》*The field under the stars (poems and prose & Essays)*，臺中市：天空數位圖書出版，2025.04，ISBN 978-626-7576-13-7，ISBN 978-626-7576-14-4（彩圖版）
39. 《文評集粹讀本》（漢英對照）*Selected Readings in Literary Reviews (Chinese-English)*，臺中市：天空數位圖書出版，2025.06，ISBN 978-626-7576-18-2，ISBN 978-626-7576-19-9（精裝本）

譯者簡介
- About the Author & Translator -

　　張智中，天津市南開大學外國語學院教授、博士研究生導師、翻譯系主任，中國翻譯協會理事，中國英漢語比較研究會典籍英譯專業委員會副會長，天津師範大學跨文化與世界文學研究院兼職教授，世界漢學·文學中國研究會理事兼英文秘書長，天津市比較文學學會理事，第五屆天津市人民政府學位委員會評議組成員、專業學位教育指導委員會委員，國家社科基金專案通訊評審專家和結項鑒定專家，天津外國語大學中央文獻翻譯研究基地兼職研究員，《國際詩歌翻譯》季刊客座總編，《世界漢學》英文主編，《中國當代詩歌導讀》編委會成員，中國當代詩歌獎評委等。已出版編、譯、著 120 餘部，發表學術論文 130 餘篇，曾獲翻譯與科研多種獎項。漢詩英譯多走向國外，獲國際著名詩人和翻譯家的廣泛好評。譯詩觀：但為傳神，不拘其形，散文筆法，詩意內容；將漢詩英譯提高到英詩的高度。

譯者簡介

Zhang Zhizhong is professor, doctoral supervisor and dean of the Translation Department of the School of Foreign Studies, Nankai University which is located in Tianjin; meanwhile, he is director of Translators' Association of China, vice chairman of the Committee for English Translation of Chinese Classics of the Association for Comparative Studies of English and Chinese, part-time professor of Cross-Culture & World Literature Academy of Tianjin Normal University, director and English secretary-general of World Sinology Literary China Seminar, director of Tianjin Comparative Literature Society, member of Tianjin Municipal Government Academic Degree Committee, member of Tianjin Municipal Government Professional Degree Education Guiding Committee, expert for the approval and evaluation of projects funded by the National Social Science Foundation of China, part-time researcher at the Central Literature Translation Research Base of Tianjin Foreign Studies University, guest editor of *Rendition of International Poetry*, English editor-in-chief of *World Sinology*, member of the editing board of *Guided Reading Series in Contemporary Chinese Poetry*, and member of the Board for Contemporary Chinese Poetry Prizes. He has published more than 120 books and 130 academic papers, and he has won a host of prizes in translation and academic research. His English translation of Chinese poetry is widely acclaimed throughout the world, and is favorably reviewed by international poets and translators. His view on poetry translation: spirit over form, prose enjambment to rewrite Chinese poetry into sterling English poetry.

推薦序
- Recommendation as a Preface -

　　有人說：文學創作比文學評論難，因文學創作必須掌握創作的技巧，尤其是遣詞用字的貼切與傳神，更需才學的深度，且要符合格律要求，故有一定的難度；而文學評論，僅就作品的文字義，加以評論即可，沒有創作的技巧、貼切、傳神，以及格律等的要求，顯然容易許多。

　　有人說：文學評論比文學創作難，因文學評論必須懂得文學創作必備的要件，以及評論的學理而加以應用，才有能力評論作品，顯然有一定的難度；而文學創作僅就個人情感加以抒發，並符合格律要求即可，故容易許多。

　　學術論文與文學創作，本截然不同的領域，也有各自不同的格律，要把兩者融會貫通並不容易。林明理是文學創作的詩人，也是跨越學術論文與文學創作的評論家，不管是創作難或是評論難，對詩人言，皆能運用自如，好無澀感。著有詩集、散文，以及詩歌評論等 39 本書，是一位多產的作家，由該等著作可看出，詩人兩者兼具的才華。

　　《文評集粹讀本》的評論極廣，盡括：學術論文與文學創作兩大類。前者包含：詩論、文論；後者包含：詩評、文評等作品。其中，當以評論周世輔大師的《回憶錄》，最令人讚賞，大師是吾輩所景仰的學者，一本《中國哲學史》成為哲學領域必讀的教材，也是教材中的圭臬。從周氏兄弟的成就與學養，可見其父母的教養，是為家庭教育的楷模。

推薦序

　　《周世輔回憶錄》非一般僅追憶過往的雲煙，它的內容多元，包含有：求學過程、從政經歷、教學研究、養育子女等的生活回顧，以至縱情山水話樂遊及詩作等的書寫。內容雖多元，然對林明理卻能一氣呵成，揮灑成章，文筆質樸，不著浮華。詩人善於直抒胸臆的白描手法，直接將感觸付諸於筆墨，而能隨流賦形，將文字之應用推至一定的高度，雖不是字字珠璣，然有一定的水準，誠屬難得。今拜讀大作，覺得有收藏價值，值得慢慢品味。當然！文中缺失，在所難免，但瑕不掩瑜。更何況！推薦序只說好不說壞，故本人樂於推薦。賦詩一首，以表讀後感！

《文評》讀後感

雙語紛飛，跨國界；
杏壇風騷，捨其誰。
畫龍點睛，龍飛去；
文海掀起，千堆雪。

國立雲林科技大學漢學研究所退休教授
天空出版社社長
蔡輝振　謹識於臺中望日臺
2025.06.12

Some say that literary writing is more difficult than literary criticism, because literary writing is indispensable with the skills of writing, especially the appropriateness and vividness of the words, in addition to the writer's talent and learning; and it must meet the requirements of rhythm, hence the difficulties. Literary criticism is comment on the literal meaning of the work, without the requirements of creative skills, appropriateness, vividness, and rhythm, so it is much easier.

Some say that literary criticism is more difficult than literary writing, because literary criticism entails the necessary elements of literary writing and the theory of criticism as well as its application, hence the difficulties. Literary writing only expresses personal emotions to meet the requirements of rhythm, which is much easier.

Literary criticism, as academic papers, and literary writing fall into completely different fields, and it is difficult to achieve mastery through a comprehensive study of the two. Lin Ming-Li is a poet of literary creation and a critic who crosses the border of academic papers and literary writing. In spite of difficulties in literary writing and in literary criticism, she can handle it with ease and adeptness. Lin is a prolific writer who has published 39 books, including poetry collections, essays, and poetry reviews, which shows the author's talent.

推薦序

Selected Readings in Literary Reviews is an extensive work, covering two categories: academic papers and literary writing. The former includes poetry theory and literary theory; the latter includes poetry reviews, literary reviews and other works. Among them, the review of Master Zhou Shifu's *Memoirs* is the most admirable. Zhou, as a master universally admired by this generation, is famous particularly for his book *A History of Chinese Philosophy*, which is a must-read textbook in the field of philosophy. From the achievements and academic accomplishments of the Zhou brothers, it can be seen that their parents' cultivation is a model of family education.

Memoirs of Zhou Shifu is not simply a recollection of the past events. Its content is diverse, including a review of life during the study process, political experience, teaching research, raising children, etc., as well as the writing of touring the landscapes, leisure travels and poems. In spite of the diverse content, Lin Ming-Li can write it at one stretch, in a simple style, and without any pomp. The poet is good at expressing her feelings directly in plain language, and can directly put her feelings into writing, and can give shape to the flow, pushing the application of words to a certain height. Although not every word in her writing is a pearl, the writing has achieved a certain level, which is admirable. After reading, I think it is worth collecting and savoring slowly. Of course, inevitable are some shortcomings in the text, which fail to obscure the merits. And, it is a common practice that in a preface, the author only compliments, which gladdens me, hence a poem:

Inspired Upon Reading This Book

Bilingual, across the borders;
Literary pieces excel, peerless.
The finishing touch touches readers;
A sea of literature, piles of snow.

Tsai Huei-Ching
Retired Professor, Institute of Sinology,
National Yunlin University of Science and Technology
President of Sky Digital Books
Written respectfully at the Wangri Terrace in Taichung
June 12, 2025.

目錄
- Contents -

01 一泓幽隱的飛瀑
——淺釋魯迅詩歌的意象藝術
A Tranquil Expanse of Waterfall: An Interpretation of the Imagerial Art of Lu Xun's Poetry ·················19

02 論丁旭輝的《台灣現代詩中的老莊身影與道家美學實踐》
On Ting Hsu-Hui's *The Influences of Lao-tzu & Chuang-tzu and Taoist Aesthetic Practices in Taiwanese Modern Poetry* ···44

03 兼備學術性和應用性的完美融合
——評《淮劇藝術通論》
Perfect Fusion of Academic and Practical Aspects: Comment on *General Theory of Huai Opera Art* ·················54

04 略談《魯拜新註》英譯本
On the English translations of *New Notes on Rubaiyat* ·········65

05 細讀張智中的一本書
Close Reading of a Book by Zhang Zhizhong ···············69

06 評蔡輝振的《魯迅小說研究》
Comment on Tsai Hueicheng's *Studies of the Novels by Lu Xun* ·················73

07 試論《周世輔回憶錄》的文學價值
On the Literary Value of *Memoirs of Zhou Shifu* ···············91

08 論周夢蝶詩中的道家美學
——以〈逍遙遊〉、〈六月〉二詩為例
On the Taoist Aesthetics in Zhou Mengdie's Poems: Taking the Poems "Free Wandering" and "June" as Examples ···97

09 簡論吳開晉詩歌的藝術思維
On Wu Kaijin's Artistic Thinking in Poetry ·················· 115

10 禪悅中的慈悲——讀星雲大師《合掌人生》
Compassion in Zen Bliss: Reading Master Hsing Yun's
Life of Praying with Hands Crossed ··············· 132

11 從孤獨中開掘出詩藝之花
——淺釋《艾蜜莉・狄金生詩選》
The Flower of Poetry from Loneliness: On *The Selected Poems of Emily Dickinson* ················· 137

12 風中銀樹碧　雨後天虹新——淺釋鄭愁予的詩三首
Trees Silver in the Wind, a New Rainbow After the Rain:
On the three poems by Zheng Chouyu ·············· 156

13 夜讀鍾玲詩集《霧在登山》
Reading Zhong Ling's Poetry Collection *The Mist Is Climbing the Mountain* at Night ················ 163

14 夜讀沈鵬詩
Reading Shen Peng's Poems at Night ·············· 174

15 夜讀《成就的祕訣：金剛經》
Night Reading *The Secret of Success: Diamond Sutra* ········· 183

16 夜讀胡爾泰《落羽松下的沉思》
Night Reading Hu Ertai's *Meditations Under the Fallen Cypress* ··················· 188

17 陳滿銘與《意象學廣論》研究述評
Review of Chen Manming and *Extensive Theory of Imagery* ·· 193

18 一隻慨然高歌的靈鳥——讀普希金詩
A Soul Bird Sings With Deep Feeling: Reading Alexander Pushkin's poetry ················· 201

19	杜國清詩歌的意象節奏 The Image Rhythm of Du Guoqing's Poems⋯⋯⋯⋯⋯	218
20	時空的哲人——淺析林亨泰的詩歌藝術 Space-time Philosopher: Brief Analysis of Lin Hengtai's Poetic Art ⋯⋯⋯⋯⋯⋯⋯⋯⋯⋯⋯⋯⋯⋯⋯⋯⋯⋯⋯	230
21	崇高的樸素——讀《高準游踪散紀》 Sublime Simplicity: Reading *Gao Zhun's Travel Notes*⋯⋯	246
22	陳義海詩歌的思想藝術成就 The Ideological and Artistic Achievements of Chen Yihai's Poetry⋯⋯⋯⋯⋯⋯⋯⋯⋯⋯⋯⋯⋯⋯⋯⋯⋯⋯⋯⋯⋯	256
23	尋找恬淡中的感性——以《魯迅圖傳》為視角 Seeking Sensibility in Tranquility: From the Perspective of *Lu Xun's Illustrated Biography*⋯⋯⋯⋯⋯⋯⋯⋯⋯⋯⋯⋯	271
24	評吳鈞的《魯迅詩歌翻譯傳播研究》 Comments on Wu Jun's *A Study of the Translation and Communication of Lu Xun's Poems*⋯⋯⋯⋯⋯⋯⋯⋯⋯⋯	282
25	簡論許達然詩的通感 On the Synaesthesia in Xu Daran's Poems⋯⋯⋯⋯⋯⋯⋯	289
26	簡論非馬的散文創作 ——讀《不為死貓寫悼歌》有感 A Brief Analysis of William Marr's Creative Essay Writing: On reading *I Will Never Write a Dirge for a Dead Cat*⋯⋯	304
27	讀東行詩集《水果之詩》 Reading Dong Xing's Poetry Collection *Poems of Fruits*⋯⋯	315
28	生命風景的畫冊——讀李若鶯詩集《謎‧事件簿》 A Picture Album of the Scenery of Life: Reading Li Ruoying's Poetry Collection *Mystery Incident Book*⋯⋯	324

29 讀《廣域圖書館》
——兼述顧敏與圖書館管理的理論與實務
Reading *Wide Area Library*: Discussing Karl Ku and the
Theory and Practice of Library Management ················· 333

30 一隻勇毅的飛鷹——讀楊宗翰《隱於詩》
A Courageous Eagle: Reading Yang Zonghan's *Hidden in
Poetry* ··· 346

31 《華痕碎影》中蘊含的魯迅審美思維
Lu Xun's Aesthetic Thoughts in *Bits & Pieces of Memories* ·· 352

32 評黃淑貞《以石傳情——談廟宇石雕意象及其美感》
Comments on Huang Shuzhen's *Using Stone to Express
Emotions: On the Imagery and Aesthetics of Temple Stone
Sculptures* ·· 358

01 一泓幽隱的飛瀑——淺釋魯迅詩歌的意象藝術
A Tranquil Expanse of Waterfall: An Interpretation of The Imagerial Art of Lu Xun's Poetry

> **摘要 Abstract**
>
> 魯迅本質上是個詩人，他的詩歌在一定程度上記述著一生的哲思與境遇。他的詩歌絕不是直白的，而是內含著豐富的意象；挖掘魯迅詩歌的意象，不僅對理解魯迅詩歌的深意，而且對現代詩歌的繁榮，都具有普遍的意義。
>
> Lu Xun, essentially, is a poet. His poetry in a certain degree records his philosophical thinking as well as his life circumstances, and has an important impact on the development of contemporary history.
>
> **關鍵詞**：魯迅、詩歌、意象藝術、白話詩、舊體詩。
> **Keywords:** Lu Xun, poetry, imagerial art, traditional poetry.

魯迅在中國近代史上占有獨特的地位，被廣泛認為是古今中外最偉大的文史學家、翻譯家、思想家之一；其詩文橫溢，內含哲思，用意深邃，語言幽默，諷刺精妙，對於五四運動以後的中國文學產生深刻的影響。魯迅本質上是個詩人，他的詩歌，反對封建主義思想的束縛，在一定程度上記述著一生的哲思與境遇；具有新鮮活潑的思想，閃爍著人文主義思想的光輝；內含著豐富的意象，給人無限遐想的空間。

一、魯迅白話詩中的意象

在五四思潮引起的白話文運動中，魯迅陸續創作出版了《吶喊》《墳》《仿徨》《野草》《朝花夕拾》等作品，表現出知識份子的精英意識和徹底的民主主義的思想特色。當時魯迅滿懷激情和信心，寫了大量白話詩，表現了廣闊、深刻、複雜的社會內容，同時也創設了豐富的意象。

先看白話詩《夢》：

> 很多的夢，趁黃昏起哄。
> 前夢才擠卻大前夢時，後夢又趕走了前夢。
> 去的前夢黑如墨，在的後夢墨一般的黑；
> 去的、在的彷彿都在說：
> 「看我真好顏色。」
> 顏色許好，暗裡不知；
> 而且不知道，說話的是誰？
> 暗裡不知，身熱頭痛。
> 你來你來，明白的夢！[1]

　　這首詩歌的形象化手法，既是現實社會、人生狀態的真實寫照，也是魯迅與「夢」進行對語交流。這些帶有喚醒的呼聲和心理，表現出黑暗中國的許多沉睡的人們被封建專制社會的扭曲，表現出其內心的焦慮；面對當時軍閥官僚作風，詩人以宏大的氣勢塑造出站起來的時代兒女改天換地的大氣魄。這與古典詩歌中的寧靜、平和形成鮮明的對照；意象帶有幽深、悲憤與尋找光明之窗的渴望，也打著十分鮮明的民族精神印記。

　　再看白話詩〈愛之神〉[2]。這首詩不是浪漫式的直抒或宣洩，而是魯迅面對瞬間的愛情陶醉，故意造成小愛神丘比特形象超現實的、富有奇幻色彩的諧趣，獨具愛情審美價值的原素：

> 一個小娃子，展開翅子在空中，
> 一手搭箭，一手張弓，
> 不知怎麼一下，一箭射著前胸。
> 「小娃子先生，謝你胡亂栽培！
> 但得告訴我：我應該愛誰？」
> 娃子著慌，搖頭說，「唉！
> 你是還有心胸的人，竟也說這宗話。
> 你應該愛誰，我怎麼知道。
> 總之我的箭是放過了！
> 你要是愛誰，便沒命的去愛他；
> 你要是誰也不愛，也可以沒命的去自己死掉。」

---

[1] 《夢》和《愛之神》、《桃花》等三首最初發表於1918年5月《新青年》第四卷第五號，署名唐俟後收入《集外集》。

[2] 本篇最初發表於1918年5月15日《新青年》第四卷第五號，署名唐俟。

在這裡，詩人毫無遲疑地提出了形象化的詰問：「你應該愛誰，我怎麼知道。」，將詩思推上了人生哲理的高度：人生總是有限的，愛要及時，否則稍縱即逝是無可避免的。

白話詩〈桃花〉（1918年5月）則是優秀的諷刺詩。詩人不但用語巧妙，而且假托了主題對現實社會中某些「文人相輕」的生活方式和對狂妄野心者的嘲弄：

春雨過了，太陽又很好，隨便走到園中。
桃花開在園西，李花開在園東。
我說，「好極了！桃花紅，李花白。」
（沒說，桃花不及李花白。）
桃花可是生了氣，滿面漲作「楊妃紅」。
好小子！真了得！竟能氣紅了面孔。
我的話可並沒得罪你，你怎的便漲紅了面孔！
唉！花有花道理，我不懂。

從思想上說，詩人用調侃的語氣寫下對傳統封建意識的背叛；詩中的物象對答是虛幻的，審美與審醜瞬間感受的矛盾，也真實地表現了魯迅的憂患和複雜心靈。

魯迅的白話詩，不僅標示著一般意義上的現實主義回歸，而且更是現實主義的豐富和深化。如這首〈他們的花園〉：

小娃子，卷螺髮，
銀黃面龐上還有微紅，——
看他意思是正要活；
走出破大門，望見鄰家：他們大花園裡，有許多好花。
用盡小心機，得了一朵百合；又白又光明，像才下的雪。
好生拿了回家，映著面龐，分外添出血色。
蒼蠅繞花飛鳴，亂在一屋子裡——
「偏愛這不乾淨花，是糊塗孩子！」
忙看百合花，卻已有幾點蠅矢。
看不得；捨不得。
瞪眼看天空，他更無話可說。
說不出話，想起鄰家：
他們大花園裡，有許多好花。

詩歌中所設置的那些景物，與時下有些文學家如花園的群花急於嘩眾取寵或自命清高的詩人挺身入世對比，叫人覺得滑稽可笑；也看得見魯迅幽默的一面，給人一種清新悅目的審美感受。

　　〈人與時〉這首詩的基調是直率而明朗的，象徵意味也很濃郁：

　　　一人說，將來勝過現在。
　　　一人說，現在遠不及從前。
　　　一人說，什麼？
　　　時道，你們都侮辱我的現在。
　　　從前好的，自己回去。
　　　將來好的，跟我前去。
　　　這說什麼的，
　　　我不和你說什麼。

　　魯迅的痛苦與希望是渾成的一片，其救國救民的夢想，不僅成為一個勇敢嘗試的榜樣；對時間的形象的描繪，有可感性。人與時間之間，外表上是分離的；但詩人天上地下，過去未來，馳騁想像，在心靈深處應是相通的。另一首白話詩〈他〉（1919年），詩裡反映了魯迅在災難歲月的孤悶情懷：

　　　一
　　　「知了」不要叫了，
　　　他在房中睡著；
　　　「知了」叫了，刻刻心頭記著。
　　　太陽去了，「知了」住了，——
　　　還沒有見他，
　　　待打門叫他，——
　　　鏽鐵鏈子繫著。

　　　二
　　　秋風起了，
　　　快吹開那家窗幕。
　　　開了窗幕，會望見他的雙靨。窗幕開了，——
　　　一望全是粉牆，
　　　白吹下許多枯葉。

三
大雪下了，掃出路尋他；
　這路連到山上，山上都是松柏，
　他是花一般，這裡如何住得！
不如回去尋他，——
　阿！回來還是我的家！

　　對詩人來說，「知了」的聲音只能成為遙遠追尋的慰藉，他設想自己站在窗的另一端，讓思念的人穿過他的心房。但隨著季節的更迭，詩人把記憶、沉哀等抽象概念變為有形之物，又把視覺轉化為觸覺，使情感的流動叫人可感。那「開了窗幕」有意的重複和詩句的顛倒，都增添了無限的惆悵和懷戀的情緒，這正是他轉向自由詩體的時候。

　　寫於 1924 年 10 月 3 日的〈我的失戀〉意象力度極強，請看最後一段：

我的所愛在豪家；
欲往尋之兮沒有汽車，
仰頭無法淚如麻。
愛人贈我玫瑰花；
回她什麼：赤練蛇。
從此翻臉不理我，
不知何故兮——由她去吧。

　　這首打油詩既有現實性內涵，又有形而上的意義。「赤練蛇」原是蛇的一種，背部黑綠色，有赤色條紋和斑點，雖無毒，但性凶猛，好捕食蛙類；在文中則比喻為心腸惡毒者。由於當時詩人的感受比較複雜，才選擇以超現實意象加以傳達，因此，這裡面求索是有目的性的。

　　儘管魯迅在他《集外集・序言》中曾說：「我其實是不喜歡做新詩的，——但也不喜歡做古詩，——只因為那時詩壇寂寞，所以打打邊鼓，湊些熱鬧；待到稱為詩上人的一出現，就洗手不作了。」但是魯迅的散文詩集《野草》，前後歷經一年零七個月（1926年 4 月 10 日－1927 年 4 月 26 日），共完成 24 篇力作，在作品結集出版之時，魯迅寫下了《野草》題辭，這是首捍衛生命的壯歌，是寫在國民黨實行「清黨」政策時期的廣州：

> 當我沉默著的時候,我覺得充實;我將開口,同時感到空虛。
>
> 過去的生命已經死亡。我對於這死亡有大歡喜,因為我借此知道它曾經存活。死亡的生命已經朽腐。我對於這朽腐有大歡喜,因為我借此知道它還非空虛。
>
> 生命的泥委棄在地面上,不生喬木,只生野草,這是我的罪過。
>
> 野草,根本不深,花葉不美,然而吸取露,吸取水,吸取陳死人的血和肉,各各奪取它的生存。當生存時,還是將遭踐踏,將遭刪刈,直至於死亡而朽腐。
>
> 但我坦然,欣然。我將大笑,我將歌唱。
>
> 我自愛我的野草,但我憎惡這以野草作裝飾的地面。
>
> 地火在地下運行,奔突;熔岩一旦噴出,將燒盡一切野草,以及喬木,於是並且無可朽腐。
>
> 但我坦然,欣然。我將大笑,我將歌唱。
>
> 天地有如此靜穆,我不能大笑而且歌唱。天地即不如此靜穆,我或者也將不能。我以這一叢野草,在明與暗,生與死,過去與未來之際,獻於友與仇,人與獸,愛者與不愛者之前作證。
>
> 為我自己,為友與仇,人與獸,愛者與不愛者,我希望這野草的朽腐,火速到來。要不然,我先就未曾生存,這實在比死亡與朽腐更其不幸。
>
> 去吧,野草,連著我的題辭!

的確,十年動亂給中國帶來深重的災難,但魯迅用他的筆與黑暗勢力進行抗爭。在這首題辭意象中蘊藏著五四時期追求光明與新生的時代精神,他崇尚榮譽,全詩運用了象徵的藝術手法,暗喻不惜以生命去奉獻給自己的追求目標,迴響著對生命和價值的追問與正義的呼聲,感人至深。

《野草》於 1927 年 7 月由北京北新書局出版,隱含著詩人正從野草地上艱難而又頑強地生存,也展示了魯迅的詩藝有了飛躍。其中,1924 年 9 月 24 日作的散文詩〈影的告別〉,對社會上漠不關心時事者居多的現象提出了強烈的批判,全詩用假托影與形的對白表現出魯迅敏銳的諷刺感,是《野草》中最出色的一篇:

人睡到不知道時候的時候，就會有影來告別，說出那些話——

有我所不樂意的在天堂裡，我不願去；有我所不樂意的在地獄裡，我不願去；有我所不樂意的在你們將來的黃金世界裡，我不願去。
然而你就是我所不樂意的。
朋友，我不想跟隨你了，我不願住。
我不願意！
嗚呼嗚呼，我不願意，我不如彷徨於無地。
我不過一個影，要別你而沉沒在黑暗裡了。然而黑暗又會吞併我，然而光明又會使我消失。
然而我不願彷徨於明暗之間，我不如在黑暗裡沉沒。
然而我終於彷徨於明暗之間，我不知道是黃昏還是黎明。我姑且舉灰黑的手裝作喝幹一杯酒，我將在不知道時候的時候獨自遠行。
嗚呼嗚呼，倘是黃昏，黑夜自然會來沉沒我，否則我要被白天消失，如果現是黎明。
朋友，時候近了。
我將向黑暗裡彷徨於無地。
你還想我的贈品。我能獻你甚麼呢？無已，則仍是黑暗和虛空而已。但是，我願意只是黑暗，或者會消失於你的白天；我願意只是虛空，決不占你的心地。
我願意這樣，朋友——
我獨自遠行，不但沒有你，並且再沒有別的影在黑暗裡。只有我被黑暗沉沒，那世界全屬於我自己。

在這首〈影的告別〉的詩情世界裡，魯迅也分別傾訴了哀厭孤獨的感情，其愛國熱血如岩漿般噴湧而出，通過影的形象，發出自己狂放不羈的呼喊。那激蕩的力量除了自然流露的情感，也深受西方象徵主義詩人波特萊爾[3]及屠格涅夫[4]等人的影響。波德

---

[3] 夏爾·波德萊爾（Charles Baudelaire, 1821-1867），法國十九世紀最著名的現代派詩人，象徵派詩歌先驅，代表作有《惡之花》。
[4] 伊凡·謝爾蓋耶維奇·屠格涅夫（Иван Сергеевич Тургенев, 1818-1883）是俄國 19 世紀批判現實主義作家，他的小說善於通過生動的情節和恰當的言語，及對大自然情境交融的描述，塑造出許多栩栩如生的人物形象。

萊爾認為，美不應該受到束縛，善並不等於美，美同樣存在於惡與醜之中；他生活在惡中，但又力圖不讓惡所吞噬，而是用批評的眼光正視惡、剖析惡。這些宏觀思路在魯迅的創作實踐中，不僅契合與強化了魯迅各種感情的抒發；而屠格涅夫從幼年時就產生了對農奴制的反感，後來形成了他精神世界中的人道主義和民主主義的因素，使他跟革命民主派的批評家們站在同線。那強烈的激情也深深地感染了魯迅；使他的這本《野草》的崇高和悲壯展現得淋漓盡致，成為中國現代散文詩的經典。

二、魯迅舊體詩中的意象

魯迅一生的後期，也是他詩歌創作的顛峰期。這一時期（1931年－1935年），他的詩歌創作主要是舊體詩。《題〈吶喊〉》《題〈仿徨〉》《無題（烟水尋常事）》《秋夜有感》《亥年殘秋偶作》等作品，因為注重借助物象或場景來間接表現詩人的心境、表現社會生活面，所以象徵涵義往往帶有多重性，把他的詩歌推到一個高致的境界。詩中的孤獨感和蒼涼感，絕非其內心軟弱的表現，反而是無畏強權的抑鬱情懷，所寫的多是他真實的悲切之聲。

魯迅的舊體詩，深受屈原的影響。屈原在《離騷》中創造了一個大求索者的形象：「路漫漫其修遠兮，吾將上下而求索。」這種探索事物的根源和不屈戰鬥的精神，在魯迅的詩歌中得到了傳承和發展。在魯迅舊體詩共六十多首中，如1912年所作的〈哀范君三章〉：

風雨飄搖日，余懷范愛農。
華顛萎寥落，白眼看鷄蟲。
世味秋荼苦，人間直道窮。
奈何三月別，竟爾失畸躬。

海草國門綠，多年老異鄉。
狐狸方去穴，桃偶已登場。
故里寒雲惡，炎天凜夜長。
獨沈清冷水，能否滌愁腸？

把酒論當世，先生小酒人。
大圜猶茗艼，微醉自沈淪。

此別成終古，從茲絕緒言。
故人雲散盡，我亦等輕塵。[5]

　　這裡的范愛農是魯迅一生的摯友，范氏在革命前不滿黑暗社會，追求革命，辛亥革命後備受打擊迫害。此詩的風格是「清逸中有悲愴」，創作的背景是魯迅到北京不久，得到了范愛農淹死的噩耗後，內心始終無法釋懷，遂而寫下此輓詩。人的感情是潛性的，而景物是顯性的。此詩以「風雨」以增強它的情味力量，然後由夜轉日，由景轉情，點明失去摯友的悲痛，亦以寥落的景像襯托出無限的愁思，以「能否滌愁腸」表現思情的無奈之苦。最後以「狐狸方去穴，桃偶已登場。」暗喻袁世凱（1859年－1916年）於1916年建立君主立憲政體，欲自立中華帝國皇帝，但終歸是失敗。這裡表現的手段是相當高明的，難怪魯迅的另一位摯友許壽裳[6]也曾感慨地表示：「魯迅吶喊衝鋒了三十年，百戰瘡痍，還是醒不了沉沉的大夢，掃不清千年淤積的穢坑。所謂右的固然靠不住，自命為左的也未必靠得住，青年們又何嘗都靠得住。」由此而知，魯迅詩歌的孕育與成熟經歷了一個較長的過程，其間受到中外許多詩學觀點的影響。在那之後，魯迅盡上天賦予他所能承受的力量，去試攀進一步的詩歌顛峰。

　　如〈無題〉（1932年）為高良富子夫人寫下一詩：「血沃中原肥勁草，寒凝大地發春華。／英雄多故謀夫病，淚灑崇陵噪暮鴉。」此乃一首投贈詩，詩的背景是寫1932年1月，廣州和南京合組的政府成立，蔣介石回奉化，汪精衛托病到上海，行政院長孫科主政，事事棘手，被迫下臺。魯迅即景抒情後，寫下心中所湧生的悠悠愁緒。他所感之「意」〈愁〉，音調諧婉，流美如珠，可以看出詩人在意象統合上的特色。

---

[5] 魯迅這首原詩最初發表於1912年8月21日紹興《民興日報》，署名黃棘。1934年魯迅把第三首編入《集外集》時題作《哭范愛農》，「當世」作「天下」，「自」作「合」，「此別成終古，從茲絕緒言」作「幽谷無窮夜，新宮自在春」。

[6] 許壽裳（1883年－1948年），字季茀，號上遂，現代著名教育家和傳記文學作家、教育家，魯迅、周作人的同學、至交。許壽裳、錢稻孫、周樹人3位中華民國教育部薦任科長1912年8月，被時任中華民國臨時大總統袁世凱指定研擬國徽圖案，3人合作設計圖樣，錢稻孫畫出圖例，魯迅執筆說明書，1913年2月發表。

再如 1932 年 12 月 31 日所作〈無題〉:「洞庭木落楚天高,眉黛猩紅浣戰袍。／澤畔有人吟不得,秋波渺渺失離騷。」這顯然是藉《楚辭‧九歌‧湘夫人》:「裊裊兮秋風,洞庭波兮木葉落。」景上所見秋葉的寥落景像〈象〉來襯托出「傷離意緒」〈意〉,這樣以景結情,詩人行吟澤畔,咏懷屈原沉於江潭之傷;也有評家認為,此詩是魯迅為勸阻郁達夫去杭州而寫的。接著這首〈吶喊〉是在 1933 年 3 月 2 日的力作:「弄文罹文網,抗世違世情。／積毀可銷骨,空留紙上聲。」在《魯迅日記》曾記載,日本人山縣初男向魯迅索取小說,魯迅不僅給他了小說,還在小說上題寫了自己的詩歌〈吶喊〉;充分傳達了詩人對抗世精神的強烈期盼以及對象徵主義藝術理想的熱情嚮往。在另一首同期之作〈仿徨〉:「寂寞新文苑,平安舊戰場。／兩間餘一卒,荷戟獨仿徨。」更是站在時代文化的最高點,然後大著膽引嗓高歌,以洩其積憤與仿徨。接著又於 1933 年 7 月 21 日寫的〈悼楊銓〉中,魯迅痛哭流涕,對楊銓[7]被害的悲憤也就十分強烈而深沉:「豈有豪情似舊時,花開花落兩由之。／何期淚灑江南雨,又為斯民哭健兒。」詩感情真誠、激昂、慷慨,且又借助於淒美的藝術想像來抒情言志,這豪情便是高漲的情調。

接著,這首在 1934 年 9 月 29 日為曾任《申報》副刊主編張梓生寫下的〈秋夜有感〉,也是難得之作:

綺羅幕後送飛光,柏栗叢邊作道場。
望帝終教芳草變,迷陽聊飾大田荒。
何來酪果供千佛,難得蓮花似六郎。
中夜雞鳴風雨集,起燃煙捲覺新涼。

詩的背景魯迅曾記載,「飛光」源自李賀《苦晝短》中的:「飛光飛光,勸爾一杯酒。」在這裡,喻杯酒光影;而「迷陽」是一種有刺的草。魯迅追求形式完美和藝術技巧,他反抗社會功利哲學、市儈習氣;詩中的「六郎」原指武則天的面首張昌宗,但在此處指梅蘭芳。創作的背景是 1934 年 4 月 28 日國民黨黨國元老之一,

---

[7] 楊銓,字杏佛,民權保障同盟執行委員,1933 年 6 月 18 日為國民黨藍衣社特務暗殺於上海,20 日魯迅曾往萬國殯儀館送殮。許壽裳《亡友魯迅印象記》:「是日大雨,魯迅送殮回去,成詩一首。這首詩才氣縱橫,富於新意,無異於龔自珍。」

任職中執委常委兼宣傳部長戴季陶（1891年－1949年）等發起請班禪九世在杭州啓建「時輪金剛法會」，曾邀梅蘭芳等人在會期內表演，但按梅蘭芳等並未參與演出。此詩寄寓詩人嚮往的社會理想，借「風雨如晦，雞鳴不已。」來訴說自己對國事如麻的酸楚；其本體論應建立在魯迅的生命活動的基石上，且很自然地成為一個生活的歌者。再如1935年12月5日為摯友許壽堂寫下的〈亥年殘秋偶作〉：「曾經秋肅臨天下，敢遣春溫上筆端。／塵海蒼茫沈百感，金風蕭瑟走千官。／老歸大澤菇蒲盡，夢墜空雲齒髮寒。／竦聽荒雞偏闃寂，起看星斗正闌幹。」，詩背景是指當時在日本帝國主義侵略軍壓迫下大批官員撤離河北省，抒寫詩人對民生之憔悴的悲觀感傷以及感慨棲身無地、悲涼孤寂的情緒。

三、魯迅詩歌意象的啓示

　　八十多年來，魯迅詩歌的意象藝術及影響這一課題的研究經歷了逐步開拓與不斷深耕的過程，越來越引起華界的高度重視；但也因為海內外先後出版過各種不同形式的賞讀或註解，其中，所涉及詩詞文字錯訛或詩意乖謬難懂，凡此，這也需要研究者作出進一步的思考。在中國現代詩史上，魯迅的詩歌具有不可替代的歷史意義；特別是留學期間的相關資料還需要繼續挖掘，研究詩裡還存在的一些特殊或疑惑問題。回溯當年魯迅對詩歌的理想追求及其實踐活動，其中包含魯迅對詩歌意象的營造，我們可以得到多方面的啓示。

1. 魯迅詩歌意象是在歷史的延續中不斷累積的，有些詩歌意象在承繼的同時還須加以變革；這也是身為一個民族的詩人心理的潛意識創造而成的。他是一個被中國歷史的傷痕武裝起來的大求索者，而我們可以由其詩歌清楚地看到中國現代啓蒙主義下知識份子的覺醒，使我們古老的民族踏上民主的新生之路。

2. 魯迅舊體詩歌意象屬於東方文化色彩，其中積澱的別情離恨或孤憤之情深長，歷來受到中國文人的咏讚。它是其高潔品格的象徵，詩心光明清瑩，具有明朗地肯定著人有追求自由的勇氣和偉大的美。雖然有許多意象帶有淒涼意味，但體現在他對國事民生的關注或重大歷史事件的省思上，他的詩能融入生命哲學的思考，詩味往往也變得厚重。

3. 魯迅是個坦蕩的愛國詩人，自然他的詩歌是不會沉默無聲的；他詩裡的情感能唱出他對人生的感悟和社會的思考，同時也開拓了現代詩學的視野。他的詩心是敞開的，但隱有一種無言的惆悵，能在傷感之餘，多一層對社會底層的關懷，也是一種痛苦的昇華。他的身影恰如一隻孤雁，誰也阻止不了越走越遠的月光，誰也阻止不了黑暗的來臨；但，他無畏風雨，絕對會持續不斷地飛，其留下的落腳點將如一泓幽隱的飛瀑，等待著春的禮讚。

4. 魯迅的詩歌意象，受到東方人文環境的浸染與激勵；但同時也汲取西方文化藝術的新奇，開拓其審美對象範圍，使之煥發詩興與激情。魯迅詩歌的意象，是在廣闊的中外文學交融的背景中生成與發展的。

【刊於中國江蘇省《鹽城師範學院學報》，第32卷，總第138期，2012年第6期，頁44-48。】

Lu Xun occupies a unique position in modern Chinese history and is widely regarded as one of the greatest historians, translators, and thinkers in ancient and modern times. His poems are filled with philosophical thoughts, profound meanings, humorous language, and exquisite satires, which have had a profound impact on Chinese literature after the May Fourth Movement. Lu Xun, essentially, is a poet. His poems oppose the constraints of feudalism and, to a certain extent, record his life's philosophical thoughts and circumstances. With fresh and lively thoughts, they shine with the brilliance of humanistic thoughts, while containing rich images, to give people endless space for imagination.

I. Imagery in Lu Xun's vernacular poetry

In the vernacular movement caused by the May Fourth Movement, Lu Xun successively created and published works such as *Call to Arms*, *Grave*, *Wandering*, *Wild Grass*, *Dawn Blossoms Plucked at Dusk*, etc., showing the elite consciousness of intellectuals and the ideological characteristics of thorough democracy. At that time, Lu Xun was full of passion and confidence, to write a large number of vernacular poems expressing broad, profound and complex social content, while creating rich imagery.

Let's first look at the vernacular poem "Dream": "Many dreams, taking advantage of the dusk to give trouble. / When the previous dream squeezes out the big previous dream, the next dream chases away the previous dream. / The previous dream, gone, is as black as ink, and the next dream, here, is as black as ink; / Those who are gone and those who are here seem to be saying: / 'Look at my really good complexion.' / The complexion may be good, but I don't know it in the dark; / And I don't know who is talking? / I don't know it in the dark, but I feel hot with a headache. / Come on, come on, you who understand the dream!"[8] The figurative technique of this poem is not only a true portrayal of the real society and life status, but also a dialogue between Lu Xun and "dreams". These awakening voices and psychology show that many sleeping people in dark China are distorted by the feudal autocratic society and their inner anxiety; facing the style of military officials at that time, the poet used a grand momentum to create the great spirit of the children of the times who stand up to change the world. This is in sharp contrast to the tranquility and peace in classical poetry; the imagery is deep, sad and eager to find a window of light, and it also bears a very clear mark of national spirit.

Let's look at the vernacular poem "God of Love"[9]. This poem is not a romantic expression or catharsis, but Lu Xun's intoxication with the momentary love, deliberately creating a surreal and fantasy-colored image of Cupid, with elements of unique aesthetic value of love: "A little kid, with wings spread in the air, / with an arrow in one hand and a bow in the other, / and somehow an arrow shot into his chest. / 'Mr. Little Kid, thank you for your random cultivation! / But

---

[8] "Dream", "God of Love" and "Peach Blossom" were first published in the fifth issue of the fourth volume of *New Youth* in May 1918, signed by Tang Qi and later included in the *Collection of Unofficial Works*.

[9] This article was first published in the fifth issue of the fourth volume of *New Youth* on May 15, 1918, signed by Tang Qi.

you have to tell me: who should I love?' / The kid panicked, shook his head and said, Oh! / You are a person with a heart, but you say such things. / Who you should love, how can I know. / Anyway, my arrow was let go! / If you love someone, love him madly; / If you don't love anyone, you can also die madly." Here, the poet raises a figurative question without hesitation: "Who should you love? How do I know?", pushing the poetic thought to the height of life philosophy: life is always limited, love must be timely, otherwise it is inevitable that it will be fleeting.

The vernacular poem "Peach Blossom" (May 1918) is an excellent satirical poem. The poet not only uses ingenious language, but also pretends to mock the theme's lifestyle of some "literati looking down on each other" in real society and the arrogant and ambitious people: "The spring rain has passed, the sun is very fair, and I just walk into the garden. / Peach blossoms bloom in the west of the garden, and plum blossoms bloom in the east of the garden. / I said, 'Great! Peach blossoms are red, and plum blossoms are white.' / (No, peach blossoms are not as white as plum blossoms.) / But the peach blossoms are angry, and their faces turn red like 'Yang Feihong'. / Good boy! Really amazing! You can even turn red with anger. / My words did not offend you, why did your face turn red! / Alas! Flowers have their own reasons, I don't understand." Ideologically, the poet writes about the betrayal of traditional feudal consciousness in a teasing tone; the dialogue between the objects in the poem is illusory, and the contradiction between aesthetics and ugliness in the moment also truly reflects Lu Xun's worries and complex mind.

Lu Xun's vernacular poetry not only marks the return of realism in a general sense, but also enriches and deepens realism. Take the poem "Their Garden" for example: "A little kid with curly hair, / A faint red on his silvery-yellow face, — it looks like he is about to live; / He walks out of the broken gate to see his neighbor's house: / There are many beautiful flowers in their big garden. / He uses all his tricks to get a lily; it is white and bright, like freshly fallen snow. / He takes it home carefully, and reflects it on his face, making it look even more rosy. / Flies fly around the flowers, making noises all over the room — / 'To prefer this dirty flower is a foolish child!' / He hurriedly looks at the lilies, but there are already a few flying arrows on them. / He cannot bear to look at them; he cannot bear to let them go. / He stares at the sky, and he has nothing to say./ He cannot speak, and thinks of his neighbors: / They have many beautiful flowers in their big garden." The scenes set in the poem are in contrast to some of the current writers who are like flowers in the garden eager to attract the public's favor or self-righteous poets who stand up to the world, which makes people feel funny; it also shows the humorous side of Lu Xun, giving people a fresh and pleasant aesthetic feeling.

The tone of the poem "Man and Time" is straight forward and clear, and the symbolism is also rich: "One person says that the future is better than the present. / One person says that the present is far inferior to the past. / One person says, what? / Time says, you all insult my present. / Those who are good in the past, go back by themselves. / Those who are good in the future, follow me. / What are you talking about? / I have nothing to say to you." Lu Xun's pain and hope are mixed together. His dream of saving the country and the people has not only become a model of brave attempts; the image of time is also sensible. On the surface, people and time are separated; but the poet's heaven and earth, past and future, and wild imagination should be connected in the depths of his heart. Another vernacular poem, "He" (1919, reflects Lu Xun's loneliness and depression during the years of disaster: "One / / 'Cicada' stops chirping, / He is asleep in the room; / 'Cicada' chirps, and I remember it every moment in my heart. / The sun has gone, the 'cicada' has stopped, — I haven't seen him yet, / Waiting to knock on the door to call him, — / It's tied with a rusty iron chain. / / Two / / The autumn wind has risen, / Quickly blow open the window of that house. / Open the window, and you will see his cheeks. / The window is opened, — All I can see is the white wall, / The white wind blows down many dead leaves. / / Three / / It's snowing heavily, clearing a way to find him; / This road leads to the mountain, the mountain is full of pines and cypresses, / He is like a flower, how can he live here! /Why not go back and look for him, — /Ah! Back to my home again!" For the poet, the sound of "cicadas" can only be a consolation for the distant pursuit. He imagines himself standing on the other side of the window, letting the person he misses pass through his heart. But with the change of seasons, the poet turns abstract concepts such as memory and sorrow into tangible things, and transforms vision into touch, making the flow of emotions perceptible. The intentional repetition of "opened the window curtain" and the inversion of the poem add infinite melancholy and nostalgic emotions. This is when he turns to free verse.

Written on October 3, 1924, "My Broken Heart" boasts vivid imagery. Please see the last stanza: "My love is in a wealthy family; / I want to go find her but there is no car, / I cannot cry when I look up. / My lover gives me roses; / What do I say to her: Red Snake. / From then on, she turns her face to ignores me, / I don't know why — let her go." This doggerel poem has both realistic connotations and metaphysical meanings. "Red Snake" is originally a kind of snake with a black-green back and red stripes and spots. Although it is not poisonous, it is ferocious and likes to prey on frogs; in the text, it is likened to a person with a vicious heart. Because the poet's feelings at the time are more complicated, he chooses to convey them with surreal images, so the search here is purposeful.

Although Lu Xun says in his "Preface to the Collection of Poems Outside the Anthology": "I actually don't like to write modern poetry, but I don't like to write ancient poetry either, just because the world of poetry has been lonely and dreary at that time, so I play a side drum to add to the excitement; when the so-called poets appear, I simply wash my hands to give it up." However, Lu Xun's prose poetry collection *Wild Grass* takes a year and seven months (April 10, 1926 - April 26, 1927) to complete a total of 24 masterpieces. When the works were published, Lu Xun wrote the title of "Wild Grass", which is a heroic song to defend life, written in Guangzhou during the KMT's "Party Purge" policy: "When I am silent, I feel fulfilled; I will speak and feel empty at the same time. / / The past life has died. I have great joy in this death, because I know it once lived. The dead life has decayed. I have great joy in this decay, because I know it is not empty. / / The mud of life is abandoned on the ground, no tall trees grow, only weeds grow, this is my sin. / / The weeds, without roots, without beautiful flowers and leaves, yet absorb dew, absorb water, absorb by taking the blood and flesh of the dead, each taking its life. While it lives, it will still be trampled on and cut down, until it dies and decays. / / But I am calm and happy. I will laugh and sing. / / I love my wild grass, but I hate the ground that is decorated with wild grass. / / The underground fire runs and rushes underground; once the molten lava erupts, it will burn all the wild grass and the trees, so that there will be no decay. / / But I am calm and happy. I will laugh and sing. / / The world is so quiet that I cannot laugh and sing. The world is not I may not be able to be so quiet. I dedicate this clump of weeds to bear witness before friends and enemies, humans and beasts, those who love and those who do not love, between light and darkness, life and death, past and future. / / For myself, for friends and enemies, humans and beasts, those who love and those who do not love, I hope that the decay of this weed will come quickly. Otherwise, I would not have lived in the first place, which is more unfortunate than death and decay. / / Go, weeds, along with my theme! "It is true that the ten years of unrest brought great disasters to China, but Lu Xun uses his pen to fight against the dark forces. The imagery of this title contains the spirit of the times of the May Fourth Movement, which pursues light and rebirth. He advocates honor. The whole poem uses symbolic artistic techniques, implying that he is ready to sacrifice his life for his own pursuit of goals, echoing the questioning of life and values and the call for justice, which was deeply touching.

Wild Grass was published by Beijing Beixin Bookstore in July 1927. It implies that the poet is surviving hard and tenaciously in the wild grass, and also shows that Lu Xun's poetry has made a leap. Among them, the prose poem "Shadow's Farewell" written on September 24, 1924 strongly criticizes the phenomenon that most people in society are indifferent to current affairs. The whole poem uses dialogues pretending to be shadows and shapes to express Lu Xun's sharp sense of irony. It is the most outstanding piece in *Wild Grass*:

When a person falls asleep and doesn't know when a shadow will come to bid farewell and say those words: / There are things I don't like in heaven, I don't want to go; there are things I don't like in hell, I don't want to go; there are things I don't like in your future golden world, I don't want to go. / But you are the one I don't like.

Friend, I don't want to follow you anymore, I don't want to live. / I don't want to! / Wuhu, wuhu, I don't want to, I'd rather wander in the nowhere. / I'm just a shadow, I'm leaving you and sinking in the darkness. But the darkness will swallow me up, but the light will make me disappear. / But I don't want to wander between light and darkness, I'd rather sink in the darkness. / But I finally wandered between light and darkness, I don't know whether it is dusk or dawn. I will raise my grayish black hand and pretend to drink a glass of wine. I will travel far away alone when I don't know the time. /Wuhu wuhu, if it is dusk, the night will naturally come to sink me, otherwise I will be disappeared by the day, if it is dawn now. /Friend, the time is near. /I will wander in the darkness without a place. /You still want my gift. What can I give you? Nothing, it will still be darkness and emptiness. However, I wish to be just darkness, or disappear in your daytime; I wish to be just emptiness, and never occupy your heart. / I wish this, friend — / I travel far away alone, not only without you, but also without other shadows in the darkness. Only I am sunken by the darkness, and the world belongs to me.

In the poetic world of "Shadow's Farewell", Lu Xun also expresses his feelings of sadness and loneliness. His patriotic passion gushes out like magma, and through the image of shadow, he issues his unrestrained cry. In addition to the natural expression of emotions, the turbulent power was also deeply influenced by Western symbolist poets such as Baudelaire[10] and Turgenev[11]. Baudelaire believes that beauty should not be constrained, goodness is not equal to beauty, and beauty also exists in evil and ugliness; he lives in evil, but tried not to be swallowed by evil, but to face and analyze evil with a critical eye. These macro-ideas not only fit and strengthen the expression of Lu Xun's various emotions in his creative practice. Turgenev has developed an aversion to serfdom since childhood, which later forms the humanistic and democratic factors in his spiritual world, making

---

[10] Charles Baudelaire (1821-1867) is the most famous modernist poet in France in the 19th century and a pioneer of symbolist poetry. His representative works include *Flowers of Evil*.

[11] Ivan Sergeyevich Turgenev (Иван Сергеевич Тургенев, 1818-1883) is a Russian critical realist writer in the 19th century. His novels are good at creating many vivid characters through vivid plots, appropriate words, and descriptions of the blending of natural situations.

him stand on the same line with the critics of the revolutionary democracy. The strong passion has also deeply influenced Lu Xun; making his book *Wild Grass* show the sublimity and tragedy vividly, to become a classic of modern Chinese prose poetry.

II. Imagery in Lu Xun's Classical Poetry

The later period of Lu Xun's life was also the peak period of his poetry creation. During this period (1931-1935), his poetry creation is mainly classical poetry. Works such as "Call to Arms", "Wandering", "Untitled (Looking for Ordinary Things in the Smoke and Water)", "Thoughts on an Autumn Night", and "Occasional Works in the Late Autumn of the Year of the Pig" often have multiple symbolic meanings because they focus on using objects or scenes to indirectly express the poet's state of mind and social life, pushing his poetry to a high level. The loneliness and desolation in the poems are by no means a manifestation of his inner weakness, but rather a depressed mood that is fearless of power, and what he writes about is mostly his true voice of sorrow.

Lu Xun's classical poetry is deeply influenced by Qu Yuan, who has created the image of a great seeker in *Li Sao*: "The road is long and far-flung, I will seek up and down." This spirit of exploring the root of things and unyielding fighting spirit has been inherited and developed in Lu Xun's poems. Among Lu Xun's more than 60 classical poems, such as "Three Chapters of Lament for Mr. Fan" written in 1912: "The wind and rain are shaking the sun, and I miss Fan Ainong. / Flowers withered and desolate, looking at chickens and insects with white eyes. / The world tastes bitter in autumn, and the straight road in the world is hard. / But why did we say goodbye in March, and you lost your body. // The seaweed is green at the gate of the country, and I have been in a foreign land for many years. / The fox has just left the den, and the peach doll has already appeared. / The cold clouds in my hometown are evil, and the summer sky is gloomy. The night is long. / Can sinking alone into the clear water clear my sorrow? // Let's talk about the present world over wine, you are a little drunkard. / The big circle is like a tea boat, I sink into the water after being slightly drunk. / This farewell will last forever, and I will stop talking from now on. / The old friends have all dispersed, and I am also waiting to be dusted."[12] Fan Ainong here is Lu Xun's lifelong friend. Before the revolution, Fan is dissatisfied with the dark society and pursues revolution. After the Revolution of 1911, he is attacked and persecuted. The style of this poem is "sadness in the clear and elegant", and the background of the creation is that Lu Xun arrives in Beijing not long ago, and after receiving the bad news that Fan Ainong is drowned, he cannot let go of his heart, so he writes this elegy. People's emotions are latent, while scenery is explicit. This poem uses "wind and rain" to enhance its emotional power, and then changes from night to day, from scenery to emotion, pointing out the grief of losing a close friend, and also using the desolate scene to highlight the infinite sorrow, and "whether it can quench the sorrow" to express the helpless pain of love. Finally, "the fox has just left the den, and the peach doll has appeared." It alludes to Yuan Shikai (1859-1916) who has established a constitutional monarchy in 1916, intending to establish himself as the emperor of the Chinese Empire, but ultimately failed. The means of expression here are quite clever. No wonder another close friend of Lu Xun, Xu Shoushang[13], once said with emotion: "Lu Xun has been shouting and charging for thirty years, and he has suffered from hundreds of battles, but he still cannot wake up from the deep dream and clear the pits accumulated for thousands of years. The so-called right is certainly unreliable, and those who claim to be left are not necessarily reliable. How can young

---

[12] This original poem by Lu Xun was first published in Shaoxing's *Minxing Daily* on August 21, 1912, signed by Huang Ji. In 1934, when Lu Xun compiled the third poem into the *Collection of Unofficial Works*, he titled it "Mourning Fan Ainong", changed "the world" to "the world", "self" to "together", and "this farewell will end in the ancient times, and from this severance" to "the endless night in the deep valley, the spring in the new palace".

[13] Xu Shoushang (1883-1948), with the courtesy name Jifu and the pseudonym Shangsui, is a famous modern educator and biographical writer, educator, classmate and close friend of Lu Xun and Zhou Zuoren. Xu Shoushang, Qian Daosun, and Zhou Shuren were recommended by the Ministry of Education of the Republic of China as section chiefs. In August 1912, they were appointed by Yuan Shikai, then the provisional president of the Republic of China, to develop the national emblem. The three worked together to design the pattern, Qian Daosun drew the illustration, and Lu Xun wrote the instructions. It was published in February 1913.

people be trusted?" From this, we can see that the gestation and maturity of Lu Xun's poetry has gone through a long process, during which he was influenced by many Chinese and foreign poetic viewpoints. After that, Lu Xun tries to climb to a higher peak of poetry with all the strength given by God.

For example, "Untitled" (1932) is a poem written for Mrs. Kora Tomiko: "Blood fertilizes the Central Plains and makes the grass grow strong, and the cold freezes the earth and makes spring flowers bloom. / Heroes often plot against their husbands' illnesses, and tears fall on the high hills and make crows cry in the evening." This is a poem for dedication. The background of the poem is that in January 1932, the government formed by Guangzhou and Nanjing was established, Chiang Kai-shek returned to Fenghua, Wang Jingwei went to Shanghai on the pretext of illness, and the Executive Yuan Minister Sun Ke was in power. Everything was difficult and he was forced to step down. After Lu Xun expressed his feelings on the spot, he records the long-lasting melancholy in his heart. The "meaning" he feels, "sorrow", has a harmonious tone and flows beautifully like pearls, which shows the poet's characteristics in the integration of images.

Another example is "Untitled" written on December 31, 1932: "The leaves on Dongting Lake are falling, the sky of Chu is high, the scarlet eyebrows have stained the battle robe. / There is someone on the bank of the river, but he cannot recite poems, his autumn eyes are vague and lost." This is obviously borrowed from "Lady Xiang from Nine Songs of the Verses of the South": "The autumn wind is blowing, the waves of Dongting Lake are rippling, and the leaves are falling." The desolate image of autumn leaves in the scene is used to highlight the "sadness and separation" (meaning). In this way, the scene is used to express the emotion. The poet walks and recites on the bank of the river, chanting the sorrow of Qu Yuan[14] who drowned himself in the

---

[14] Yang Quan, also known as Xingfo, is an executive member of the Civil Rights Protection League. He was assassinated by the Kuomintang Blue Shirts Society spies in Shanghai on June 18, 1933. Lu Xun went to the International Funeral Home to bury him on the 20th. Xu Shoushang's "Impressions of My Late Friend Lu Xun": "It was raining heavily that day, and Lu Xun came back from the funeral procession and wrote a poem. This poem is full of talent and originality, just like the piece by Gong Zizhen."

river. Some critics also believe that this poem was written by Lu Xun to dissuade Yu Dafu from going to Hangzhou. Next is the masterpiece "Call to Arms" written on March 2, 1933: "Writing is caught in the literary trap, resisting the world and going against the world's feelings. / The accumulated destruction can destroy the body, leaving only the sound on the paper." It is recorded in *Lu Xun's Diary* that the Japanese Yamagata Hatsuo asks Lu Xun for a novel. Lu Xun not only gives him the novel, but also writes his own poem "Call to Arms" on the novel. It fully conveyed the poet's strong expectation for the spirit of resisting the world and his passionate yearning for the ideal of symbolist art. In another work of the same period, "Wandering": "The new literary garden is lonely, and the old battlefield is peaceful. / There is only one soldier left in the two rooms, carrying a spear and wandering alone." It is standing at the highest point of the culture of the era, and then singing boldly to vent his accumulated anger and hesitation. In the poem "Mourning Yang Quan" written on June 21, 1933, Lu Xun burst into tears, and his grief over Yang Quan's death was very strong and deep: "How can there be the same heroic sentiment as in the old days, when flowers bloom and fall as they please. / Who would have thought that tears would fall in the rain south of the Yangtze River, and I would mourn for the brave men of this country." The poem is sincere, passionate, and generous, and it uses tragic artistic imagination to express emotions and aspirations. This heroic sentiment is the high mood.

Next, this poem "Thoughts on an Autumn Night" written by Zhang Zisheng, an editor-in-chief of the supplement of *Shen Bao* on September 29, 1934, is also a rare work: "Behind the curtain of Qiluo, flying light is sent, and a temple is built beside the cypress and chestnut bushes. / King Wang finally taught the fragrant grass to change, and the Mi Yang was used to decorate the barren fields. / Where can I find yogurt to offer to thousands of Buddhas, and it is rare to find lotus flowers like Liu Lang. / In the middle of the night, the cocks chirp and the wind and rain gather, and the smoke rolls up to feel the new coolness." The background of the poem Lu Xun once recorded that "flying light" comes from Li He's "Bitter Days Are Short": "Flying light, flying light, advise you to drink a glass of wine." Here, it refers to the light and shadow of a glass of wine; and "Mi Yang" is a kind of thorny grass. Lu Xun pursues perfection in form and artistic skills. He resisted the utilitarian philosophy and mercenary habits of society. The "Liu Lang" in the poem originally refers to Zhang Changzong, Wu Zetian's male concubine, but here it refers to Mei Lanfang. The background of the creation was that on April 28, 1934, Dai Jitao (1891-1949), one of the elders of the Kuomintang, who serves as a member of the Central Executive Committee and Minister of Propaganda, and others initiated the "Kalachakra Dharma Assembly" in Hangzhou to invite Panchen Lama IX. Mei Lanfang and others were invited to perform during the meeting, but Mei Lanfang and others did not participate in the performance. This poem expresses the poet's longed social ideals, and uses "The wind and rain are dark, and the cocks are singing" to express his bitterness about the complicated national affairs. Its ontology should be based on the cornerstone of Lu Xun's life activities, and he naturally becomes a singer of life. Another example is the poem "Occasional Poems in the Late Autumn of the Year of the Pig" written for his close friend Xu Shoutang on December 5, 1935: "Having experienced the coldness of autumn, how dare I write about the warmth of spring. / The vast sea of dust makes me feel a hundred emotions, the golden wind makes thousands of officials run away. / When I return to the big lake in old age, the mushrooms and cattails are all gone, and my teeth are cold when I fall into the empty clouds in my dream. / I listen to the lonely chicks in the lonely house, and I get up to see the stars." The background of the poem refers to the large number of officials evacuating Hebei Province under the oppression of the Japanese imperialist invaders at that time. The poet expresses his pessimistic sadness about the people's livelihood and his feeling of being homeless, desolate and lonely.

III. The Enlightenment of Lu Xun's Poetry Imagery

For more than 80 years, the research on the imagery art and influence of Lu Xun's poetry has undergone a process of gradual development and continuous deepening, and has attracted more and more attention from the Chinese community; but also because various forms of appreciation or annotations have been published at home and abroad, among which the poems involve misunderstandings or the meaning of the poems are obscure and difficult to understand, all of which also require researchers to make further reflections. In the history of modern Chinese poetry, Lu Xun's poems have irreplaceable historical significance; especially the relevant materials during his study abroad need to continue to be excavated to study some special or puzzling problems in the poems. Looking back at Lu Xun's ideal pursuit of poetry and his practical activities, including his creation of poetic images, we can get many inspirations.

1. Lu Xun's poetic images are constantly accumulated in the continuation of history. Some poetic images need to be transformed while being inherited; this is also created by the subconscious psychology of poets as a nation. He is a great seeker armed with the scars of Chinese history, and we can clearly see from his poems the awakening of intellectuals under modern enlightenment in China, which has enabled our ancient nation to embark on the road of democratic rebirth.

2. The imagery of Lu Xun's classical poetry is of oriental culture. The deep feelings of separation and loneliness in it have always been praised by Chinese literati. It is a symbol of his noble character. The poetic heart is bright and clear, and it clearly affirms that people have the courage and great beauty to pursue freedom. Although many images are sad, they are reflected in his concern for national affairs and people's livelihood or his reflection on major historical events. His poetry can be integrated with the thinking of life philosophy, and the poetic flavor often becomes heavy.

3. Lu Xun is a frank patriotic poet, so naturally his poetry will not be silent. The emotions in his poems can sing his perception of life and his thinking about society, and at the same time, it also opens up the vision of modern poetics. His poetic heart is open, but it contains a kind of silent melancholy. Besides sadness, he can also show his concern for the lower classes of society, which is also a kind of painful sublimation. His figure is just like a lone goose. No one can stop the moonlight from going farther and farther, and no one can stop the coming of darkness. However, he is fearless of wind and rain, and will definitely continue to fly. The footsteps he leaves behind will be like a hidden waterfall, waiting for the praise of spring.

4. Lu Xun's poetic imagery is influenced and inspired by the oriental humanistic environment; but at the same time, he also absorbs the novelty of Western culture and art, expands the scope of his aesthetic objects, and makes it glow with poetry and passion. The imagery of Lu Xun's poetry is generated and developed in the context of the vast fusion of Chinese and foreign literature.

〔Published in *Journal of Yancheng Teachers College*, Jiangsu Province, China, Vol. 32, No. 138, No. 6, 2012, pp. 44-48.〕

02 論丁旭輝的《台灣現代詩中的老莊身影與道家美學實踐》
On Ting Hsu-Hui's *The Influences Of Lao-Tzu & Chuang-Tzu And Taoist Aesthetic Practices In Taiwanese Modern Poetry*

摘要 Abstract

丁旭輝是台灣詩壇評論的學者之一，此書以臺灣現代詩對老子、莊子的接受與轉化情形與道家美學實踐，作一闡述，有其獨特的時代價值。

Ting Hsu-hui is one of the commentary scholars in Taiwan's poetry circles. This book elaborates on the acceptance and transformation of Lao-tse and Chuang-tzu and Taoist aesthetic practices in Taiwanese modern poetry. It has a unique value of the times.

關鍵詞：美學、老子、莊子、現代詩、自然。
Keywords: aesthetics, Lao-tzu, Chuang-tzu, modern poetry, nature.

一、其人其書

丁旭輝（1967 年－　）臺灣省雲林縣人，中山大學文學博士，現任「國立高雄應用科技大學」人文學院院長，曾獲「國科會研究獎」、巫永福基金會臺灣文學論文獎，著有現代詩〈新詩〉評論、研究專著等多種。

《台灣現代詩中的老莊身影與道家美學實踐》的時間斷限自 1949 年起至 2009 年寫作完成為止共約 60 年間，丁旭輝所論述的臺灣現代詩影響的來源與接受的對象，重在體認感悟，而非著眼於考證老莊哲學的駁辨。他以《老子》、《莊子》及道家美學為主要範疇，藉由詩話的故事情節裡的想像或感受賦予詩作丰采的意涵。全書共分八章，由老莊形象的現代書寫起，經由「道家美學的生命演出」等單元的佳例，我們不難看出，丁旭輝在以「魚意象的發展與忘我美學的形成」，及「蝶意象的擴張與物化美學的闡揚」中實我的體認，也清楚地表述了他的審美自然觀；這種以老莊美學的正面詮釋開啓了臺灣現代詩史上以「自得境界與消遙神韻」為最高美的思想先河。無論是從「以物觀物的無我美學」到「無我美學的作品實踐」，丁旭輝由老、莊語言的發想創新，感悟到天地自然無為而成的大美存在，以之推移於詩想的多種關係之中。他認為，「詩意的想像」是臺灣的現代詩人們不斷主動接近老、莊思想並把他們消化、轉化為詩作形式的主因；最後，更渴望與期待道家美學的研究對臺灣現代詩的影響能持續發展，臻於新的時代價值。

二、道家美學中的詩想與詮釋（Interpretation）

在道論中，一切行為關係都應取法天地，唯貼近本然，才能合於人的生命生存自由自適要求，並可以從煩擾之下解脫出來，實現難得的「自樂」與「消遙」。或說，「有我之境」是「以情觀物」，即詩人看到了與自己無利害關係的景物，為之感動而把自我情感移加到景物上去。而無我之境」是「情以物興」、「心隨物以宛轉」，即詩人以靜虛之心觀物，這就打破了人與物的界限，也打破了心靈與現實時空閾限。

這不是一部應時之作。雖然在我看來，僅僅注意到中國傳統老、莊以及以他們為主體的道家美學，似乎無法呈現現代詩與古典文學、哲學之間關係的全貌。然而，為了集中呈現存在於臺灣現代詩與老、莊、道家美學之間的接受轉化關係；丁旭輝的思考遠遠超出了美學研究範圍，其視野寬闊，確實也提供了臺灣現代詩壇上少見的佳作。這部論著結構宏偉，既表現在取材收集上，也表現在立意上。他把研究範疇從老、莊著眼，才能認識道家美學之遠，逐步開展臺灣現代詩的生命。在一定意義上，他深化了詩的涵義，確實是對美的境界性揭示。在發展方向上，他力求超越了對象所表現的意義，純粹以道家美學去領略對象的形式美，並為詩的真諦留下了深刻印記。最後，他把握了時間斷限的無限性，便體悟了詮釋詩作中奧妙無窮的意味和志趣。

丁旭輝以詩作論證道家藝術精神在詩歌上的顯現，書中，他引用了許多臺灣現代詩人接受了老、莊的自我隱喻意象，並沿著詩人自喻的軌跡，加以轉化而展開了反思，在藝術上給人以新的啟示。誠然，任何一種美的創造並非局限於一種具體事物的描摹，否則最多只能給人一種感性的知識或片刻的愉悅，而不能從更高的層次上領悟美或進而體驗到自由聯想之趣味。如果說，世俗之美重在形象的話，那麼，道家美學則超越於形象。因為，老、莊哲學的基本特徵是「無為而又無不為」，大美起始於美又超越於美。丁旭輝由詩作範例中逐步勾勒出道家美學的特質，其論述是對美的詩想加以詮釋；他對詩學追求的玄遠哲理、時空意識等審美體驗，這是道家美學思想的一種集中表現。細品之中，這是文化藝術的漫遊，全書也注重詩作的哲理意蘊，語言鮮明豐滿，常能直抒胸臆，也極大地拓展了臺灣現代詩的時空。

　　在丁旭輝看來，莊子以直覺體物而感知魚樂，人亦如魚。他提出許多位詩人接受《莊子》魚樂與否的故事，從而加深了臺灣的時代背景的想像或悲辛形象。他發現，莊子有兩個內在的美學樞紐，即「忘我」與「物化」。然後論述這兩者於魚、蝶意象之外在臺灣現代詩中的滲透與交融，及上溯老子的道家整體美學。文中也提出，蝶意象很單純的來自於《齊物論》。《齊物論》中的蝶，自是想像的蝶、夢境的蝶、虛構的蝶，臺灣現代詩接受了此一想像的蝶，而轉化為多方隱喻，甚至納入現實之蝶、真實之蝶。他舉證了許多詩作中，其實與詩人追求一個解脫形體的永恆靈魂的心靈是與莊蝶意象一致的。在論述中重複出現的莊蝶意象之「形體解脫」、「新生喜悅」、「實我體認」、「隔世追尋」等深刻隱喻，即構成一種典型的、反覆出現的意象。丁旭輝擅用這些意象中的原型意義加以串連或擴散，形成在華語文學中的象徵體系的雛形，對臺灣現代詩的內涵與發展，產生了一定的影響。他認為，臺灣現代詩中，老、莊的忘我、物化美學落實到生命實踐，成為人生自我救贖的心靈對策與苦難解藥。最後在總結裡，他期待，此書一方面提供了老、莊解詩的方法學示範，一方面能實際提供了閱讀的路徑。

　　筆者以為，老、莊的審美自然觀，是從參悟天地之美而推及人的行為。而丁旭輝對審美和藝術創造規律的認識，也大多來自老、莊及道家美學思想。在臺灣詩論上，他對於道家美學思想的運用與闡釋，已蘊含著他的審美觀、審美情趣和審美判斷，具有十分深刻的美學意義。因此，丁旭輝詩想範疇的審美生成，常能引喻貼切，很形象地表達出原詩的旨意。

三、丁旭輝：默默筆耕不息的詩評家

丁旭輝沉浸於現代詩學十餘年，對老莊思想十分熟稔，又長時間閱讀西方哲學著作。嚴格說來，在老、莊思想系統並沒有一套專門針對美學的理論，但老莊思想的價值旨趣、運思與言說的方式，常蘊含著豐富的美學資源。也正是在老莊思想的啟發下，丁旭輝開創了審美意識自覺之門；而研究現代詩一直都是他心靈不竭的種子。他以道家美學作為詩美的出發點和歸宿，無疑也宣告了臺灣美學系統理論的誕生。

這十多年來，他體現了老、莊的審美觀念，為之默默的，是用真誠的筆觸，寫下具有豐富深刻的詩美內涵，其學術價值是從道家美學嵌結詩人與自然的和諧關係。所以，可以說，這是一部重新詮釋臺灣現代詩中老、莊及道家美學的探索之作。丁旭輝也是位不可多得的追求美學境界的教授，長期以來，他把研究詩論視為他孜孜以求的人生境界。我認為，此書的價值既體現在對西方傳統美學的超越上，又體現在對老、莊道家美學思想的理論建構上。他從多方面闡述了老、莊美學思想的價值基礎、哲學範式、終極旨歸及實踐範例，實為臺灣現代詩詮釋的選擇提供了一種依據與思路。

此書給當代臺灣現代詩的重要啟示，是確立道家美學與現代詩相契合的價值觀，此外，丁旭輝也為此書提供了理論相映的實踐。這不僅為道家美學實踐增添了許多的色彩，也對道家美學思想中的老莊身影的原生態思想，作一大理想描述。丁旭輝詩論的特色在於專注於詩的解讀，傾心於內在理路的剖析與建構；其評論的對象，包括台灣當代詩人、也評論過中國詩人等。他開啟用道家美學的眼光看待現代詩的意涵，自覺「返樸歸真」到本初之美與樸真之美的優態境域，以道家淡定、寧靜的心境，積極尋找和皈依審美生存的詩美家園。因而，此書對研究現代詩的啟示有著終極的價值意義。

－2011.10.17 作

【刊河南省《商丘師範學院學報》，第 28 卷，2012 年第 1 期，總第 205 期，書評〈論丁旭輝的《台灣現代詩中的老莊身影與道家美學實踐》〉，頁 22-23。】

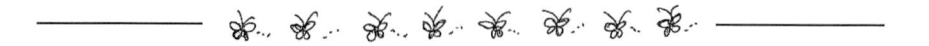

I. The man and his book

Ding Xuhui (1967-) is from Yunlin County, Taiwan Province. He holds a doctorate in literature from Sun Yat-sen University and is currently the dean of the College of Humanities at the National Kaohsiung University of Applied Sciences. He has won the National Science Council Research Award and the Wu Yung-fu Foundation Taiwan Literature Paper Award. He has written many books, including reviews of modern poetry (New Poetry) and research monographs.

The period of *The Influences of Lao-tzu & Chuang-tzu and Taoist Aesthetic Practices in Taiwanese Modern Poetry* is about 60 years from 1949 to 2009. Ding Xuhui discusses the sources of influence and the objects of acceptance of modern Taiwanese poetry, focusing on understanding and perception rather than focusing on the research and debate of Laozi and Zhuangzi's philosophy. He takes *Laozi*, *Zhuangzi* and Taoist aesthetics as the main categories, and uses the imagination or feelings in the storyline of the poem to give the poem a rich connotation. The book is divided into eight chapters, starting with the modern writing of Laozi and Zhuangzi's images, and through the excellent examples of the unit "The Life Performance of Taoist Aesthetics", it is not difficult to see that Ding Xuhui has realized the self in "The Development of Fish Image and the Formation of Selfless Aesthetics" and "The Expansion of Butterfly Image and the Exposition of Materialized Aesthetics", and has also clearly expressed his aesthetic view of nature. This positive interpretation of Laozi and Zhuangzi's aesthetics has opened up the precedent of the thought of "self-satisfaction and dissipated spirit" as the highest beauty in the history of modern Taiwanese poetry. Whether from "selfless aesthetics of viewing things with things" to "the practice of selfless aesthetics in works", Ding Xuhui, through the innovation of Laozi and Zhuangzi's language, come to realize the great beauty of the natural world and nature, and to use it to move forward in various relationships of poetry. He believes that "poetic imagination" is the main reason why modern Taiwanese poets continue to actively approach Laozi and Zhuangzi's thoughts and digest and transform them into poetic forms. Finally, it is his hope that the influence of Taoist aesthetics research on modern Taiwanese poetry can continue to develop to achieve new era values.

II. Poetic imagination and interpretation in Taoist aesthetics

In Taoist theory, all behavioral relationships should follow the example of heaven and earth. Only by being close to nature can we meet the requirements of human life, survival, freedom and self-adaptation, and be freed from troubles to achieve the rare "self-joy" and "disappearance". In other words, "the state of having myself" is "viewing things with emotion", that is, the poet sees the scenery that has nothing to do with himself, is moved by it and transfers his own emotions to the scenery. The state of "selflessness" is "emotions are inspired by things" and "heart follows things in a roundabout way". That is, the poet observes things with a quiet and empty heart, which breaks the boundary between people and things, and also breaks the time and space barriers between the mind and reality.

It is not a work to suit the time, in spite of my opinion that only paying attention to the traditional Chinese Laozi, Zhuangzi and Taoist aesthetics with them as the main body seems to be unable to present the full picture of the relationship between modern poetry and classical literature and philosophy, in order to focus on the acceptance and transformation relationship between modern Taiwanese poetry and Laozi, Zhuangzi and Taoist aesthetics. Ding Xuhui's thinking far exceeds the scope of aesthetic research, and his broad vision does provide rare masterpieces in the modern Taiwanese poetry circle. This treatise has a grand structure, which is reflected in both the collection of materials and the conception. He focuses on the scope of research from Laozi and Zhuangzi, so that he could understand the far-reaching Taoist aesthetics and gradually develop the life of modern Taiwanese poetry. In a certain sense, he has deepened the meaning of poetry, which is indeed a revelation of the realm of beauty. In terms of development direction, he strives to transcend the meaning expressed by the object, purely appreciate the formal beauty of the object with Taoist aesthetics, and leave a deep impression on the true meaning of poetry. Finally, he has grasped the infinity of time to realize the infinite meaning and interest in interpreting poetry.

Ding Xuhui uses poetry to demonstrate the manifestation of the Taoist artistic spirit in poetry. In the book, he quotes many modern Taiwanese poets who have accepted the self-metaphorical images of Laozi and Zhuangzi, and followed the path of the poets' self-metaphors, transformed them, and started to reflect, giving people new inspiration in art. Indeed, the creation of any kind of beauty is not limited to the description of a specific thing; otherwise, it can only give people a kind of perceptual knowledge or a moment of pleasure, but cannot comprehend beauty from a higher level or further experience the fun of free association. If it is said that secular beauty focuses on the image, then Taoist aesthetics transcends the image. Because the basic characteristics of Laozi and Zhuangzi's philosophy are "doing nothing and doing everything", great beauty begins with beauty and transcends beauty. Ding Xuhui gradually outlines the characteristics of Taoist aesthetics from the examples of poetry. His discussion is an interpretation of the poetic idea of beauty. His aesthetic experience of the profound philosophy and time & space consciousness in the pursuit of poetry is a concentrated expression of Taoist aesthetic thought. In the details, this is a wandering of culture and art. The whole book also focuses on the philosophical meaning of poetry. The language is bright and rich, often able to express one's feelings directly, and it also greatly expands the time and space of modern Taiwanese poetry.

In Ding Xuhui's view, Zhuangzi perceives the joy of fish by intuition, and people are also like fish. He proposed that many poets accept the story of whether the fish in "Zhuangzi" is happy or not, thereby deepening the imagination or tragic image of the era background of Taiwan. He finds that Zhuangzi has two inner aesthetics, namely "selflessness" and "objectification". He then discusses the penetration and integration of these two in modern Taiwanese poetry, in addition to the images of fish and butterfly, and traces back to Laozi's overall Taoist aesthetics. The article also proposes that the butterfly image comes simply from "On the Equality of Things". The butterfly in "On the Equality of Things" is an imaginary butterfly, a butterfly in dreams, and a fictional butterfly. Modern Taiwanese poetry accepts this imaginary butterfly and transforms it into many metaphors, even incorporating real butterflies. He has cited many poems to prove that the poet's pursuit of an eternal soul free from the body is consistent with Zhuangzi's butterfly image. The repeated metaphors of Zhuangdie's image of "body liberation", "new joy", "real self-realization", "separate pursuit" and so on in the discussion constitute a typical and recurring image. Ding Xuhui is good at connecting or diffusing the archetypal meanings in these images to form the prototype of the symbolic system in Chinese literature, which has a certain impact on the connotation and development of modern Taiwanese poetry. He believes that in modern Taiwanese poetry, Laozi and Zhuangzi's selflessness and materialization aesthetics are implemented in life practice, becoming a spiritual countermeasure and antidote for self-salvation in life. Finally, in the summary, he hopes that this book can provide a methodological demonstration of Laozi and Zhuangzi's poetry interpretation on the one hand, and a practical reading path on the other hand.

The author believes that Laozi and Zhuangzi's aesthetic view of nature is to extend from the beauty of heaven and earth to human behavior. Ding Xuhui's understanding of the laws of aesthetics and artistic creation also mostly comes from Laozi, Zhuangzi and Taoist aesthetics. In Taiwanese poetry theory, his application and interpretation of Taoist aesthetics already implies his aesthetic view, aesthetic taste and aesthetic judgment, and has a very profound aesthetic significance. Therefore, the aesthetic generation of Ding

Xuhui's poetic category can often be used to aptly express the original poem's intention very vividly.

III. Ding Xuhui: A poetry critic who works silently

Ding Xuhui has been immersed in modern poetry for over ten years. He is very familiar with Laozi and Zhuangzi's thoughts and has been reading Western philosophical works for a long time. Strictly speaking, there is no theory specifically targeting aesthetics in the Laozi & Zhuangzi thought system, but the value, purpose, thinking and expression methods of Laozi & Zhuangzi's thoughts often contain rich aesthetic resources. It was also inspired by Laozi & Zhuangzi's thoughts that Ding Xuhui has opened the door to aesthetic consciousness; studying modern poetry has always been an inexhaustible seed in his mind. He takes Taoist aesthetics as the starting point and destination of poetic beauty, which undoubtedly announces the birth of Taiwan's aesthetic system theory.

Over the past decade, he has embodied the aesthetic concepts of Laozi and Zhuangzi, and has done so silently, using sincere brushstrokes to write down the rich and profound poetic connotations. Its academic value lies in the harmonious relationship between the poet and nature embedded in Taoist aesthetics. Therefore, it can be said that this is an exploratory work that reinterprets the aesthetics of Laozi, Zhuangzi and Taoism in modern Taiwanese poetry. Ding Xuhui is also a rare professor who is pursuing the realm of aesthetics. For a long time, he has regarded the study of poetry theory as the realm of life he has been striving for. I believe that the value of this book is reflected both in the transcendence of Western traditional aesthetics and in the theoretical construction of the Taoist aesthetic thoughts of Laozi & Zhuangzi. He expounds on the value foundation, philosophical paradigm, ultimate purpose and practical examples of Laozi and Zhuangzi's aesthetic thoughts from many aspects, which actually provids a basis and idea for the choice of interpretation of modern Taiwanese poetry.

This book provides an important inspiration for contemporary Taiwanese modern poetry, which is to establish the values that Taoist aesthetics and modern poetry are consistent. In addition, Ding Xuhui also provided the book with the practice of theory. This not only adds a lot of color to the practice of Taoist aesthetics, but also makes a great ideal of description of the original ecological thought of Laozi & Zhuangzi in Taoist aesthetic thought. The characteristic of Ding Xuhui's poetry theory is that he focuses on the interpretation of poetry and is devoted to the analysis and construction of the inner logic. The objects of his comments include contemporary Taiwanese poets and Chinese poets. He starts to look at the connotation of modern poetry from the perspective of Taoist aesthetics, and consciously "returns to simplicity and truth" to the optimal realm of original beauty and simple beauty. With the Taoist calm and peaceful state of mind, he actively seeks and converts to the poetic homeland of aesthetic survival. Therefore, this book has ultimate value and significance for the enlightenment of studying modern poetry.

—Written on October 17, 2011

【Published on Henan Province's *Journal of Shangqiu Normal University*, Vol. 28, No. 1, 2012, No. 205; Book Review "*On Ding Xuhui's The Influences of Lao-tzu & Chuang-tzu and Taoist Aesthetic Practices in Taiwanese Modern Poetry*", pp. 22-23.】

03 兼備學術性和應用性的完美融合——評《淮劇藝術通論》
Perfect Fusion of Academic and Practical Aspects: Comment on *General Theory of Huai Opera Art*

淮劇[1]是在民間說唱「門嘆詞」與蘇北「香火戲」結合的基礎上，吸收里下河「徽班」和京劇的一些藝術精華發展而成的地方劇種，具有非常鮮明的蘇北地域文化特色。2008年6月淮劇正式列入國家非物質文化遺產名錄。

孫曉東[2]教授是精於戲劇文學的學者，尤其對中國非物質文化遺產淮劇史的考察、江蘇省內各淮劇團的調查及持續地在戲曲領域耕耘播種或推廣上，都有著深厚的影響與貢獻。光明日報出版社2016年12月出版的《淮劇藝術通論》，是一部影響深遠、兼備學術性和應用性著作。著者為了學術研究對戲曲史料加以悉心收集並拓寬領域，廣泛涉獵淮劇音樂、唱腔流派、鑼鼓、知名劇作、表演藝術家等專題研究，對淮劇藝術進行了多方面探討，極具可讀性；同時他這一淮劇的研究成果，也是對淮劇藝術和中國戲曲文化關係領域進行深度研究的一項新收獲。

本書的基礎內容是對江蘇省「最具代表性的地方劇種——「淮劇」發展史的細膩撰述和現況之研究。著者之所以將淮劇的美學特徵及其文學性、表演的演技、音樂及舞台進行系統描述，是因為在此之前的十九世紀以後迄今，文獻對淮劇作品集、地方戲曲通論或淮劇發展史較為鮮見，而著者經過多年的論證與探源，將史料與文論結合，讓淮劇總體研究脈絡清晰，體現出一種重構淮劇史的意識。

---

[1] 淮劇，又名江淮劇，是江蘇省「最具代表性的地方劇種」之一，至今已有200多年的歷史，是中國非物質文化遺產。

[2] 孫曉東，江蘇鹽城人，現為鹽城師範學院文學院教授，主要從事中國戲劇文學與藝術研究。

兼備學術性和應用性的完美融合——評《淮劇藝術通論》

一、豐富詳實的主體內容

　　著者在「導論」中對已有二百多年歷史、並在 2008 年 6 月被正式列入國家非物質文化遺產名錄的淮劇做了扼要的宏觀描述，說明了本書的主體結構，充分地傳承了戲曲藝術精髓，也為本書論述提供了必要的鋪墊。書中的主體內容共九章，主要論述了這樣幾個方面的內容：

1. 淮劇發展歷史。著者首先通過對淮劇定義的考辨：進一步明晰了淮劇以江淮方言為基礎，是屬流傳於江蘇、安徽以及上海部分地區的地方性戲曲；接著通過對淮劇產生時的起源期、雛形期、早期、成熟期這四個階段的疏理，揭示了淮劇從「門嘆詞」到「江淮戲」的孕育過程，論述了淮劇在建國後正式定名之後的發展：指出了淮劇在政治引導下的繁盛、十年浩劫中的一息生機及上世紀七八十代淮劇重建的努力，並分析了淮劇在九十年代面臨的觀眾日益變少、隊伍日趨變小、地域日漸委縮的困境與原因及應對的措施。

2. 淮劇的美學特徵。淮劇是戲劇的一種，不僅具有戲曲共同的綜合性、通俗性、地方性及寫意性的美學特徵，而且同時作為一種地方戲劇還具有著一些個性化美學特徵。著者在對淮劇具有戲劇共性的美學特徵詳加論述的同時，著重指出淮劇所獨具的悲情特徵及具備的文藝的本真性。

3. 淮劇劇目及其文學性。劇目是一個劇種重要的核心組成，著者在對淮劇傳統劇目、現代劇目進行概要介紹的同時，又從抒情性、審美性、教化性、通俗性等四個方面論述淮劇文本的文學性。這樣的探索十分重要，也是前人研究中較為薄弱的一個方面。

4. 淮劇表演。著作分為演技、音樂、舞台等三個篇章對淮劇表演藝術的歷史演變、表演特點、角色行當、音樂形態與流派及服飾、臉譜、舞台布景等方面進行了全面系統、深入細緻地研究，尤其書中對採用許多本土的一些民間音樂素材及重要的曲譜、唱腔的探討更具地方特色。

5. 淮劇經典作品賞析。淮劇是通過音樂、舞蹈、語言來表演故事，歷經兩百餘年的演繹，保留下了許多代表性的劇目，著者對劇種的古典、現代、都市新淮劇這三種較為代表性的劇目類型進行了細緻地賞析，尤其對經典作品的唱腔藝術的論述較為獨到。

6. 淮劇表演藝術家。淮劇藝術的發展離不開一代又一代淮劇藝術家的智慧和努力，對他們藝術貢獻的評述無疑會使人們對淮劇的認識更加全面。著者選取了淮劇發展史上具有代表性的筱文艷、何叫天、馬秀英、劉少峰、陳德林、梁偉平、陳澄等老、中、青三代共七位表演藝術家，對他們的從藝道路，創立的流派唱腔及對社會的貢獻與影響等方面加以深入撰述與評述，充分彰顯了他們對於淮劇藝術發展的意義和價值。

7. 淮劇傳承發展與保護。在外來文化、新的傳播方式等的衝擊下，淮劇也與全國其他地方性劇種一樣，面臨著觀眾人數銳減、人才供應不足等種種窘境，面臨著傳承發展與保護的考量和問題，為此，著者曾專門組織調研組對江蘇、上海兩個省（市）的一些淮劇團、淮劇學習班、從事淮劇研究工作的相關人員以及部分普通民眾進行了調閱，並對所搜集到的資料進行了分析、總結，客觀分析了淮劇現在面臨的生存狀況，提出了有針對性的非物質文化遺產的保護措施。這種立足於田野調查的研究，使得著作有別於一般理論論述的空泛，而具有了較強的實踐操作性。

二、獨具創新的研究體系

1. 本書的研究價值，主要顯示在致力於探索淮劇所出現的重大發展經歷及目前存在的問題。書中特別是對的淮劇表演的特點、服飾、臉譜、音樂流派及經典作品進行了考察，並深入瞭解淮劇的形成背景、實質及其在現實生活中所起的影響及作用，並給予其適當的社會地位，試圖讓讀者瞭解，淮劇除了是庶民文化的表現及延伸特定族群的情感記憶以外，也可提升為一種區域文化的認同，從而使全書具有了文化價值與歷史價值。

2. 本書在研究方法的運用上，著者有著獨到的理解與原則，以一種特有的「歷史還原法」和「歷史的美評與批評」去思考，同時還打破了舊思維，廣泛地用敘事學和美學等研究方法，充分收集第一手原文資料，並認真梳理和引述重要文獻後進行論述。他開啟了廣博而細膩的研究視野，讓淮劇文化滲透札根到

兼備學術性和應用性的完美融合——評《淮劇藝術通論》

鹽城人民的血脈裡，並務實地提出淮劇具有文化滲透及文化認同的深刻內涵的新見解。

3. 在內容上具有前瞻性，填補了以往國內同類文獻著作的某些空白，顯示出二十一世紀淮劇發展史的新視野。著者致力於淮劇研究的完整面貌，史論結合，特別是以往淮劇史著作所缺失的劇作文本的文學性等幾個方面進行了系統的論述，因而獲得諸多學者的肯定及公正的學術評價。書中對筱文艷、何叫天、馬秀英、劉少峰、陳德林、梁偉平、陳澄等淮劇傑出的表演藝術家的評述及經典作品的解讀更顯著者的研究功力。

淮劇藝術源遠流長，是蘇北人傳統文化最為立體的展現，它曾是百姓生活中喜慶堂會中的娛樂，將真善美滲透到民心，也實現了族群的文化記憶之間的情感交流。著者長期以來不遺餘力地推動淮劇藝術的傳承、保護和發展，並為鹽城這塊熱土孕育滋生的淮劇劇團貢獻才智，協助打造一個藝術品牌，碩果累累。目前，新淮劇多以講述大時代的小故事為主流，著者在撰述中將淮劇的演變及目前問題加以呈現，期許未來將現代台詞、配樂、流行語加以應用或借用影視、魔幻等現代藝術品種的元素與淮劇固有的藝術手法相融合，使觀者產生了共振，進而提昇審美文化內涵與品性。同時，著者也在舞台燈光、戲曲音樂、人物服裝及舞台道具等方面進行了新探索。因而，此書是著者不斷推出的具有創新性和實際應用價值的研究成果，弘揚了淮劇文化。此外，著者亦十分重視文本的藝術本體，包括故事性、傳奇性及著名人物形象塑造的典型性描述等，讓文本得以提高臻於完善的創作水平，同時這也是著者總結、觀察與研究成功經驗，並為攀登淮劇藝術研究打好更深厚基礎所做出的努力。

著者近年來，除了教學與專於這項研究之外，他幾乎臻於完善，宏觀把握並對淮劇藝術研究提供了這一個重要的文本，也廣泛地對中國戲曲文化提供了幫助。他讓讀者充分瞭解到淮劇紮根於農村、貼進百姓的淮劇音樂力的表現以及具有清新的鄉土氣息與粗狂奔放的陽剛魅力的同時，也看到淮劇所具有的豐富的藝術形態，既樸素而優美。而著者對淮劇洞見及文化史述、戲曲美學、經典曲調選錄等客觀性的撰述，以及在文本最後對淮劇出路的探索與革新，讓此書有了更深的文化內涵。因而，此書具有獨特的理論價值和史料價值，對淮劇愛好者及研究者來說，無疑是最有益的啟示。

因此，由於淮劇戲曲本身的價值，並取決於戲劇的本體的重要性，未來如何讓傳統的價值與現代淮劇之間融合，讓這項文化傳承具有了思想深度及普及性，這是著者需要加以深切體會的。著者如能再繼續研究，加以推廣至國際的學界交流，並再多多關注淮劇發展的新困難和如何改善經營形式的新挑戰以及其在蘊含的族群認知問題上加以深入研究，讓淮劇藝術研究真正地成為地域文化研究，使其更具有文化傳承的典範價值及現實意義，這或許是淮劇這一非物質文化遺產傳承發展、再現輝煌的真正關鍵所在。

【刊遼寧省，《文化學刊》*Culture Journal*，遼寧社會科學院主辦，總第84期，刊〈兼備學術性和應用性的完美融合——評《淮劇藝術通論》〉，2017年第10期，頁234-236。】

Huai Opera[3] is a local opera that was developed on the basis of combining the folk storytelling "Mentanci" with the "Xianghuo Opera" of northern Jiangsu province, absorbing some of the artistic essence of the Lixiahe "Huiban" and Peking Opera. It has very distinct northern Jiangsu regional cultural characteristics. In June 2008, Huai Opera was officially included in the National Intangible Cultural Heritage List.

Professor Sun Xiaodong[4] is a scholar who is proficient in drama literature. He has made profound influence and contributions, especially in his research on the history of Huai Opera, a Chinese intangible cultural heritage, his investigation of various Huai Opera troupes in

---

[3] Huai Opera, also known as Jianghuai Opera, is one of the "most representative local operas" in Jiangsu province. It has a history of more than 200 years and is a Chinese intangible cultural heritage.

[4] Sun Xiaodong, a native of Yancheng, Jiangsu Province, is currently a professor at the School of Literature of Yancheng Normal University, mainly engaged in the research of Chinese drama literature and art.

兼備學術性和應用性的完美融合——評《淮劇藝術通論》

Jiangsu province, and his continuous efforts in cultivating, sowing and promoting the field of opera. *General Theory of Huai Opera Art*, published by Guangming Daily Press in December 2016, is a far-reaching monograph that combines both academic and practical value. For academic research, the author carefully collected and expanded the scope of opera historical materials, and extensively studied topics such as Huai opera music, singing styles, gongs and drums, famous plays, and performing artists. He conducted a multi-faceted discussion on Huai opera art, which is quite readable. At the same time, his research results on Huai opera are also a new achievement in the in-depth study of the relationship between Huai opera art and Chinese opera culture.

The basic content of this book is a detailed description of the development history and current status of Huai Opera, the most representative local opera in Jiangsu province. The author systematically describes the aesthetic characteristics of Huai Opera and its literary nature, acting skills, music and stage performance because there have been few documents on Huai Opera collections, local opera general theories or the history of Huai Opera development since the 19th century. After years of argumentation and exploration, the author has combined historical materials with literary theory to make the overall research of Huai Opera clear, to reflect a consciousness of reconstructing the history of Huai Opera.

I. Rich and detailed main content

In the "Introduction", the author gives a concise and macroscopic description of the Huai Opera, which has a history of over 200 years and was officially included in the National Intangible Cultural Heritage List in June 2008. It explains the main structure of the book, fully inherits the essence of opera art, and also provides the necessary foundation for the book's discussion. The main content of the book consists of nine chapters, which mainly discuss the following aspects:

1. The development history of Huai Opera. The author first examines the definition of Huai Opera: further clarifying that Huai Opera is based on the Jianghuai dialect and is a local opera that is circulated

in Jiangsu, Anhui and parts of Shanghai; then, by sorting out the four stages of Huai Opera's origin, embryonic stage, early stage and mature stage, the author reveals the gestation process of Huai Opera from "Mentanci" to "Jianghuai Opera", and discusses the development of Huai Opera after it was officially named after the founding of the People's Republic of China: pointing out the prosperity of Huai Opera under political guidance, the breath of life during the ten-year catastrophe, and the efforts to rebuild Huai Opera in the 1970s and 1980s, and analyzing the difficulties and reasons faced by Huai Opera in the 1990s, such as the decreasing audience, the shrinking team and the shrinking region, as well as the corresponding measures.

2. The aesthetic characteristics of Huai Opera. Huai Opera is a type of drama that not only possesses the common aesthetic characteristics of opera, namely, comprehensiveness, popularity, locality and freehand style, but also, as a local drama, it also possesses some personalized aesthetic characteristics. While elaborating on the common aesthetic features of Huai Opera, the author also emphasizes the unique tragic features of Huai Opera and its literary and artistic authenticity.

3. Huai Opera repertoires and their literary qualities. Repertoire is an important core component of a drama genre. While giving a brief introduction to traditional and modern Huai opera repertoires, the author also discusses the literary nature of Huai opera texts from four aspects: lyricism, aesthetics, education, and popularity. Such exploration is very important and is also a relatively weak aspect in previous research.

4. Huai Opera performance. The book is divided into three chapters: acting, music, and stage. It conducts a comprehensive, systematic, in-depth and meticulous study of the historical evolution, performance characteristics, role roles, musical forms and schools, costumes, facial makeup, stage settings and other aspects of Huai Opera performing arts. In particular, the book's discussion of the use of many local folk music materials and important scores and singing styles is more local in character.

5. Appreciation of classic works of Huai Opera. Huai Opera tells stories through music, dance and language. After over two hundred years of performance, many representative repertoires have been preserved. The author has made a detailed appreciation of the three more representative repertoire types of the opera: classical, modern and urban new Huai Opera, and his discussion on the singing art of classic works is particularly unique.

6. Huai opera performing artist. The development of Huai Opera art is inseparable from the wisdom and efforts of generations of Huai Opera artists. Comments on their artistic contributions will undoubtedly make people's understanding of Huai Opera more comprehensive. The author selects seven performing artists from the old, middle-aged and young generations, including Xiao Wenyan, He Jiaotian, Ma Xiuying, Liu Shaofeng, Chen Delin, Liang Weiping and Chen Cheng, who are representative in the history of Huai Opera, and gives in-depth descriptions and comments on their artistic paths, the singing styles they created, and their contributions and influences on society, fully demonstrating their significance and value to the development of Huai Opera art.

7. Inheritance, development and protection of Huai Opera. Under the impact of foreign culture and new modes of communication, Huai Opera, like other local operas in the country, is faced with various difficulties such as a sharp decline in audience numbers and insufficient talent supply. It is also faced with considerations and problems of inheritance, development and protection. For this reason, the author has specially organized a research team to survey some Huai Opera troupes, Huai Opera training classes, relevant personnel engaged in Huai Opera research and some ordinary people in Jiangsu and Shanghai provinces or cities, and has analyzed and summarized the collected information, objectively analyzed the current survival situation of Huai Opera, while proposing targeted protection measures for intangible cultural heritage. This kind of research based on field investigation makes the work different from the empty general theoretical discussions and has strong practical operability.

II. Unique and innovative research system

1. The research value of this book lies mainly in its commitment to exploring the major development experiences and current problems of Huai Opera. The book especially examines the characteristics, costumes, facial makeup, music schools and classic works of Huai Opera performances, and has an in-depth understanding of the formation background, essence, influence and role of Huai Opera in real life, and gives it an appropriate social status, trying to let readers understand that Huai Opera is not only a manifestation of common people's culture and an extension of the emotional memory of a specific ethnic group, but can also be promoted to a regional cultural identity, thus giving the whole book cultural and historical value.

2. The author has a unique understanding and principles in the application of research methods in this book. He thinks in a unique way of "historical restoration" and "historical aesthetics and criticism". At the same time, he breaks the old thinking and widely uses research methods such as narratology and aesthetics. He fully collects first-hand original materials, and carefully sorts out and quotes important documents for discussion. He has opened up a broad and detailed research perspective, allowing Huai Opera culture to penetrate and take root in the blood of the people of Yancheng, and pragmatically put forward new insights that Huai Opera has profound connotations of cultural penetration and cultural identity.

3. It is forward-looking in content, filling certain gaps in previous domestic literature of the same kind and showing a new perspective on the history of the development of Huai Opera in the 21st century. The author is committed to the complete picture of Huai Opera research, combining history and theory, and especially systematically discussing several aspects such as the literary nature of the play texts that were missing in previous Huai Opera history works, and has therefore won recognition from many scholars and fair academic evaluation. The book's comments on outstanding Huai Opera performing artists such as Xiao Wenyan, He Jiaotian, Ma Xiuying, Liu Shaofeng, Chen

兼備學術性和應用性的完美融合——評《淮劇藝術通論》

Delin, Liang Weiping, and Chen Cheng, as well as their interpretation of classic works, further demonstrate the author's research skills.

Huai Opera art has a long history and is the most three-dimensional display of the traditional culture of the people of northern Jiangsu. It was once entertainment in festive gatherings in the lives of the people, infiltrating truth, goodness and beauty into the hearts of the people and realizing emotional exchanges between the cultural memories of ethnic groups. The author has been working tirelessly to promote the inheritance, protection and development of Huai Opera art.

The Huai Opera Troupe, nurtured in the fertile land of Yancheng, has contributed its talents and wisdom to help create an art brand and has achieved fruitful results. At present, the mainstream of the new Huai Opera is to tell small stories of the great era. In his writing, the author presents the evolution and current problems of Huai Opera, hoping that in the future modern lines, soundtracks, buzzwords will be applied, or elements of modern art forms such as film and television, magic, etc., will be borrowed to integrate with the inherent artistic techniques of Huai Opera, so as to resonate with the audience and enhance the aesthetic and cultural connotation and quality. At the same time, the author also made new explorations in stage lighting, opera music, character costumes and stage props. Therefore, this book is the author's continuous research result with innovativeness and practical application value, which promotes Huai Opera culture. In addition, the author also attaches great importance to the artistic essence of the text, including its storytelling, legendary nature and typical descriptions of famous characters, so that the text can be improved to a perfect creative level. At the same time, this is also the author's effort to summarize, observe and study successful experiences, and lay a deeper foundation for the research of Huai Opera art.

In recent years, in addition to teaching and focusing on this research, the author has almost perfected it, and has provided this important text for the study of Huai Opera art with a macro grasp, and has also provided extensive help to Chinese opera culture. He allows readers to fully understand the Huai Opera's musical power, which is rooted in the countryside and close to the people, as well as its fresh rural flavor and rough and unrestrained masculine charm. At the same time, he also allows readers to see the rich artistic forms of the Huai Opera, which are both simple and beautiful. The author's objective writing on Huai Opera's insights and cultural history, opera aesthetics, and selection of classic tunes, as well as the exploration and innovation of the future of Huai Opera at the end of the text, give this book a deeper cultural connotation. Therefore, this book has unique theoretical and historical value, and is undoubtedly the most beneficial inspiration for Huai Opera enthusiasts and researchers.

Therefore, since the value of Huai Opera itself depends on the importance of the drama itself, the author needs to have a deep understanding of how to integrate traditional values with modern Huai Opera in the future, so that this cultural heritage can have ideological depth and popularity. If the author continues his research, promotes it to international academic exchanges, and pays more attention to the new difficulties in the development of Huai Opera and the new challenges in how to improve its business model, as well as conducting in-depth research on the ethnic cognition issues it contains, so that the research on Huai Opera art can truly become a regional cultural research, and give it more exemplary value and practical significance for cultural heritage. This may be the real key to the inheritance and development of Huai Opera, an intangible cultural heritage, and the restoration of its glory.

【Published in Liaoning Province, *Cultural Journal*, sponsored by Liaoning Academy of Social Sciences, Issue 84, published "Perfect Fusion of Academic and Practical Aspects: Comment on *General Theory of Huai Opera Art*", Issue 10, 2017, pp. 234-236.】

04 略談《魯拜新註》英譯本
On the English translations of *New Notes on Rubaiyat*

《魯拜集》（The Rubaiyat of Omar khayyam）是波斯十一世紀的詩人奧瑪・珈音（Omar Khayyám, 1048-1122）的四行詩集，其特徵是每首四行，一、二、四行押韻，第三行通常不押韻，跟中國的絕句頗為相似。此書在華人世界的譯本以十九世紀英國作家愛德華・費滋傑羅（Edward Fitzgerald）的英譯本，廣泛流傳。《魯拜》原名 Rubaiyat，意「四行詩」，非指一首分成一百零一節的長詩；而是每一首都有獨立存在的價值，且佳作如林。他的詩大部分關於命運、死亡、享樂、不朽，用筆墨來探索來世及宗教，意境高遠，數百年來啟發無數讀者。

奧瑪・珈音是個詩哲、著名的天文學家、數學家，一生研究各門學問，尤精天文學。他留下詩集《柔巴依集》（Rubaiyat，又譯《魯拜集》），是寫其思想深度與世界，歌咏天意無常、生命短暫、美好事物如過眼雲煙、命運難以捉摸等體悟，因而是部人生感悟的詩化結晶。繼胡適、郭沫若、聞一多、徐志摩、吳劍嵐、孫毓堂等人英譯衍譯本之後，台大外文系梁欣榮教授，自幼受父親的啟蒙，愛讀舊詩，自美國德州 A&M 大學英美文學博士畢業後，在教授之餘，用畢生的心血創作了大量豐盈的著作，獲梁實秋翻譯獎、林語堂翻譯獎及台大文學翻譯獎評審等殊榮。他在 2013 年亦推出譯本《魯拜新詮》，以古典七言絕句形式重新詮釋《魯拜集》，當代學者給予極高評價，在翻譯內容上也有較大的延伸。

在諸家翻譯的原著中，梁欣榮的《魯拜新詮》非但強化了文本中的詩體，以仰視的角度出現在翻譯家的平台上，讓讀者看到更多的是他深厚的文學底子，得以「凝視」奧瑪・珈音詩歌裡最深層的寂寞，並帶著一種對他生命價值的敬意，而我們也確定了這位不朽的詩人生存的價值。

文評集粹讀本
-Selected Readings in Literary Reviews-

　　正如德國偉大的美學思想家、哲學家阿多諾（Heodor Ludwig Wiesengrund Adorno, 1903-1969）所說：「有必要讓苦難發出聲音，這是一切真理的條件。」[1]奧瑪・珈音的人生感悟是有其人生體驗的深厚基礎的，他的博深學養與廣闊的視野，對自然世界、人生場景、生死的超然與社會面貌等都帶著一種探索、求知的感覺，與此同時也陸續接受了一些新思想，並發出一些與眾不同的新見解。他能用波斯文及阿拉伯文寫詩，其四行詩雖無關政治與批判，也曾遭批評為「無恥腐敗」，但我以為，神的恩典，總是夠他用的，他的卓越成就與盛名是無庸置疑的。而我在梁欣榮教授的書中，聽見他在翻譯此書與詩人時空中心靈的撞擊與情感的交流,其中，也蘊涵了梁教授對詩歌特殊的審美要求，從而輔助塑造奧瑪・珈音的完整形象。這是本值得我珍藏的好書。有幸拜讀，因而為文。

【刊香港先鋒詩歌協會主辦，《流派》詩報，第二期，2017.03。】

　　The Rubaiyat of Omar Khayyam is a collection of four-line poems by the 11th century Persian poet Omar Khayyám (1048-1122). Its characteristic is that each poem has four lines, with the first, second, and fourth rhyming lines, while the third line usually does not rhyme, which is quite similar to the Chinese quatrain. The English translation of this book by the 19th century British writer Edward Fitzgerald is widely circulated in the Chinese world. The original name of the work is "Rubaiyat", which means "four-line poem". It does not refer to a long poem divided into 101 stanzas; rather, each poem has its own value, and there are many excellent works. Most of his poems are about fate, death, enjoyment, and immortality. He uses pen and ink to explore the afterlife and religion. His profound artistic conception has inspired countless readers through hundreds of years.

　　Omar Kayin is a poet-philosopher, a famous astronomer, and a mathematician. He studied various subjects throughout his life, especially astronomy. He left behind a collection of poems entitled

---

[1] Theodor Adomo. Negative Dialectics [M]. Continuum Press. 1987.
　-2016.10.17 Taiwan.

Rubaiyat, which describes the depth of his thoughts and the world, singing about the impermanence of God's will, the brevity of life, the fleetingness of beautiful things, and the unpredictability of fate. Therefore, it is a poetic crystallization of his understanding of life. Following the English translations of Hu Shi, Guo Moruo, Wen Yiduo, Xu Zhimo, Wu Jianlan, Sun Yutang and others, professor Liang Xinrong of the Department of Foreign Languages at National Taiwan University, who was inspired by his father to read old poems since childhood, has devoted his life to creating a host of works after graduating from Texas A&M University with a doctorate in British & American literature. He has won the Liang Shiqiu Translation Award, the Lin Yutang Translation Award and the National Taiwan University Literature Translation Award. In 2013, he made a translation, *A New Interpretation of the Rubaiyat*, which reinterpreted the *Rubaiyat* in the form of classical seven-character quatrains. Contemporary scholars have given it high praise, and the translation content has also been greatly extended.

Among the original works translated by various people, Liang Xinrong's *A New Interpretation of Rubaiyat* not only strengthens the poetic style in the text, but also appears on the platform of the translator from an upward perspective, allowing readers to see more of his profound literary foundation, and to "gaze" at the deepest loneliness in Omar Kayin's poems, and with a kind of respect for the value of his life, we also confirm the value of the existence of this immortal poet.

As the great German aesthetic thinker and philosopher Adorno (1903-1969) said, "It is necessary to give voice to suffering. This is the condition of all truth."[2] Omar Kayin's life is based on his own life experience. His profound knowledge and broad vision have brought him a sense of exploration and knowledge of the natural world, life scenes, the transcendence of life and death, and the social outlook. At the same time, he has gradually accepted some new ideas and put forward some new and different insights. He writes poetry in Persian and Arabic. Although his quatrains have nothing to do with politics and criticism, they have been criticized as "shameless and corrupt", but I

---

[2] Theodor Adomo. Negative Dialectics [M]. Continuum Press. 1987.
— October 17, 2016, Taiwan

think that God's grace is always enough for him. His outstanding achievements and fame are beyond doubt. In Professor Liang Xinrong's book, I heard the collision and emotional exchange between his translation of this book and the poet's soul in time and space. It also contains Professor Liang's special aesthetic requirements for poetry, which helps to shape the complete image of Omar Kayin. This is a good book worth collecting, and it is a luck for me to read it and write about it.

【Published in the second issue of *School* Poetry News, hosted by the Hong Kong Pioneer Poetry Association, March, 2017.】

05 細讀張智中的一本書
Close Reading of a Book by Zhang Zhizhong

長年以來致力於中國詩詞的翻譯與教學的張智中教授，已出版編、譯、著一百二十餘部，並獲翻譯與科研獎項等多種，是廣受海峽兩岸好評的翻譯家。智中是土生土長的河南博愛人，是農民的兒子，因而熱愛詩詞的他始終懷有鄉土情懷；目前是天津市南開大學外國語學院教授、博士研究生導師，已將漢詩英譯提高到英詩的高度，也保有一顆赤子之心的審美情愫。

日前閱讀了智中寄來的一本早期的著作《毛澤東詩詞英譯比較研究》。全書體現的主要特點有：一是詩歌形式和翻譯策略的創新性，既有不拘其形，散文筆法，也有詩意內容，讀者盡可以遐想。二是將修辭格與意象、文化因素結合，並採取多樣的詩詞翻譯版本進行比較研究，大量考據，是他在更廣泛翻譯研究上的一種嚴謹的學習態度與其力圖通過史料勾勒出翻譯詩詞美學的情感概括。三是詩詞翻譯傳神的體悟與為詩作添增了思想深度。在大量的翻譯詩中，也包孕智中對詩詞創作的追求，確是此書的一大特色。

印象中，在近年來中國大陸的英譯詩詞發展上，鮮少有人像張智中一樣，時刻努力以赴，在英譯古詩的審美心理結構上產生如此傳神的翻譯風格；並能夠超脫世俗，靜觀自在。我還記得有首《五古・詠指甲花》詩云：

百花皆競春，指甲獨靜眠。
春季葉始生，炎夏花正鮮。

葉小枝又弱，種類多且妍。
萬草被日出，惟婢傲火天。
淵明獨愛菊，敦頤好青蓮。
我獨愛指甲，取其志更堅。

揭示了毛澤東偏愛枝葉弱小，卻能頑強生長的鳳仙花（亦稱：指甲花），顯見他在少年時代就含有深邃的思想及藝術表現。

但最令我感動的是，文本的最後一頁，張智中為此書寫了一首詩：

晴川一片消遙遊，
芳草常青伴左右。
日出學海何處帆，
烟波江上我不愁。

詩情濃郁，能彰顯張智中熱切求知、奮進的精神，也把持著與師長、同學在校園裡相守互勉的感懷，並多了點詩人為教育獻身的崇高感。

在我所認識的教師之中，智中是位對漢詩英譯與教學深深關注的學者。就像俄國大作家陀思妥耶夫斯基認為，意志力可以帶給我們能力、機智和知識。智中也是帶有堅強意志的詩人，他已通過生命的淬鍊，又以謙遜、博學的面貌呈現於廣大讀者面前。對我來說，他是一位可敬的友人，而其詩作也有一種自然之美，恰如日出的晨光，有著一種清新內斂的沉穩度，遂成為全書之中最獨特的音響。

—2024.9.8寫於清晨

【刊登臺灣《更生日報》*Keng Sheng Daily News*，副刊，2024.12.21 林明理書評（細讀張智中的一本書），及林明理畫作3幅（晨曦），（帆影），（蓮）。】

Professor Zhang Zhizhong, who has been devoted to the translation and teaching of Chinese poetry for years, has published over 120 books, and has won a host of translation and research awards. He is widely praised by both sides of the Taiwan Straits. Zhizhong is a native of Henan Province, the son of farmers, so he loves poetry with local feelings. At present, he is a professor in the School of Foreign Studies of Nankai University, Tianjin, and is supervisor of doctoral students. He has raised the English translation of Chinese poetry to the height of English poetry, while retaining a childlike aesthetic feeling.

Recently I have finished reading a book entitled *A Comparative Study of the English Translations of Mao Zedong Poems* by Zhang. The main features of the book are as follows: First, it is innovative in poetic form and translation strategy, with both unrestrained forms, prose style and poetic content. Second, he combines figures of speech with images and cultural factors, and adopts a variety of translated versions of poems for comparative study. His extensive research is a rigorous learning attitude in broader translation studies and his attempt to outline the emotional summary of translated poetry aesthetics through historical materials. The third is the understanding of poetry translation and the depth of thought added to the poetry. In a large number of translated poems, there is also his pursuit of poetry creation, which is indeed a major feature of this book.

In my impression, it is rare thing, in the history of English translation of ancient Chinese poems in China, for Zhang Zhizhong to be constantly painstaking, so much so that he produces vivid and expressive translations in the light of C-E poetry translation aesthetics, while remaining detached from the unquiet world. I still remember a poem by Mao Zedong which entitled *Ode to Camphire Flowers*:

> A hundred flowers vie for the beauty of spring,
> when the camphire flower is asleep in quietude.
> In spring it begins to be alive with tender leaves;
> the height of summer sees the height of flowering.
> Small leaves on tender twigs, a variety of them
> with a variety of beauties. Myriads of grasses are

> bathed in sunshine — only the camphire flower
> is heat-proof. Tao Yuanming, a poet-recluse, loves
> chrysanthemums; Zhou Dunyi is a writer famous
> for his Love of Lotus Flowers; as for me, I singularly
> love the camphire flower, which distinguishes itself
> for its will which is strong, stubborn, and unyielding.

The poem exhibits Mao Zedong's love of the camphire flower which is fragile and stubborn, as well as his profound thought expressed in artistic pieces in his childhood.

But what touches me most is a poem by him on the last page of the book:

> In a stretch of boundless sunny land I roam in leisure:
> green grass is lush here, and fair there. Sunrise, an
> academic sail is sailing at the limitless sea — where?
> Facing misty water and waves, I'm free from any worry.

The poem is rich in poetry, fully revealing Zhang Zhizhong's unslackening spirit in seeking knowledge and forging ahead, the feeling of mutual encouragement between teachers and students on the campus, as well as a sense of loftiness concerning the poet's dedication to education and translation.

Among all the teachers I know, Zhang Zhizhong is a scholar who is deeply concerned about the teaching and translation of classical Chinese poetry into English. As the great Russian writer Fyodor Dostoyevsky believed, the willpower can bring us power, wit and knowledge. Zhizhong is also a poet with a strong will. He has been through the tempering of life before presenting himself to the readers with a humble and knowledgeable appearance. To me, he is a respectable friend, and his poems have a natural beauty, like the morning light of sunrise, with a fresh, introspective calmness that produces a most unique sound.

—Written in the morning of September 8, 2024.

【Carried on the Supplement of *Keng Sheng Daily News* (KSDN) in Taiwan, December 21, 2024.】

06 評蔡輝振的《魯迅小說研究》
Comment on Tsai Hueicheng's *Studies of the Novels by Lu Xun*

摘要 Abstract

《魯迅小說研究》係蔡輝振一生力作，他從〈創作背景〉、〈作品分類〉、〈寫作技巧〉、〈思想探討〉、〈風格地位〉五範疇，探討魯迅小說的實際成就與評點，值得研究。

Studies of the Novels by Lu Xun is Tsai Hueicheng's life-long undertaking. He analyzes the actual accomplishments and critical points of Lu Xun's novels from five points: his creative backgrounds, classification of his works, his writing techniques, exploration of his thoughts, and the status of his styles. It is worthy of further investigation.

關鍵詞：魯迅、小說、美學思想。
Keywords: Lu Xun, novels, aesthetical thoughts.

一、其人其書

蔡輝振（1955年－ ）是個特別的人，他出生於彰化縣臨海僻鄉的小村，個性樸實剛毅；自幼窮困，堅忍苦讀，奮鬥歷程，幾多浮沉，十分令人感動。他有情而且創意十足，曾是兼具理性、感性和知性的成功企業家，但最後公司被倒債而拖垮。他毅然選擇棄商從文，再度拾起書本攻讀，42歲畢業於香港珠海大學文學博士，目前是臺灣省雲林科技大學教授。26至28歲之間，連續三年參加德國、美國及瑞士國際發明展，獲金牌獎等多項殊榮。學術專長於創意研發、文獻數位典藏科際整合、台灣文學、魯迅研究等；並成立「魯迅數位博物館」資料庫、「麗文線上教學」數位學習平台，勤於教學與專案研究。

《魯迅小說研究》是蔡輝振的博士論文，高雄復文出版；內容充實，很重視文獻資料整理的精華點。文筆自然流暢，能準確的提綱挈領，有著他自己實事求是的科學態度。他親自走訪中國多地,也介紹了很多不同學家的評點。這些都啟發於蔡振輝他個人的智慧才華、毅力和學派的觀念及感覺上的優劣。他在第七章總結裡,歸納出魯迅具有「沉鬱、冷峻又執著偏激」的性格,以致於使他在小說作品上,所表現的便是「憂憤沉鬱、幽默精煉」,呈現著他「冷雋尖刻」的藝術風格。在評論裡作者也提到,他認為魯迅只不過是個社會病理學家,而非社會病療學家。最後,作者研究發現,魯迅及其作品確實很富感染力與煽動力,尤其對於血氣方剛的年輕人更是易受其影響的。作者引用當年名作家蘇雪林、夏志清及梁實秋等對魯迅的批判之詞後,他在建議中提出,大陸今後對魯迅研究方向的修正觀點及對魯迅小說應還以純粹的文學風貌、勿泛政治化的期許。細讀全書,俯仰之間,皆成心得。顯然地,蔡輝振的努力和才情,已經得到了豐富的收穫。

然而,筆者以為,魯迅在歷史上的成就,後代越是遮掩,越是明亮,正像彎月因蒙上黑紗而倍感動人;因為魯迅寫作的熱情曾戰勝艱辛的歲月,在中國兵荒馬亂的苦味中間,魯迅小說的出現才得以呈現無限甘甜。魯迅小說,雖非全然的科學真理,不必過度的迷戀崇拜;但它也不是純粹的偏激,可以被簡單地否定。唯從美學思想上講,魯迅小說確有值得借鏡和學習之處。因此,筆者僅就文本的內容見解,加以分析評述。

二、魯迅小說研究的實質和特點

魯迅(1881年－1936)原名周樟壽,1898年改為周樹人,是中國重要文學家、思想家、評論家。生於清光緒七年,浙江省紹興市的一個書香門弟。祖父曾在北京任官員,父親是名秀才。12歲時,祖父因科舉舞弊案而被革職下獄,魯迅兄弟隨即離城被安插到大舅父家中避難;自此,家道衰落,但童年的境遇、紹興十七年的生活場景,也造就了魯迅日後完成的小說《吶喊》、《彷徨》和散文集《朝花夕拾》的思想靈泉。之後,魯迅入南京四年,20歲畢業於南京的礦路鐵路學堂,翌年赴日本七年,入仙台醫學專門學校,學習現代醫學。一年後,因觀看日俄戰爭紀錄片,深感於要救國救民,需先救思想。遂而棄醫從文,

他希望用文學改造中國人的「國民劣根性」。這些在作者的第二章裡更有細膩的詳述。

　　尤令我注目的是，魯迅 19 至 20 歲之間，在南京求學階段寫下的詩歌，其中，〈別諸弟三首〉之三：「從來一別又經年，萬里長風送客船。我有一言應記取，文章得失不由天」這是首思鄉情切、寄語其弟周作人寫作上的叮嚀與期勉。而〈蓮蓬人〉是首深刻的美學詩作：「芰裳荇帶處仙鄉，風定猶聞碧玉香。鷺影不來秋瑟瑟，葦花伴宿露瀼瀼。掃除膩粉呈風骨，褪卻紅衣學淡妝。好向濂溪稱淨植，莫隨殘葉墮寒塘。」這首詩確實有自己的內在邏輯，藉蓮來呈現自己，而不失其藝術之為藝術的本質。從這個角度來看，魯迅在 20 歲時，其美學思想即涵蓋東西文化的洗禮，已能創造出很耐人尋味的詩美境界。魯迅是宋代的周敦頤〈字濂溪〉的後裔子孫，原詩的核心思想是：文學是活的，有生成變化，就如同濂溪先生的獨愛蓮之出淤泥而不染，此詩主題不同於周敦頤細膩的寫實表現，而在流露出賞蓮的自己，也有恬靜的生命力。

　　而魯迅 22 歲時在日本留學時寫下的另一首〈自題小像〉詩：「靈臺無計逃神矢，風雨如磐暗故園。寄意寒星荃不察，我以我血荐軒轅。」詩裡滿是張力、悲憤的動勢，其背後隱藏的訊息，明言之，是魯迅對於中國抗戰的記憶映像的綜合呈現與憂思性格的鋪現。其中就有魯迅生命的動態和歷史的向度，更賦予古典美學的特性。然而，魯迅總是能多元思想，超越羈絆，而這也是他備受尊崇，不被歷史遺忘的原因。

　　魯迅歸國後，自創作文學起，直到 55 歲因肺結核和肺氣腫誘發的嚴重氣胸而病世。一生的作品在未來探討魯迅研究上，有不可替代的歷史價值。蔡振輝對魯迅小說的專注、投入、鍥而不捨的收集、整理，是基於對研究主體的觀察入微與真知遠見。他認為，魯迅較擅長於現代白話文的短篇作品，尤其是以諷刺、鄉土小說為主。他雖同意魯迅是國際名作家、文學家，更是新文學運動以來中國最偉大的文藝創作家；但就作品單篇而言，魯迅並非每篇都是傑作。但我隨著研究的深入，反芻在魯迅小說的領域裡，跳脫學派的推崇或輕蔑，留下理性嚴謹深思後的是什麼…？筆者認為只有回歸美學思想（Esthetics thought）才能還原其傑作生命力。

　　魯迅誕生於中國內憂外患之際，對國力衰微有更直接的切膚之痛，其憤世嫉俗的激情，盡傾注於文學創作之中。他自幼喜好書畫，愛好文藝的傾向源自於其與生俱來的美學思想，既存中國古典文學形迹，又具西方美學風範，深受俄國的果戈理、波蘭的顯克微支以及日本的夏日漱石、森鷗外…等外國文學的影響。故他的小說，決然不會趨時媚俗，而是一種獨闢蹊徑、帶有很強化浪漫愛國思想的主觀相契合。他運用人對事物的美的認識能力和審美評價能力的凝聚，融入了自己的思想感情和審美偏好，從而體現了對揭開舊社會的黑暗的審美理想和抨擊舊思想的腐朽的審美氣質，自創「言簡義重」的新奇風格。魯迅的美學思想主要表現在他擅長的小說中，其特點概括起來有以下兩方面：

1. 人物鮮明　寓意深刻

德國古典美學家康德（Immanuel Kant, 1724-1804）認為，審美判斷不是一種知識，不是一種認知活動，而是一種感覺。而魯迅小說裡的人物塑造，有通俗性及常為悲劇性情節的內容；在很大程度上體現了他天性哲學、破除迷信的宗教理念及文藝思想體系的有機成分。如果說盧梭是法國啟蒙哲學的最主要代表之一，是法國大革命的精神導師；那麼，魯迅他便是愛國主義的崇拜者，他也同樣是中國近代文藝美學的奠基者。

比如《徬徨‧在酒樓上》介紹主角「呂緯甫」的描繪：「…細看他相貌，也還是亂蓬蓬的鬚髮；蒼白的長方臉，然而衰瘦了。精神很沉靜，或者卻是頹唐；又濃又黑的眉毛底下的眼睛也失了精采。」這段裡，開啟了中國小說用白話書寫的藝術表現；字的生命可比之於魯迅的精神；他的美學思索並不是純粹的當下，隨即揭示歷史的變動與文化的傷痕。

捷克漢學家雅羅斯拉夫‧普實克（Prusek, Jaroslav）曾說過，魯迅的興趣顯然不在於創造所能刺激讀者幻想的激動人心的情節，而在別處。這感觸也反映出，魯迅的小說是有目的性的自由創造活動的藝術，且不受制於傳統。他跳脫鏡花水月般的浪漫（如《紅樓夢》），也不取材於幻想（如《西遊記》或傳奇〈李娃傳〉等）通俗體材；反而專以社會基層的平凡小人物為主，用心描繪出當下生活經驗的反照，藉以喚起人們對意蘊空間的想像及對美感的社會性的重視。另外，〈頭髮的故事〉、〈示眾〉等等膾炙人口的小說，作品也具有真實度與想像的拓展，能刻劃多重人物的性格，時而溫馨與詼諧、時而帶有童稚般的熱情、時而感人熱淚；

能拉進與讀者間的距離,隱約表露出魯迅的熱血與創作中最平常的快樂。

2. 布局連綿 鄉土意趣

其實,魯迅是很重視小說的節奏和意趣的,在動人的意象及融匯鄉土語言的表達上,也獨具匠心。如《吶喊‧故鄉》裡〈故鄉〉的開頭:「我冒著嚴寒,回到相隔二千餘里,別了二十餘年的故鄉。→現在」,與一般散文家散發出的激盪難平情愫有所不同,他把這種鄉土意趣當是他歸國創作心境趨於平靜後的一種反映。作品中經由布局的細膩處理,產生了一種新的建築美學風格。文字精簡,排列創新,→語言符號可以變成包含許多詮釋的模子,也可以將空間與時間延伸化,賦予該內容新鮮的聯想;它更需要讀者的聽、視、觸的多種感覺之投入參與。

如魯迅筆下寫的紹興風情中,有篇〈出關〉的主角「老子」說:「我橫豎沒有牙齒,咬不動。」或者,《故事新編》中〈理水〉的「愚人」說:「真也比螺螄殼裡道場還難」暗喻極困難。這些語言具有歷史懷舊感的鄉土氣圍,也就形成了一種少見的諧趣,應該說這是魯迅完整清晰地表達了個人創作的風格,文字間偶爾也透露出英雄式的樂觀精神。

總而言之,研究魯迅小說不同於科學,科學是一種知識或理論能力。而魯迅把審美現象中的矛盾揭露出來,儘管他最終並未能有效地解決中國人的陋習、也無力改造積弊的社會。然而,魯迅一生不但精通日、德、俄等語言、熟識中國古典詩詞外,散文、翻譯、評論等創作之影響源遠流長。尤以小說為最,常能赤誠的吶喊,既有真情,又有形象。此外,魯迅小說中的美感,雖是感情經驗,卻具有理性基礎。他在中國小說歷史上的地位多半無人質疑,但也由於有時在文字表現的批判上過於犀利,強烈呈現反封建色彩,雖未走到個人主義的極端路線,還是在死後難逃被後世韃韃的命運。

蔡輝振在此書第六章第二節裡,明確地記錄下蘇雪林在《我論魯迅》中檢討了魯迅思想中的特異性。其中有段:「魯迅心理是病態的,性格大家公認是陰賊、刻薄、氣量偏狹、多疑善妒、復仇心堅韌強烈、領袖慾旺盛,思想陰暗空虛、憎恨哲學,可以說是個虛無哲學者,他的學力文才僅及叔本華、尼采、陀思妥耶夫斯基等人的一半。」後來又批評說魯迅是「流氓」、「土匪」等激憤之詞。

　　曾記得法國存在主義者沙特 Satre 的哲學觀點,他認為人生是絕對的自由,是可以完全的選擇。在選擇時,可以真誠的面對自己,也可欺騙自己。筆者以為,魯迅生前是把精神的自由當作創作的最高原則,在他眼底,雖然並不贊成尼采（Nietzsche, 1844-1900）的充滿懷疑主義和虛無主義的翻譯哲學,但魯迅與尼采都有多災多難的人生經歷和孤獨的心靈,似存有心靈相通的一面;所以,魯迅對一生都被病痛和孤獨所折磨的天才尼采的理論是有選擇的接受的。至於魯迅的才氣是否如蘇雪林或其他批評者所說那般,則見人見智。

　　筆者以為,魯迅在付出自己畢生的精力後,他仍企圖透過文學將中國的苦痛與絕望反射出來,盼能重新建構一種新氣象;這就是他在小說裡所要表現的有關人性的掙扎與博鬥,怎不令人敬佩他的作法？他的小說,文如行雲流水,是中國現代語言的肯定,文字之中有一種對時代無限抗力的持續或嘲諷,或幽默或無奈心酸,也蘊含著某些喻象與力量。至於其它的翻譯文學及創作,也是為了絕大多數人的熱愛和一份孤獨的尊嚴而寫的。當然,這也並非全然無缺憾,魯迅有時憤恨的情緒,混雜了難以言說的苦味,字語間難免偏激,抑是更陷於孤獨和寂寞。然而,相信有智慧的讀者,當能體會魯迅敢於創造生存的希望,這份勇氣,畢竟是現代小說家們少有的現象。至於如果他的才氣不是如此,那歷史將被剪下這些片斷的頌揚和欽讚的。

三、結語：含蓄的批評

　　今年十一月初,收到蔡輝振寄來的《魯迅小說研究》時,讚美的呼聲迎接著他的這本學術著作,但同時也要指出其中的優缺:

　　其一、作者在研究方法上,引述分析、歸納,雖企圖統一他從前人學說中所看到的論述,卻未能完全如他所願。他只作到將魯迅小說的文獻整理分析的程度,象徵地試圖在各家批評之聲浪中,僅提出對未來研究方向的期許,並未能深入調和各家之說,或就魯迅小說的觀點,提出更創新的評論。

　　其二、在研究文本的態度上,蔡輝振的科學精神及務實態度是絕對無庸置疑的;我們可看出作者在求知過程時所下的苦功。

他十分重視魯迅小說人物的歷史性,也逐步地探索魯迅創作的時代背景和性格形成的內在過程。他運用許許多多有關魯迅小說的寫作技巧,把故事的情節摘錄下來,在其思想的探討及藝術風格的塑造上,都表現得非常成功。

綜上而言,魯迅已經離開我們整整 74 年了,世界的潮流無止境的、又繼續向前逐流。如果要真正瞭解魯迅小說的價值性,就必須要去揭示他心理活動的奧祕。這既是剖析的根本目的,也是近幾十年來各學派對其正負面評價問題的癥結。筆者以為,除分析魯迅的潛意識、動機及人格等更深一層的內容外,其中,魯迅的美學思想遠比其意識生活更為重要。

從科學背景看,魯迅重視文學的力量是為企圖解決中國當時社會的病態現象、為改變民族的劣根性。這就反映出他是位有強度和有效率的心理系統。他的人格的形成並不是一個無衝突的徑直的過程,相反的,他因幼年家庭遭變故及外在環境的影響,確是一個充滿矛盾憤慨與悲涼的過程,也嘗盡世間冷暖。尤其是他的奉母成婚的悲劇婚姻,更讓他感到人生的孤寂與無奈。他曾說:「愛情是我所不知道的。」然而,在他的小說裡似乎也可以找到愛和建設性的能量;而且還成為創造用白話文寫小說的重要動力。魯迅十分推崇屈原著作《離騷》中的「浪漫的愛國精神」,也很喜歡幫助年輕人於求知。在文藝的本質上,他的文學正是中國國力衰微時期對於人性的尊嚴與藝術美的頌歌。他開闢了中國最早用西式新體寫小說的新領域,用文學去說明歷史、見證歷史。他的翻譯文學也通達流暢,堅持忠實原文,又力爭文字優雅風範。

依照這些觀點,筆者以為魯迅的美學思想就是他創造小說的主要表徵,對他的一生命運具有決定性的意義。魯迅的童年愛好閱讀較有趣味的野史、漫畫小說;也透過聽祖母說故事,開始著意把美、藝術與故事內容聯繫起來。這就不難看出,他的美學思想性格主導了日後創作的表現。而他在詩學上,也有種突發的藝術直覺,這是非有大氣魄、大力量的人所不能的。

再從小說的創作角度看,少有不具情感價值的東西。在德國美學家黑格爾(Hegel, 1770-1831)的《美學》書中,即把藝術直覺稱為「充滿敏感的觀照。」他有句名言:「美是一種無目的快樂。」也可解釋說,心靈的愉悅才是最重要的。如果筆者對魯迅小說的上述理解合乎實際的話，那麼我認為閱讀魯迅小說，對絕大部份的人來說，仍是中國現代小說中對美學表現相當完整、最龐大也最確切的表述。它源生於魯迅感性與理性思維的完整的統一，在美學思想上，是一種最輕靈的飛躍。最後，僅以一首詩致魯迅—這位掌握白話文學的優秀舵手：

〈雨后的夜晚〉

雪松寂寂
風裏我
聲音在輕喚著沉睡的星群
梧桐也悄然若思

路盡處，燈火迷茫
霧中
一個孤獨的身影
靜聽蟲鳴

雕像上的歌雀
狡黠又溫煦地環伺著
突然，一陣樂音
隨夜幕飛來⋯拉長了小徑

—〈觀上海魯迅公園有感〉

寫於 2010.11.23 夜

【刊登臺灣佛光大學文學院中國歷史學會《史學集刊》，第 43 集，2011 年 10 月，頁 181-190。】

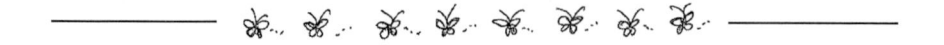

I. The person and his book

　　Tsai Hueicheng (1955-) is a person of specialty. He was born in a small village near the sea in Changhua County. With a simple and resolute personality, he has been poor since childhood, but he has perseveredin studying hard. His struggles and ups and downs are very touching, and he is passionate and creative. He was a successful entrepreneur with rationality, sensibility and intellect, but his company was eventually dragged down by debt. He resolutely chose to give up business and pursue literature. He picked up books again and graduated with a doctorate in literature from Zhuhai University in Hong Kong at the age of 42. He is currently a professor at Yunlin University of Science and Technology in Taiwan. Between the ages of 26 and 28, he participated in the International Invention Exhibitions in Germany, the United States and Switzerland for three consecutive years and won many awards including gold medals. His academic expertise is in creative research and development, interdisciplinary integration of digital collections of literature, Taiwanese literature, and Lu Xun research. He also established the "Lu Xun Digital Museum" database and the "Liwen Online Teaching" digital learning platform, and is diligent in teaching and project research.

A Study of Lu Xun's Novels is Tsai Hueicheng's doctoral dissertation, published by Kaohsiung Fuwen Publishing House. It is rich in content and pays great attention to the essence of the literature and data compilation. The writing is natural and fluent, and can accurately summarize the main points, with his own pragmatic scientific attitude. He personally visited many places in China and introduced the comments of many different scholars. These are all inspired by Cai Zhenhui's personal wisdom, perseverance, and the strengths and weaknesses of the school's concepts and feelings. In the summary of Chapter 7, he concluded that Lu Xun has a "depressed, cold and stubborn" personality, so that what he expresses in his novels is something "angry and melancholy, humorous and refined", presenting his "cold and sharp" artistic style. In the review, the author also mentioned that he thought Lu Xun was just a social pathologist, instead of a sociologist. Finally, the author found that Lu Xun and his works were indeed very infectious and inflammatory, especially for young people who were full of vigor and vitality. After quoting the criticisms of Lu Xun by famous writers of the time, such as Su Xuelin, Xia Zhiqing and Liang Shiqiu, the author proposed in his suggestion that the mainland should revise its views on the direction of Lu Xun's research in the future and that Lu Xun's novels should be given a pure literary style and not be politicized. Read the whole book carefully, and you will gain a lot from it. Obviously, Tsai Hueicheng's efforts and talents have yielded rich rewards.

However, I think that the more Lu Xun's achievements in history are covered up by later generations, the brighter they become, just like the crescent moon turning more attractive when covered with a black veil. Because Lu Xun's passion for writing has overcome the hard years, and in the bitterness of China's chaos and war, the emergence of Lu Xun's novels can present infinite sweetness. Although Lu Xun's novels are not completely scientific truths, there is no need to be overly obsessed with them; but they are not purely radical and can be simply denied. Only from the perspective of aesthetic thought, Lu Xun's novels are indeed worth study and research. Therefore, I only analyze and comment on the contents of the text.

II. The essence and characteristics of Lu Xun's novel research

Lu Xun (1881-1936) was originally named Zhou Zhangshou, and changed his name to Zhou Shuren in 1898. He is an important Chinese writer, thinker, and critic. He was born in the seventh year of Emperor Guangxu's reign in the Qing dynasty, in a scholarly family in Shaoxing City, Zhejiang Province. His grandfather was an official in Beijing, and his father was a scholar. When he was 12 years old, his grandfather was dismissed from office and imprisoned for cheating in the imperial examinations. Lu Xun and his brothers left the city and were placed in the home of their eldest uncle for refuge. Since then, the family has declined, but the circumstances of his childhood and the life scenes of the 17 years in Shaoxing also created the ideological inspiration for Lu Xun's novels *The Scream*, *Wandering* and the prose collection *Dawn Blossoms Plucked at Dusk* that he completed later. Afterwards, Lu Xun went to Nanjing for four years and graduated from the Mining and Railway School in Nanjing at the age of 20. The following year, he went to Japan for seven years and entered Sendai Medical School to study modern medicine. One year later, after watching a documentary about the Russian-Japanese War, he felt that in order to save the country and the people, we must first save our thoughts. So he gave up medicine to turn to literature. He hoped to use literature to transform the "bad national character" of the Chinese. These are more carefully described in the second chapter of the book.

評蔡輝振的《魯迅小說研究》

What particularly caught my attention were the poems written by Lu Xun when he was 19-20 years old and studying in Nanjing. Among them, the third of "Three Farewell Poems to My Brothers" goes like this: "It has been many years since we parted, and the long wind sends the passenger ship off for thousands of miles. I have a word that you should remember, the success or failure of an article is not determined by fate." This is a poem that expresses his homesickness and is a reminder and encouragement to his younger brother Zhou Zuoren on writing. The Lotus Man is a profound aesthetic poem: "The lotus dress and water chestnut belt are in the fairyland, and the fragrance of jade can still be smelled when the wind stops. The shadow of the egret does not come, and the autumn is rustling, and the reed flowers are accompanied by the night dew. Sweep off the greasy powder to show your character, and take off the red clothes to learn light makeup. It is better to be called a pure plant in Lianxi, and don't fall into the cold pond with the dead leaves." This poem does have its own internal logic, using the lotus to present itself without losing art itself. From this perspective, when Lu Xun was 20 years old, his aesthetic thoughts included the baptism of Eastern and Western cultures, and he was able to create a very intriguing poetic realm. Lu Xun is a descendant of Zhou Dunyi (also known as Lianxi) of the Song dynasty. The core idea of the original poem is that literature is alive and has generation and change, just like Mr. Lianxi's love for the lotus that grows out of the mud without being stained. The theme of this poem is different from Zhou Dunyi's delicate realistic expression, and it reveals the tranquil vitality of himself who appreciates lotus.

Another poem, "Self-titled Portrait", written by Lu Xun when he was 22 years old and studying in Japan, reads: "There is no way to escape the divine arrows in the spirit platform, the wind and rain are like a rock and darken the hometown. I send my thoughts to the cold stars, but I don't know, I will sacrifice my blood to the heavens." The poem is full of tension and sad movements. The hidden message behind it is, to put it bluntly, a comprehensive presentation of Lu Xun's memory of the Chinese War of Resistance against Japan and a display of his thoughtful character. It contains the dynamics of Lu Xun's life and the dimension of history, and is endowed with the characteristics of classical aesthetics. However, Lu Xun is always able to think in multiple ways and transcend shackles, and this is also the reason why he is highly respected, instead of being forgotten, by history.

After returning to China, Lu Xun started his own literary career until he died of severe pneumothorax caused by tuberculosis and emphysema at the age of 55. His life's works have irreplaceable historical value in future research on Lu Xun. Cai Zhenhui's focus, dedication, and perseverance in collecting and organizing Lu Xun's novels are based on his meticulous observation and far-sightedness of the research subject. He believes that Lu Xun is better at short stories in modern vernacular, especially satire and local novels. Although he agrees that Lu Xun is an internationally renowned writer, and the greatest literary creator in China since the New Literature Movement. But in terms of individual works, not every single work of Lu Xun is a masterpiece. But as I studied more, I realized that in the field of Lu Xun's novels, what is left after rational and rigorous thinking, beyond the praise or contempt of the school? The author believes that only by returning to aesthetic thought can the vitality of his masterpieces be restored.

Lu Xun was born at a time when China was troubled by internal and external troubles. He felt the pain of the decline of national strength more directly. His passion for worldly cynicism was devoted to literary creation. He liked calligraphy and painting since he was a child. His inclination to love literature and art originated from his innate aesthetic thought. He has both the traces of classical Chinese literature and the style of Western aesthetics. He was deeply influenced by foreign literature such as Gogol of Russia, Sienkiewicz of Poland, and Natsume Soseki and Mori Ogai of Japan. Therefore, his novels will never be vulgar and trendy, but will be unique and in line with the subjective concept of strengthening romantic patriotism. He used the cohesion of people's ability to recognize the beauty of things and their ability to evaluate aesthetics, and integrated his own thoughts, feelings and aesthetic preferences, thus reflecting his aesthetic ideal of uncovering the darkness of the old society and criticizing the decadent aesthetic temperament of old ideas, and created a novel style of "simple words and heavy meaning". Lu Xun's aesthetic thoughts are mainly reflected in the novels he is good at, and its characteristics can be summarized in the following two aspects:

1. Vivid characters and profound meanings

The German classical aesthetician Immanuel Kant (1724-1804) believed that aesthetic judgment is not a kind of knowledge, not a cognitive activity, but a feeling. The characterization in Lu Xun's novels is popular and often tragic; to a large extent, it reflects the organic components of his philosophy of nature, religious ideas that break superstition, and literary and artistic thought system. If Rousseau is one of the most important representatives of French Enlightenment philosophy and the spiritual mentor of the French Revolution; then Lu Xun is an admirer of patriotism, and he is also the founder of modern Chinese literary and artistic aesthetics.

For example, the description of the protagonist "Lu Weifu" in "Wandering in the Tavern" is: "…Looking closely at his appearance, he still has unkempt hair. His pale rectangular face has become thinner. His spirit is very calm, or even decadent; his eyes under his thick and black eyebrows have lost their brilliance." This paragraph opens up the artistic expression of Chinese novels written in vernacular Chinese; the life of words can be compared to Lu Xun's spirit. His aesthetic thinking is not purely present, but immediately reveals the changes in history and the scars of culture.

Czech sinologist Jaroslav Prusek once said that Lu Xun's interest is obviously not in creating exciting plots that can stimulate readers' imaginations, but elsewhere. This feeling also reflects that Lu Xun's novels are art of purposeful and free creative activities, and are not constrained by tradition. He escapes from the romanticism of mirror-like flowers and water moons (such as *Dream of the Red Chamber*), and does not draw on popular materials such as fantasy (such as *Journey to the West* or legends such as *The Story of Li Wa*). Instead, he focuses on ordinary people at the grassroots level of society, carefully depicting the reflection of current life experience, in order to arouse people's imagination of the space of meaning and the emphasis on the social nature of beauty. In addition, his popular novels such as "The Story of Hair" and "Showing the Public" also have the extension of authenticity and imagination, and can portray the personalities of multiple characters, sometimes warm and humorous, sometimes with childish enthusiasm, and sometimes touching tears. They can narrow the distance between readers and implicitly reveal Lu Xun's passion and the most ordinary happiness in his creation.

2. Continuous layout and local interest

In fact, Lu Xun attaches great importance to the rhythm and interest of the novel, and is also ingenious in the expression of moving images and the integration of local language. For example, the beginning of "Hometown" in "Hometown Scream" is: "I braved the severe cold and returned to my hometown, which is more than 2,000 miles away and I have not seen for more than 20 years", which is different from the turbulent emotions exuded by general essayists. He regarded this hometown interest as a reflection of his calm creative mood after returning to China. The delicate layout of the work has produced a new architectural aesthetic style. The text is concise and the arrangement is innovative. Language symbols can become a model with many interpretations, and can also extend space and time to give the content fresh associations. It requires the reader's multiple senses of hearing, seeing, and touching to participate.

For example, in the Shaoxing style written by Lu Xun, the protagonist "Laozi" in "Out of the Pass" said: "I have no teeth, so I can't bite." Or, in "The Fool" in "Managing Water" in *New Stories*, he said: "It's really harder than the dojo in the snail shell", which is a metaphor for extreme difficulty. These languages have a rural atmosphere with a sense of historical nostalgia, which also forms a rare harmony. It should be said that this is Lu Xun's complete and clear expression of his personal creative style, and the words occasionally reveal a heroic optimism. In short, studying Lu Xun's novels is different from science. Science is a kind of knowledge or theoretical ability. Lu Xun exposed the contradictions in the aesthetic phenomenon, although he ultimately failed to effectively solve the bad habits of the Chinese and was unable to transform the society with accumulated problems. However, Lu Xun was not only proficient in Japanese, German, Russian and other languages, and familiar with classical Chinese poetry, but also had a long-lasting influence in his prose, translation, and commentary. Especially in his novels, he could often shout out sincerely, with both true feelings and images. In addition, the aesthetics in Lu Xun's novels, although emotional experience, has a rational basis. His position in the history of Chinese novels is mostly unquestionable, but because of his sometimes too sharp criticism in textual expression, and his strong anti-feudal color, although he did not go to the extreme line of individualism, he still could not escape the fate of being slandered by later generations after his death.

In the second section of Chapter 6 of this book, Tsai Hueicheng clearly recorded that Su Xuelin reviewed the peculiarities of Lu Xun's thoughts in *My View On Lu Xun*. There is a paragraph: "Lu Xun is mentally ill. His character is generally recognized as being treacherous, mean, narrow-minded, suspicious, jealous, vengeful, and strong. He has a strong desire for leadership, dark and empty thoughts, and hates philosophy. He can be said to be a nihilistic philosopher. His academic ability and literary talent are only half of Schopenhauer, Nietzsche, Dostoyevsky, etc." Later, he criticized Lu Xun as a "hooligan" and "bandit".

I remember the philosophical viewpoint of the French existentialist Satre. He believed that life is absolutely free and can be completely chosen. When choosing, you can face yourself honestly or deceive yourself. The author believes that Lu Xun regarded spiritual freedom as the highest principle of creation during his lifetime. In his eyes, although he did not agree with Nietzsche's translation philosophy full of skepticism and nihilism in Nietzsche's 1844-1900, Lu Xun and Nietzsche both had disastrous life experiences and lonely hearts, and they seemed to have a spiritual connection. Therefore, Lu Xun selectively accepted the theories of Nietzsche, a genius who was tortured by illness and loneliness throughout his life. As for whether Lu Xun's talent is as Su Xuelin or other critics say, it depends on one's opinion.

The author believes that after Lu Xun devoted his entire life to this work, he still attempted to reflect China's suffering and despair through literature, hoping to reconstruct a new atmosphere; this is the struggle and fight of human nature that he wanted to express in his novels. How can we not admire his approach? His novels are as smooth as flowing water, and are an affirmation of modern Chinese language. There is a kind of continuation or ridicule of the infinite resistance of the times in his words, or humor or helplessness and sadness, and it also contains certain metaphors and power. As for other translated literature and creations, they were also written for the love of the vast majority of people and a kind of lonely dignity. Of course, this is not entirely without flaws. Lu Xun's emotions of resentment are sometimes mixed with unspeakable bitterness, and his words are inevitably extreme, which makes him even more lonely and isolated. However, I believe that wise readers can appreciate Lu Xun's courage to create hope for survival. After all, this courage is rare among modern novelists. As for if his talent was not like this, history would be cut out of these fragments of praise and admiration.

III. Conclusion: implicit criticism

In early November this year, when I received the *Study on Lu Xun's Novels* sent by Tsai Hueicheng, I was greeted with praise for this academic work, but at the same time, I also want to point out its strengths and weaknesses:

First, in terms of research methods, the author quoted, analyzed, and summarized. Although he attempted to unify the arguments he saw from the theories of his predecessors, he was not able to do it completely as he wished. He only managed to organize and analyze the literature on Lu Xun's novels, symbolically trying to put forward expectations for future research directions amid the waves of criticism from various sources, but was unable to deeply reconcile the opinions of various sources, or to put forward more innovative comments on the viewpoints of Lu Xun's novels.

Second, in terms of the attitude towards researching texts, Tsai Hueicheng's scientific spirit and pragmatic attitude are absolutely unquestionable. We can see the hard work the author put in the process of seeking knowledge. He attaches great importance to the historical nature of the characters in Lu Xun's novels, and gradually explores the historical background of Lu Xun's creation and the internal process of character formation. He uses many writing techniques related to Lu Xun's novels to extract the plot of the story, and is very successful in exploring his thoughts and shaping his artistic style.

In general, Lu Xun has left us for 74 years, and the trend of the world is endless and continues to move forward. If you want to truly understand the value of Lu Xun's novels, you must reveal the mystery of his psychological activities. This is not only the fundamental purpose of the analysis, but also the crux of the problem of positive and negative evaluation of him by various schools in recent decades. The author believes that in addition to analyzing Lu Xun's subconscious, motivation and personality and other deeper contents, Lu Xun's aesthetic thoughts are far more important than his conscious life.

From a scientific background, Lu Xun attaches importance to the power of literature in an attempt to solve the pathological phenomena of Chinese society at that time and to change the bad habits of the nation. This reflects that he is a strong and efficient psychological system. The formation of his personality is not a conflict-free and straight process. On the contrary, due to the changes in his family in his childhood and the influence of the external environment, it is indeed a process full of contradictions, anger and sadness, and he has also experienced the ups and downs of life. Especially his tragic marriage for his mother made him feel lonely and helpless in life. He once said, "love is something I don't know." However, love and constructive energy seem to be found in his novels, and it has become an important driving force for creating novels written in vernacular Chinese. Lu Xun highly praised the "romantic patriotic spirit" in Qu Yuan's work "Li Sao", and he also liked to help young people learn. In the essence of literature and art, his literature is a hymn to the dignity of human nature and artistic beauty during the period of China's national decline. He opened up a new field in China that was the first to write novels in a new Western style, using literature to explain and witness history. His translated literature is also fluent, insisting on being faithful to the original text, and striving for an elegant style of writing.

According to these viewpoints, I think Lu Xun's aesthetic thought is the main manifestation of his novel creation, which has a decisive significance for his life. Lu Xun liked reading interesting unofficial history and comic novels in his childhood. He also began to pay attention to linking beauty, art and story content through listening to his grandmother's storytelling. It is not difficult to see that his aesthetic thought and personality dominated the expression of his future creation. And he also has a sudden artistic intuition in poetry, which is impossible for people with great courage and strength.

From the perspective of novel creation, there are few things that do not have emotional value. In the book "Aesthetics" written by

German aesthetician Hegel (1770-1831), artistic intuition is called "sensitive observation." He has a famous saying: "Beauty is a purposeless happiness." It can also be explained that the joy of the soul is the most important. If the author's understanding of Lu Xun's novels is in line with reality, then I think that reading Lu Xun's novels is still the most complete, largest and most accurate expression of aesthetics in modern Chinese novels for most people. It originates from the complete unity of Lu Xun's sensibility and rational thinking. In terms of aesthetic thought, it is a most light-hearted leap. Finally, I would like to dedicate a poem to Lu Xun, the excellent helmsman who mastered vernacular literature:

After the Rain

The cedars are silent
The wind wraps me
The sound is gently calling the sleeping stars
The parasol trees are also thinking quietly
At the end of the road, the lights are dim
In the mist
A lonely figure
Listens to the insects
The singing sparrow on the statue
Cunningly and warmly
Suddenly, a burst of music
Flying in with the night... lengthening the path

—**Thoughts on Visiting Shanghai Lu Xun Park**

Written on the night of November 23, 2010

【Published on the *Journal of Historical Papers* by of the Chinese History Society of the College of Literature, Fo Guang University, Taiwan, Vol. 43, October 2011, pp. 181-190.】

07 試論《周世輔回憶錄》的文學價值
On the Literary Value of *Memoirs of Zhou Shifu*

　　周世輔（1906年－1988年），湖南省茶陵鄉周陂水頭村人，著名文學家、哲學家，國父思想研究的奠基人。享年83歲。國立暨南大學文學士，韓國東國大學名譽哲學博士，曾先後任湖南一中校長、湖南大學、政治大學、師範大學等校執教，長達50年。著有《中國哲學史》、《國父思想》等書，共四十本。獲教育部學術著作獎、資深教授獎等殊榮。

　　2011年10月5日，周世輔的次子周玉山教授邀請古遠清等三人在台北江浙餐廳用餐後，他高大俊秀、為人嚴謹中帶著幾分俏皮。在長達一小時的訪談中，話題曾轉向他與父親生前留下的這本《周世輔回憶錄》上，我好奇地表示想深入探究。別後數日，竟能收到此書。在我閱讀的視野中，這部回憶錄記敘了周世輔一生八十三年滄海生涯裡，有求學過程、從政經歷到教書及研究、教育子女等生活回顧，也有縱情山水話遊樂的一面。就中國歷史體裁言，本書以傳記體為主，紀事本末體為副；有些地方行文很直率，但總體仍以經過細密組織的措辭為主。正如他在《中國哲學史》完成後，曾撰數聯。其中，「道傳一脈，堯舜禹湯文武。／學無常師，儒墨道法縱橫。」周世輔所體現的是以儒學為經，百家為緯，在百家學中，行師禹墨，學宗黃老。他對中國哲學研究的信念力量，以先秦學說與宋明理學為主；而不是依賴於理性與現實政治。他精研中山學說、涉及中西哲學領域，將自己置於歷史的正確一面，在艱苦卓絕中得到了許多鼓舞。曾撰一聯以自慰：「文積千篇堪稱富，／書藏萬卷不言貧。」這是對堅強靈魂的頌歌，而我們也看到堅守者的姿態和努力的背影。

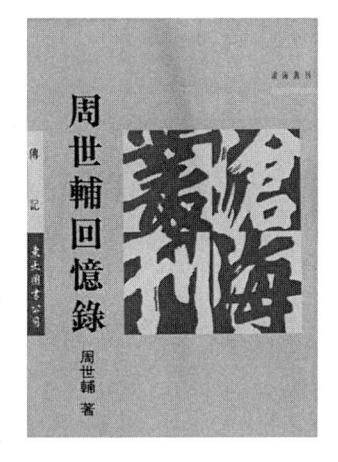

　　在書中，周世輔在教育方面不遺餘力，對子女的愛護，還表現在因材施教的方法上，結果各有不同的成就。尤其在描述對玉

山小時候個性倔強與陽山的教導在情感的表達上，極大地豐富了書整體的蘊涵。這也難外這兩兄弟在最後結論對父親的追悼文，情思魂然一體，字字句句盡是思切與感懷，當然，這一切歸功於他們從小在充滿了人文氣息的熏染與慈母周關淑卿的養育之恩，讓子女們個個在社會上均足稱道。周世輔生前以其清峻之風骨，引起海內外文壇的注目。他勤奮教書，既寫詩文，又寫論著，用自己的心血建構起「中山學術」的不倦探求者。此書裡描述的壯麗風光及許多古蹟，還體現在人與自然的和諧統一上，也收錄許多詩文史話。在他客觀的山水世界與人的精神世界，通過意象的融合。如他的《秋水連天洞庭湖》、《君山名勝古蹟》，都堪稱上品。

　　目前為止，周世輔的生平故事已廣為人知。據他自己承認，他喜遊山玩水，本書在記述名勝古蹟中，先講到古聖先賢的勳業，其滿腔熱血，鮮明地表現出了回歸自然、回歸東方的美學趨向。書寫歷史詩文，亦包含人事與風景的記載或風雲際會與慷慨悲歌的歷史事蹟。這些回憶是記下了生活在他生命旅途中的刻痕，記下他生命中的體悟和感動，也使讀者感受到其文學創作水平和詩藝鑒賞力不斷提高。周世輔編這本書，初衷確實就是想從文學、歷史、傳略與遊記中，分屬敘事、敘時、敘人、敘景不同體裁的作品，選出以故事發生的時間編排或特殊背景為寫作對象，使讀者從中獲得多種學識與樂趣。他對文學的關注在他的人生中發揮了重要作用，同時，也造就了周玉山、周陽山這兩兄弟亦追隨其父親進入教界，先後於政治大學及臺灣大學任教。在物欲橫流的環境裡，他始終堅持著自己的精神追求；從此書的開端起，我們看到一個敞亮的內心世界，走到無比輝煌的終點。至少就書所紀錄來說，他的回憶錄是別出心裁的。

　　截取敘述中的某些生平事功為橫面加以章節分析，是一般出版回憶錄的慣用手法之一，然而作為個人回憶錄能以涵蓋歷史人物，集散文、韻文為一體，溶傳記於一爐者卻鮮有兼備學識與樂趣的研究文章。然而，在《周世輔回憶錄》裡，周世輔的話語果敢而堅定。他博取文、史、傳、遊的資料，前後歷經五年，在撰寫回憶錄時倒下，令人動容。他對自己評價說，「進無以立功，退無以補過，庸庸碌碌，流傳著千萬章文字，桃李復多姿，宜無憾矣！」這是我認為，周世輔一生最有意義的成就。如今，「周世輔形象」將長久活在後人心中。為什麼？因為在中國現代文學史上，真正寫出自傳却並不採取傳記形式的，除魯迅外，周世輔是少數的學者之一。他的文學就是他的回憶錄。但須說明，真正擔得起這本回憶錄不過想幫助讀者更方便地瞭解中國歷史的人物事，用訴說的方式，啓發讀者在閱讀時更自覺地想起歷史人物。這是他此書的不竭的源泉！因此，從這個意義上來看，此書的價值或許不只是普通的賞析著作了。

—2011.10.20 作

【刊登臺灣《大海洋》詩雜誌，第 85 期，2012.07。】

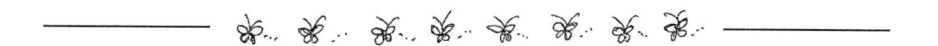

Zhou Shifu (1906-1988), a native of Zhoupi Shuitou Village, Chaling Township, Hunan Province, is a famous writer and philosopher, as well as the founder of the study of the Father of the Nation's thoughts. He died at the age of 83. Receiving a Bachelor of Arts from National Chi Nan University and an Honorary Doctor of Philosophy from Dongguk University in South Korea, he served as the principal of Hunan No. 1 Middle School, Hunan University, National Chengchi University, and Normal University for 50 years. He wrote a total of 40 books, including *History of Chinese Philosophy* and *Thoughts of the Father of the Nation*. He won the Ministry of Education's Academic Book Award and Senior Professor Award.

On October 5, 2011, Professor Zhou Yushan, the second son of Zhou Shifu, invited Gu Yuanqing and three other people to dine at Jiangzhe Restaurant in Taipei. He was tall, handsome, austere yet playful. During the one-hour interview, the topic turned to the book *Memoirs of Zhou Shifu* left by him and his father. I was curious and wanted to explore it in depth. I received this book a few days after we parted. In my reading, this memoir recounted Zhou Shifu's 83-year life, including his study, political experience, teaching and research, educating his children, and other life reviews, as well as his leisure time in the mountains and rivers. Concerning the style of Chinese history, this book is mainly biographical, with a secondary style of chronicle. In some places, the writing is very straightforward, but overall it is still mainly based on carefully organized rhetoric. Just as he wrote several couplets after completing *History of Chinese Philosophy*; among them, "The Tao is passed down in one vein, from Shun, Yu, Tang, Wen and Wu. / Learning has no permanent teacher, Confucianism, Mohism, Taoism and Legalism are all over the place." Zhou Shifu embodies Confucianism as the classic and the Hundred Schools of Thought as the latitude. Among the Hundred Schools of Thought, he follows Yu and Mo, and studies Huang and Lao. His belief in the study of Chinese philosophy is mainly based on the pre-Qin doctrine and Song and Ming Neo-Confucianism; rather than relying on reason and real politics. He studied Sun Yat-sen's doctrine and involved in the fields of Chinese and Western philosophy, placing himself on the right side of history, and was encouraged by many hardships. He once wrote a couplet to comfort himself: "A collection of thousands of articles is rich, / A collection of ten thousand books is not poor." This is an ode to a strong soul, and we can also see the posture and hard work of the persevering person.

In the book, Zhou Shifu spared no effort in education, and his love for his children was also reflected in the method of teaching students in accordance with their aptitude, with different results. In particular, the description of Yushan's stubborn personality when he was a child and the emotional expression of Yangshan's teaching greatly enriched the overall connotation of the book. This is also true of the two brothers' final eulogy for their father. Their emotions and souls are one, and every word and sentence is full of deep thoughts and feelings. Of course, this is attributed to the humanistic atmosphere they have been exposed to since childhood and the kindness of their loving mother Zhou Guan Shuqing, which has made each of their children worthy of praise in society. Zhou Shifu's clear and upright character attracted the attention of the literary circles at home and abroad during his lifetime. He was diligent in teaching, writing both poetry and essays, and was a tireless explorer who built the "Sun Yat-sen Scholarship" through his own efforts. The magnificent scenery and many historical sites described in this book also reflect the harmonious unity of man and nature, and also include many poems and historical stories. In his objective world of mountains and rivers and the spiritual world of people, through the fusion of images. For example, his "Autumn Waters Connecting the Sky to Dongting Lake" and "Junshan Scenic Spots and Historic Sites" are both top-notch.

So far, Zhou Shifu's life story is widely known. According to his own admission, he likes to travel around. In recording scenic spots and historical sites, this book first talks about the achievements of ancient sages and wise men. His passion clearly shows the aesthetic trend of returning to nature and returning to the East. Writing historical poems also includes records of human affairs and landscapes or historical events of wind and cloud and generous and tragic songs. These memories record the traces of life on his life journey, record his understanding and emotions in life, and also make readers feel that his literary creation level and poetry appreciation are constantly improving. Zhou Shifu's original intention in compiling this book was to select works of different genres, including narrative, time, character, and scenery, from literature, history, biography, and travelogues, and write about the time arrangement or special background of the story, so that readers can gain a lot of knowledge and fun from it. His focus on literature played an important role in his life. At the same time, it also led to the two brothers Zhou Yushan and Zhou Yangshan following their father into the church, teaching at National Chengchi University and National Taiwan University respectively. In an environment full of material desires, he always insisted on his spiritual pursuit. From the beginning of this book, we see a bright inner world, and reach an incomparably glorious end. At least in terms of what is recorded in the book, his memoirs are original.

It is a common practice to extract certain life events from the narrative and analyze them in chapters. However, as a personal memoir, it is rare to find a research article that is both knowledgeable and interesting, covering historical figures, combining prose and rhyme, and melting biography into one. However, in *Memoirs of Zhou Shifu*, Zhou Shifu's words are bold and firm. He collected materials from literature, history, biography, and travel, and spent five years. He collapsed while writing his memoirs, which is touching. He said of himself, "I have not achieved anything if I advance, and I have not made up for my mistakes if I retreat. I have lived a mediocre life, but

I have left behind thousands of chapters of writings, and my students are many and varied. I should have no regrets!" This is, in my opinion, the most meaningful achievement of Zhou Shifu's life. Today, the "image of Zhou Shifu" will live long in the hearts of future generations. Why? Because in the history of modern Chinese literature, Zhou Shifu is one of the few scholars who truly wrote an autobiography but did not adopt the form of a biography, except for Lu Xun. His literature is his memoirs. But it should be explained that the only reason he could afford this memoir was to help readers understand the people and events of Chinese history more conveniently, and to inspire readers to think of historical figures more consciously when reading in a narrative method. This is the inexhaustible source of his book! Therefore, from this point of view, the value of this book may not only be an ordinary work for appreciation.

—Written on October 20, 2011

【Published on Taiwan's *Big Ocean* Poetry Magazine, Issue 85, July 2012.】

08 論周夢蝶詩中的道家美學——以〈逍遙遊〉、〈六月〉二詩為例
On the Taoist Aesthetics in Zhou Mengdie's Poems: Taking the Poems "Free Wandering" and "June" as Examples

摘要 Abstract

周夢蝶是當代重要的詩人，他的詩用語豐富而多義，善以莊子思想撥見對其哲學與美學形成的敏感，在孤獨中鋪陳出不凡的思維與想像。以周夢蝶的《逍遙遊》、《六月》二詩為例，分析詩中所展露的道家美學的生命演出，進而建構出臺灣現代詩史上的新創價值。

Zhou Mengdie is an important contemporary poet. His poetic language is rich with multi-meanings. He is good at using Zhuangzi's thoughts to reveal his sensitivity to the formation of philosophy and aesthetics, and lays out extraordinary thoughts and imaginations in solitude. Taking Zhou Mengdie's poems "Free Wandering" and "June" as examples, this paper analyzes the life performance of Taoist aesthetics revealed in the poems, and then constructs new values in the history of modern Taiwanese poetry.

關鍵詞：莊子、美學、周夢蝶、道家、詩。
Keywords: Zhuangzi, aesthetics, Zhou Mengdie, Taoism, poetry.

　　周夢蝶（1921.12.29- ），本名周起述，河南淅川縣人；童年失怙，個性沉靜且獨善其身。自幼熟讀古典詩文，曾就讀開封師範、宛西鄉村師範學校；因戰亂，中途輟學。隨軍來臺時，家鄉遺有髮妻和二子一女。1952 年開始在報上發表詩集，十五歲時，偷偷替自己取筆名為『夢蝶』，其實是源自莊周夢蝴蝶，表示崇尚自由的無限嚮往。自軍中退伍，加入「藍星詩社」；後又於 1959 年起在臺北市著名的明星咖啡廳門前擺書攤渡日，長達 21 年。出版的第一本詩集《孤獨國》，被選為「台灣文學經典」。1962 年開始有佛禪、與莊子共融的明顯傾向，常默坐書攤前，成為「市景」一隅，晚年似「苦行僧」般，過著幾近孤隱的生活。

1980年美國 Orientations 雜誌記者專訪於他,並以古希臘時期代神發佈神諭的 Oracle 為喻,撰文稱許他為「廈門街上的先知」(Oracle on Amoy Street)。同年因胃潰瘍開刀,以致歇業。曾獲臺灣「中國文藝協會」新詩特別獎、笠詩社「詩創作」獎、中央日報文學成就獎、第一屆「國家文化藝術基金會」文藝獎、「中國詩歌藝術學會」藝術貢獻獎等。著有《孤獨國》、《還魂草》、《周夢蝶世紀詩選》、《約會》、《十三朵白菊花》、《周夢蝶詩文集》等。他對作品的要求相當高,常透過「虛實相生」等方法使讀者的視覺與感知達到平衡,畫面空靈純淨;並以自我靈魂為起點,引禪意入詩,這是對莊子道家美學思想的藝術實踐。

一、〈消遙遊〉與忘我美學

　　《莊子》書中不乏「超以象外」與具備詩意想像的畫面。其中,強調的包括「虛」與「實」需時時體現的,在概念上雖是相對立;但在創作中,周夢蝶對天地自然的感受和表達,則選擇語言超越了拘泥於物象的階段,而直入司空圖在《詩品》中提出了「超以象外,得其寰中,離形得似」的境界。正是這種「超以象外」的創作方法,才能「得其寰中」,從而達到莊子美學中永恆追求的至極表現。如今,周夢蝶的詩是華人文學寶庫中的奇葩,單從畫面形式的表層意義上看,他常體現出自我美學素養來啟迪觀衆的思維,藉以享受審美愉悅。

　　正如莊子生於戰亂之世,認為「道」的性質即自然,它是虛無和永恆的、是一種心靈與精神的境界,也是萬物與生命之美產生和存在的本原。在〈至樂〉中,曾說:「人之生也,與憂俱生」,這就是莊子出於苦難而能超越苦難的生活美學。周夢蝶也在思考具體的物象與抽象之中,力求「美」與「真」的和諧統一,他接受《莊子》,也冀望借助《莊子・刻意》之說:「淡然無極,而眾美從之,此天地之道,聖人之德也。」他常透過對自然的細膩觀察,去瞭解美、尋找美、體悟美,從而使自己能夠減少痛苦,忘懷得失。也就是說,周夢蝶將體道為一種自我修養,其強烈的生命精神與澹泊的詩性、特有的直覺性,使他能處於清靜無為的境界中得以體驗天籟、地籟、人籟等萬殊聲音。其目的是為追求一種宇宙精神,追求物我相融的心態;又或許,也只有在自然的靜默中才是他對神聖感覺的最好回應。

然而，道家「物我俱忘」的思想也影響周夢蝶甚廣。在創作理念上，他看到了《莊子》的深刻本質，對現象世界的超越，亦必然是其推動藝術發展的根本動力。按莊子所言，道不僅存在於客觀世界中，更存在於得道者的心中。於是，周夢蝶也以詩尋求心靈的解脫為對策，在虛靜、孤寂而自由的生活中，終結出千古永垂的佳作〈消遙遊〉。他將「道」賦予了強烈的審美特徵，首先，題下先引《莊子‧消遙遊》：「北溟有魚，其名為鯤。鯤之大，不知其幾千里也。化而為鳥，其名為鵬，鵬之背，不知其幾千里也，怒而飛……」其全詩如下：

　　絕塵而逸。回眸處
　　亂雲翻白，波濤千起；
　　無邊與蒼茫與空曠
　　展笑著如回響
　　遺落於我蹤影底有無中。

　　從冷冷的北溟來
　　我底長背與長爪
　　猶滯留看昨夜底濡濕；
　　夢終有醒時——
　　陰霾撥開，是百尺雷嘯。

　　昨日已沉陷了，
　　甚至鮫人底雪淚也滴乾了；
　　飛躍啊，我心在高寒
　　高寒是大化底眼神
　　我是那眼神沒遮攔的一瞬。

　　不是追尋，必須追尋
　　不是超越，必須超越——
　　雲倦了，有風扶著
　　風倦了，有海托著
　　海倦了呢？堤倦了呢？

　　以飛為歸止的
　　仍須歸止於飛。

> 世界在我翅上
> 一如歷歷星河之在我膽邊
> 浩浩天籟之出我脇下……[1]

從題下引言開篇寫景，細味卻不止是簡單寫景，同時還速寫出詩人的主觀感受原是渴求消遙；即著重視覺意象，藉由自喻為鯤鵬的飄逸身影而給人於空靜中傳出動蕩的波濤、平淡中透出幽深而自在的印象。在詩人回眸處，看似寫眼前蒼茫與空曠之景，其實是把他的孤獨寫盡了；如同那鵬鳥高飛遠去，直至無影無蹤。而那展笑著如回響，造成懸疑落合的效果，正是情思所在。詩人開始回想起自己從彼岸跨海而來，以「我底長背與長爪」純然是鯤鵬的神奇英姿，以及「陰霾撥開，是百尺雷嘯」的遄飛氣勢，用誇張比喻，逸想自己生命中曾經有過濡濕的淚光、在飽經喪亂之後隨之而來的淒清與無可奈何的遣悶，使詩人陷入一個不可預知的陰霾……直到夢醒時，那羈旅他鄉、欲歸未得的愁思方得以獲得了片刻寧靜。

第三段，詩人繼以擬人手法，描摹「鮫人底雪淚」已滴乾的「善等待」與「我是那眼神沒遮攔的一瞬」的「愛凝望」，鮮明塑造出翹首盼望故鄉與愛人的癡情。詩行至第四段，已去掉了「沉鬱頓挫」的尾巴，透過移覺把視覺印象轉換為聽覺，呈現一種迷離憂傷的意緒。然而，「不是超越，必須超越——」，這遠近交錯的情感，能精妙傳神地烘托出一線「蕭散自然」的生機，而讓詩的傳意活動無礙自發的顯現。其深含之意則暗示大化之中，已無過往的責難與懺悔，轉而渴望追求完全擺脫塵世之累的寧靜心境；在頻頻提問中，怎不動人心眼而啟遙念之思。詩至此，連結成不息的音韻與節奏，把「不是追尋，必須追尋」的愛整個流洩出來，反而有一種「渾然無雕飾」的清新之美。到了最後一段，「以飛為歸止的／仍須歸止於飛。」為全詩鋪墊了詩人藝術自覺追求的目標——超以象外，甚而想達到「世界在我翅上」的那種無限壯闊的天境。於是，詩人從有言、具象可感知的藝術空間，慢慢昇華到「一如歷歷星河之在我膽邊／浩浩天籟之出我脇下……」形象以外的「忘我」境界，思念至此已是徹底的形象化了。

---

[1] 周夢蝶，《還魂草》，臺北，領導出版社，1978年，頁 66-67。

二、〈六月〉的詩境與「道美」

　　要閱讀周夢蝶詩的唯美、意蘊，就得借重莊子美學的智識，記得《莊子‧天道》曾說：「夫虛靜恬淡寂寞無為者，萬物之本也。」這也應驗了周夢蝶的詩風表現在文學創作上就是抒情樸真。其實樸就是淡雅，淡就是樸，就是自然；也正因為「心繫鄉土」的深厚情結，致使詩人的不少作品充滿了思辨的色彩。有時雖因形象發展常見以末段接回首段的「迴旋書寫」手法，似有趨於悲傷之勢，但通常到最後總能剎見曙光、體現出詩人對美好事物的嚮往。

　　由道出發的莊子美學自然也是「無言」的美學——「天地有大美而不言」(《莊子‧知北遊》)。然而，這種最高境界的美，如同《莊子‧外物》所言：「言者所以在意，得意而忘言」，意旨詩歌之美，不僅在有盡之言，尤在「無聲勝有聲」或「無窮之意」的層面。這些道家的美學思想，也同樣深深影響著周夢蝶的思維方式及對生命哲學的把握。其中，莊子審美自由論集中體現在「神遊」的理論上，主要宗旨是，要實現對客觀世界的超越，「心遊」才是最重要的。它需要想像，讓精神在超越時空的宇宙中無拘無束的「逍遙」。這與前詩欣賞中的「逍遙遊」對感覺的覺醒有其關聯性。莊子在《逍遙遊》中，構想了無功、無名、無我的神人、聖人、至人，又使他們成為他人生審美的對象——人融合於自然。也就是這個深刻思考，再度讓周夢蝶注入了全部思想、情緒、語言的花朵，而成為一個淵深的哲人。再就他的另一首早年之作〈六月〉，我們可以清楚地看到詩人欲解脫這形體束縛的莊蝶意象。一首詩的形神、平奇、隱顯……等，是否能構成統一和諧的藝術整體，關係著詩之所以優劣的主因；而從這兒也得到了最佳證明：

　　　蓬然醒來
　　　繽紛的花雨打得我底影子好濕！
　　　是夢？是真？
　　　面對珊瑚礁下覆舟的今夕。

　　　一粒舍利等於多少堅忍？世尊
　　　你底心很亮，而六月底心很暖——
　　　我有幾個六月？

我將如何安放我底固執？
在你與六月之間。

據說蛇底血脈是沒有年齡的！
縱使你鑄永夜為秋，永夜為冬
縱使黑暗挖去自己底眼睛……
蛇知道：它仍能自水裡喊出火底消息。

死亡在我掌上旋舞
一個蹉跌，她流星般落下
我欲翻身拾起再拚圓
虹斷霞飛，她已紛紛化為蝴蝶。

【附註】釋迦既卒，焚其身，得骨子累萬，光瑩如五色珠，搗之不碎。名曰舍利子。[2]

　　縱觀此詩氣韻生動，深遠難盡。一開始，詩人給我們描繪的就是他在創作時所進入的「物我相融」、「物我統一」的境界；其思想核心則是講求現實世界的「空」與超現實世界的「真如」。若就詩的結構而言，首先從聽覺起筆，花雨成全詩的底色，凸出詩人孤獨的身影、珊瑚礁、舟子這些圖景；也體現了「蓬然醒來」與夢境意象的空靈與超脫塵俗之美。這與道家美學首先表現在道的朦朧美和不可捉摸的神秘極為相似，但這種神秘却給人想像的聲響、一種美的享受；又似是人生幻化的莊周之蝶，是夢亦真中自我的物化，足見詩人意象經營之用心。

　　在《莊子・齊物論》篇末「莊周夢蝶」：「夢飲酒者，旦而哭泣；夢哭泣者，旦而田獵。方其夢也，不知其夢也。夢之中又占其夢焉，覺而後知其夢也。且有大覺而後知此其大夢也，而愚者自以為覺，竊竊然知之。君乎，牧乎，固哉！丘也與女，皆夢也；予謂女夢，亦夢也。是其言也，其名為吊詭。萬世之後而一遇大聖，知其解者，是旦暮遇之也。」在這裡，或許周夢蝶將莊子具有濃重「超越」、「形上」、「虛靜無為」等意味和特點，從他心理的感受，蘊育出〈六月〉這首詩的背景。而這首詩亦有莊子美學思想「覺夢如一」的觀念呈現。如此說來，「莊周夢蝶」的審美化

---

[2] 周夢蝶，《還魂草》，臺北，領導出版社，1978年，頁 48-19。

是無庸置疑的，周夢蝶亦是藉由夢覺狀態的不分來象徵認識主體與客體即「我」與物界限消融。亦即，以揚棄主體對於形軀、生死、人我之執著，進而覺知自由、超越的生命真境。

　　緊接著，自然又是一種道家之思了。「一粒舍利等於多少堅忍？」詩人默問著，也描寫出詩人在現實矛盾衝擊中造成的內心痛苦與失落。但這只是一種相對的圓〈你底心很亮〉與相對的寂〈我有幾個六月〉，正蘊含著詩人渴望明日的再生。詩人將「安放我底固執」，如同生命體的太陽，其沉落亦如佛僧之圓寂。由於此詩並沒有出現理語，又頗能彰顯現代詩這一體裁特有的音韻。但在第三段，則寄託主旨於言外，其力勢變化轉為由痛苦而沉靜、和緩，有著對生命獲得了悟的辨思。這裡，其深層次的含義，卻是以靜定之心，欲解脫情愛與死永恆搏鬥的主題，抵達無欲無求幸福的彼岸，恰如舟航。到了末段，「死亡在我掌上旋舞」及前兩句呈現的是偏於調和性陰柔風格。後兩句，則表現出詩人已把自我修持的疑惑與對罪惡、誘惑與慾望的恐懼，透過夢中幻化的頓悟之後，形體已把世俗之愛宗教化，亦含有人生必須經過痛苦的修行及磨難與血火冶煉，方能趨於永恆不滅的禪意。至此，詩人的心靈便得以自在遨遊。之後，詩人的作品，也常以莊子為宗師，著力描寫出一種「天人合一」中的東方哲人的智慧。

三、周夢蝶：以生命為詩的歌者

　　周夢蝶的一生，在藝術上，充滿了傳奇式的浪漫主義色彩。記得德國存在主義哲學家海德格（Heidegger, 1889-1976）曾說：「心境愈是自由，愈能得到美的享受。」個人以為，凡是優美的詩歌都是時代的鏡子和回聲，只有形象，才能給藝術以血液和呼吸。在過去的評論界，多認為周夢蝶是講究詩的形象化和多種修辭手段的運用，因而使人感到空靈逸秀，富有質感。他很少在詩中講些大道理，而總是通過形象化的描寫和語言的複雜變化來抒情。其詩的可貴之處，恰恰在於：他既能以澎湃的詩情為命運所帶來的痛苦與愛憐和追求光明的即將到來而高歌，又具有一種抑揚頓挫的節奏感以及以感情注入物象的繪畫美。而莊子美學不但體現了詩人所要表達的深層思想，又造成了一個完整的藝術世界。他總是運用自己豐富的想像力，使無形的變為有形，無聲的變為有聲，無色的使人可見，甚至把沒有生命的變為有生命。當然，從詩的內容上來講，其基調的深情低吟、溫婉淒美，也擅以矛盾語法或用「蝴蝶」、「雪」、「火」來暗示禪機。似乎自苦的詩心遠離了塵世，而生活又很早就鍛煉了他堅強的意志和樸實；但是，從探求詩美來講，不能不使人讚嘆詩人的藝術匠心。

　　事實上，周夢蝶的詩早期受莊子影響較深，對生死的感悟，亦莊亦禪，是那樣深邃又空濛，使人讀後有一種惘然若失之感，這正是詩的魅力所在。不過他對佛學、甚至回教可蘭經中的哲學都用心研究過；而從小所受的古典文化的影響也是潛移默化、形成一種新古典的語言風貌，進入到他靈魂深處的。如〈消遙遊〉詩裡的前幾句，有宋詞的頓挫語音節。所以，莊子美學是哲學，也是周夢蝶所尋求的精神家園；他用自己的藝術實踐使得詩體獲得了新的生命。這點，與道家美學本質上的要求是可以相匯通的。

　　正如德國哲學家康德（Immanuel Kant, 1724-1804）所說，凡最高的美都使人惆悵，忽忽若有所失，如羈旅之思念家鄉。也正是這種思鄉愁思反映在周夢蝶詩中便是追尋精神的超越與失落情緒的並存，常直接藉由夢中或物我冥合所產生的經驗，論證生命的片刻愉悅或自由精神之可得。這無異於符合莊子美學的遊世情懷，也是詩人在詩美探索上企以達到「物化」即主客體相互混合的境界或藝術追求。從總體看，詩人晚期之作更趨於寧靜、恬淡、感情轉向對人生哲理的開掘；在詩的形式上，韻律感增強。本文試圖運用莊子美學內涵作為現代詩〈消遙遊〉及〈六月〉的閱讀策略，並嘗試對文本中所透顯的詩性特質和生命情調作一詮釋。總之，無論是以此來探析長於形象描繪，或可加深瞭解字句多有來歷復有禪思的周夢蝶的詩歌。

－2012.5.7 作

【刊中國河南省《商丘師範學院學報》，2013 年第 1 期，頁 24-27。】

　　Zhou Mengdie (1921.12.29-), whose real name is Zhou Qishu, was born in Xichuan County, Henan Province. He lost his father in childhood and was quiet and self-centered. He was familiar with classical poetry and prose since childhood and studied at Kaifeng

Normal School and Wanxi Rural Normal School. He dropped out of school due to the war. When he came to Taiwan with the army, his first wife and two sons and one daughter were left behind in his hometown. He began to publish poetry collections in newspapers in 1952. At the age of 15, he secretly gave himself the pen name "Mengdie", literally "dreaming of butterflies", which actually came from Zhuang Zhou Mengdie (dreaming of butterflies by Zhuangzi), expressing his infinite yearning for freedom. After leaving the army, he joined the Blue Star Poetry Society. He then set up a book stall in front of the famous Star Cafe in Taipei City from 1959 onwards, which lasted for 21 years. His first poetry collection, *Lonely Country*, was selected as a "Taiwanese literary classic". In 1962, he began to have a clear inclination towards Buddhism and integration with the village. He often sat in front of the book stall in silence, becoming a corner of the "city scene". In his later years, he lived a life of almost solitude like an "ascetic monk".

In 1980, a reporter from the American Orientations magazine interviewed him and compared him to the Oracle who issued oracles on behalf of gods in ancient Greece, and wrote an article praising him as "Oracle on Amoy Street". In the same year, he had surgery for a gastric ulcer, which led to his closure. He has won the Taiwan "Chinese Literature and Art Association" New Poetry Special Award, the Lishi Society "Poetry Creation" Award, the Central Daily News Literary Achievement Award, the first "National Cultural and Art Foundation" Literature Award, and the "Chinese Poetry Art Society" Art Contribution Award. He has written *Lonely Country, Resurrection Grass, Zhou Mengdie Century Poetry Selection, Date, Thirteen White Chrysanthemums, Zhou Mengdie Poetry Collection* and so on. He has high requirements for his works, and often uses methods such as "virtual and real coexistence" to balance the reader's vision and perception, and the picture is ethereal and pure; and starting from the self-soul, he introduces Zen into poetry, which is an artistic practice of Zhuangzi's Taoist aesthetics.

I. "Free Wandering" and the aesthetics of selflessness

There are many scenes in the book *Zhuangzi* to "transcend the image" and have poetic imagination. Among them, the emphasis is on the need for "virtual" and "real" to be reflected at all times. Although they are opposite in concept, in his creation, Zhou Mengdie's feelings and expressions of the natural world and nature are beyond the stage of sticking to the image, and directly enter the realm proposed by Sikong Tu in "Shipin" that can "transcend the image, get its world, and get likeness without form". It is this creative method of "transcending the image" that can "get its world", thereby achieving the ultimate expression of the eternal pursuit in Zhuangzi's aesthetics. Today, Zhou Mengdie's poems are a treasure trove of Chinese literature. Judging from the superficial meaning of the form of the picture, he often embodies his own aesthetic qualities to enlighten the audience's thinking and enjoy aesthetic pleasure.

Just as Zhuangzi was born in a war-torn world, he believed that the nature of "Tao" is nature, which is nothingness and eternity, a state of mind and spirit, and the origin of the beauty of all things and life. In "The Greatest Happiness", he once said: "When people are born, they are born with sorrow". This is Zhuangzi's life aesthetics that can transcend suffering from suffering. Zhou Mengdie also seeks the harmonious unity of "beauty" and "truth" in his thinking about concrete objects and abstractions. He accepts *Zhuangzi* and hopes to use the words in *Zhuangzi*: "Be indifferent and boundless, and all beauty will follow. This is the way of heaven and earth and the virtue of saints." He often understands, seeks and realizes beauty through meticulous observation of nature, so that he can reduce pain and forget gains and losses. In other words, Zhou Mengdie regards the realization of Tao as a kind of self-cultivation. His strong life spirit, indifferent poetic nature and unique intuition enable him to experience the sounds of heaven, earth and human beings in a state of tranquility and inaction. The purpose is to pursue a kind of cosmic spirit, a state of mind that is harmonious with the self; or perhaps, only in the silence of nature can he best respond to the sacred feeling.

However, the Taoist idea of "forgetting both the self and the world" also has a great influence on Zhou Mengdie. In terms of creative concept, he saw the profound essence of *Zhuangzi*, and the transcendence of the phenomenal world must be the fundamental driving force for his artistic development. According to Zhuangzi, Taoism exists not only in the objective world, but also in the hearts of those who have attained Taoism. Therefore, Zhou Mengdie also used poetry to seek spiritual liberation as a countermeasure. In the empty, lonely and free life, he finally created the masterpiece "Free

Wandering" that will be passed down through the ages. He endowed "Tao" with strong aesthetic characteristics. First, the title first quoted "Zhuangzi·Free Wandering": "There is a fish in the North Sea, its name is Kun. Kun is so big that no one knows how many thousands of miles it is. It turns into a bird, whose name is Peng. Peng's back is so big that no one knows how many thousands of miles it is. It flies away in anger..." The full poem is as follows:

> Escape from the dust. Looking back
> The chaotic clouds are white, and the waves are rising;
> The boundlessness, the vastness, and the emptiness
> are smiling like an echo
> left in the existence and non-existence of my traces.
>
> Coming from the cold North Sea/My long back and long claws
> Still linger to see the wetness of last night;
> The dream will eventually wake up —
> The haze is dispelled, and it is a hundred-foot thunder.
>
> Yesterday has sunk,
> even the snow tears of the fish have dried up;
> flying, my heart is in the cold
> the cold is the eyes of the great changes
> I am the moment when that eyes are not covered.
>
> Not to pursue, must pursue
> Not to surpass, must surpass —
> the clouds are tired, the wind supports
> the wind is tired, the sea supports
> the sea is tired? Is the embankment tired?
>
> Those who fly as their destination
> must still return to flying.
> The world is on my wings
> Just like the stars are at my side
> The vast sky is under my limbs...[3]

---

[3] Zhou Mengdie, *Resurrection Grass*, Taipei, Leader Press, 1978, pp. 66-67.

The poem begins with a description of the scenery in the quotation under the title. If you savor it carefully, you will find that it is not just a simple description of the scenery, but also a quick sketch of the poet's subjective feeling of longing for detachment. That is, it focuses on visual imagery, and by comparing himself to the floating figure of a phoenix, it gives people the impression of turbulent waves in the silence and deep and comfortable in the plainness. When the poet looks back, it seems to be describing the vast and empty scene in front of him, but in fact it is describing his loneliness — just like the phoenix flying high and far away, until it disappears without a trace. And the smile that echoes like an echo, creating a suspenseful effect, is exactly where the emotion lies. The poet began to recall that he had come across the sea from the other side, with "my long back and long claws" being the miraculous and heroic figure of a phoenix, and "the haze was cleared away, and there was a thunderous roar of a hundred feet". He used exaggerated metaphors to imagine that he had been wet with tears in his life, and the sadness and helplessness that followed after the fullness of grief, which made the poet fall into an unpredictable haze... until he woke up from the dream, the sorrow of being trapped in a foreign land and wanting to return but not being able to get a moment of peace.

In the third paragraph, the poet continues to use personification to depict the "good waiting" of the "tears of snow at the bottom of the fish" that have dried up and the "loving gaze" of "I am the moment when the eyes are not covered", vividly shaping the infatuation of looking forward to the hometown and the lover. In the fourth paragraph, the "depressed and frustrated" tail has been removed, and the visual impression is transformed into the auditory impression through telepathy, presenting a kind of confused and sad mood. However, "not transcending, must transcend —", this intertwined emotion of near and far can exquisitely and vividly set off a line of "sparse and natural" vitality, allowing the poem's communication activity to appear spontaneously without hindrance. Its deep meaning implies that in the great changes, there is no longer any blame or repentance for the past, but a desire to pursue a peaceful state of mind that is completely free from the burdens of the world. In the frequent questions, how can it not move people's hearts and inspire thoughts of the distant past. At this point, the poem is connected into an endless rhythm, which fully expresses the love of "not pursuing, but must pursue", and instead has a kind of "pure and unadorned" fresh beauty. In the last paragraph, "those who fly as their destination / must still return to flying." The goal of the poet's conscious pursuit of art is paved for the whole poem — to go beyond the image, and even want to reach the infinite and magnificent heaven of "the world is on my wings". Thus, the poet gradually sublimated from the artistic space of words and concrete perception to the "selflessness" realm beyond the image, "Just like the clear stars in my heart / the vast sky out of my arms...", and the thoughts have been completely visualized.

II. The poetic realm and "Tao beauty" of "June"

To read the beauty and meaning of Zhou Mengdie's poems, we must rely on the wisdom of Zhuangzi's aesthetics. Remember that "Zhuangzi·Heavenly Dao" once said: "The empty, quiet, lonely and inactive are the root of all things." This also proves that Zhou Mengdie's poetic style is lyrical and simple in literary creation. In fact, simplicity means elegance, simplicity means simplicity, and simplicity means nature; it is precisely because of the deep complex of "being attached to the hometown" that many of the poet's works are full of speculative colors. Sometimes, although the "circular writing" technique of connecting the last paragraph to the first paragraph seems to be sad due to the development of the image, it usually always sees the light at the end, reflecting the poet's yearning for beautiful things.

Zhuangzi's aesthetics, which starts from Taoism, is naturally a "silent" aesthetics — "The world has great beauty but does not speak" (Zhuangzi·Zhi Beiyou) However, this highest level of beauty, as stated in "Zhuangzi: External Things", is "the reason why people talk is to care about things, and when they are satisfied, they forget the words", which means that the beauty of poetry is not only in the limited words, but also in the level of "silence is better than sound" or "infinite meaning". These Taoist aesthetic thoughts also deeply influenced Zhou Mengdie's way of thinking and grasp of the philosophy of life. Among them, Zhuangzi's aesthetic freedom theory is concentrated in the theory of "spiritual wandering", the main purpose of which is that to achieve transcendence of the objective world, "heart wandering" is the most important. It requires imagination, allowing the spirit to "wander" freely in the universe beyond time and space. This is related to the awakening of feelings in the appreciation of the previous poem. In "Free Wandering", Zhuangzi imagined gods, saints, and perfect people who were meritless, nameless, and selfless, and made them the objects of his aesthetics of life — people integrated into nature. It was this profound thinking that once again injected Zhou Mengdie with all the flowers of thoughts, emotions, and language, and became a profound philosopher. In his other early work "June", we can clearly see that the poet wanted to break free from the image of Zhuangdie, which was bound by the form. Whether the form, spirit, plainness, strangeness, and implicitness of a poem can constitute a unified and harmonious artistic whole is related to the main reason why the poem is good or bad; and this is also the best proof:

> I woke up
> The colorful rain of flowers made my shadow so wet!
> Is it a dream? Is it true?
> Facing the boat capsized under the coral reef tonight.
>
> How much perseverance is equal to one relic? Buddha
> Your heart is bright, and the heart of June is warm —
> How many Junes do I have?
> How will I place my stubbornness?
> Between you and June.
>
> It is said that the blood of snakes has no age!
> Even if you cast the eternal night into autumn and the eternal night into winter
> Even if darkness digs out its own eyes...
> The snake knows: it can still shout out the news of fire from the water.
>
> Death dances in my palm
> One stumble, she falls like a meteor
> I want to turn over and pick her up and put her together again
> The rainbow breaks and the clouds fly away, she has turned into butterflies.
>
> 【Note】After the death of Sakyamuni, his body was burned and his bones were obtained. There are tens of thousands of

bones, shining like five-colored beads, which cannot be broken even if they are shaken. They are called relics.[4]

The poem is full of vividness and profoundness. At the beginning, the poet describes the state of "the fusion of the self and the world" and "the unity of the self and the world" that he entered when he was creating. The core of his thought is to pursue the "emptiness" of the real world and the "truth" of the surreal world. In terms of the structure of the poem, it starts with hearing, and the rain of flowers forms the background of the poem, highlighting the poet's lonely figure, coral reefs, and boatmen. It also reflects the ethereal and otherworldly beauty of "suddenly waking up" and the dream image. This is very similar to the Taoist aesthetics, which first manifests itself in the hazy beauty and elusive mystery of Taoism, but this mystery gives people an imaginary sound and a kind of aesthetic enjoyment. It is also like the butterfly of Zhuang Zhou, which is the materialization of the self in the dream and reality, which fully shows the poet's intention in managing the image.

At the end of "Zhuangzi Qiwu Lun" and "Zhuangzi Dreaming of Butterflies": "those who dream of drinking will cry in the morning; those who dream of crying will hunt in the morning. When they are dreaming, they don't know that they are dreaming. In the dream, they interpret their dreams again. Only when they wake up do they know that it is a dream. Moreover, only when they have a great awakening can they know that this is a great dream, but the fools think they are awake and know it secretly. My lord, my shepherd, how solid! I and you are both dreaming. Yes; I say that a female dream is also a dream. This is what he said, and his name is paradoxical. After all eternity, if you meet a great sage once, you will know his explanation, and you will meet him at dusk." Here, perhaps Zhou Mengdie took Zhuangzi's strong meaning and characteristics of "transcendence", "metaphysical", and "quietness and inaction" and derived the background of the poem "June" from his psychological feelings. This poem also embodies the concept of Zhuangzi's aesthetic thought of "dreaming as one". In this way, there is no doubt that "Zhuang Zhou Mengdie" is aesthetic. Zhou Mengdie

---

[4] Zhou Mengdie, *Resurrection Grass*, Taipei, Leader Press, 1978, pp. 48-19.

also uses the indistinguishability of the dream state to symbolize the understanding of the subject and the object, that is, the dissolution of the boundary between "I" and things. That is, by abandoning the subject's obsession with the body, life and death, and the self, one can then realize the true state of life that is free and transcendent.

Next, it is naturally a Taoist thought. "How much perseverance is equal to one relic?" The poet asked silently, and also described the poet's inner pain and loss caused by the impact of the contradictions in reality. But this is only a relative circle (Your heart is very bright) and a relative silence (How many Junes do I have), which implies the poet's desire for rebirth tomorrow. The poet will "place my obsession" like the sun of a living body, and its sinking is like the nirvana of a Buddhist monk. Since this poem does not appear in rational language, it can also highlight the unique rhythm of the genre of modern poetry. But in the third paragraph, the theme is placed beyond words, and the change of power turns from pain to calmness and gentleness, with a reflection on the enlightenment of life. Here, the deeper meaning is to use a calm heart to get rid of the theme of the eternal struggle between love and death, and reach the other side of happiness without desire, just like sailing. In the last paragraph, "death dances in my palm" and the first two sentences present a more harmonious and feminine style. The last two lines show that the poet has transformed the doubts about self-cultivation and the fear of sin, temptation and desire through the sudden enlightenment in the dream. The form has turned secular love into religion, and it also contains the idea that life must go through painful practice and suffering and be refined by blood and fire before it can reach eternal Zen. At this point, the poet's mind can roam freely. After that, the poet's works often take Zhuangzi as the master, and strive to describe the wisdom of the Eastern philosopher in the "unity of man and nature".

III. Zhou Mengdie: A singer who uses life as poetry

Zhou Mengdie's life is full of legendary romanticism in art. I remember that German existentialist philosopher Heidegger (1889-1976) once said: "The freer the mind is, the more beauty can be enjoyed." I personally think that all beautiful poems are mirrors and echoes of the times. Only images can give art blood and breath. In the past, critics believed that Zhou Mengdie was particular about the imagery of poetry and the use of various rhetorical means, which made people feel ethereal, elegant and rich in texture. He rarely talked about great truths in his poems, but always expressed his emotions through figurative descriptions and complex changes in language. The value of his poetry lies in the fact that he can sing with surging poetic emotions about the pain and pity brought by fate and the pursuit of the coming of light, and also has a rhythmic sense of ups and downs and a pictorial beauty that injects emotion into the image. Zhuangzi's aesthetics not only reflects the deep thoughts that the poet wants to express, but also creates a complete artistic world. He always uses rich imagination to make the invisible visible, the silent audible, the colorless visible, and even the lifeless alive. Of course, in terms of the content of the poem, its tone is affectionate and gentle, and it is also good at using contradictory grammar or using "butterflies", "snow" and "fire" to imply Zen. It seems that his self-tortured poetic heart is far away from the world, and life has tempered his strong will and simplicity very early. However, from the perspective of exploring the beauty of poetry, one cannot help but admire the poet's artistic ingenuity.

In fact, Zhou Mengdie's early poems were deeply influenced by Zhuangzi. His perception of life and death is both Zhuangzi and Zen, so profound and hazy that people feel lost after reading it, which is the charm of poetry. However, he has studied Buddhism and even the philosophy in the Islamic Koran carefully; and the influence of classical culture he has received since childhood has also subtly formed a neoclassical language style and entered the depths of his soul. For example, the first few lines of the poem "Free Wandering" have the rhythmic syllables of Song dynasty poetry. Therefore, Zhuangzi aesthetics is philosophy, and it is also the spiritual homeland that Zhou Mengdie seeks. He uses his artistic practice to give the poetic form a new life. This is consistent with the essential requirements of Taoist aesthetics.

As the German philosopher Immanuel Kant (1724-1804) said, the highest beauty makes people melancholy, as if they have lost something, like a traveler missing his hometown. It is precisely this kind of homesickness that is reflected in Zhou Mengdie's poems, which is the coexistence of the pursuit of spiritual transcendence and the feeling of loss. He often directly uses the experience generated in dreams or the fusion of the self and the object to prove the momentary joy of life or the availability of free spirit. This is no difference from the wandering sentiment that conforms to Zhuangzi's aesthetics, and it is also the poet's attempt to achieve "materialization" in the exploration of poetic beauty, that is, the realm or artistic pursuit of the mutual fusion of subject and object. Generally speaking, the poet's late works tend to be more tranquil and calm, and the emotions turn to the exploration of the philosophy of life. In the form of poetry, the sense of rhythm is enhanced. This article attempts to use the connotation of Zhuangzi's aesthetics as a reading strategy for the modern poems "Free Wandering" and "June", and attempts to interpret the poetic characteristics and life sentiment revealed in the text. In short, whether it is to explore the poems of Zhou Mengdie, who is good at describing images, or to deepen the understanding of the poems of Zhou Mengdie, whose words and sentences, with a history, and are full of Zen meditation.

—2012.5.7 Author

【Published in *Journal of Shangqiu Normal University*, Henan Province, China, No. 1, 2013, pp. 24-27.】

09 簡論吳開晉詩歌的藝術思維
On Wu Kaijin's Artistic Thinking in Poetry

摘要 Abstract

本文闡述了吳開晉詩歌的詩化意象，及其藝術思維的過程及意義，揭示出吳開晉對當代美學的深刻影響。論文以三階段作品從中回溯歷史，將其藝術與人生緊密地聯繫起來，藉以體驗其現代詩歌的價值歸宿。

This paper expounds the poetic imagery of Wu Kaijin's poetry, the process and significance of his artistic thinking, and reveals Wu Kaijin's profound influence on contemporary aesthetics. The paper traces back history through three stages of his works, closely linking his art with his life, so as to experience the value of his modern poetry.

關鍵詞：吳開晉、藝術思維、詩人、意象。
Keywords: Wu Kaijin, artistic thinking, poet, imagery.

一、其人其詩

吳開晉（1934- ）是山東省沾化縣知名的詩人，為山東大學文學院教授。從1994年出版的第一本詩集《月牙泉》，繼而1998年《傾聽春天》和2004年《遊心集》開始，到2008年《吳開晉詩文選集》，就顯示了自己獨特的新詩風格；他有著自己的文學理論思想，多表現在具體的作品之中。詩性優雅、靈動中又充滿了濃郁的溫婉氣息和堅毅的思想感情，這是他的風格標誌。

今年過年後，再次收到遠從北京吳老師寄來的詩文集，我看了又看，它帶給我多麼寶貴的財富；每當我心境空虛或沉思之際，那是我生活中無上的歡愉。深入細讀，彷彿置身在大自然，從靜謐的天體中讓我思想之湧流忽地光明起來，隱約在神聖的樹林彼處，像銀屑般閃爍。

吳開晉初期詩作，清純、真樸，人物刻劃情真意切，大多以寫實為主。中期作品則是旅遊情思、人物緬懷，與現實生活貼得很近。晚期的創作加入了更多的細節和敘事的因素。其中，尤以〈土地的記憶〉這首詩獲得 1996 年以色列米瑞姆‧林德勃哥詩歌和平獎，評委會評語寫道：「吳開晉教授所著《土地的記憶》是一篇扣人心弦的，凝聚了反對惡勢力的、充滿感情的詩篇。詩歌通過非凡的隱喻手法，表現了犧牲者的痛苦和對惡魔的愁恨」。看得出，他努力地將自己的感悟用簡單與莊嚴的方式描繪出對史實理解的高度。從根本上來說，正由於吳開晉藝術想像的獨特思維，儘管晚年身體遭遇了些許磨難，而對藝術活動卻之所以一直保持著不衰的興趣，歸根究底，也正是與藝術思維的獨特功能和想像力有關。他始終將詩情融注於形象，而伴隨時間而來的智慧和經驗的包容力，都存在著喜於寫詩的火花。所以，在我們面前樹立的，乃是一位堅強而慈祥、超越性的詩人的形象。

二、詩歌裡的自然意象與內涵

記得愛爾蘭詩人葉慈（William Butler Yeats, 1865-1939）曾寫下：

時光流逝時但睿智緊隨
枝葉即便繁茂卻靠孤根支持
青春歲月我虛誇矯飾
曾經我恣意炫耀
如今且讓我枯萎成真理。

詩句是多麼溫柔又充滿力量！也是一種美感的表達。可以說，這是透過審美活動而展示了詩人的自然審美的成就。在我看來，吳開晉最奇絕的力量就在於他把寫實寫意的思想與真樸無華的詩性元素結合為一體，把靈思一瞬間的透徹與美學精神結合為一體；由此更深刻體味生活與藝術兩相促進，更見其才情橫溢的詩華。

吳開晉也是個早慧的詩人，這首〈電車上〉是 22 歲時的作品，是首難得的溫馨之作：

為什麼人們全都站起來，
到了什麼地方？
啊，走來一位將作媽媽的少婦，
她全身落滿了尊敬的目光。

她輕倚著窗玻璃坐下，
羞澀感激在眸子間深藏；
也許小生命正撞打母親喜悅的心，
看，她已把微笑的眼睛閉上。

這首詩是純粹的自然，乃是詩人長期以來根植於心中悲憫的本然。一部電車上的小故事，更反映出人與人間，唯有真情，才能讓社會變得更美好；而少婦孕育一個小生命的羞澀表情與人們紛紛想讓座的互動，更讓這幅畫面，常存讀者心中。可以說，吳開晉不僅是注重情感的詩人，更應該說是客觀敏銳地觀察社會人生的人。

吳開晉中期作品《月牙泉》詩集，記錄許多旅遊詩，其中，與夫人明岩女士到千佛山留照，寫下：

雙足深深繫入岩石
變幻的雲作村景
不管春雨秋霜
不管月月年年
讓我們站成永恆

首先，詩人吟唱出自己的愛意及期許，彷彿我們也可以看到他們並肩地依偎著。雖然人間沒有人為他們建造永恆的殿堂，但詩人這段刻骨銘心的愛情，卻遠比千佛山上的雲景都要美。英國著名詩人華茲華斯（William Wordsworth, 1770-1850），也這樣深有體會地指出：「詩是強烈情感的自然流露。它起源於在平靜中回憶起來的情感。」[1]這首詩裡，詩人也思考著如何讓「愛」化為永恆，情感真切、聖潔；不僅能夠創造出美的樂音，從而激起讀者深刻的印象。

另一本《傾聽春天》詩集中，大多收錄自然、旅遊、人物寫實等題材。其中《與妻懷舊》是63歲所寫：

回憶是一把銼
銼動了疼痛和傷悲
粉末飄飛

---

[1] 《西方文論選》（下），上海譯文出版社1979年版，第17頁。

> 遮蓋了天空
> 歲月的年輪
> 貯滿了淚水
> 澆灌著要枯萎的希望
> 將熄的燈燭
> 黎明前發出一聲嘆息

　　這是詩人與妻憶起文革時期的舊事。吳開晉有別於文革時期詩人的因素在於，他關心當時社會上的某些不公義情事，但選擇以詩釋放壓抑的情感；對詩人而言，詩可以創造出一種純粹的感染力，進而引起對社會的省思。這首詩表現出一股深沉的哀傷，道出詩人回憶起往事那一刻和親人分離的哀嘆；而妻子明岩始終是個傾聽心聲的良伴。此詩真摯感人，承繼而來的，能擴大我們的想像力，製造出詩的強音。最重要的是，裡面找不到文革的軼事，或那種對時代的焦灼感及無所依託的精神困惑。有的只是以未稀釋和不裝飾的詩語，最後延伸出來的畫面，卻能讓讀者感受得到文革的「傷痕」。

　　另一首〈土地的記憶─獻給反法西斯戰爭勝利紀念日〉收錄在《吳開晉詩文選集》四卷中的第一卷裡，這裡面凝聚了吳開晉畢生的心血，是一套很有學術價值之著作，尤以此詩最具代表性，也奠定了詩壇的重要地位，是詩人61歲所寫：

> 土地是有記憶的
> 正如樹木的年輪
> 一年一道溝壑
> 貯存著億萬種聲音
> 當太陽的磁針把它劃撥
> 便會發出歷史的回聲
>
> 聽！那隆隆作響的
> 是盧溝橋和諾曼地的炮聲
> 還夾著萬千染血的吶喊
> 那裂人心肺的
> 是奧斯威辛和南京城千萬冤魂的呻吟
> 還有野獸們的狂呼亂叫
> 那震人心魄的

是攻佔柏林和平型關的號角
還有槍刺上閃耀的復仇怒吼

莫要說那驅除魔鬼的炮聲
已化為節日的焰火，高高升入雲端
莫要說那焚屍爐內的骨灰
已築入摩天大樓的基礎，深深埋入地層
莫要說被野獸剖腹孕婦的哀嚎
已化為伴隨嬰兒的和諧音符
莫要說被試驗毒菌吞噬的痛苦掙紮
已化為無影燈下寧靜的微笑
這些早已過去
如煙雲飄浮太空
安樂是一種麻醉劑
人們也許把過去遺忘
但土地不會忘記
它身上留有法西斯鐵蹄踐踏的傷痛
留有無數反抗者澆鑄的紀念碑裡的呼喊
每當黎明到來
它便在疼痛中驚醒

寫這首詩的力量是由內生起的，在第一個詩節中，已體現出他對二次大戰整體中國東北百姓被德國納粹黨毒害、日軍進攻蘆溝橋事變、南京大屠殺等畫面，他從自然之道反觀人世之道的視角，用心控訴戰爭對人類無辜百姓的破壞及影響。

詩人的感覺與表現的交融，使他成為一個敏銳靈動的詩才。每年9月3日是中國人民抗日戰爭勝利紀念日，也是世界反法西斯戰爭勝利紀念日。這是近代百年以來，中華民族反抗帝國主義侵略取得的第一次全面勝利，也是中華民族由衰敗走向振興的重大轉捩點。最後一節告訴我們，可以瞭解到作者的感傷，同時也慶幸法西斯政權的崩解。雖然這段歷史迄今已超過一世紀，作者每一回憶，仍不能擺脫戰爭的陰影，對日、德暴行的記憶就像被感染的傷口一樣，依然在流血。從1937年南京大屠殺到納粹黨的活人試驗，其野蠻、狂暴的行徑仍深深銘刻在中國人的記憶中。

吳開晉對歷史的細緻觀察，這其中既有現代詩人超越時空的體會和哲思，也有對土地的無限敬畏和民族性的自覺。那些穿越光陰以探索歷史的詩句，直面人生；而去勇敢追求的人文關懷，純粹而敏感，幽微而堅毅，感性又悲壯。在這裡，作者已作出直抵歷史本真的真實抒寫和靈魂的詮釋。在這裡，也可以看出吳開晉對詩的貢獻，一方面，他讓詩人得以運用戰爭的醜陋來發掘人性的愛與良善；另一方面，他讓讀者明瞭詩人的任務，在於運用其創造能力，修復殘缺的世界中僅存的溫暖—愛，並使它恢復生氣，讓人僅記歷史的教訓，重新去感知這個世界，去體會土地被戰爭蹂躪的傷痕。

除了上述詩集，吳開晉期晚期詩歌的成果已漸為世界詩歌界關注。由於受到禪道精神的薰陶，偏向以視野的廣度以及對自然有一種敏銳靈躍的感受力，使他體現出含蓄的感性及清新淡雅的風格。在詩人追隨靈性、不同的體悟中，能引起讀者對它興發一種高貴的情感或充分發揮了想像力。詩人於64歲寫下的〈密密的梧桐葉〉，就是一首清澈明亮的詩，風景瞬間成為一首交響曲，一種沒有富麗氣息、沒有歷史，卻運用蘊含詩意的方式去描述：

> 密密的梧桐葉
> 在微風中親熱地交談
> 它們互相觸摸、拍打
> 讓笑語在雲空傳遍
>
> 每一片都有自己的故事——
> 關於布穀鳥的賽唱，或斑鳩的苦戀
> 它們從不保留什麼
> 一點一滴，都講給夥伴
>
> 當暴風雨來襲
> 它們便互相警告和吶喊
> 有誰支撐不住那無情地擊打
> 留下的便珠淚潸潸
>
> 它們祝願它早日化為泥土
> 再從樹根潛入樹幹
> 當春天的風笛在雲中吹響
> 它們便重新相會在樹巔

詩句捨棄清麗精緻,將對自然現象的關注,以追求原始樸素的直接呈現,富哲思。梧桐葉顫動的各種意象,在周圍自然保護的溫柔中顯露出來,能讓我們觀賞到天地間所包容的萬物之美。對詩人來說,一花一木,春秋輪代,更迭有序;樹葉也必須經歷暴風雨的洗煉愈見重生傲然。由此而知,他的藝術思維並不是受到表面上或視覺上的景觀所吸引;反之他看重的是作品中蘊含其中的哲理。另一首〈長木公園的雲松〉是詩人67歲前往馬里蘭大學講學時,是一首輕盈又有音樂性的小詩:

　　用陽光的金線,撥弄白雲
　　去打破雲空的寂靜
　　多少人仰視你
　　都難看到你真實的面容
　　你的根也一定很深很深
　　可穿透厚厚的地層
　　那長在香山紅葉間同樣高大的一株
　　定是你連體的身影
　　只是那掛在翠葉間的一顆顆松果裡
　　綴滿了我思念祖國的眼睛

一道漫射的光線,平靜而不凝聚,點醒了異國秋天雲松的笑容,也傳遞釋出詩人的思鄉輕愁;那北京西郊的香山園林的紅葉和眼前這雲松高大的表面連結在一起,傳達出古典主義派的美學,整個公園有種我無法言傳的祥和寧靜,平靜地接受詩人共有的視覺回憶。詩人已經覺悟,不論距離有多遠,詩人想念祖國及家鄉的心卻拉得很近。另一首〈威明頓森林公園的天鵝〉,更以一種近乎經典規律的方式寫出:

　　一隻腳掌
　　佇立於湖面
　　凝神靜聽
　　雲空飄來的
　　柴可夫斯基的旋律
　　忽然展開銀翅
　　做三百六十度的旋舞

這是首完全顛覆了學院式拘泥古板的傳統作風的詩，我既看不到森林公園以其美麗的風景來構築詩的嗜好，也看不到詩人把夢想的而非看到的事物賦予神秘的光環；相反地，如果你想詩能達到感人的悲愴境地，只能以一種真實中肯，以宗教般虔誠的心去觀察，直到想起生命的廣被，一隻單飛的天鵝，在內心裡的呼喚，就會在心中燃起一股抒情的靈火，含容著淡淡的憂淒與哀傷。而天鵝泛起漣漪，沒有任何騷動；更顯露牠的舞姿，是如此優美，致使詩人的繆斯沉默了。至此，可見吳開晉相信藝術的本質唯有透過創作與自我的精神世界進行直接的接觸或溝通；晚期詩風崇尚樸實的原始風格，又有清雅悠然的現代感。

　　《遊心集》也多集中旅遊詩及人物素描，其中，65歲時寫下〈憶友人〉：

　　　　似荷葉上的一絲風
　　　　似松林間的一片雪
　　　　你清麗的身影飄去了一個夢
　　　　在心的年輪上
　　　　永遠鑲嵌著那雙明亮的星斗

　　這首詩寫得輕靈、清新；詩的語言是從繆思女神激發想像，輕鬆自然地降臨詩人感性的心田。詩人在尋求古典性唯美的聖潔以及建構起一種雋永的回憶中，能坦率地流溢真情，營造令人驚異的效果。無疑，他為愛情加上浪漫冥思的想像到詩性生成的貫通，提供了一個內蘊豐厚的精神國度；足見他也是一位在畫面構圖的處理上充滿詩意的詩人。

三、結語：詩美是吳開晉藝術思維中的精神表現

　　雖然吳開晉教授前年面臨喪妻之痛及病疾所苦，但對他而言，這正展現了自己生命的強度。在鼓勵我的創作中，我發現，他的藝術思維關鍵在於美學，其美學思想不僅是知性與邏輯思考的活動，對於讓讀者產生知識的生活磨練，或愛的詮釋也有很深的著墨。他在淳厚溫儒的外表下，卻能善用時間研究美學，除創造了許多精闢的評論外，也能以詩描繪了一個清新自然、優美深邃、和諧統一的藝術世界。他的詩歌創作尤以旅遊感事抒懷題材居多，內容豐富，思想澄澈，抒情色彩，也能從歷史軌跡進行宏觀考察。

要找出吳開晉詩歌創作的主要思想脈絡，唯有探尋通向其詩文之廣博思想，得以認識其詩歌的內涵。

吳開晉也是一位感情豐沛的詩人，他的詩還可以被研究出許多方面的成果，在保持自己特殊情感的條件下，他真正發現了詩最主要的原素是愛；他智慧的地方是將事物的真實性重新整建欲引導我們深入這些東西所代表的深層意義中。詩是自然界裡最美最偉大的景致，而吳開晉的詩，有另一種禪風，暗喻著美麗的事物不是永恆的，而更懂得珍惜平和中的寧靜是幸福的。最後，謹向遠在北京養病中的老師致上我最誠真的謝意，這是對我最具鼓舞作用的詩文集。

—2010.5.23

【刊江蘇省《鹽城師範學院學報》人文社會科學版，第 31 卷，總第 127 期，2011.01 期，書評〈簡論吳開晉詩歌的藝術思維〉，頁 65-68。】

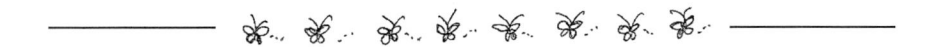

I. His person and his poetry

Wu Kaijin (1934-) is a well-known poet from Zhanhua County, Shandong Province, and a professor at the College of Literature of Shandong University. From the first collection of poems *Crescent Moon Lake* published in 1994, followed by *Listening to Spring* in 1998 and *Youxin Collection* in 2004, to *Selected Poems of Wu Kaijin* in 2008, he has shown his unique style of new poetry. He has his own literary theory and thought, which is mostly reflected in specific works. The poetry is elegant and agile, full of rich gentle breath and resolute thoughts and feelings, which is his style.

After this Chinese New Year, I received the collection of poems sent by Mr. Wu from Beijing again. I read it again and again, which brought me such precious wealth. Whenever I feel empty or contemplative, it is the supreme joy in my life. Reading it carefully, I feel as if I am in nature. From the quiet celestial bodies, my thoughts suddenly become bright, hidden in the sacred forest, glittering like silver dust.

Wu Kaijin's early poems are pure and simple, with sincere and heartfelt character portrayals, mostly based on realism. His middle-period works are about travel feelings and character nostalgia, and are very close to real life. His late works add more details and narrative elements. Among them, the poem "Memory of the Land" won the 1996 Israel Miriam Lindbergh Poetry Peace Prize. The judges commented: "Professor Wu Kaijin's *Memory of the Land* is a gripping, emotional poem that condenses the opposition to evil forces. The poem expresses the pain of the victims and the hatred of the devil through extraordinary metaphors." It can be seen that he tried hard to describe his understanding of historical facts in a simple and solemn way. Fundamentally speaking, it is precisely because of Wu Kaijin's unique thinking in artistic imagination that he has maintained an unfailing interest in artistic activities despite some physical hardships in his later years. In the final analysis, it is also related to the unique function and imagination of artistic thinking. He always integrates poetic emotions into images, and the wisdom and tolerance of experience that come with time all have the spark of love for writing poetry. Therefore, what stands before us is the image of a strong, kind, and transcendent poet.

II. Natural images and connotations in poetry

I remember that the Irish poet William Butler Yeats (1865-1939) once wrote: "Time passes but wisdom follows / Even if the branches and leaves are luxuriant, they are supported by lonely roots / In my youth I was vain and embellished / Once I showed off at will / Now let me wither into truth." How gentle and powerful the poem is! It is also an expression of beauty. It can be said that this is a display of the poet's achievement in natural aesthetics through aesthetic activities. In my opinion, Wu Kaijin's most amazing strength lies in his combination of realistic and freehand ideas with simple and unadorned poetic elements, as well as his instantaneous insight with aesthetic spirit. This allows us to appreciate more deeply the mutual promotion of life and art, and to see his overflowing poetic talent.

Wu Kaijin was also a precocious poet. This poem "On the Tram" was written when he was 22 years old. And it is a rare and heartwarming piece:

> Why did everyone stand up?
> Where did they go?

> Ah, here comes a young woman who will be a mother.
> She is covered with respectful eyes.
>
> She sat down lightly leaning against the window glass,
> with shyness and gratitude hidden in her eyes;
> Perhaps the little life was hitting the mother's happy heart,
> Look, she has closed her smiling eyes.

This poem is pure and natural, and it is the poet's inherent sadness that has been rooted in his heart for a long time. A small story on the tram also reflects that only true feelings between people can make society better; and the shy expression of the young woman giving birth to a little life and the interaction between people who want to give up their seats make this picture always remain in the readers' hearts. It can be said that Wu Kaijin is not only a poet who pays attention to emotions, but also a person who observes society and life objectively and keenly.

Wu Kaijin's mid-period collection *Crescent Moon Lake* records many travel poems, including a photo he took with his wife, Ms. Mingyan, at Thousand Buddha Mountain, where he wrote: "Our feet are deeply embedded in the rocks / The changing clouds make the village scenery / Regardless of spring rain and autumn frost / Regardless of the months and years / Let us stand forever." First, the poet sings out his love and expectations, as if we can also see them leaning against each other side by side. Although no one in the world has built an eternal temple for them, the poet's unforgettable love is far more beautiful than the cloud scenery on Thousand Buddha Mountain. William Wordsworth (1770-1850), a famous British poet, also pointed out with deep understanding: "Poetry is the natural expression of strong emotions. It originates from emotions recalled in peace."[2] In this poem, the poet also thinks about how to make "love" eternal. The emotions are true and holy; not only can it create beautiful music, but also arouse a deep impression on readers.

Another collection of poems, *Listening to Spring*, mostly with the themes of nature, travel, and realistic characters. Among them,

---

[2] *Selected Western Literary Theories (Volume 2)*, Shanghai Translation Publishing House, 1979, p. 17.

"Reminiscing with My Wife" was written when he was 63 years old: "Memories are a file / It stirs up pain and sorrow / Powder flies / Covers the sky / The annual rings of the years / Filled with tears / Watering the withering hope / The extinguished candle / Lets out a sigh before dawn." This is the poet and his wife recalling the old days during the Cultural Revolution. What makes Wu Kaijin different from the poets during the Cultural Revolution is that he is concerned about some unjust things in society at that time, but chooses to release his repressed emotions through poetry. For the poet, poetry can create an appeal, which in turn causes reflection on society. This poem expresses a deep sorrow, expressing the poet's lament of separation from his loved ones at the moment of recalling the past; and his wife Mingyan is always a good companion who listens to his heart. This poem is truly touching, and what follows can expand our imagination and create a strong voice of poetry. Most importantly, there are no anecdotes of the Cultural Revolution, or the kind of anxiety about the times and the spiritual confusion of having nowhere to rely on. There are only undiluted and undecorated poetic words, and the final extended picture can make readers feel the "scars" of the Cultural Revolution.

Another poem, "Memory of the Land: Dedicated to the Anniversary of the Victory of the Anti-Fascist War", is included in the first of the four volumes of *Selected Poems and Essays of Wu Kaijin*. This poem embodies Wu Kaijin's life-long efforts and is a set of works of great academic value. This poem is the most representative and has established an important position in the poetry world. It was written by the poet at the age of 61: "The land has a memory. Memories / are like the annual rings of a tree / a ravine every year / storing millions of sounds / when the sun's compass moves it / it will echo history / listen! The rumbling sound / is the sound of the Lugou Bridge and the Normandy artillery / and the screams of thousands of bloodstained people / the heart-wrenching sound / is the groaning of thousands of innocent souls in Auschwitz and Nanjing / and the screams of the beasts The screams / That thrilling sound / Was the trumpet of the capture of Berlin's Peace Pass / And the roar of revenge flashing on the bayonet / / Don't say that the sound of the cannon that exorcises the devil / Has turned into festive fireworks, rising high into the clouds / Don't say that the ashes in the crematorium / Have been built into the foundation of the skyscraper, buried deep in the ground / Don't say that the wailing of the pregnant woman who was cut open by the beast / Has turned into a companion Following the harmonious notes of the baby/Don't mention the painful struggle of being devoured by experimental toxins/It has turned into a peaceful smile under the shadowless lamp/These are long gone/Like smoke floating in space/Comfort is an anesthetic/People may forget the past/But the land will not forget/It bears the pain of the fascist iron hoofs trampling on it/And the cries in the monuments cast by countless resisters/Every time dawn comes/It wakes up in pain". The power to write this poem was internal. In the first stanza, he has already shown his feelings about the entire Northeast China being poisoned by the German Nazis during World War II, the Japanese attack on Lugou Bridge, the Nanjing Massacre, etc. He reflects on the way of the world from the perspective of the way of nature, and carefully denounces the destruction and impact of war on innocent people.

The fusion of the poet's feelings and expressions makes him a sharp and agile poet. September 3rd each year is the anniversary of the victory of the Chinese People's War of Resistance Against Japanese Aggression and the anniversary of the victory of the World Anti-Fascist War. This is the first comprehensive victory of the Chinese nation in resisting imperialist aggression in the past 100 years, and it is also a major turning point for the Chinese nation from decline to revitalization. The last section tells us that we can understand the author's sadness, and at the same time we are glad that the fascist regime collapsed. Although this period of history has lasted for more than a century, the author still cannot get rid of the shadow of war in every memory. The memory of the atrocities of Japan and Germany is like an infected wound, still bleeding. From the Nanjing Massacre in 1937 to the Nazi Party's human trials, its barbaric and violent behavior is still deeply engraved in the memory of the Chinese.

Wu Kaijin's meticulous observation of history includes both the experience and philosophy of a modern poet that transcends time and space, as well as his infinite awe of the land and his national consciousness. Those poems that travel through time to explore history face life directly, and the humanistic care that is bravely pursued is pure and sensitive, subtle and resolute, emotional and tragic. Here, the author has made a true expression and soul interpretation that goes straight to the true history. Here, we can also see Wu Kaijin's contribution to poetry. On the one hand, he allows poets to use the ugliness of war to explore the love and kindness of human nature; on the other hand, he allows readers to understand the poet's mission, which is to use his creative ability to repair the only remaining warmth in the broken world-love, and restore it to life, so that people only remember the lessons of history, re-perceive this world, and experience the scars of the land ravaged by war.

In addition to the above-mentioned poetry collections, the achievements of Wu Kaijin's late poetry have gradually attracted the attention of the world poetry community. Influenced by the spirit of Zen, he tends to have a broad vision and a keen and lively perception of nature, which makes him show implicit sensibility and a fresh and elegant style. In the poet's pursuit of spirituality and different realizations, it can arouse readers' noble emotions or fully develop their imagination. The poem "Dense Plane Leaves" written by the poet at the age of 64 is a clear and bright poem. The scenery instantly becomes a symphony, a way of describing without grandeur and history, but with poetic meaning:

> Dense Plane Leaves
> Chatting affectionately in the breeze
> They touch and clap each other
> Let laughter spread across the sky
>
> Each leaf has its own story —
> About the singing competition of the crowing bird, or the bitter love of the spotted pigeon.

They come from without holding back anything, they tell their partners every bit of it. When a storm hits, they warn and shout at each other. If someone can't stand the ruthless beating, they will shed tears. They hope that it will turn into soil soon, and then dive into the trunk from the roots. When the spring bagpipes sound in the clouds, they will meet again at the top of the tree.

The poem abandons elegance and refinement, and pays attention to natural phenomena in order to pursue the direct presentation of primitive simplicity, which is full of philosophical thoughts. The various images of the trembling leaves of the sycamore tree are revealed in the gentleness of the surrounding natural protection, allowing us to appreciate the beauty of all things contained in the world. For the poet, every flower and every tree has its own seasons, and they change in an orderly manner. Leaves must also experience the baptism of storms to be reborn with pride. From this, we can see that his artistic thinking is not attracted by the superficial or visual landscape; on the contrary, he values the philosophy contained in his works. Another poem, "Cloud Pine in Longwood Park", was written by the poet when he was 67 years old and went to the University of Maryland to give a lecture. It is a light and musical poem:

> Use the golden thread of the sun to play with the white clouds
> To break the silence of the sky
> How many people look up at you
> It is difficult to see your true face
> Your roots must be very deep
> Can penetrate the thick stratum
> The equally tall tree growing among the red leaves of the Fragrant Hill
> Must be your conjoined figure
> It's just that the one hanging among the green leaves in each pine cone
> My eyes are filled with longing for my motherland

A diffuse light, calm and uncondensed, awakens the smile of the foreign autumn pine, and also conveys the poet's homesickness. The red leaves of the Fragrant Hill Garden in the western suburbs of Beijing are connected with the tall surface of the pine in front of me, conveying the aesthetics of classicalism. The whole park has a kind of peace and tranquility that I can't describe, quietly accepting the poet's shared visual memories. The poet has realized that no matter how far the distance is, the poet's heart that misses his motherland and hometown is very close. Another poem, "Swans in Wilmington Forest Park", is written in a nearly classic style:

> One foot
> Standing on the lake
> Listening intently

> The clouds
> Tchaikovsky's melody
> Suddenly spread its silver wings
> Doing a 360-degree spin

This is a poem that completely subverts the traditional style of academic and rigid writing. I can neither see the forest park's hobby of constructing poetry with its beautiful scenery, nor can I see the poet endowing things that are dreamed rather than seen with a mysterious aura. On the contrary, if you want the poem to reach a touching and tragic state, you can only observe it with a true and pertinent, religious-like piety, until you think of the vastness of life, a swan flying alone, and the call in your heart will ignite a lyrical spiritual fire in your heart, containing a faint sadness and sorrow. The swan's ripples are not agitated; it also reveals its dancing posture, which is so beautiful that the poet's muse is silent. At this point, it can be seen that Wu Kaijin believed that the essence of art can only be directly contacted or communicated with the spiritual world of the self through creation. The late poetry style advocates a simple primitive style, with a modern sense of elegance and leisure.

Youxin Collection also focuses on travel poems and character sketches. Among them, "Remembering Friends" was written at the age of 65: "Like a breeze on a lotus leaf/Like a piece of snow in a pine forest/Your beautiful figure has drifted away a dream/On the annual rings of the heart/Forever embedded with the two bright stars." This poem is written in a light and fresh style; the language of the poem is inspired by the imagination of the goddess Muse, and it descends easily and naturally into the poet's emotional heart. In his pursuit of the sanctity of classical aesthetics and the construction of a timeless memory, the poet can frankly express his true feelings and create a surprising effect. Undoubtedly, his love, romantic meditation, imagination and poetic generation provide a rich spiritual realm; it shows that he is also a poet with poetic meaning in the treatment of picture composition.

III. Conclusion: Poetic beauty is the spiritual expression of Wu Kaijin's artistic thinking

Although Professor Wu Kaijin faced the pain of losing his wife and suffering from illness two years ago, for him, this just showed the strength of his life. In encouraging my creation, I found that the key to his artistic thinking lies in aesthetics. His aesthetic thought is not only the activity of intellectual and logical thinking, but also deeply focuses on the life training or the interpretation of love that allows readers to generate knowledge. Under his simple and gentle appearance, he can make good use of his time to study aesthetics. In addition to creating many insightful comments, he can also use poetry to describe a fresh, natural, beautiful, profound, harmonious and unified artistic world. His poetry creation is mostly about themes of expressing feelings about travel, with rich content, clear thoughts, lyrical colors, and can also conduct macroscopic investigations from the historical track. To find out the main ideological thread of Wu Kaijin's poetry creation, we can only explore the broad thoughts leading to his poetry and understand the connotation of his poetry.

Wu Kaijin is also a poet with rich emotions. His poetry can be studied in many aspects. Under the condition of maintaining his special emotions, he truly discovered that the most important element of poetry is love. His wisdom is to reconstruct the reality of things and guide us to go deep into the deep meaning represented by these things. Poetry is the most beautiful and greatest scenery in nature, and Wu Kaijin's poetry has another kind of Zen style, implying that beautiful things are not eternal, and that we know better to cherish the tranquility in peace and happiness. Finally, I would like to express my sincerest gratitude to my teacher-friend who is recovering from illness in Beijing. This is the most inspiring collection of poems and essays for me.

—2010.5.23

〔Published in Jiangsu Province's *Journal of Yancheng Teachers College*, Humanities and Social Sciences Edition, Vol. 31, No. 127, 2011.01, Book Review "On the Artistic Thinking of Wu Kaijin's Poetry", pp. 65-68.〕

10 禪悅中的慈悲——讀星雲大師《合掌人生》
Compassion in Zen Bliss: Reading Master Hsing Yun's
Life of Praying with Hands Crossed

　　星雲大師（1927- ），江蘇江都人。12 歲出家，23 歲到臺灣，40 歲創建佛光山，現任國際佛光會世界總會長，獲文學榮譽博士等殊榮。他是當代佛學界難得的大才，一生不曾虛耗過尺寸光陰，其行履思想，對世界佛教界有深遠的影響。其著作開闊浩瀚，正是其偉大人格的體現。大師書法的創作隨靈感源源不絕而日益累積，也蘊涵著文人情懷的素雅之韻。在他所有的著作中，《合掌人生》令人感動和震撼，這裡不擬對大師的禪淨同歸的淨土思想作全盤考察，只以《合掌人生》為例，對其一生弘法心路歷程作一簡評。

　　對星雲大師的經歷，我希望看到的是，在當時的環境底下，大師是怎樣面臨現實挑戰與生死哲學命題？又如何將生活禪法與哲思緊實地連接？所幸這套《合掌人生》，給了我想要尋索的問題，一個勇毅而清晰的圖像。

　　大師出生於江都一個純樸的農家，出家後，縱然歷經戰亂、顛沛流離，飽嘗饑餓與困頓；也曾幾度處於生死邊緣或無妄的牢獄之災；但總能在關鍵時刻值遇善緣，化險為夷，並從中汲取智慧。他一生信順佛祖，決志弘法，從無疑惑；其寫作的靈感，源自生活中的體驗，隨緣喜捨，終日不變。佛光山自 1967 年開山，大師擔任主管 18 年後退位，一生多奉行「以無為有、以退為進、以眾為我、以空為樂」的人生觀，也絕無誑語。他也重視文化弘法，雖然主張佛教要革新，但也不排斥傳統；其解析生活禪或生命禪的例證，更是不勝枚舉。如說：「求觀音、拜觀音，更要自己做觀音。」這短短的一段話，融攝各家佛性思想於一爐，可見大師對各家思想的融合是很成功的。

　　印象最深刻的一段描述是，大師的外婆 18 歲就開始茹素，她勤奮敦厚、慈祥助人、仗義執言，是大師記憶中最溫馨的回憶，也影響其簡樸與臨危不亂的性格。輾轉來台後，既發深信佛陀教義，便起切願。他說，人生的意義，應該是在於奉獻、服務、結緣，其信願堅固，更認為，修行應該從人格完成，從道德的增長做起，修行是明心見性的功夫。其中有許多哲思，能提升到大乘佛教的殊勝基礎菩提心的高度。他始終祈望讓眾生在禪法中懂得慈悲喜捨，在禪悅中獲得智慧清明。如他為 95 歲的母親李劉玉英居士（大家稱她老奶奶）送行寫下一副輓聯：「歷經民國締造，北伐統一，國共戰爭，吾母即為現代史；走遍大陸河山，遊行美日，終歸淨土，慈親好似活地圖。」除抒寫出自己無盡的追思外，這實際是大師以信方便激勵人認真念佛的善方便。在「六信的信果」中有一句話「深信淨土，皆以念佛三昧得生」。而我也深信，依心所現的十方世界亦不可盡，應有極樂國，在十萬億土外，最為清淨莊嚴。

大師的行腳走過無數的弘法歷練、走過開闢佛光山的荊棘、走過世界、走過多少風風雨雨……，唯一不變的，仍是大師勤勉不懈之寫作風格，這種樸實真摯的論述，對國際佛教起了非常重要的作用，成為弘法的中流砥柱。無論事持或理持，他皆以倡導「三好、四和」（做好事、說好話、存好心；家庭和諧、人我和敬、社會和諧、世界和平）為己任。在佈教的基礎上作出心中的期望。大師 50 多歲時，查出得了糖尿病，10 年前又罹患心肌梗塞，近些年來因病多次動了手術。在他一一梳理過去的種種記憶中的人、物、事中，我看見了大師一腔弘法為眾的熱血，也瞭解到，大師的淨土思想源於「心佛眾生，但俱信願」。他一生為弘揚佛法，不遺餘力；其願力堪與日月爭輝。

星雲大師的近作《合掌人生》，是他以現身說法進，而對自我處世原則及重要的回憶作出了更為詳盡的詮釋。大師的心性思想，為攝取學人的一種非常智慧的思想。他曾說：「慈悲沒有怨敵，施捨必有收穫。」他的佛法是生活佛法，以「小故事、富哲理」聞名於世。在其諸多著作中，以教導大眾在生活中實踐佛法為主，為建設人間淨土的理想，他奉獻一生，無悔無私。謹以此文對大師表達最深切的祈福。

—2012.1.10 作

【刊福建《莆田學院學報》，第 19 卷第 1 期，總第 78 期，2012.02】

Master Hsing Yun (1927-) was born in Jiangdu, Jiangsu province of China. He became a monk at the age of 12, and came to Taiwan at the age of 23, to found Fo Guang Shan at the age of 40, and is currently the World President of the International Buddhist Association. He has been awarded the honorary doctorate in literature as well as other honors. He is a rare talent in the contemporary Buddhist community. He has never wasted a single moment of his life. His conduct and thoughts have had a profound impact on the world Buddhist community. His works are broad and vast, which is the embodiment of his lofty personality. The master's calligraphy has accumulated day by day with endless inspiration, containing the simple and elegant rhyme of the feelings of literati. Among all his works, *The Life of Gathering Palms* is the most touching and shocking. I will not make a comprehensive study of the master's Pure Land thought of Zen and Pure Land Buddhism here, but only use "The Life of Gathering Palms" as an example to make a brief comment on his life-long journey of spreading Buddhism.

What I want to see about Master Hsing Yun's experience is how the master faced the challenges of reality and the philosophical propositions of life and death under the environment at that time? How to closely connect the living Zen with philosophical thinking? Fortunately, this set of *The Life of Gathering Palms* gave me a courageous and clear picture of the question I wanted to seek.

The master was born in a simple farmer's family in Jiangdu. After becoming a monk, he experienced war, displacement, hunger and hardship. He was on the verge of life and death, and have been imprisoned for several times. However, he always encountered good fortune at critical moments, turned danger into safety, and gained wisdom from it. He believed in the Buddha all his life and was determined to spread the Dharma without any doubt. The inspiration for his writing came from his experience in life, and he gave as the circumstances dictated. Fo Guang Shan was founded in 1967. The master served as the director for 18 years before resigning. Throughout his life, he pursued the life philosophy of "taking nothing as something, retreat as progress, taking the masses as myself, and taking emptiness as happiness", and he never talked nonsense. He also attached great importance to the spread of Buddhism through culture. Although he advocated the reform of Buddhism, he did not reject tradition. His examples of analyzing living Zen or life Zen are too numerous to count. For example, he said: "Pray to Guanyin, worship Guanyin, and be Guanyin yourself." This short sentence integrates various Buddhist thoughts into one, which shows that the master's integration of various thoughts is very successful.

The most impressive description is that the master's grandmother started to be a vegetarian at the age of 18. She was diligent, kind, helpful, and righteous. She is the warmest memory in the master's memory, and also influenced his simple and calm character. After coming to Taiwan, he had a deep belief in the Buddha's teachings and made a fond wish. He said that the meaning of life should be dedication, service, and establishing relationships. His faith and aspirations are firm, and he believes that practice should start with the completion of personality and the growth of morality. Practice is the effort to see the mind and nature. There are many philosophical thoughts that can be elevated to the height of bodhisattva, the special foundation of Mahayana Buddhism. He always hopes that sentient beings can understand compassion, joy, and generosity in meditation, and gain wisdom and clarity in meditation. For example, he wrote a couplet for his 95-year-old mother, Ms. Li Liu Yuying (everyone called her grandma), who passed away: "She experienced the founding of the Republic of China, the Northern Expedition, the Kuomintang-Communist War, and my mother is modern history; she traveled all over the country, visited the United States and Japan, and finally returned to the Pure Land. My kind mother is like a living map." In addition to expressing his endless remembrance, this is actually the Master's good convenience to encourage people to recite the Buddha's name seriously with the convenience of faith. There is a sentence in "the Fruit of the Six Faiths" that "those who have deep faith in the Pure Land can be reborn by reciting the Buddha's name in Samadhi." And I also firmly believe that the ten directions of the world that appear in the mind are also inexhaustible, and there should be a Pure Land, which is the most pure and solemn outside the 100 trillion lands.

The Master's journey has taken him through countless experiences in spreading the Dharma, through the thorns of opening up Fo Guang Shan, through the world, through many ups and downs... The only thing that remains unchanged is the Master's diligent and unremitting writing style. This simple and sincere discussion has played a very important role in international Buddhism and has become the mainstay of spreading the Dharma. Whether it is practical or theoretical, he advocates "Three Goods and Four Harmonies" (doing good deeds, saying good words, and having good intentions; family harmony, mutual respect, social harmony, and world peace). He made his expectations in his heart on the basis of preaching. When the Master was in his 50s, he was diagnosed with diabetes. Ten years ago, he suffered a myocardial infarction. In recent years, he has undergone many operations due to illness. In the people, things and events in his past memories, I saw the master's passion to spread the Dharma for the benefit of all, and I also understood that the master's Pure Land thought originated from "the mind, Buddha and sentient beings, all with faith and aspiration". He spared no effort in his life to spread the Dharma. His aspirations were comparable to the sun and the moon.

Master Hsing Yun's recent work *The Life of Gathering Palms* is a more detailed interpretation of his principles of conduct and important memories through his own experience. The master's mind and nature thoughts are a very wise thought for students. He once said: "Compassion has no enemies, and charity will definitely bring rewards." His Dharma is a living Dharma, famous for "small stories and rich philosophy". In his many works, he mainly teaches people to practice Buddhism in their daily lives. He dedicated his life to the ideal of building a pure land on earth without regrets and selflessness. This article expresses my deepest wishes to the master.

—Written on January 10, 2012

【Published on Fujian province *Journal of Futian College*, Vol. 19, No. 1, Total No. 78, 2012.02】

11 從孤獨中開掘出詩藝之花——淺釋《艾蜜莉·狄金生詩選》

The Flower of Poetry from Loneliness: On *The Selected Poems of Emily Dickinson*

摘要 Abstract

艾蜜莉·狄金生被譽為「自但丁以來，除莎士比亞之外，西方最具原創性的詩人」。她的詩歌凸顯了孤獨中的靈魂慰藉，呈現出單純的內心獨白與真樸的睿智，從而對世界文學做出了貢獻。

Emily Dickinson is praised as "the most original poet, except Shakespeare, in the West since Dante". Her poetry highlights the soul comfort in loneliness, presents pure inner monologue and genuine wisdom, thus making contributions to world literature.

關鍵詞：艾蜜莉·狄金生、詩人、孤獨、意境。
Keywords: Emily Dickinson, poet, loneliness, artistic conception.

一、傳略

艾蜜莉·狄金生（Emily Dickinson, 1830-1886）一個響亮而有力度的名字，生於美國麻州小鎮。其父為執業律師，曾是當地的望族；因一時經濟拮据，不得已賣掉了祖產的磚房，喬遷到一間木造屋，狄金生的三兄妹都在那裡出世。生前只發表過10首詩的狄金生，感情內向，不喜露面。她是大自然的女兒，因而，她的許多詩歌始終和生態、愛與存在的鄉愁緊緊相連。她也溯源追尋死亡和永生，而這些主題也反覆出現在她寄給朋友的信裡。年輕時，她在安默斯特學院（Amherst Academy）學習了七年，此後，又在霍約克（Mount Holyoke）女子學院度過了一段短暫的時光，最終返回到位於安默斯特的家中。狄金生開始對人生的種種煩惱和孤獨狀況進行了詩意的再現與挖掘。其詩風簡煉而富意境美，譬喻尖新；既有具象的嘲諷，有時也用調侃式的語氣，寫出那獨特的畫境。

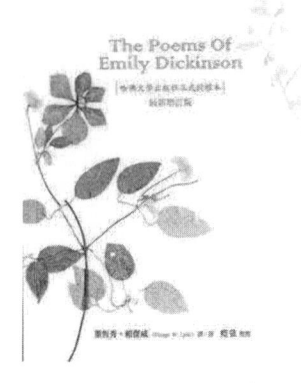

身為一個孤僻的女詩人，狄金生晚年很少邁出自己家門一步，因此，與友人間都靠通信維繫。她一生共寫了 1800 多首詩，善於運用反思維調動詩行，充滿了哲理性和思辨性；但僅有十幾首在生前獲得了出版。直到狄金生逝世後，其妹妹拉維尼亞才發現了她藏匿的作品。在她死後近七十年才得到文學界的認真關注，被現代派詩人追認為先驅。艾蜜莉・狄金生也被譽為「自但丁以來，除莎士比亞之外，西方最具原創性的詩人」。她的詩歌凸顯了孤獨中的靈魂慰藉，呈現出單純的內心獨白與真樸的睿智，從而對世界文學做出了貢獻。

二、作品的哲思與情趣

　　對狄金生詩藝詩美的探索，是貫穿這本《艾蜜莉・狄金生詩選》的一根紅線。拜讀這部詩集，除了深深感佩董恆秀銳準確的藝術洞察力和藝術感受力以外；也為賴傑威譯者對狄金生詩歌所做的序文更有精到的評析而感動。在這本精選的六十首作品中，採中英對照呈現。內容包括對狄金生的寫作技巧與詩學的探討並附有狄金生生平詳介與校訂年表，以及對每首詩歌的短評寫得精彩是最大特點。除得益於他們兩位精湛通博的學術功力和求真求是的研究態度外，還得益於對狄金生詩學的真知灼見。總的看來，狄金生的創作之路是從孤獨中開掘出詩藝之花的。而此書裡的詩歌最突出的特色，是以純真的情懷，唱出的生命之歌。更可貴的是，她善於捕捉瞬間的靈魂閃光，哪怕只是短小的生活片斷，都能使情感之河泊泊湧動。此外，她還善於以哲理性的語言去揭示生死的超脫和對人生中孤獨處境的逆向思考，從而增加了作品的力度。

　　如這首〈在路上獨自漫遊的小石頭〉，寫得很集中精煉。內裡所觀境不是一種孤絕，而是富有情趣和幽默感，能激起讀者更深的思考：

　　　　在路上獨自漫遊的小石頭
　　　　是多麼快樂，

從孤獨中開掘出詩藝之花——淺釋《艾蜜莉・狄金生詩選》

既不憂事業，
也無懼急務——
素樸的棕色外衣上
隨意披著路過的宇宙，
自主若太陽——
結友或自愉，
順應天理
以儉樸之道——

當然，這種帶有浪漫色彩偽裝其叛叛的基調；已不是單純的對生存環境的揶揄，而是把對詩中說的這塊小石，不屑與功利主義者為伍，只在宇宙路過它時，才願意將之隨手披上；內裡能把追求儉樸之道，去洗掉一切偽善虛榮的毒素的精神滲入其中。實際上，狄金生在經過種種社會和心理的衝擊之後，一如蟬蛻般脫掉那些離開社會需要也離開詩的本體要求的陳舊外殼，而開始嚮往新的簡靜生活以走向新生。如〈一陣暴風雨擣碎了空氣〉，正是有了這種信念，詩人才能保持孤高和簡樸，甘心與自然為鄰，繆斯為伴：

一陣暴風雨擣碎了空氣——
疏雲瘦骨嶙峋——
一抹黑雲似幽靈的斗篷
遮蔽天與地。

群魔在屋頂咯咯獰笑——
空中呼嘯——
揮動拳頭——
咬牙切齒——
狂甩亂髮。

晨光照射——雀鳥醒躍——
妖怪凋萎的眼睛
遲緩地望向他的故鄉——
啊，寧靜就是樂園！

這首詩是把周圍的暴風雨的襲擊與退去戲劇化，烘托得很真切，使人有身臨其境之感。

正因狄金生常以新奇的目光看大自然的生息,也用了不少現代詩常用的藝術手法,如意象的選擇或象徵的運用。其中,詩人嚮往著一種恬淡美好的禪境,但更多地是在寫自己的「悟」。如〈夏日遠逸〉,就很有代表性,寫得很輕盈雋永:

> 夏日遠逸
> 悄然如憂傷離去───
> 如此纖靜難覺
> 不像是背信───
> 午後已感薄暮微光靜透
> 一種濃厚的寂靜,
> 或是大自然消磨
> 隱居的下午───
> 黃昏早臨───
> 晨光陌生───
> 像急欲離去的客人,
> 那種多禮惱人的風度───
> 就這樣,無需翅膀
> 或小船勞送
> 我們的夏日飄然逃逸
> 進入了美之地。

這是寫夏日感悟的詩,現實即便是孤獨,等待和守望也毫無結局;但是,詩人卻從夏日飄然逃逸中,悟出了某種禪機。原來:自然會有更替,美麗總是短暫的。詩人本是淡泊的,又何必去為昨日猶糾結的憂傷而懊惱或去追求為愛而轟轟烈烈的聲響呢!

記得印度詩人泰戈爾(1861-1941)曾說:「藝術家是自然的情人,所以他是自然的奴隸,也是自然的主人。」[1]狄金生也忘情於自然,追求返樸歸真。雖然十九世紀美國文評家希更生(Thomas Wentworth Higginson)不懂狄金生詩篇的原創,令人愕腕;然而,狄金生自二十歲起就已理解到她之為詩人的天命。這部詩集中,有許多曲折迂迴的表現方法,或隱喻,或象徵,或嘲諷,或造境,詩人都想創造出一種純淨的詩美,力圖擺脫功利性。如這首小詩

---

[1] 泰戈爾著,《生如夏花:泰戈爾經典詩選》,臺北,遠足文化,2011.12,頁 99。

從孤獨中開掘出詩藝之花——淺釋《艾蜜莉‧狄金生詩選》

〈無法知道曙光何時來〉，至純，至淨，映照曙光或者神的啟示的降臨，是如鳥羽般輕靈，還是如岸濤般拍擊而來？這也是對污濁塵世的一種否定：

> 無法知道曙光何時來，
> 我打開每一扇門，
> 是如鳥有羽，
> 還是如岸有濤——

詩人早期作品中也曾質疑過宇宙的創生者和統治者——神——的慈愛，並大膽地將之視為苦鬥、申斥的對象。因而對自然界裡到處充滿的死亡與磨難，能很快轉換成藝術想像。如這首〈任何快樂的花朵〉，詩裡有她深刻的喜悅和灰色的絕望交織的複雜心情。詩人把愛的神秘、驚恐和幸福感化為一種心靈的反光，去揭示出對人生、社會、神的觀點和認知，也可說是情境的反諷：

> 任何快樂的花朵
> 似都不感驚異
> 在它嬉戲時，白霜將它斬首——
> 以偶然的力量——
> 白色殺手繼續走——
> 太陽無動於衷依舊運行
> 為了替一個表贊同的神
> 區劃另一天。

如果說重意境和語言的形象性是一般詩歌的重要特徵的話，那麼重意象和情感的嫁接跳躍則是狄金生詩的特點之一。清秀而外表嚴謹的狄金生喜歡長年素裝，始終擁有詩人的氣質，連他的日記、甚至書信也都充滿了詩味。29歲的她，在書信中曾透露了喜愛獨居和對做一個家庭主婦的不自在；而其一生的感情世界和隱居的關連，也總讓人無限遐思。如這首〈沒有戰艦像書卷〉，是狄金生生活中的真正的形象，用永恆的真理顯現出閱讀一本書或一首詩的力量，寫得比較大氣和有力度：

> 沒有戰艦像書卷
> 領我們航向遙遠的國土
> 也沒有駿馬像頁

> 跳躍奔馳的詩篇——
> 最窮的人也可以做此遊——
> 不用負擔過路費
> 乘載人之靈魂的戰車
> 是多麼儉樸。

　　此詩從另一側面來看，則表現了狄金生傲世不群的生命力；其奔馳的想像力也與空間時間相一致而取得了永恆，讀來給人一種豁達清爽之感。在 1870 年 8 月，希更生第一次造訪狄金生後，他寫給妻子信中轉述狄金生說過的一句話：「如果我讀到一本書，它能讓我全身冰冷到任何火燄都不能使我溫暖，我知道那就是詩。又倘使我肉體上感覺到彷彿我的頭頂被拿掉，我知道那就是詩。這些是我僅知的方式。還有其他的方式嗎？」[2]從這裡可以看出狄金生勇於逆向思考的藝術叛逆性。再如這首小詩〈凝望夏空〉：

> 凝望夏空
> 即是詩，它未見於書中——
> 真正的詩飛逝——

　　這寂靜、優美的藝術境界，自然是詩人嚮往的心靈「清淨」境界；這也是此詩玲瓏剔透的根源。

　　狄金生自 1860 年開始隱居，除了 1864 年，因眼疾而前往波士頓接受七個月的治療外，幾乎足不出戶。這首〈心靈選擇了她的社群〉，具有某些神秘色彩，是生命感悟體現最為集中之處。作為一生與詩為伴的人，其心靈即為帝王；對詩神繆斯的共同崇敬，其中隱含哲理思考是不言而喻的：

> 心靈選擇了她的社群
> 然後——深鎖門扉——
> 毋需再向她的神聖選擇權
> 薦舉人選——
>
> 心堅靜，就算見到馬車暫停——
> 在她簡陋的矮門邊——

---

[2] 《艾蜜莉·狄金生詩選》，譯／評：董恆秀、賴傑威，台灣，木馬文化出版，2006 年 11 月，頁 345-346。

從孤獨中開掘出詩藝之花——淺釋《艾蜜莉·狄金生詩選》

心堅靜，就算是帝王下跪
在她蓆上——

我曾見她——從一廣大國家——
擇取一個——
然後關閉她目注的門閥——
如默石——

狄金生是一個喜愛閱讀及孤獨寫作的人，正因經歷過多少風風雨雨和受盡苦戀的折磨，但最終還是選擇了一個寧靜地並埋首於詩作，向後世展示出她的執著與純真。如這首〈我喜愛烈痛的臉孔〉，詩人滿懷激情、揶揄地描寫了有些人不善於誠實地面對自己的情感，唯有等到在烈痛或將死前才可能做到。在今天看來，這應是詩人自己悲苦生活的真實寫照：

我喜愛烈痛的臉孔，
因我深知其真實——
人不假裝抽搐，
或佯裝劇痛——

當目光呆滯——即是死亡——
無從偽裝
額上汗珠
真樸的苦悶串成。

此詩讀來自由流暢，讓人在靜靜的思索中，感受到詩人感情浪潮的衝擊。

由此，我們看到詩人感情的抒發，都離不開文學的第一要素——語言。關於狄金生對信仰與人生的苦悶與愛的追尋與精神的解脫，由這首四行小詩〈愛〉，或許從中可看到她對「愛」這個字進行了精心的構建：

愛只能以自己衡量自己——
「我與我同大」——試著向從未
感受太陽的烈焰者說太陽是什麼——
它自己是它唯一的準繩——

狄金生用自己的藝術實踐使「愛」這一詩體獲得了新的詮釋：愛是它自己唯一的衡量。其中愛情帶給她的痛苦與歡喜，或渴望與傷感，含有無限深意。而最能代表她對死亡與永恆之間的探索的當是這首被稱讚的〈就像我們愛坐在死者身邊〉，在狄金生身上也有一顆勇敢的種子，那就是「愛」。此詩則體現使理與象、與情結合的諧趣美：

　　就像我們愛坐在死者身旁，
　　他們變得無上珍貴——
　　就像我們極力要爭回失去的
　　雖然其他的都在這裡——

　　我們用破碎的算術
　　評估我們的獎品
　　對我們如豆的眼睛
　　它漸逝的比例——巨大無比！

　　內裡暗喻著人要珍惜當下，因為生命不能重新來過，為何要等到失去或死亡時才懂得珍惜呢？狄金生的諷刺詩的創作雖不如抒情詩量多，但影響也不小。不過她的晚期之作，已不似早期那樣與神〈或稱上帝〉處於敵對狀態。如這一首〈除死亡之外〉，同樣給人一種藝術快感，這種快感就是帶有俏皮的諧謔美。再加上它對死亡的坦然與不排除永生的信念了，理應受到人們的關注：

　　除死亡之外，餘皆可予調整——
　　朝代再興——
　　體系——安置在他們孔上——
　　堡壘——瓦解——

　　生命的荒漠——被繼來的春天——
　　再次播種了色彩——
　　而死亡是其自身的特例——
　　身處變遷之外

　　這是詩人在苦心尋找思想和情感飽和交凝的聚點。狄金生對詩歌要求謹嚴、脫俗，正由於她在藝術上有著自己獨立不依的追求，所以才能成為偉大的詩人。最後是以幻想和擬人化手法，寫下這首〈她飛向明亮的東方〉，這是在狄金生母親過世之後而作：

從孤獨中開掘出詩藝之花——淺釋《艾蜜莉·狄金生詩選》

她飛向明亮的東方，
天堂的弟兄們
接引她回家，
沒帶另一雙替換的翅膀，
或是愛之方便物，
就這樣被吸引走。

想像她現在是何光景，
推想她過去的模樣，
我們認為我們在做夢——
這樣就會使那些漫無目的的日子
淡逝化於無形
在已不是家的家。

　　狄金生的母親因中風而臥病七年期間，多由狄金生傾力照料。在這裡，詩人表達了失親後才真正體會到「沒有母親」的苦味，並以此詩向母親表達強烈的思念與關懷。那種直透天國的目光使詩歌所達到的思想高度，就已具一定的意義了。

三、狄金生：神秘而隱逸的行者

　　這本詩集是耐人尋味的佳品，只有細細揣摩，才能體會到狄金生從孤獨的行吟到獲得靈魂的新生的過程。我們以此來閱讀狄金生的詩作，不難發現，她是個神秘而逸靜的詩人。在1862年這一年裡，是她創作生涯裡最豐盛之年，共寫了366首詩。其中不但充滿了奇妙的聯想和豐富的想像，而且更可以窺見，在她想像力的支配下，所運用的多種藝術方法，這就給作品帶來了獨特的藝術魅力。儘管她也寫了些諷刺詩，較為明朗和犀利；但可貴之處，是她總是不自覺地把自己的個性融入了詩作。寫詩可說是狄金生為釋放心中的焦慮或說是發抒情感壓力的一種方式。語言都是言既無盡，意又無窮，而這也是她內心的潛台詞。

　　這位神祕而隱逸的行者，可惜在她的母親於1883年去世時過於憂傷，加以她最疼愛的侄子也死於傷寒，年僅八歲。狄金生在悲痛之餘，因而病倒。原本醫生診斷為「精神衰竭」，也可能是腎臟炎發病，總之，就在她重病三年後竟奪走了她的生命，身後葬於她父母墓旁。

對狄金生而言，她要讀者親自去感受她所經歷的種種情感，無論是充滿著愛或自責的感情，或是恐懼、驚異和困惑，我們從中都可以體會到一種情緒上的消長和抑揚頓挫。她也是個追求榮譽與為真理而獻身的歌者，其一生心志雖說相當不可思議，甚至連她的兄長都表明了狄金生十五年從未踏返家門的事實。但她從不是個素樸的詩人，而是能領會世間的真與美、善與惡的哲人。其詩中展現的心境，特別是在信裡的感情是那樣真實和迫切。後人雖不清楚她為何絕世獨立？又或許狄金生認為，生活才是最高的藝術；而想要對她進一步瞭解的讀者，無疑地，此書的結集已取得了可喜的成績；不但使人從其詩作中領略到狄金生大半生的心靈歷程，且可讓人感受到其獨特的哲思與情趣之美。在這裡，我已聽到詩人心靈中那以生命與世俗博鬥的強音，相信在二十一世紀內，在詩人們、評論家、編輯家的共同努力下，在狄金生詩歌愛好者的支持下，迪金生的心已和大自然的融合中獲得了永恆的平靜。

—2013.3.15 作

【刊登於中國安徽省馬鞍市《大江詩壇 2014 中國詩選》，中國電影出版社，2014.10，頁 91-94。】

I. Biography

Emily Dickinson (1830-1886), a resounding and powerful name, was born in a small town in Massachusetts, USA. Her father was a practicing lawyer and was once a prominent family in the local area. Due to temporary financial difficulties, they were forced to sell the ancestral brick house and move to a wooden house, where Dickinson's three siblings were born. Dickinson, who published only 10 poems during her lifetime, was introverted and did not like to show up in public. She is the daughter of nature, and therefore many of her poems are closely linked to ecology, love and existential nostalgia. She also explored the origins of death and immortality, themes that recurred in the letters she sent to friends. As a young woman, she attended

Amherst Academy for seven years, then briefly attended Mount Holyoke College before returning home to Amherst. Dickinson began to poetically reproduce and explore the various troubles and loneliness in life. Her poetry is concise yet rich in artistic conception, with sharp and novel metaphors. It contains concrete sarcasm and sometimes a teasing tone to write about that unique painting scene.

As a solitary female poet, Dickinson seldom left her home in her later years, so she maintained contact with her friends through correspondence. She wrote more than 1,800 poems in her lifetime. She was good at using reverse thinking to mobilize the lines of poetry, which were full of philosophy and speculation. But only a dozen of them were published during her lifetime. It was not until after Dickinson's death that her sister Lavinia discovered her hidden works. It was not until nearly seventy years after her death that she received serious attention from the literary world and was recognized as a pioneer by modernist poets. Emily Dickinson is also known as "the most original poet, except Shakespeare, in the West since Dante." Her poetry highlights the soul comfort in loneliness, presents pure inner monologue and genuine wisdom, thus making contributions to world literature.

II. The philosophy and interest of the work

The exploration of Dickinson's poetic art and beauty is a red thread running through book of *The Selected Poems of Emily Dickinson*. After reading this collection of poems, I was deeply impressed by Dong Hengxiu's keen and accurate artistic insight and sensibility. I was also moved by the insightful analysis of Dickinson's poems in the preface written by translator Lai Jiewei. This collection of sixty selected works is given in both Chinese and English. The content includes a discussion of Dickinson's writing skills and poetics, with a detailed introduction to Dickinson's life and a chronology of revisions, as well as short reviews of each poem, which are brilliantly written. In addition to benefiting from their superb academic skills and truth-seeking research attitude, we also benefited from their profound insights into Dickinson's poetics. In general, Dickinson's creative path is to dig out the flower of poetry from loneliness. The most prominent feature of the poems in this book is that they sing the songs of life with pure feelings. What is more valuable is that she is good at capturing the momentary flash of the soul. Even if it is just a short fragment of life, it can make the river of emotions surge. In addition, she is also good at using philosophical language to reveal the transcendence of life and death and reverse thinking about the lonely situation in life, thus increasing the power of her works.

For example, the poem "A Little Stone Wandering Alone on the Road" is written in a very concentrated and concise manner. The scene inside is not lonely, but full of interest and humor, which can inspire readers to think more deeply:

> A small stone wandering alone on the road
> How happy it is,
> Not worrying about career,
> Nor fear of urgency —
> On a plain brown coat
> casually wrapped in the passing universe,
> Autonomous like the sun
> Make friends or enjoy yourself,
> Follow the will of nature
> With the way of frugality

Of course, this tone of rebellion is disguised with romantic colors. It is no longer a simple mockery of the living environment, but a poem about the little stone that disdains to associate with utilitarians and is only willing to cover itself with the universe when it passes by. It can infiltrate into it the spirit of pursuing frugality and washing away all the toxins of hypocrisy and vanity. In fact, after experiencing various social and psychological shocks, Dickinson shed her old shell, which was separated from the social needs and the essential requirements of poetry, like a cicada shedding its shell, and began to yearn for a new simple and quiet life to move towards a new life. For example, in "A Storm Shattered the Air", it is with this belief that the poet can maintain her solitude and simplicity, and be willing to live next to nature and be accompanied by the Muse: "A storm shattered the air— / The sparse clouds were bony — / A black cloud was like a ghost's cloak / covering the sky and the earth. // The demons cackled on the roof — / Howling in the air — / Waving their fists — / Gnashing their teeth — / Shaking their hair wildly. // The morning light shines — Birds wake up — / The monster's withered eyes / Look slowly towards his hometown — / Ah, tranquility is paradise!" This poem dramatizes the attack and retreat of the surrounding storm, and sets off the scene so vividly that people feel as if they are there.

Because Dickinson often looked at the life of nature with a novel eye, she also used many artistic techniques commonly used in modern poetry, such as the selection of images or the use of symbols. Among them, the poet yearns for a tranquil and beautiful state of Zen, but she is writing more about her own "enlightenment". For example, "Summer's Escape" is very representative, written in a light and timeless manner: "Summer's escape / As quiet as sorrow leaving — / So subtle and hard to notice / Not like a betrayal — / The afternoon has already felt the twilight and the faint light is penetrating / A thick silence, / Or maybe it's Nature spending / The secluded afternoon — / Dusk comes early — / The morning light is unfamiliar — / Like a guest eager to leave, / With that kind of polite and annoying demeanor — / Just like this, without wings / or boats to send us off / our summer escapes / Into a beautiful land." This is a poem about the perception of summer. Even if the reality is lonely, waiting and watching will have no end; however, the poet has realized some kind of Zen from the summer's escape. It turns out: nature will change, and beauty is always short-lived. Poets are inherently indifferent, so why should they worry about the sorrow of yesterday or pursue the passionate sound of love?

I remember that the Indian poet Rabindranath Tagore (1861-1941) once said: "The artist is the lover of nature, so he is both the slave of nature and the master of nature."[3] Dickinson was also fascinated by nature and pursued a return to nature. Although it was surprising that the 19th century American literary critic Thomas Wentworth Higginson did not understand the originality of Dickinson's poems, Dickinson had understood her destiny as a poet since she was 20 years old. In this collection of poems, there are many tortuous and circuitous ways of expression, whether metaphor, symbol, irony, or creation of a scene. The poet wants to create a pure poetic beauty and try to get rid of utilitarianism. Like this little poem "I Can't Know When the Dawn Will Come", the purest and cleanest thing, reflecting the coming of dawn or

---

[3] Rabindranath Tagore, *Life is like a Summer Flower: Selected Classic Poems of Rabindranath Tagore*, Taipei, Hiking Culture, December 2011, p. 99.

God's revelation, is it as light as a bird's feather, or as crashing as waves on the shore? This is also a denial of the filthy world: "I don't know when the dawn will come, / I open every door, / is it like a bird with feathers, / or like the shore with waves —". In the poet's early works, she also questioned the kindness of God, the creator and ruler of the universe, and boldly regarded him as the object of struggle and rebuke. Therefore, the death and suffering that are everywhere in nature can be quickly transformed into artistic imagination. Like the poem "Any Happy Flower", the poem contains her complex emotions of deep joy and gray despair. The poet transforms the mystery, fear and happiness of love into a reflection of the soul to reveal her views and cognition of life, society and God. It can also be said to be an irony of the situation:

> Any happy flower
> Doesn't seem surprised
> As it played, the frost decapitated it —
> By the power of chance —
> The White Killer continued to walk —
> The sun is indifferent and keeps moving
> For a god who approves
> Zoning for another day.

If the emphasis on artistic conception and the imagery of language is an important feature of general poetry, then the emphasis on the grafting and jumping of images and emotions is one of the characteristics of Dickinson's poetry. Dickinson, who was handsome and serious in appearance, liked to wear plain clothes all year round and always had the temperament of a poet. Even her diary and letters were full of poetry. At the age of 29, she revealed in her letters that she loved living alone and was uncomfortable with being a housewife. The relationship between her emotional world and seclusion throughout her life always makes people think about it. For example, the poem "No Battleship Like a Book" is a true image of Dickinson's life, which uses eternal truth to show the power of reading a book or a poem. It is written in a more majestic and powerful way:

> No warship is like a scroll
> Lead us to a distant land

> There is no horse image page
> The poem of leaping and running —
> Even the poorest people can do this tour.
> No need to pay tolls
> The chariot of the human soul
> How frugal.

Viewed from another perspective, this poem expresses Dickinson's unique vitality; her running imagination is consistent with space and time and achieves eternity, which gives people a sense of openness and freshness when reading it. In August 1870, after Higgins visited Dickinson for the first time, he wrote to his wife, quoting Dickinson's words: "If I read a book that chills me so much that no fire could warm me, I know that is poetry. And if I feel physically as if the top of my head were taken off, I know that is poetry. These are the only ways I know. Are there any other ways?"[4] From this we can see Dickinson's artistic rebelliousness in daring to think in reverse. Another example is this short poem "Gazing at the Summer Sky": "Gazing at the summer sky / is poetry, it is not found in books — / real poetry flies away —", this quiet and beautiful artistic realm is naturally the "pure" realm of the soul that the poet yearns for; this is also the source of the exquisiteness of this poem.

Dickinson began living in seclusion in 1860 and rarely left her house except for a seven-month stay in Boston in 1864 for treatment of an eye disease. The poem of "The Soul Chooses Her Community" has a certain mysterious quality and is the most concentrated expression of life perception. As a person who has been accompanied by poetry all her life, her soul is the emperor; the common reverence for the Muse of poetry contains philosophical thinking that is self-evident:

> The soul chooses her community
> Then — lock the door tightly —
> No need to ask her for her divine right to choose
> Recommended candidates —

---

[4] *The Selected Poems of Emily Dickinson*, translated/reviewed by Dong Hengxiu and Lai Jiewei, published by Trojan Horse Publishing in Taiwan, November 2006, pp. 345-346.

With a firm heart, even if you see the carriage stop —
At her humble low door —
With a firm heart, even the emperor kneels down
At her table —

I have seen her — from a vast country —
Choose one —
Then she closed the door she was looking at.
Like Silent Stone

Dickinson was a person who loved reading and writing alone. Although she had experienced many ups and downs and suffered from bitter love, she finally chose a quiet place to bury herself in poetry, showing her persistence and innocence to future generations. For example, in the poem "I Love the Face of Severe Pain", the poet describes passionately and ironically that some people are not good at facing their emotions honestly, and can only do so when they are in severe pain or are about to die. From today's perspective, this should be a true portrayal of the poet's own miserable life:

I love faces of intense pain,
Because I know the truth —
People don't fake twitches.
Or feigning severe pain —

When the eyes are dull — that is death —
No disguise
Sweat beads on forehead
It's a string of really simple anguish.

This poem reads freely and fluently, allowing one to feel the impact of the poet's emotional waves in quiet contemplation.

From this, we can see that the expression of poet's emotions is inseparable from the first element of literature — language. Regarding Dickinson's anguish over faith and life, her pursuit of love, and her spiritual liberation, this four-line poem "Love" may reveal her careful construction of the word "love":

Love can only measure itself by itself.
"I am as big as I am" — Try to

> Those who feel the flame of the sun say what the sun is —
> Itself is its only criterion —

Dickinson used her artistic practice to give a new interpretation to the poetic form of "love": love is its own only measure. The pain and joy, or desire and sadness, that love brings her contain infinite meaning. The song that best represents her exploration of death and eternity is the praised "As We Love to Sit by the Side of the Dead". There is also a brave seed in Dickinson, that is "love". This poem embodies the harmonious beauty of combining reason, image and emotion:

> Just as we love to sit beside the dead,
> They become extremely precious.
> Just like we try to regain what we lost
> Although the others are here —
>
> We use broken arithmetic
> Evaluating our prizes
> To our small eyes
> Its vanishing proportions — enormous!

The inner metaphor is that people should cherish the present, because life cannot be repeated, so why wait until loss or death to appreciate it? Although Dickinson's satirical poems were not as numerous as her lyric poems, their influence was still considerable. However, her later works are no longer hostile to God as in her early works. For example, the poem of "Except Death" also gives people a kind of artistic pleasure, which is a kind of playful and humorous beauty. Coupled with its calm attitude towards death and its belief in immortality, it deserves people's attention:

> Except for death, everything else can be adjusted —
> The dynasty is reborn
> System — placed in their holes —
> The fortress collapses
>
> The Desert of Life — The Spring That Came
> Sowing colors again —
> And death is its own special case —
> Outside the Change

This is the poet's painstaking search for the point where her thoughts and emotions are saturated and condensed. Dickinson had strict and unconventional requirements for poetry. It was precisely because she had her own independent pursuit in art that she became a great poet. Finally, the poem "She Flies to the Bright East" was written using fantasy and personification. It was written after Dickinson's mother passed away:

> She flew to the bright east,
> Brothers in Heaven
> Lead her home,
> Without a replacement pair of wings,
> Or a convenient thing of love,
> Just like that, I was attracted away.
>
> Imagine what she is like now.
> Imagine what she looked like in the past.
> We think we are dreaming —
> This will make those aimless days
> Fading into the invisible
> In a home that is no longer home.

Dickinson took care of her mother during the seven years when she was bedridden due to a stroke. Here, the poet expresses that it was only after the loss of her parents that she truly experienced the bitterness of "being without a mother", and uses this poem to express her strong longing and care for her mother. The ideological height reached by the poem due to its gaze that penetrates the heavens has a certain significance.

III. Dickinson: A mysterious and reclusive traveler

This collection of poems is an intriguing masterpiece. Only by careful reading can one appreciate Dickinson's journey from lonely wandering to the rebirth of the soul. When we read Dickinson's poems in this light, it is not difficult to discover that she is a mysterious and quiet poet. In 1862, the most productive year in her creative career, she wrote a total of 366 poems. Not only are they full of wonderful associations and rich imagination, but one can also see the various artistic methods she used under the control of her imagination, which gives the works a unique artistic charm. Although she also wrote some satirical poems, which were relatively clear and sharp, what was valuable was that she always unconsciously incorporated her own personality into her poems. Writing poetry can be said to be a way for Dickinson to release her anxiety or express her emotional pressure. Language is endless in words and infinite in meaning, and this is also her inner subtext.

This mysterious and reclusive traveler was unfortunately too sad when her mother died in 1883, and her favorite nephew also died of typhoid fever at the age of eight. Dee Jinsheng fell ill due to grief. The doctor originally diagnosed her with "mental exhaustion", or possibly nephritis. In short, her life was taken away three years after she became seriously ill, and she was buried next to her parents' grave.

For Dickinson, she wants readers to personally feel the emotions she experienced, whether it was feelings of love or self-blame, or fear, surprise and confusion, we can all experience the ups and downs of emotions. She was also a singer who pursued honor and dedicated herself to the truth. Although her lifelong determination was quite incredible, even her brother pointed out the fact that Dickinson had never returned home for fifteen years. But she was never a naive poet, but a philosopher who could understand the truth and beauty, good and evil in the world. The moods expressed in her poems, and especially the emotions in her letters, are quite real and urgent. Although later generations do not know why she was so unique and independent? Or perhaps Dickinson believed that life was the highest art; and for readers who want to know more about her, this collection of books has undoubtedly achieved gratifying results. It not only allows people to appreciate Dickinson's spiritual journey for most of her life from her poems, but also allows people to feel the beauty of her unique philosophy and interest. Here, I have heard the strong voice in the poet's heart that fights against the world with life. I believe that in the 21st century, with the joint efforts of poets, critics, and editors, and with the support of Dickinson's poetry lovers, Dickinson's heart has achieved eternal peace in its fusion with nature.

—Written on March 15, 2013

〔Published in *Dajiang Poetry Forum 2014 Chinese Poetry Selection* in Ma'an City, Anhui Province, China, China Film Publishing House, October, 2014, pages 91-94.〕

12 風中銀樹碧 雨後天虹新——淺釋鄭愁予的詩三首
Trees Silver in the Wind, a New Rainbow After the Rain: On the three poems by Zheng Chouyu

　　在現代詩歌藝術史中，1933年誕生於山東濟南的鄭愁予—是個響亮的名字。童年隨父征戰南北，遷徙避難途中由母親親授古典詩詞；1949年舉家隨國民政府赴臺。曾任教於愛荷華大學、耶魯大學、香港大學等校；2005年返臺擔任東華大學駐校作家、榮譽教授及金門大學講座教授等職。

　　鄭愁予寫詩並無固定的模式，但具象中有抽象，格調清俊如風中銀樹，逸秀如雨後彩虹；總是志趣高雅，很有情韻，能傳達出詩人的人生體驗。他不重視名利、為人慷慨仁慈；喜歡漫遊山水，通過借鑒與融合古今中西的詩歌藝術，意象極為鮮活，視像美強烈。不僅廣泛而充分地吸收了藝術的精髓，在作品中常用情節化的敘述使詩意靈動起來；並把熱情、寬宏的本性中的一些心理波動、歡樂與痛苦均真誠表現。多採用歷史題材、鄉愁或浪漫的抒情手法，有著藝術上的開拓性；更深知俄國哲學家別林斯基所說的「藝術是形象思維」內容之妙。即「用生動而美麗的形象」來表現「具有繁複的多種多樣的現象的大千世界」。如作於1956年的〈當西風走過〉：

　　　　僅圖這樣走過的，西風——
　　　　僅吹熄我的蠟燭就這樣走過了
　　　　徒留一葉未讀完的書冊在手
　　　　卻使一室的黝暗，反印了窗外的幽藍。

　　　　當落桐飄如遠年的回音，恰似指間輕掩的一葉
　　　　當晚景的情愁因燭火的冥滅而凝於眼底
　　　　此刻，我是這樣油然地記取，那年少的時光
　　　　哎，那時光，愛情的走過一如西風的走過。

　　詩人筆下有一個典型的世界，在這個世界裡是無際的心靈宇宙與有限的物質空間的統一。他常在色彩中尋求自己的靈感，而充滿懸念的那種不可觸摸的感受所傳達給讀者的，是現實的一個

片段、整個微觀世界，和愛情那永遠輪迴的一種神奇而縹緲的感覺。當愛遠離，詩人選擇在蒼涼中又透射出達觀，恰如西風走過……而大自然的撫慰終能凌駕於這一世界之上。讀鄭愁予的詩，你不由自主地會沉靜下來，想去捕捉那靜寂宇宙中的詩性光芒。比如詩人 20 歲寫下的〈小小的島〉，全詩妙在詩人的深情想望，意象如連環，綿延不斷；其豐富的詩味，讓讀者不知不覺地從海和天空構成的背景中走出來：

您住的小小的島我正思念
那兒屬於熱帶，屬於青青的國度
淺沙上，老是棲息著五色的魚群
小鳥跳響在枝上，如琴鍵的起落

那兒的山崖都愛凝望，批垂著長藤如髮
那兒的草地都善等待，鋪綴著野花如菓盤
那兒浴你的陽光是藍的，海風是綠的
則你的健康是鬱鬱的，愛情是徐徐的

雲的幽默與隱隱的雷笑
林叢的舞樂與冷冷的流歌
你住的那小小的島我難描繪
難繪那兒的午寐有輕輕的地震

如果，我去了，將帶著我的笛杖
那時我是牧童而你是小羊
要不，我去了，我便化做螢火蟲
以我的一生為你點盞燈

　　詩象就是心象。這裡，詩人借景抒情，翹首企盼之情，含而不露，比喻貼切；其格調寧靜淡雅，但仍然彌漫著一股濃郁的古典韻味。從詩中「小鳥跳響」、「琴鍵的起落」的段落轉折，詩人藉以使內在的情感與外界的境況，得以有機的連結、影響。其尋求的不是未經過思考的過濾的心意活動的形相，而是昇華到純潔世界裡讓讀者細細咀嚼去感出思念的奧秘。全詩運用倒裝、類疊等修辭法，間接詮釋了主題的含義：愛，是守護的勇氣。最後以螢火蟲為喻象表達出對愛的堅守，很形象地傳達出詩意。鄭愁予雖然擁有許多飄泊的記憶，但不管時光如何流變，並沒有沖淡他對大海的嚮往。詩人的心境是浪漫而自由的，也如海一樣寬闊而包容。在他 24 歲所寫的一首短詩〈下午〉，我們仍可以讀出詩人一生對愛的執著追求，意象輕靈，如天使純真的聲音：

> 啄木鳥不停的啄著，如過橋人的鞋聲
> 整個的下午，啄木鳥啄著
> 小山的影，已移過小河的對岸
> 我們也坐過整個的下午，也踱著
> 若是過橋的鞋聲，當已遠去
> 遠到夕陽的居處，啊，我們
> 我們將投宿，在天上，在沒有星星的那面

此詩一開始，感情的直抒轉化為意象的表達，橋上那些啄木鳥的聲音與鞋聲，頗具動感與靜謐中的愉悅。而「我們也坐過整個的下午」，詩人不用陳言，把感覺化為鮮活的意象。太陽光束過濾過的暖色調和最後月夜下的想像，富有生氣又有構思的神秘性。這首詩與前兩首相比，更顯得流暢自然；清新的詩境和樸真的語言，強化了兩者的親近性，也更多了些民歌的音韻。

對許多讀者來說，鄭愁予是個雄健秉異的詩人。早期的詩歌浪漫而鮮明，作過許多絕妙的描寫，完美的程度更是讓讀者驚訝莫名，極具超脫的想像。他所揭櫫對愛情真諦的表現與生命動感等概念，「感性」仍是他創作中最大的靈感根源。在詩藝方面也擅於表現自我，他寫詩擅長描繪大自然的細緻，始終保留著對海的美好回憶；其高度抒情風格和巨大的感染力，總在視覺上的盛宴留下深刻印象，也真正能從中挖掘出思想的寶藏。

—2011.9.8 作

【刊登臺灣《海星》詩刊，2012 春季號，第 3 期，頁 16-19。】

In the art history of modern poetry, Zheng Chouyu, born in Jinan, Shandong in 1933, is a celebrity. He followed his father to fight in the north and south in his childhood, and his mother taught him classical poetry during his migration. In 1949, he followed his family with the

Nationalist Government to Taiwan. He taught at the University of Iowa, Yale University, and the University of Hong Kong. In 2005, he returned to Taiwan to serve as a resident writer, honorary professor, and lecturer at Kinmen University at National Dong Hwa University.

   Zheng Chouyu's poetry writing has no fixed pattern, but it is abstract in the concrete, and his style is as elegant as a silver tree in the wind, and as elegant as a rainbow after the rain. He cherishes a noble aspiration and is very sentimental, and can convey the poet's life experience. He does not value fame and wealth, and is generous and kind; he likes to roam the mountains and rivers, and through the reference and integration of ancient and modern Chinese and Western poetry art, the imagery is very vivid and the visual beauty is distinct. Not only has he widely and fully absorbed the essence of art, he often uses episodic narration in his works to make the poetry lively. He sincerely expresses some psychological fluctuations, joys and pains in his passionate and magnanimous nature. He often uses historical themes, nostalgia or romantic lyrical techniques, which is pioneering in art; he also understands the wonderful content of "art is image thinking" as said by Russian philosopher Belinsky. That is, "using vivid and beautiful images" to express "the world with complex and diverse phenomena". For example, "When the West Wind Passes By" written in 1956:

> Just trying to pass by like this, the west wind —
> Just blowing out my candle and passing by like this
> Leaving only an unfinished book in my hand
> But making the darkness of the room reflect the faint blue outside the window.
>
> When the falling tung tree floats like an echo of the past, just like a leaf gently covered between fingers
> When the sadness of the evening scene condenses in the eyes because of the extinguishing of the candlelight
> At this moment, I remember the time of my youth like this
> Ah, at that time, love passed by just like the passing of the west wind.

   The poet's pen has a typical world, in which the infinite spiritual universe and the limited material space are unified. He often seeks his inspiration in colors, and the intangible feeling full of suspense conveys to the reader a fragment of reality, the entire microcosm, and a magical and delicate feeling of the eternal reincarnation of love. When love is far away, the poet chooses to show optimism in the coolness, just like the west wind passing by... And the comfort of nature can finally transcend this world. Reading Zheng Chouyu's poems, you will involuntarily calm down and want to capture the poetic light in the silent universe. For example, the poem "Little Island" written by the poet when he was 20 years old, the whole poem is wonderful because of the poet's deep affection and longing, and the imagery is like a chain, stretching endlessly. Its rich poetic flavor makes readers unconsciously walk out of the background formed by the sea and the sky:

>I am missing the little island where you live
>It belongs to the tropics, to the green country
>There are always colorful fish inhabiting on the shallow sand
>The birds jump on the branches, like the rise and fall of piano keys
>
>The cliffs there love to gaze, with long vines hanging like hair
>The grass there is good at waiting, covered with wild flowers like fruit plates
>The sunshine that bathes you there is blue, and the sea breeze is green
>Then your health is depressed, and love is slow
>
>The humor of the clouds and the hidden thunder laughter
>The dance and music of the forest and the cold flowing songs
>The small island where you live is hard for me to describe
>It is hard to describe the gentle earthquakes during the afternoon nap there
>
>If I go, I will bring my flute stick
>At that time I was a shepherd boy and you were a lamb
>If not, if I go, I will turn into a firefly
>I will light a lamp for you with my whole life

Poetic images are mental images. Here, the poet uses the scenery to express his emotions, and his expectation is implicit but not revealed, and the metaphor is appropriate. The style is quiet and elegant, but it is still filled with a strong classical flavor. From the paragraphs of "birds jumping" and "the rise and fall of the piano keys" in the poem, the poet makes the inner emotions and the external situation organically connected and influenced. What he seeks is not the form of unfiltered mental activities without thinking, but sublimation to the pure world for readers to chew and feel the mystery of longing. The whole poem uses inversion, superposition and other rhetoric methods to indirectly interpret the meaning of the theme: love is the courage to protect. Finally, the firefly is used as a metaphor to express the persistence of love, which conveys the meaning of the poem very vividly. Although Zheng Chouyu has many wandering memories, no matter how time changes, it has not diluted his yearning for the sea. The poet's state of mind is romantic and free, and as broad and tolerant as the sea. In a short poem he wrote when he was 24, "Afternoon", we can still read the poet's lifelong pursuit of love. The imagery is light and ethereal, like the innocent voice of an angel:

> The woodpecker keeps pecking, like the sound of shoes of people crossing the bridge
> The whole afternoon, the woodpecker pecked
> The shadow of the hill has moved to the other side of the stream
> We also sat for the whole afternoon, and also walked
> If it were the sound of shoes crossing the bridge, it would have gone far away
> Far away to the place where the sunset lives, ah, we
> We will stay in the sky, on the side without stars

At the beginning of this poem, the direct expression of emotion is transformed into the expression of imagery. The sound of the woodpeckers and the sound of shoes on the bridge are quite dynamic and quiet. In "We Also Sat All Afternoon", the poet turns his feelings into vivid images without exposition. The warm tones filtered by the sun's beams and the imagination under the last moonlight are full of vitality and mysteriousness. Compared with the previous two poems, this poem is more fluent and natural. The fresh poetic scene and simple language strengthen the intimacy between the two, and also have more folk song rhythm.

文評集粹讀本
Selected Readings in Literary Reviews

For many readers, Zheng Chouyu is a strong and unique poet. His early poems are romantic and vivid, with many wonderful descriptions, and the degree of perfection makes readers amazed and extremely imaginative. He reveals the true meaning of love and the concept of life dynamics. "Sensibility" is still the biggest source of inspiration in his creation. He is also good at expressing himself in poetry. He is good at describing the details of nature in his poems, and always retains the beautiful memories of the sea. His highly lyrical style and great appeal always leave a deep impression as a visual feast, which contains the treasure of thought.

— Written on September 8, 2011

【Published in Taiwan's *Starfish* Poetry Magazine, Spring 2012, Issue 3, Pages 16-19.】

13 夜讀鍾玲詩集《霧在登山》
Reading Zhong Ling's Poetry Collection *The Mist Is Climbing the Mountain* at Night

鍾玲（1945- ）是跨越臺、美、港三地的著名學者，更是擅長小說、散文的作家，也是在文學之路上跋涉的詩人。在她第二本《霧在登山》的詩集裡，人們從中可以不斷地揣摩其內心深層情感的秘密；也可以看到她對九位古典美人的造像與遐思，其中的後記與箋注，是極有見地的。此外，還有為她敬愛的人及緬懷遊地景物等創作。豐富的內容和優美的詩的形式的結合，讓我看到的是一個孤獨的愛情守望者，在細雪的窗前感受著寂寞，在與心徘徊之後是渴盼恆定的力量和內心如秋葉般詩意的柔情。或許只有她自己才能深悟到行走中的痛苦，才能聽得見摯愛的人毫不留情地踏向死亡的足音。走進她一生感情的城池的疼痛，也促使她活得更加豐實且更有意義。現就我感受最深的幾首詩作略談體會。

首先是寫詩應有自己的深刻體驗，應全心地投入詩的構思和感受創作的過程。在她 1999 年十月寫下貼近現實，關注民生的〈安魂曲—致九二一地震的死難者〉，她感慨萬端，因而賦詩一首。其所表現的是她詩歌創作中的新的高度，是其崇高人格和堅強生命力的放射。此詩曾由名作曲家黃友棣與賴德和分別譜成曲：

　　世界末日的震動晃醒你
　　意識方脫離夢境
　　磚塊石塊已經壓上身
　　打破你的頭、折斷你的腿
　　壓碎你的肋骨你的心
　　飛來的黑色死亡
　　像巨大的隕石壓下
　　願親人長流的淚水

洗淨你滿身的傷口
願兩千萬人的心酸心痛
沖淡你孤獨承受的驚恐

如果這個島的罪孽深重
重如堆在你身上如山的石塊
你替我們大家承受天譴

你累世的路
今生最崎嶇
可以起程了，不要驚怕
前面是明亮的坦途

　　這可說是一首表達對社會悲憫的詩，而死難者意象象徵著人生的生存的本質，蘊涵著玄思和感慨。來自成長於臺灣的鍾玲的那份真摯與同情，卻不時流露出同胞間一種高貴的情操——彼此關懷，令人仰視。且讓死難者生命與死亡在同一墓中歇息，靈魂得以平靜，這正是鍾玲詩意之所在。

　　詩人自是多情客，高雄家鄉草木、異域風情等皆成為她詩歌中的華彩樂章，表達出她的感事傷懷。鍾玲認為，人是覺醒－成長－成熟，然後得到智慧。人的身體卅歲就開始衰退，但內心可不斷年輕和成長。它的啟示性是顯而易見的。雖然世人常道，鍾玲是個女強人。其實，她是個摯愛文學、做事極認真又感情執著的人。她自小希望能表現具有偉大抱負、廣闊視野；表現不倦地寫作精神、嚮往追求愛與美的崇高。而這種感情和風格，是體現出詩人一生的美學追求。如 2001 年秋，鍾玲寫下的〈你駐足的草地〉一詩，是為前夫名導演胡金銓上墳後而作：

來到這片你駐足的草地，
遙望煙籠的洛杉磯，
你近到可以觸及我的手指，
卻遠隔一千個明暗的日子。

想到你飄盪而鮮明的一生，
由北方的古都到南方的海域，
你的映像照亮五湖四海，

最後落腳煙籠的洛杉磯，
暮色四合中追逐一個夢想，
一個夢，刻畫異鄉人的飄盪。

一股力量催我來這片草地——
那十年同行、十年的糾結，
來整理兩人之間千絲萬縷：
什麼是以為付出其實收受，
什麼是以為脫離其實滲透。

來到你最後駐足的地方——
一片片碑石平鑲草地上
像千萬片巨廈的玻璃窗，
躺著望去一片也看不見，
一個名字一個日期也看不見，
你真的已經融入風景，
正像你鏡頭下的畫面。

穿越朝鮮看外景那年
你教我用眼睛框架山水；
二十年來你的色彩和構圖、
你的叮嚀、滲透我的生命。
這一刻、在這寧靜的下午，
我依然用你的品味四顧。

我來到這片幽綠的草地
探訪到寧靜自得的你，
那不寧靜的出了遠門。

　　詩人目光東流，靜靜地坐在空寂之外；想像自己遇到了前夫並與之交談。她看著記憶，與時間並肩行走⋯⋯。詩中有幽綠的草地、由北方的古都到南方的海域、巨廈的玻璃窗、穿越朝鮮，意象的轉換幅度大，時空跳躍強，傳達出一種哀思和憂鬱。越是在現實的世界裡，越是感到個人的無助與徬徨，精神的困境因此而生。此刻，詩人的影子是靜的，只沉浸在回憶與現實、自然與時空相交融的境界裡，其身姿也是孤獨的。在靜穆的沉思中，她的心靈展開翅膀輕柔地在幽遠的時空裡翱翔。而最後一段有兩層意義：一方面，象徵著死亡，再者也有靈魂洗淨之意。這兩個意義是一體兩面。詩人把幽綠的草地在時間上拉長，使節奏慢下來，類似電影中的高速攝影所製造出來的慢鏡頭。這時詩人的心裡已被寧靜的陽光曬暖，於是，她發現了自己未來該走的路。當年情感失意時，鍾玲也曾在學佛、探求智慧的過程中了悟到，那深藏於內心的律動與在夜空中的憧憬，原本都是未完成的生命形式。於今，她以往對心靈的信任，現已轉為佛教精義的信心。此詩雖讓人看到「美麗得使人痛苦」的瞬間，但也有著禪家智慧的妙語。她想像中的前夫已然獲得了寧靜，回到豐足永恆的世界了。

　　中年以後的鍾玲，是個人教學與創作的強力放射時期。她在2004年七月寫下的〈陌地生故居〉一詩的背景，據其自述是在1967-1972年間於陌生地（Madison）就讀威士康辛大學研究所，在那裡，她經歷過苦讀與情感的風暴。三十多年後，詩人再度回到陌生地故居，有感而作：

　　　　細雨怎會那麼黏人？
　　　　不像記憶中爽身。
　　　　我不得不踏著雨向南
　　　　回到小紅樓前面。
　　　　三十年前就是座老木屋
　　　　如今竟一點也不肯傾斜，
　　　　依舊棗紅同樣的棗紅。
　　　　細雨靜靜裏住各式折騰：
　　　　第一次心悸，第一次心許
　　　　第一次折磨自己的淚水，
　　　　接下去是半甲子重複
　　　　心悸心許和淚水。
　　　　紅樓是一種循環的起點。
　　　　我看見一個女孩爬出前窗，
　　　　後門正激烈地搖晃，
　　　　她逃離的是生命的強烈。
　　　　有一天當我不再逃離，
　　　　我將打開門穿入小樓
　　　　走進茫茫的細雪。

這裡，暗示著詩人在喧嘩與回憶中的內心苦悶與孤獨。鍾玲自美國威斯康辛大學取得比較文學博士學位後，1972 年起曾在紐約、臺灣、香港等名校任教。此詩含蓋在她讀書時的青春勃動期，充滿著對人生、愛情的美好嚮往，也有著青年人的憂鬱和悲傷。她把自己最天真純摯的哀愁與熱情全注入到喜愛的詩中，她的愛又是真誠的，深沈而傷感的。誠然，詩歌理應借景抒情，托物言志。鍾玲也用歌聲親吻著陌地生故居，她對昔時的生活與往事，縱是痛苦與歡樂參和著，又是那樣懷念；所以說，沒有愛就沒有真正的詩人。

在這瞬息萬變的世上，鍾玲認為，她是靠自己堅強的個性，想做的事就一定能做到，亦肯定世間存有真實的愛情。如詩人在 2008 年六月寫下的這首〈太陽的面貌〉，讓讀者了解，影響詩人一生的情感世界就存在於兩個重要的人之間：

我的世界有兩種太陽

有一個人雖然在遠方
卻恆久給我力量
溫暖我，用他對世界灑下的光熱

穩定我，像不動的太陽

有一個人
他的心總是在遊走
卻循著一定的軌跡
試探我，以變幻不定的光芒
扶持我，像風推動飄帆

這個宇宙有無數太陽
隱藏在心的深處
我們看不見的地方

鍾玲把感受和思考意象化，是此詩的核心；同時，亦將世俗和精神的愛混合起來，以證實自己對愛的哲學見解。當然，說它內裡寓含著對一位傑出的胡導演的悼念，是不可否認的。而與余光中師生間的知遇之情，是那樣真切感人，也是真實生活的寫照，從而將具體的形象與幻想化的精神融合，創造出富有張力的意象。

鐘玲自己一再強調，她原來就想好好當一個作家。她的思想敏銳而寬廣，很顯然地，此詩的藝術情境也是展示得成功的。

—2013.2.23

【刊臺灣《海星》詩刊，2014.06，第 12 期夏季號，頁 15-19。】

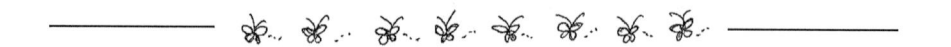

    Zhong Ling (1945-) is a famous scholar in Taiwan, the United States, and Hong Kong. She is also a writer good at novels and essays, and a poet who has traveled on the road of literature. In her second collection of poems *The Mist Is Climbing the Mountain*, people can constantly guess the secret of her deep emotions, and they can also see her images and reveries of nine classical beauties. The postscripts and notes are very insightful. In addition, there are also works for her beloved people and the scenery of the places she visited in Myanmar. The combination of rich content and beautiful poetic form makes me see a lonely watcher of love, feeling lonely in front of the window with fine snow, and after wandering with her heart, she longs for the power of constancy and the tenderness of her heart as poetic as autumn leaves. Perhaps only she herself can deeply understand the pain of walking, and can hear the footsteps of her beloved stepping towards death without mercy. The pain of walking into the city of her lifelong emotions also prompted her to live a richer and more meaningful life. Now a brief talk about my feelings about the poems which touch me the most deeply.

    First of all, when writing poetry, one should have one's own profound experience, and should devote oneself to the conception of poetry and the process of feeling creation. When she wrote "Requiem — To the Victims of the 921 Earthquake" in October 1999, which was close to reality and concerned about people's livelihood, she was deeply moved and thus wrote a poem. It shows the new height of her poetry creation, and is the radiation of her noble personality and strong vitality. This poem was composed by the famous composers Huang Youdi and Lai Dehe respectively:

夜讀鍾玲詩集《霧在登山》

> The vibration of the end of the world wakes you up
> your consciousness has just left the dream
> bricks and stones have already pressed on your body
> breaking your head, breaking your legs
> crushing your ribs and your heart
> the flying black death
> is like a huge meteorite pressing down
> may the tears of your loved ones
> wash away the wounds on your body
> may the sadness and pain of 20 million people
> dilute The fear you bear alone
>
> If the sins of this island are as heavy as the mountains of rocks
> piled on you
> You bear the damnation for all of us
>
> Your path through many lives
> This life is the most rugged
> You can set off now, don't be afraid
> There is a bright and smooth road ahead.

This can be said to be a poem expressing sadness for society, and the image of the victims symbolizes the essence of life, implying profound thoughts and feelings. The sincerity and sympathy from Zhong Ling, who grew up in Taiwan, often reveal a noble sentiment among compatriots — caring for each other, which makes people look up to them. Let the lives and deaths of the victims rest in the same tomb, so that their souls can be at peace — this is exactly what Zhong Ling meant by the poem.

The poet is a sentimental person. The plants and trees of her hometown of Kaohsiung, the exotic customs, etc., have become the colorful movements in her poems, expressing her feelings and sorrows. Zhong Ling believes that people awaken, grow, mature, and then gain wisdom. The body of a person begins to decline at the age of 30, but the heart continues to be young and growing. Its enlightenment is obvious. Although people often say that Zhong Ling is a strong woman. In fact, she is a person who loves literature, is very serious about doing things, and is emotionally persistent. Since she was a child, she hopes to show great ambitions and broad vision, to show the spirit of tireless writing, and to yearn for the pursuit of love and beauty. And this kind of emotion and style reflects the poet's lifelong aesthetic pursuit. For example, in the fall of 2001, Zhong Ling wrote the poem "The Grassland Where You Stayed" for her ex-husband, the famous director King Hu, after he passed away:

> Coming to this grassland where you stay,
> Looking at the smoky Los Angeles from afar,
> You are so close that I can touch my fingers,
> But you are a thousand days away.
>
> Thinking of your turbulent and vivid life,
> From the ancient capital in the north to the sea in the south,
> Your image illuminates the world,
> Finally landing in the smoky Los Angeles,
> Chasing a dream in the twilight,
> A dream that depicts the turbulence of a stranger.
>
> A force urged me to come to this grassland —
> the ten years of walking together, the ten years of entanglement,
> to sort out the myriad connections between the two of us:
> what is thought to be giving is actually receiving,
> what is thought to be detached is actually permeating.
>
> I came to the place where you last stayed —
> pieces of stone tablets are flat on the grassland
> like thousands of glass windows of a huge building,
> lying down and looking at it, you can't see a single piece,
> you can't see a name or a date,
> you have really merged into the scenery,
> just like the picture under your lens.
>
> The year I traveled through North Korea to see the exterior
> you taught me to frame the landscape with my eyes;
> for twenty years, your colors and composition,
> your exhortations, have permeated my life.
> At this moment, in this quiet afternoon,
> I still look around with your taste.

夜讀鍾玲詩集《霧在登山》

> I came to this green meadow
> to visit you who are peaceful and contented,
> and then left the distant door without peace.

The poet's eyes drifted eastward, sitting quietly outside the emptiness. She imagined that she met her ex-husband and talked to him. She looked at her memory and walked side by side with time.... In the poem, there are green meadows, from the ancient capital in the north to the sea in the south, the glass windows of the giant building, and crossing North Korea. The image transformation is large, and the time and space jump is strong, conveying a kind of grief and depression. The more you are in the real world, the more you feel your own helplessness and hesitation, and the spiritual dilemma arises from this. At this moment, the poet's shadow is still, immersed only in the realm where memories and reality, nature and time and space blend together, and his posture is also lonely. In quiet contemplation, her soul spreads its wings and soars gently in the distant time and space. The last paragraph has two meanings: on the one hand, it symbolizes death, and on the other hand, it also means the cleansing of the soul. These two meanings are two sides of the same coin. The poet stretches the green grass in time and slows down the rhythm, similar to the slow motion created by high-speed photography in movies. At this time, the poet's heart has been warmed by the peaceful sunshine, so she found the path she should take in the future. When she was frustrated in her love life, Zhong Ling also realized in the process of studying Buddhism and seeking wisdom that the rhythm hidden deep in her heart and the vision in the night sky were originally unfinished forms of life. Today, her previous trust in the soul has turned into faith in the essence of Buddhism. Although this poem shows a moment of "painfully beautiful", it also contains the wisdom of Zen. Her imaginary ex-husband has already found peace and returned to a world of abundance and eternity.

After middle age, Zhong Ling is in a period of strong radiation of personal teaching and creation. The background of the poem "Strange Place, Old Residence" she wrote in July 2004 was that she studied in the strange place "Madison" at the University of Wisconsin Graduate School from 1967 to 1972, where she experienced hard study and emotional storms. Over 30 years later, the poet returned to the strange place and wrote this poem:

> How can the drizzle be so sticky?
> It's not as refreshing as in my memory.
> I had to walk south in the rain
> and return to the front of the Little Red Building.
> Thirty years ago, it was an old wooden house.
> Now it refuses to lean at all,
> Still the same red date.
> The drizzle quietly wrapped up all kinds of torments:
> The first palpitations, the first promises
> The first time to torture myself with tears,
> Then it was repeated for half a century
> Palpitations, promises and tears.
> The Red Mansion is the starting point of a cycle.
> I saw a girl climb out of the front window,
> The back door was shaking violently,
> She was running away from the intensity of life.
> One day when I no longer run away,
> I will open the door and walk into the small building
> Walk into the vast drizzle.

Here, it hints at the poet's inner depression and loneliness in the noise and memories. After obtaining a doctorate in comparative literature from the University of Wisconsin, Zhong Ling has taught at prestigious universities in New York, Taiwan, and Hong Kong since 1972. This poem covers her youthful vigor when she was studying, full of beautiful yearnings for life and love, as well as the melancholy and sadness of young people. She poured all her most innocent sorrow and passion into her favorite poems, and her love was sincere, deep and sad. Indeed, poetry should express emotions through scenery and express aspirations through objects. Zhong Ling also kissed her hometown with her singing. She missed her past life and past events, even though they were mixed with pain and joy. Therefore, there is no real poet without love.

In this ever-changing world, Zhong Ling believes that she can achieve whatever she wants to do with her strong character, and she is sure that true love exists in the world. For example, the poem "The Face of the Sun" written by the poet in June 2008 allows readers to understand that the emotional world that affects the poet's life exists between two important people:

> There are two kinds of suns in my world
>
> There is a person who, although far away, always gives me strength, warms me, and uses the light and heat he sheds on the world
>
> Stabilizes me, like an unmoving sun
>
> There is a person
> whose heart is always wandering
> but follows a certain trajectory
> tests me, supports me with his ever-changing light, like the wind pushing a sail
>
> There are countless suns in this universe
> hidden in the depths of the heart
> where we cannot see

  The core of this poem is that Zhong Ling visualizes her feelings and thoughts; at the same time, she also mixes secular and spiritual love to confirm her philosophical views on love. Of course, it is undeniable that it contains a mourning for an outstanding director Hu. The friendship between Yu Guangzhong and his teacher is so real and touching, and it is also a portrayal of real life, thus integrating the concrete image with the fantasy spirit to create a tense image. Zhong Ling herself repeatedly emphasized that she originally wanted to be a writer. With her sharp and broad thoughts, it is obvious that the artistic situation of this poem is successfully exhibited.

—February 23, 2013.

【Published in Taiwan *Starfish* Poetry Magazine, June, 2014, Summer Issue 12, Pages 15-19.】

14 夜讀沈鵬詩
Reading Shen Peng's Poems at Night

沈鵬（1931- ），江蘇省江陰市人，係近代中國重要的書法家、美術評論家兼詩人。主要代表著作有《當代書法精品集·沈鵬卷》、《故宮博物院藏畫》等三十餘種。曾獲聯合國 Academy 世界和平藝術權威獎等殊榮，列入多種名人傳記與辭書。

今年元月十五日，筆者有幸參與 2013 年的「海峽兩岸作家藝術家水墨丹青大展」活動中，收到沈鵬大師贈予《三餘再吟》，頗感新鮮。不僅書名獨特，詩詞也別具一格。詩人以情為帆，在精湛的書法筆下，對詩藝上的精心探索，在兩岸文界上是罕見的；其詩詞所達到的思想藝術高度也廣為人們所公認。細讀其中的一篇〈重上阿里山〉，不禁被詩人對臺灣熱烈的情懷所感動，在詩中他唱道：

盤旋九千九，曲折走龍蛇。
雲自身前過，山從霧裡賒。
目窮通五岳，日落入無涯。
樸野多真味，重嚐阿里茶。

這是沈鵬再次赴台訪遊時寫下的詩詞。他飛越重山，長途跋涉而來；在情緒上自是一環扣一環的。詩人選用了抱韻形式，以旅行中快速變幻的窗景來襯托嚮往阿里山的壯美與樸真，更增詩意。還不止於此，詩人特別感觸的是，兩岸能以書藝交流的可貴，並生發出人生的哲理，意在抒發歲月催人老的緬懷之情。

詩的本質雖在於抒情，但它總離不開形象思維的範疇。就像沈鵬從小就在古典詩詞中吸取了不少有價值的詞彙，但他總似法國浪漫派（Romantic School）傑出的雕刻家羅丹所創作的沉思者（The Thinker），習慣把自己的詩當作一件造型藝術品去雕塑，並以此去折射出自己的心靈之光。如這首在 2002 年十月寫下〈太湖包山寺題聯〉，其新穎的視角就給人一種富有禪味的意象美：

夜讀沈鵬詩

禪寺包山山包寺
太湖浴佛佛浴湖

　　蘇州包山寺，為唐肅宗李亨所賜名。因西山四面為水所包，俗稱包山； 又名「顯慶禪寺」，聞名天下。惜毀於十年浩劫，1995年使得重建。沈鵬在鳥語泉聲中，如一棵伐不倒的青松，讓靈魂走出山寺，達到與自然一種完美的契合。這就是從平凡中寫出了不平凡，語言也幽默風趣。而最能代表他這一詩藝探索的，當是被書詩界稱讚的〈夜讀〉，這首寫於 2004 年元月，這是借咏夜讀友人詩書來傾吐他對世事炎涼和創作的甘苦；用哲理式的諷刺，針砭現實，寫得委婉而不流於直白：

　　　好友遺我書，助我度歲除。
　　　往事塵封隔，閉目不自驅。
　　　一言重九鼎，陰晴磬咳殊。
　　　萬馬齊躍進，向隅千里駒。
　　　人情異冷暖，飲水便如魚。
　　　得意忘江海，失意沫相濡。
　　　席上多佳餚，歲朝遠庖廚。

　　據考究，此詩最後一句背景，源自孟子曰：「無傷也，是乃仁術也，見牛未見羊也。君子之於禽獸也，見其生，不忍見其死；聞其聲，不忍食其肉。是以君子遠庖廚也。」〈參見孟子《梁惠王上》篇〉。如果沈鵬不是熟讀古書，是寫不出這樣生動的詩行的。此外，這裡頭還透露出詩人極其反感訛言我詐的隱秘心理。凡是詩人沒有不愛惜自然生物的，一定要努力做到遠離貪求才是。時至晚年，詩人早已有了書藝上的飛騰，但仍孜孜不息於編輯與創作，四處遊訪各國後，2005 年夏也寫下了這首〈上海黃浦江夜遊〉，雖是旅遊詩，但沈鵬還善於以幽默的語言去揭示生命的真諦和以愛去戰勝孤獨：

　　　十里洋場夜未央，樓船來往織梭忙。
　　　驕陽消息尋何處？散入吳淞七彩光。

　　黃浦江，位於上海市，被稱為「上海的母親河」。沿岸的上海外灘，掏盡了古今多少風流人物的夢。這「十里洋場」特指舊時上海、天津等洋商聚集、歌舞昇平之地。而吳淞在上海市北部，曾為鴉片戰爭、抗日戰爭及解放戰爭時期戰場，如今卻是上海市集裝箱運輸的重要作業區。沈鵬的詩，對歷史的傷痕與現實生活的無奈，常體現在寫旅遊的文字中；人們可以從中看到詩人那顆真誠無私的心。比如他在 2006 年六月寫下〈岳麓山愛晚亭〉，詩人不僅愛女兒，愛其夫人的素雅端莊；而且有一顆童心，因而他的旅遊詩也不時滲入童趣：

  瀟湘靈氣此雲山，古木清雅香草妍。
  我與樊川共車馬，何須霜葉盛時看？

  岳麓山位於湖南長沙市的湘江西岸，緊鄰古城長沙，自古以來便是文人墨客必遊之地，亦是中國四大名亭之一。記得唐代杜牧有句詩「停車坐愛楓林晚，霜葉紅於二月花」。而沈鵬詩裡的旅遊勝地「愛晚亭」，應是與杜牧撰樊川文集時的才情聯到一塊兒。他的詩思馳騁，早與杜牧齊駕車，奔騰雲山去了。其實，在沈鵬許多優美動人的旅遊詩中，〈詠泰山〉應是他最為膾炙人口的一篇，詩句氣象深厚而博大。這首完成於 2007 年十一月的作品所呈現的，不僅是心清如水的藝術風格，更表達了超邁雄奇的個性和意志，以及詩人對「閒淡清雅」、對生活美學的一種追求：

  博大不讓土，崇高不求同。
  不以群山小，群山仰一宗。

  作為才情橫溢的沈鵬，這種追求並不足為奇。特別是晚年，當他懷想起泰山的雄姿，未嘗不思念。閒居也絕非與世隔離，不與外界人事相接；而是寄詩語意古樸莊重，並專以韻勝。沈鵬詩詞也強調音樂美和抒情性，如這首在 2009 年三月寫下的〈寒山寺題壁〉，他從歷史發展的高度，來讚美寒山寺：

  鐘聲迴盪夜遲遲，過往客船江月思。
  閱盡古今無限事，寒山化育一身詩。

夜讀沈鵬詩

　　自來評家能道得人心中事者少爾，沈鵬的詩，重在妙悟。此詩詩意淺露，大意是，世道艱辛，詩人以詩題壁，反映了他想以唐朝詩人張繼的《楓橋夜泊》的詩為楷模，加以推崇和效仿的精神。言志乃沈鵬的本意。他佇立江畔，歌咏江蘇城西外的一幕幕美景…借物寓情，眼處心生句自神。而夜半鐘聲迴盪，詩人如不繫之舟的情懷，也呈現出一種撲朔迷離的幻象之美。最後，這首在 2011 年四月八日寫下〈悼周海嬰〉，是為其老友海嬰，在全國政協開會時因病缺席，竟成永訣；詩人傷痛之餘，便寫下了自己獨特的感慨，含有無限深意：

　　　　滿座群英君席賒，何期背影走天涯！
　　　　迅翁一語終身誓：「不做空頭文學家」。

　　周海嬰（1929-2011）是魯迅和愛人許廣平僅有的 1 個兒子，畢業於北京大學物理系。僅管詩人內心籠罩悲傷、沉重；但沈鵬也是個勤奮的歌者，他對身邊的友輩乃至國家、社會或需要援助的人，總是默默地付出他的愛。詩人觀察之細，聯想之巧；是近代中國書藝史中的佼佼者。那魯迅生前所發的一句重誓「不做空頭文學家」，或許也正是沈鵬一生所追求的藝術實踐，從而為中國書詩的發展，注入了新的活力，其晚年之作也就獲得國際上更大的矚目了。

　　　　　　　　　　　　　　　　　　　　　　－2013.1.17 作

【刊臺灣《人間福報》副刊 Merit Times，2013.1.29 副刊及沈鵬、魯光贈書畫圖 2 張。】

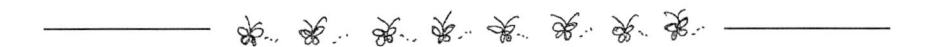

　　Shen Peng (1931-), a native of Jiangyin City, Jiangsu province, is an important calligrapher, art critic and poet in modern China. His major representative works include more than 30 titles such as *Collection of Contemporary Calligraphy Masterpieces: Chen Peng Volume* and *Paintings in the Palace Museum*. He has won many honors, including the United Nations Academy World Peace Art Authority Award, and has been included in many celebrity biographies and dictionaries.

文評集粹讀本
Selected Readings in Literary Reviews

On January 15th this year, I had the honor to participate in the 2013 "Cross-Strait Writers and Artists Ink and Color Exhibition" and received the *Sanyu Zaiyin* from Master Chen Peng, which was quite refreshing. Not only is the title of the book unique, but the poems are also distinctive. The poet uses emotion as a sail, and his meticulous exploration of poetry art in his exquisite calligraphy is rare in the literary circles on both sides of the Taiwan Strait. The ideological and artistic heights reached by his poems are also widely recognized by people. Reading one of the poems, "Revisiting Alishan", I could not help but be moved by the poet's passionate feelings for Taiwan. In the poem, he sings:

> Circling nine thousand nine,
> twisting and turning like a dragon or snake.
> The clouds passing by,
> the mountains emerging in the fog.
> The sight extends to the five mountains,
> and the sun sets into the boundless sky.
> Simple and authentic taste,
> try Ali tea again.

This is a poem written by Shen Peng when he visited Taiwan again. He flew over mountains and traveled a long distance to get here; his emotions were naturally connected. The poet chose the form of hugging rhyme, using the rapidly changing window views during the journey to highlight the grandeur and simplicity of Alishan, adding to the poetic flavor. Not only that, the poet was particularly touched by the preciousness of the exchange of calligraphy between the two sides of the Taiwan Strait, which gave rise to the philosophy of life, and intended to express the nostalgia for the passage of time.

Although the essence of poetry lies in lyricism, it is always inseparable from the scope of figurative thinking. Just like Shen Peng has absorbed many valuable words from classical poetry since he was a child, he is always like "The Thinker" created by Rodin, an outstanding sculptor of the French Romantic School. He is used to sculpting his poems as a piece of plastic art and using it to reflect the light of his soul. For example, this poem, "Couplet for Baoshan Temple in Taihu Lake", written in October 2002, has a novel perspective that gives people a kind of imagery beauty full of Zen flavor:

夜讀沈鵬詩

> Zen Temple encircles the Mountain which encircles the Temple
> Taihu Lake bathing Buddha which is bathing Taihu Lake

Baoshan Temple in Suzhou was named after Emperor Suzong of the Tang Dynasty, Li Heng. Because West Mountain is surrounded by water on all sides, it is commonly known as Bao Mountain. It is also known as "Xianqing Zen Temple" and is famous all over the world. Unfortunately it was destroyed during the ten-year catastrophe of the Cultural Revolution and was rebuilt in 1995. Amid the chirping of birds and the sound of springs, Chen Peng is like an uncuttable green pine tree, allowing the soul to walk out of the mountain temple and achieve a perfect harmony with nature. This is how the extraordinary is written from the ordinary, and the language is also humorous and witty. The poem that best represents his exploration of poetry is "Night Reading", which was praised by the poetry community. This poem was written in January 2004. It expresses his feelings about the vicissitudes of life and the joys and sorrows of writing by quoting the poem of a friend at night. It uses philosophical satire to criticize reality, and is written in a tactful way without being too straightforward:

> A good friend left me a letter
> to help me get through the New Year.
> The past is sealed away, and
> I cannot help but close my eyes.
> A word is as heavy as nine tripods,
> and the mood may change with the weather.
> Ten thousand horses are galloping together,
> and a thousand-mile horse is approaching.
> People's feelings are different,
> and they are like fish drinking water.
> When you are successful, you forget the world;
> when you are unsuccessful, you support each other.
> There are many delicious dishes on the table,
> but the kitchen is far away during the New Year.

According to research, the background of the last sentence of this poem comes from what Mencius said: "Doing no harm is the way of benevolence, just like seeing the cow but not the sheep. As for the gentlemen, when they see the animals alive, they cannot bear to see them die. When they hear their cries, they cannot bear to eat their flesh. That is why gentlemen stay away from the kitchen." (See Mencius' "The King Hui of Liang, Part I"). If Shen Peng had not been familiar with ancient books, he would not have been able to write such vivid lines of poetry. In addition, this also reveals the poet's secret psychological state of being extremely disgusted with false accusations and deceptions. All poets cherish natural creatures and must strive to stay away from greed. In his later years, the poet had already achieved great success in calligraphy, but he still worked tirelessly on editing and creation. After traveling around the world, he wrote this poem "Night Cruise on the Huangpu River in Shanghai" in the summer of 2005. Although it is a travel poem, Shen Peng is also good at using humorous language to reveal the true meaning of life and to overcome loneliness with love:

> The night is still long in the foreign concessions,
> and the ships are busy coming and going.
> Where can I find news about the scorching sun?
> Scattered into the colorful light of Wusong.

Huangpu River, located in Shanghai, is known as the "Mother River of Shanghai". The Bund along the coast of Shanghai has filled the dreams of countless famous figures from ancient times to the present. The "Ten Miles of Foreign Concessions" refers specifically to Shanghai, Tianjin and other places where foreign merchants gathered and lived in peace and prosperity in the old days. Wusong is located in the north of Shanghai. It was once a battlefield during the Opium War, the Anti-Japanese War and the War of Liberation. Now it is an important operating area for container transportation in Shanghai. Shen Peng's poems, which express the scars of history and the helplessness of real life, are often reflected in his travel writings; people can see the poet's sincere and selfless heart from them. For example, in June 2006, he wrote "Yuelu Mountain Love Evening Pavilion". The poet not only loves his daughter, but also loves his wife for her elegance and dignity. He also has a childlike heart, so his travel poems are often infiltrated with childlike interest:

> The spiritual energy of Xiaoxiang is reflected in this cloud mountain,
> with elegant ancient trees and beautiful fragrant herbs.

夜讀沈鵬詩

> Fanchuan and I were riding together, so
> why should we watch the leaves in full frost?

Yuelu Mountain is located on the west bank of the Xiangjiang River in Changsha, Hunan province, close to the ancient city of Changsha. It has been a must-visit place for literati and poets since ancient times, and is also one of the four famous pavilions in China. I remember a poem by Du Mu from the Tang Dynasty, "I stop my car and sit to enjoy the maple forest in the evening, and the frosted leaves are redder than the flowers of February." The tourist attraction "Aiwan Pavilion" in Chen Peng's poem should be associated with Du Mu's talent when he wrote the Fanchuan Collection. His poetic thoughts were running wild, just like Du Mu, riding a chariot through the clouds and mountains. In fact, among Shen Peng's many beautiful and moving travel poems, "Ode to Mount Tai" should be his most popular one, with profound and broad verses. This work, completed in November 2007, not only presents an artistic style of a heart as clear as water, but also expresses a transcendent and magnificent personality and will, as well as the poet's pursuit of "leisure and elegance" and the aesthetics of life:

> Being broad-minded does not shy away from being humble,
> and being lofty does not seek to be the same as others.
> Do not think the mountains are small,
> for all mountains look up to one ancestor.

As a talented person like Shen Peng, this pursuit is not surprising. Especially in his later years, when he recalled the majestic appearance of Mount Tai, he always missed it. Living in seclusion does not mean being isolated from the world or having no contact with the outside world. Instead, it means making the language of poetry simple and solemn, and focusing on rhyme. Shen Peng's poems also emphasize musical beauty and lyricism. For example, in "Wall Inscription of Hanshan Temple" written in March 2009, he praised Hanshan Temple from the perspective of historical development:

> The sound of bells echoes in the late night,
> and I miss the moon on the river as the passenger ships pass by.
> After reading countless events from ancient times to the present,
> Hanshan has developed a poetic spirit.

There have always been few critics who can express what is in people's hearts. Shen Peng's poems focus on wonderful insights. The meaning of this poem is simple and concise. The general idea is that life in this world is difficult. The poet wrote the poem on the wall, reflecting his desire to promote and emulate the poem "Night Mooring at Maple Bridge" by Tang Dynasty poet Zhang Ji. Expressing one's aspirations was Shen Peng's original intention. He stood by the river, singing the beautiful scenes outside the west of Jiangsu city.... He used objects to express his emotions, and his words were inspired by his eyes and heart. As the midnight bells echo, the poet's feelings, like an untied boat, also present a kind of confusing and illusory beauty. Finally, this poem, "Mourning Zhou Haiying", was written on April 8, 2011. It was written for his old friend Haiying, who was absent from the National Committee of the Chinese People's Political Consultative Conference due to illness, and it became a farewell forever. The poet was heartbroken and wrote down his unique feelings, which contained infinite deep meaning:

> The seats are filled with all the heroes,
> but who would think your form would leave for the end of the world?
> Mr. Lu Xun made a lifelong vow:
> "I will never be an empty-headed writer."

Zhou Haiying (1929-2011) was the only son of Lu Xun and his wife Xu Guangping. He graduated from the Department of Physics at Peking University. Although the poet is filled with sadness and heaviness in his heart, Shen Peng is also a diligent singer. He always silently gives his love to his friends, the country, the society or people in need. The poet's observation is meticulous and his associations are ingenious, and he is a leader in the history of modern Chinese calligraphy. Lu Xun's solemn vow before his death, "not to be a literary empty talker", may be exactly the artistic practice that Shen Peng pursued throughout his life, thus injecting new vitality into the development of Chinese calligraphy and poetry, and his works in his later years have attracted greater international attention.

— Written on January 17, 2013

【Published in the supplement of Taiwan's *Merit Times* on January 29, 2013, and two paintings and calligraphy presented by Shen Peng and Lu Guang.】

15 夜讀《成就的祕訣：金剛經》
Night Reading *The Secret of Success: Diamond Sutra*

在國際佛教學界接受教義，並進行《金剛經》專門研究者不乏其人，也大多取得了一些成果；然而，我們卻可從這本《成就的秘訣：金剛經》書中去感受星雲大師的身影與佛陀傳教的精神情懷。當然，透過大師賦予此書不凡的內涵，將其中的疑難之處，於中剖析得淋漓盡致；並依循原典，力圖讓大家共享佛法實踐於人間的信念，進而貼近整部《金剛經》的本然面貌。

大師除了以擅長說故事的天份，以原典為本，保留了最接近佛陀傳法時的完整概念外，也添加些情節，讓讀者在追隨真樸的文字而不受文字翻譯的侷限之際，不免也會想像「佛教出世的精神」和「入世的實用」到底該如何修持與慧解並重？而美學大師蔣勳更在書前推薦說：「我對《金剛經》沒有研究，不敢詮釋解讀。但是每天的念誦帶給我平靜喜悅，是一天裡最開心的時刻。」由此，更加好奇於我，會不會也因書中內容而有所悟道？或因《金剛經》而得到不可思議的感動？又為什麼星雲大師提倡《金剛經》？這些或可作為我想揭開《金剛經》之謎的鑰匙。

然而，這一切的懷想，對我這初聞佛法者而言，在文字裡，一個面貌慈藹的大師，從開山階段的辛勞到海內外數百萬信徒的同體共生的成就，一幕一幕地……瞬間浮現腦海。他以重建佛陀的教義為己任，以莊嚴又不失幽默的筆觸完成了這一部貫通古今中外學家的自然思想，這也是他多年來的自我體悟與研究，而不只是他在書中對如何實踐般若的哲學主張，或是對「發心當下，無限可能」的道德勸示，這使得全書所詮釋《金剛經》為何是初期大乘佛教的代表性經典之一，也是般若類佛經的綱要書，又為何在華人地域流傳最廣，變得更為清晰的展現。

在此書於2010年秋問世之後，迄今已增版了十多次，可見在社會上的廣泛流傳。其實諸多大家對《金剛經》的纂要、注解、夾頌、宣演、義記、採微、集解、科釋、宗通、決疑、大意、直說等各種註疏，早已高達一百餘種；由此可見，其註釋之豐，為群經之妙典。

　　一般人認為，《金剛經》乍看之下不易索解，然而，透過大師給自己進入《金剛經》的境界以一個充滿崇敬的開頭，再逐步導引，讓讀者看得到經裡闡明的脈絡；而究其實，他也的確是位無可企及的心靈導師。首先他教導我們先從什麼是「般若」，又如何實踐「般若」做起。然而，我畢竟是現實之我，雖然現實之我仍無法超越世間的痛苦、矛盾和困惑，但大師要我們相信，只要發揮人的無限潛能，學習《金剛經》就是般若，就是斷除一切煩惱；而成就讓人得到幸福的秘訣，就是：「應無所住而生其心」，也就是「般若」，是佛智慧，能明澈身心的一部寶典。由大師再度執筆寫下了精深獨創的書中，就是以《金剛經》所蘊含的真義，穿插故事的對白得以拓展，並闡發自己的研究心得，遂而轉化為佛教叢書的新經典。

　　大師告訴了我們，要相信自己本具佛性，相信自身光明，相信自己潛能無限。如是，心，就會堅實如金剛。而這些詮釋各得一端，也見證了「佛在人間，人成即佛成」的內涵；書後還附錄了《金剛經》原典與白話譯釋。原來《金剛經》不以出家為理想，認為只要有心求道，皆可達到解脫的境界。因此，透過《金剛經》的誘導，使善男信女發菩提心，而人人由此發心，皆可進至菩薩的實踐階段。書裡有許多菩提與世尊的問答，倡導新理想的故事。全書講解得出神入化，淺顯易明，促使《金剛經》的內涵不斷地增廣，受到讀者們普遍的喜愛。昨日好友琇月醫師的突來贈書，便雀躍歡喜。不待深夜，手捧此書，窗前燈下，在大師靈動而嚴密的筆法與寧靜意境中，讀來興味盎然，也深感《金剛經》的感染力而震撼於心。

　　這部書，無論對個人還是對社會都是一種力量的源泉，或許這正是大師的樸素、誠懇和奮進不息的人生使然，他的筆法才如此真切，從而體現出佛家獨特的學理價值。而他撰寫中的每一故事一些溫暖的底色與智慧的語錄，才更令我們動容。

—2013.05.01

【刊臺灣《人間福報》*Merit Times* 副刊，2013.6.16。】

夜讀《成就的祕訣：金剛經》

There are many people in the international Buddhist community who have accepted the teachings and conducted specialized research on the *Diamond Sutra*, and most of them have achieved fruitfully. however, we can feel the figure of Master Hsing Yun and the spiritual sentiments of the Buddha's preaching from this book *The Secret of Achievement: Diamond Sutra*. Of course, through the extraordinary connotations that the Master has endowed this book, the difficult points therein have been analyzed thoroughly. Following the original text, he strives to let everyone share the belief of practicing Buddhism in the world, and thus get closer to the true appearance of the entire *Diamond Sutra*.

In addition to using his talent for storytelling to retain the complete concepts closest to the Buddha's teachings based on the original text, the master also added some plots so that readers can follow the genuine and simple text without being limited by the translation of the text. They will inevitably wonder how the "Buddhist spirit of transcendence" and "worldly practicality" should be cultivated and understood in a balanced way. The aesthetics master Jiang Xun even recommended the book in the beginning: "I have not studied the Diamond Sutra and dare not interpret it. But reciting it every day brings me peace and joy, and it is the happiest moment of the day." This made me even more curious about whether I would also gain some enlightenment from the content of the book? Or have you been incredibly moved by the Diamond Sutra? Why does Master Hsing Yun promote the *Diamond Sutra*? These may serve as the key to unlocking the mystery of the *Diamond Sutra*.

However, for me, who is new to Buddhism, all these memories, in the text, of a kind-faced master, from the hard work in the early stages of founding the school to the achievements of the coexistence and harmony of millions of believers at home and abroad, scene by scene... instantly emerged in my mind. He took it as his mission to reconstruct the Buddha's teachings, and completed this book of natural thoughts that spanned ancient and modern Chinese and foreign scholars with a solemn yet humorous touch. This is also the result of his self-realization and research over the years, and not just his philosophical proposition on how to practice Prajna in the book, or his moral exhortation of "infinite possibilities in the present moment of aspiration". This makes the book's interpretation of why the *Diamond Sutra* is one of the representative classics of early Mahayana Buddhism, an outline book of Prajna Buddhist scriptures, and why it is most widely circulated in the Chinese region more clearly displayed.

Since this book was published in the fall of 2010, it has been reprinted over ten times, which shows that it is widely circulated in the society. In fact, there are already more than one hundred kinds of annotations and commentaries on the *Diamond Sutra*, including compilations, annotations, additional verses, expositions, meaning notes, collections of details, collections of explanations, classifications, general explanations, solutions to doubts, general ideas, and direct explanations. It can be seen that the richness of the annotations makes it a wonderful classic among all sutras.

Most people think that the *Diamond Sutra* is difficult to understand at first glance. However, the master gives himself a respectful beginning to enter the realm of the Diamond Sutra, and then gradually guides readers to see the context of the sutra. In fact, he is indeed an unattainable spiritual mentor. First, he taught us what "Prajna" is and how to practice "Prajna". However, I am only my real self after all. Although my real self is still unable to transcend the pain, contradictions and confusions of the world, the Master wants us to believe that as long as we give full play to our infinite potential, learning the Diamond Sutra is Prajna, which is to eliminate all troubles. The secret to achieving happiness is: "One should not dwell on anything and give rise to the mind", which is "Prajna", a treasure book of Buddha's wisdom that can illuminate the body and mind. The master once again wrote a profound and original book, which expanded the dialogues of the story based on the true meaning of the *Diamond Sutra*, expounded his own research experience, and transformed it into a new classic in the Buddhist series.

The Master told us to believe in our inherent Buddha nature, believe in our own light, and believe in our unlimited potential. In this way, the mind will be as solid as a diamond. These interpretations each have their own side, and also bear witness to the connotation of "Buddha is in the human world, and when man becomes enlightened, Buddha becomes enlightened"; the book also includes an appendix of the original text of the *Diamond Sutra* and its vernacular translation. It turns out that the *Diamond Sutra* does not regard becoming a monk as an ideal. It believes that as long as one is determined to seek the truth, one can achieve the state of liberation. Therefore, through the guidance of the *Diamond Sutra*, good men and women can develop the Bodhicitta, and everyone who develops this bodhi mind can advance to the Bodhisattva's practice stage. The book contains many questions and answers between Bodhi and the Buddha, as well as stories advocating new ideals. The whole book is explained in a fascinating and easy-to-understand manner, which has continuously expanded the connotation of the *Diamond Sutra* and is widely loved by readers. Yesterday, my good friend Dr. Xiu Yue suddenly gave me a book as a gift, and I was so happy. I don't wait until late at night to hold this book in my hands, read it under the lamplight in front of the window, and I will be very interested in reading the master's lively and rigorous writing style and tranquil artistic conception. I will also be deeply shocked by the appeal of the *Diamond Sutra*.

This book is a source of strength for both individuals and society. Perhaps it is because of the master's simplicity, sincerity and unremitting efforts in life that his writing style is so genuine, thus reflecting the unique academic value of Buddhism. What makes us even more moved is the warm background and wise quotes in each story he wrote.

—May 1, 2013.

【Published on the supplement of Taiwan's *Merit Times*, June 16, 2013.】

16 夜讀胡爾泰《落羽松下的沉思》
Night Reading Hu Ertai's *Meditations Under the Fallen Cypress*

　　曾任教於臺灣師大的文學博士胡其德（筆名胡爾泰，1951－　），是臺灣文壇上少數的學者詩人。在初冬一個涼爽的午後，很榮幸地收到他寄贈的新詩集，也想起了一些生趣盎然的事。其詩大多具有浪漫情味，也有知識份子憂患之想，更與他豪邁的才氣、優雅的氣度結合。

　　正如詩人在〈雲中書〉中將懷友之情寫得清新脫俗，都是直接而無矯情的，還有的是意象的轉化、通感手法的運用，都增添了此詩的力度：

　　　　美人住在雲端
　　　　一個雲深不知處的地方
　　　　當她梳起秀髮
　　　　雲瀑就從天飛奔而下
　　　　越過山巒直到靈魂的窗臺
　　　　當雲朵冉冉飄過
　　　　美人的笑容就從回憶的池中展開

　　　　春蠶吐的絲
　　　　搭起的相思橋
　　　　連接了前山和後山
　　　　青鳥是殷勤的天使
　　　　傳遞雲端的消息
　　　　銀鈴的笑聲曾經跌落蓮花池

　　　　我的思念是池邊的草
　　　　滋長於春雨的霏霏
　　　　青色的浪漫
　　　　是一帖不凋的狂草
　　　　漫過光陰的原野
　　　　一直到
　　　　天之涯　雲之端

夜讀胡爾泰《落羽松下的沉思》

詩人在教學期間，曾遊學法、德、荷蘭三國，長達三年，先後兩次獲得教育部文藝創作獎，平日除了教學與研究之餘，也喜歡徜徉於山水之間，寄情於詩，是一位具有獨特風格的詩人。此詩裡的畫面美，是時空藝術的融合，也有著詩人內心的獨白，情感真摯，因而能使人憶起豐富的聯想。這是他在詩美上的探索，也很具神韻。他在許多詩篇中關於景物和大自然的描繪，都給人一種綺麗多姿的意象美。比如這首〈鳶尾花〉，詩的筆調是抒情而明朗的，更是別出心裁：

　　寶藍羽毛的鳶鳥呀
　　挾著春天的尾巴
　　飛到了埤塘邊
　　給綠色的花梗叢
　　添了幾道彩虹

　　伊人戴著呢帽
　　來到小橋
　　看著綠池中的垂瓣
　　搖出扇形的光
　　彩虹的影子跌落
　　鳶尾花在水中綻放

　　鳶尾花呀
　　也在我思念的土壤綻放
　　在櫻花未謝
　　流蘇飛著粉白的
　　暮春三月

在這兒，詩人把池畔的一次際遇譜寫成詩——讓想像的翅膀在夢幻與現實中飛行，並描繪出對詩美的嚮往與追求；讀起來音韻優美，充滿了聽覺上的動感。值得一提的是，二〇一七年四月下旬，詩人因急性胰臟炎住院，他依然有感而思，遂寫下一首〈病中手記〉，在最後一句裡，詩人仍幽默地說：「我只知道在草地上看雲比在病床上看天多了」。這是一首頗有思想深度的詩，也是詩人勇於戰勝病魔後的故事。誠如他在〈落羽松下的沉思〉最後段的詩裡寫道：

189

千縷的思緒拉長了樹影
延伸到夜的邊界
夢的國度
我隱約聽到
枯澀的枝幹迸出的
翠綠的葉音

　　這是詩人壯心不已的力作,也寫出了詩人對愛與生存的勇氣、生命中濃郁的回憶及關懷鄉土之情,都已烙印在讀者的心中;而我也由衷地希望他在古稀之年以後繼續寫出更多的優美詩篇。

—2021.11.10

【刊臺灣《金門日報》*Kenmen Daily News* 副刊,2021.11.20 刊書評及林明理畫作 1 幅。】

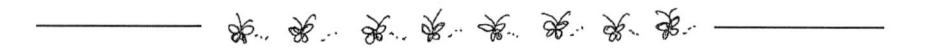

　　Hu Qide (pen name Hu Ertai, 1951-), a PhD in literature who once taught at National Taiwan Normal University, is one of the few scholar-poets in Taiwan's literary circle. On a cool afternoon in early winter, I was honored to receive his new collection of poems, which also reminded me of some interesting things. Most of his poems are romantic and reflect the worries of intellectuals, and are combined with his heroic talent and elegant demeanor.

　　Just as the poet writes about his feelings for his friends in "The Book in the Clouds" in a fresh and refined way, it is direct and unpretentious. In addition, the transformation of imagery and the use of synaesthesia add to the power of this poem:

Beauty lives in the clouds
A place deep in the clouds
When she combed her hair
The cloud waterfall rushes down from the sky
Over the mountains to the windowsill of the soul
As the clouds drift by
The beauty's smile unfolds from the pool of memories

夜讀胡爾泰《落羽松下的沉思》

Silk spun by spring silkworms
Acacia Bridge
Connects the front and back mountains
The bluebird is a diligent angel
Delivering messages in the cloud
The laughter of silver bells once fell into the lotus pond

My thoughts are the grass by the pond
Growing in the spring rain
Cyan Romance
It is a piece of everlasting wild grass
The Fields of Time
Until
The End of the Sky, The End of the Cloud

During his teaching period, the poet studied in France, Germany and the Netherlands for three years and won the Ministry of Education's Literary Creation Award twice. In addition to teaching and research, he also likes to wander among mountains and rivers and express his feelings in poetry. He is a poet with a unique style. The beautiful pictures in this poem are a combination of the art of time and space. They also contain the poet's inner monologue and sincere emotions, which can arouse rich associations in people. This is his exploration of poetic beauty, and it is also very poetic. His descriptions of plants and nature in many of his poems give people a colorful and beautiful imagery. For example, this poem "Iris" has a lyrical and bright tone, and is even more original:

The kite with royal blue feathers
Holding the tail of spring
Flying to the edge of the pond
Give the green stalks
Added a few rainbows

Yiren is wearing a felt hat
Come to the bridge
Looking at the drooping petals in the green pond
Shake out fan-shaped light
The shadow of the rainbow falls
Iris blooming in water

> Iris
> Also blooming in the soil of my longing
> Before the cherry blossoms fade
> The tassels are flying pink and white
> Late Spring March

Here, the poet composes a poem about an encounter by the pool — letting the wings of imagination fly between dreams and reality, and depicting the yearning and pursuit for poetic beauty; it reads beautifully and is full of auditory dynamics. It is worth mentioning that in late April 2017, the poet was hospitalized due to acute pancreatitis. He suddenly felt inspired and wrote a poem "Ward Notes". In the last sentence, the poet still said humorously: "I only know that watching the clouds on the lawn is much more comfortable than lying on the hospital bed." This is a poem with great thought depth, and also the story of the poet's courageous victory over illness. As he wrote in the last section of his poem "Meditations under the Bald Cypress":

> Thousands of thoughts lengthen the shadows of the trees
> Extending to the edge of night
> Dreamland
> I vaguely heard
> The dry branches burst out
> Green leaf sound

This is the poet's ambitious masterpiece, which also expresses the poet's courage for love and survival, the rich memories in life and his care for his hometown, all of which have been imprinted in the hearts of readers; and I sincerely hope that he will continue to write more beautiful poems after he is over 70 years old.

— November 10, 2021.

【Published in the supplement of Taiwan's *Kenmen Daily News*, a book review and a painting by Lin Ming-li were published on November 20, 2021.】

17 陳滿銘與《意象學廣論》研究述評
Review of Chen Manming and *Extensive Theory of Imagery*

一、其人其書

陳滿銘（1935－　），臺灣苗栗縣頭份鎮人。去年自臺灣師大國文系教授退休後，現為《萬卷樓》圖書股份有限公司董事長、《國文天地》雜誌社社長兼總編輯。專長含儒學、詞學、章法學、意象學、國文教學等。出版有二十幾種專著，編撰十餘冊。曾被遴選入《中華名人大典》、英文版《世界專業人才名典》（美國 ABI）、《21世紀2000世界傑出思想家》（英國 IBC）等典籍，殊榮無數。

21世紀意象學研究正蔚為學術上新貴，而融貫《意象學廣論》這部書中層次邏輯與意象系統的核心理念，是作為一種「現代性哲學體系的美學觀」。近10年來，臺灣在臺師大陳滿銘教授及其高足仇小屏、陳佳君等的引導下，不但建立了「辭章章法學」等新學科，提供了中國文學研究的精神向度，也把漢語章法學的研究轉向科學的道路，備受海峽兩岸研討會矚目。他們孜孜以求的就是為意象學、辭章章法學構築一個宏大的闡釋框架，期能透過豐富的審美視野與邏輯理念相融和，最大極限地呈現文體的變化規律，從而得出某種結論。

從這個意義上說，作者對意象學的思想模型中，它是有廣義與狹義之別的。這之中，當我們構思或閱讀時，經過觀察、審思與美的蘊釀階段，如何成為有意境的景像的創造，就成為進入文學領域的焦點；而探索《意象學廣論》，就是開始對詩文藝術最高境界的一種探尋。由於思維在經與外界的物象相交會時，有一個聯想、想像的過程，其間可能會發生抽離出「意象系統」；所以，當本身設計其表現技巧的，都屬於「形象思維」，而愈發呈現有關「措詞」等問題。是故，如以此為研究對象的，即為狹義意象學。再者，如以「形象思維」與「邏輯思維」合而為一，繼而探討與

「綜合思維」此三方面，如何統和等相關問題，而以此為主要研究對象的，即為廣義意象學。這些思想在當代的哲學或美學等學科研究，既取決於意象學自身的內容，也取決於中國儒家的哲學範疇以及與語文螺旋結構的關係。

二、審美視野中的意象學廣論

《意象學廣論》涵蓋思想的基本方式，有著深奧的哲學與美學形態，對中國詩歌意象觀念的理解與意象藝術形成了一種鮮明的影響力。中國先賢對詩歌創作常強調情景相融的整體思維，其意象詩學觀，向來都主張「意」與「象」的應合，主客體和諧一致。而此書對傳統詩歌情志的感發、邏輯和思維的闡釋，都有著承載作用。作者論述的重點簡述如下：

1. 邏輯層次，通常都由多樣的「二元對待」為基礎，經「移位與轉位」之過程與「多」、「二」、「一〈0〉」螺旋結構」之終極統合，形成其完整系統；這可由《周易》與《老子》等哲學典籍中找到它的理論根源。個別意象擴展到整體意象，以呈現「意象系統」，有的甚至推本於「思維」，加以統攝、融貫；是反映宇宙人生生生不息的基本規律，用以探討其哲學意涵、辭章表現與美學詮釋。

2. 「形象思維」與「邏輯思維」為「二」，「主題」、「文題」、「風格」為「一〈0〉」。由「〈0〉一」而「二」而「多」，凸顯的是創作〈寫〉的順向過程；而由「多」而「二」而「〈0〉」，凸顯的是鑑賞的逆向過程。

3. 辭章乃結合「意象」之形成、表現、組織與統合而形成的一個綜合體。其中，意象之形成與表現是由「形象思維」加以呈現的；意象之組織是由「邏輯思維」加以呈現的；意象之統合是由「形象思維」與「邏輯思維」和而為一加以呈現的。這些都可以由「多、二、一〈0〉結構加以統一，形成一個綜合體。」這〈0〉〈風格、韻律、氣象、境界〉之美，統合了「多」〈層次、變化〉、〈二〉〈陽剛、陰柔或調和、對比〉、「一」〈統一、和諧〉所形成的。

4. 「意象」是一切思維〈含形象、邏輯、綜合〉的基本單元，原有著「二而一」、「一而二」的關係，藉以形成「思維系統」或「意象系統」。作者用「景」與「景」〈同形同構〉、「景」與「事」

〈異形同構〉、「景」與「情」〈異質同構〉的結構類型為實例，解說甚詳。

綜合而言，《意象學廣論》不僅表現為詩歌的意象營構從古典詩詞開始就一直沿著「意隨象出」的方向展開，也形成一種感物寄興的思維研究模式。另一方面，它自覺地接受了中國文學美學與西方現代美學的表現策略。書中每種研究都能概括出某種規律；每一種實例或闡釋，也都能得出一種結論。而這些意象學進程的經驗描述與邏輯思維，是思想性與審美性的交融與互動。其中第八章，在「意象包孕式結構的美學詮釋」章節裡，作者引用中國諸家美學概論，表達了意象學也追求中國傳統的最高境界的美。這種美的形成都可溯源到《周易》與《老子》的哲學層面，它根植於宇宙的元氣和作者的思維本體。

三、陳滿銘：結合科學與人文的辭章學泰斗

《意象學廣論》思想是陳滿銘教授在臺師大 40 年教學過程中，經他觀察、分析、研究而得的碩果，也是當代意象論中一個重要範疇。它包括了辭章意象論的寫成和意象與聯想、想像互動論、意象「多」、「二」、「一〈0〉螺旋結構論」以及意象包孕式結構論等共十章論述。此書從文本的角度精闢地以中國古典詩歌實例解析，並印證了作者所說的以「構」連結「意象」成篇的理論基礎，以見它們在辭章上所造成的變化與奧妙。

2009.11.07
作者與臺師大陳滿銘教授於臺灣師範大學校園合照
the author and Professor Chen Manying of National Taiwan Normal University took a group photo on the campus of National Taiwan Normal University

我很慶幸，由作者手中收到這本書。我們知道，任何一種理論對古典詩詞的闡釋都意味著對既定規律的詩思；意象學也不例外。在 2002 年 5 月的一場由蘇州舉辦的《海峽兩岸中華傳統文化與現代化研討會》上，中國知名的學者鄭頤壽教授就在其論文發表中讚許：「臺灣的辭章章法學體系完整、科學…陳滿銘研究成果豐碩。」

而我從書中，深刻地瞭解到，這位辭章學學者的儒者風範及獨特的思維方式。他一生都在不斷地豐富自己，對求學問的細審深論，是極有見地的；但很少人知道，他的古詩也寫得神韻悠然。

比如《停雲》詩友選集這本書裡，作者寫下這首〈訪烏衣巷古址〉：「赫赫烏衣古，尋常屋幾重，橋邊追勝跡，燕子杳無蹤。」描繪出對詩人劉禹錫的懷古詩情、融合對自然、社會、歷史的感觸。再如〈舟遊維也納近郊人工湖〉：「輕舸入迷津，神工歎絕倫。清歌聲不住，漾就一湖春。」描繪出一幅富有詩情畫意的圖景。詩人以心去擁抱自然，回顧這美麗的音樂之都，當年於二次大戰期間，遭受戰火嚴重破壞，戰後更被美、英、法、蘇聯四國共同占領了十年之久。這段歷史的滄桑，使詩人心物交融，眼前也呈現出人工湖儀態萬千的風姿。彷彿中，綠樹環遶、維也納清歌餘音綿長⋯我們也感覺遠離了塵世的煩囂、見到天鵝在憩息的湖畔。這樣，我們也就不難理解滿銘老師為什麼是學界的瑰寶了。

—2010.05.12

【刊於 2010 年 10 月，臺灣臺北的「國圖」刊物《全國新書資訊月刊》，第 142 期，頁 90-93，合照 1 張，頁 90-93，合照 1 張。】

I. The person and the book

Chen Manming (1935-) is from Toufen Town, Miaoli County, Taiwan. After retiring from the Chinese Department of National Taiwan Normal University last year, he is now the chairman of Wanjuanlou Book Co., Ltd. and the president and editor-in-chief of the magazine "Guowen Tiandi". His expertise includes Confucianism, Ci-form poetry studies, composition, imagery, Chinese teaching, etc. He has published more than 20 monographs and compiled more than 10 books. He has been selected into the "Chinese Celebrity Dictionary", the English version of the "World Professional Talent Dictionary" (ABI in the United States), and the "21st Century 2,000 Outstanding World Thinkers" (IBC in the United Kingdom), and has received numerous honors.

The study of imagery is becoming a new academic hot topic in the 21st century, and the core concept of the hierarchical logic and imagery system in the book *Extensive Theory of Imagery* is a "modern philosophical system of aesthetics". In the past 10 years, under the guidance of Professor Chen Manying of National Taiwan Normal University and his students Qiu Xiaoping and Chen Jiajun, Taiwan has not only established new disciplines such as "lexicon and chapter law", providing a spiritual dimension for the study of Chinese literature, but also turned the study of Chinese chapter law to a scientific path, which has attracted much attention at seminars on both sides of the Taiwan Strait. What they strive for is to build a grand explanatory framework for imagism and rhetoric, hoping to present the changing rules of the style to the greatest extent through the integration of rich aesthetic vision and logical concepts, and thus draw a certain conclusion.

In this sense, the author's thought model of imagism is divided into broad and narrow meanings. Among them, when we conceive or read, after the stages of observation, reflection and the incubation of beauty, how to create a scene with artistic conception becomes the focus of entering the field of literature. Exploring *Extensive Theory of Imagery* is to begin a search for the highest realm of poetic art. When thinking intersects with external objects, there is a process of association and imagination, during which the "image system" may be extracted; therefore, when the expression techniques are designed, they belong to "image thinking", and more and more problems such as "wording" are presented. Therefore, if this is the research object, it is narrow imageology. Furthermore, if "image thinking" and "logical thinking" are combined into one, and then the three aspects of "comprehensive thinking" are explored, how to integrate them and other related issues, this is the main research object, and it is broad imageology. The research of these ideas in contemporary philosophy or aesthetics depends not only on the content of imageology itself, but also on the philosophical categories of Chinese Confucianism and its relationship with the spiral structure of language.

II. A Broad Treatise on Imagery in the Aesthetic Perspective

The Broad Treatise on Imagery covers the basic way of thinking, has profound philosophical and aesthetic forms, and has formed a distinct influence on the understanding of the concept of imagery in Chinese poetry and imagery art. Chinese sages often emphasize the overall thinking of the integration of scene and mood in poetry creation. Their imagery poetics have always advocated the correspondence of "meaning" and "image", and the harmony between subject and object. This book has a role in carrying the inspiration, logic and thinking of traditional poetry. The author's key points are briefly summarized as follows:

1. Logical level, usually based on various "binary oppositions", through the process of "displacement and transposition" and the ultimate integration of "many", "two", "one (0) spiral structure", to form a complete system; this can be found in the "Book of Changes" and "Laozi" and other philosophical classics. Individual images are expanded to the overall image to present the "image system", and some are even based on "thinking", integrated and integrated. It reflects the basic laws of the endless cycle of the universe and life, and is used to explore its philosophical implications, rhetorical expressions and aesthetic interpretations.

2. "Image thinking" and "logical thinking" are "2", "Theme", "Topic", and "Style" are "1 (0)". From "(0)1" to "2" to "Many", it highlights the forward process of creation (writing); and from "Many" to "2" to "(0)", it highlights the reverse process of appreciation.

3. Rhetoric is a comprehensive body formed by combining the formation, expression, organization and integration of "image". Among them, the formation and expression of image is presented by "image thinking". The organization of image is presented by "logical thinking". The integration of image is presented by the combination of "image thinking" and "logical thinking". All of these can be unified by the "many, two, one (0) structure to form a comprehensive whole." The beauty of (0) (style, rhythm, atmosphere, realm) integrates the "many" (level, change), (two) (masculine, feminine or harmony, contrast), and "one" (unity, harmony).

4. "Image" is the basic unit of all thinking (including image, logic, and synthesis), and originally has the relationship of "two in one" and "one in two" to form a "thinking system" or "image system". The author uses the structural types of "scene" and "scene" (same shape

and same structure), "scene" and "event" (heterogeneous shape and same structure), and "scene" and "emotion" (heterogeneous same structure) as examples, and explains them in detail.

In summary, *Extensive Theory of Imagery* not only shows that the construction of poetic imagery has been developing in the direction of "meaning follows imagery" since classical poetry, but also forms a thinking research model of expressing feelings through objects. On the other hand, it consciously accepts the expression strategies of Chinese literary aesthetics and Western modern aesthetics. Each study in the book can summarize a certain law; each example or explanation can also draw a conclusion. The empirical description and logical thinking of these imagistic processes are the fusion and interaction of thought and aesthetics. In Chapter 8, in the section "Aesthetic Interpretation of Image-Encompassing Structure", the author quotes the general theories of aesthetics of various Chinese scholars to express that imagism also pursues the highest level of beauty in Chinese tradition. The formation of this kind of beauty can be traced back to the philosophical aspects of the *Book of Changes* and *Laozi*, which are rooted in the vitality of the universe and the author's thinking.

III. Chen Manying: A master of rhetoric who combines science and humanities

The idea of *Extensive Theory of Imagery* is the result of Professor Chen Manying's observation, analysis, and research during his 40 years of teaching at National Taiwan Normal University. It is also an important category in contemporary imagery. It includes ten chapters on the writing of rhetoric imagery theory and imagery and association, imagination interaction theory, image "many", "two", "one (0) spiral structure theory" and image inclusive structure theory. This book analyzes Chinese classical poetry from the perspective of text, and confirms the author's theoretical basis of connecting "image" with "structure" to form a chapter, showing the changes and mysteries they have caused in the rhetoric.

I am very fortunate to receive this book from the author. We know that any theory that interprets classical poetry means poetic thinking about established rules; imagism is no exception. At the "Cross-Strait

Chinese Traditional Culture and Modernization Seminar" held in Suzhou in May 2002, Professor Zheng Yishou, a well-known Chinese scholar, praised in his paper: "Taiwan's rhetoric system is complete and scientific... Chen Manming has made fruitful research achievements." From the book, I deeply understand the Confucian style and unique way of thinking of this rhetoric scholar. He has been constantly enriching himself throughout his life, and his careful and in-depth discussion on the pursuit of knowledge is very insightful; but few people know that he also wrote ancient poems with a magical and leisurely charm.

For example, in the book *Tingyun*, the author wrote the poem "Visiting the Ancient Site of Wuyi Lane": "The magnificent Wuyi Lane is ancient, and the houses are just a few layers high. I followed the traces of the victory by the bridge, but the swallows are gone." It depicts the poet Liu Yuxi's nostalgic poetry and his feelings about nature, society, and history. Another example is "Boating in the Artificial Lake in the Suburbs of Vienna": "The light boat enters the maze, and the divine work is unparalleled. The clear singing voice never stops, and the lake is full of spring." It depicts a poetic and picturesque picture. The poet embraces nature with his heart and looks back at this beautiful music capital, which was severely damaged by war during World War II. After the war, it was jointly occupied by the United States, Britain, France, and the Soviet Union for ten years. The vicissitudes of this period of history made the poet's mind and body blend together, and the man-made lake presented its various graceful appearances before his eyes. It seemed that we were surrounded by green trees and the lingering sound of Vienna's clear songs.... We also felt far away from the troubles of the world and saw swans resting by the lake. In this way, it is not difficult for us to understand why Professor Man Ming is a treasure in the academic world.

— May 12, 2010.

【Published in October 2010, "National Library" publication *National New Book Information Monthly* in Taipei, Taiwan, No. 142, pages 90-93, 1 group photo, pages 90-93, 1 group photo.】

18 一隻慨然高歌的靈鳥——讀普希金詩
A Soul Bird Sings With Deep Feeling: Reading Alexander Pushkin's poetry

摘要 Abstract

普希金以詩真實地反映內心的深沉思想及豐沛感情與當年俄國社會背景嚴酷的真實境遇；作品無不至情至性，深具魅力。其中蘊含的溫柔、豐盛與美好，正如他自己流星般燦爛卻短暫的一生，給予人無限遐思；也表達了他深信光明必勝黑暗，人類的博愛必能戰勝奴役和壓迫的反抗精神和崇尚自由的詩意生活。

Pushkin used his poems not only to reflect his deep thought and rich feeling but also to portray the cruel reality of the Russian society of his time. With great sincerity and compassion, his works are full of artistic charm. Just like his brilliant yet short life of a shooting star, the gentleness, richness and goodness imbedded in his works captivated the imagination of the readers. His works also expressed his firm belief that light would conquer darkness, and that universal love would overcome enslavement and oppression, leading to a poetic life of freedom.

關鍵詞：普希金、詩人、俄羅斯、詩歌。
Keywords: Pushkin, poet, Russia, poetry.

一、傳略

普希金（Aleksandr Pushkin, 1799-1837）是享譽世界的俄國詩人、最偉大的文豪。1799 年生於莫斯科一個富有詩文修養的貴族家庭，八歲即能以法文寫詩，十五歲寫下詩歌〈沙皇村回憶〉，清新雋永，展現他非凡的天賦，獲老詩人德札文（Gavriil Romanovic Derzavin, 1743-1816）激賞。1817 年畢業後入外交部任職，開始與十二月黨人[1]文藝圈接近；當時因俄國民族意識高漲，遂而寫了多

---

[1] 1825 年，俄國貴族革命家發動了反對農奴制度和沙皇專制制度的武裝起義，因起義時間是俄曆 12 月，所以領導這次起義的俄國貴族革命家在俄國歷史上被稱為「十二月黨人」，即 Decembrist。

首政治抒情詩，如〈致查阿達耶夫〉（1818）、〈自由頌〉（1817）等，是貴族革命運動在文學上的反映。不料，在 1820 年，竟因此遭到遠調南俄。然而，高加索 Caucasus 與克里米亞 Crimean 的美麗而寧靜的山水景物與豪邁風情，卻引起了普希金崇仰自由的情感，在那裡生活了四年，也完成多首長篇敘事詩、戲劇及讚美了純潔的愛情詩和美妙的大自然。

1824 年，普希金在南方期間，因愛上敖德塞 Odessa 總督沃隆佐夫之美貌的妻子伊莉莎白，與總督發生衝突，又被沙皇革職，轉而幽禁於其父親領地米哈夫斯特村兩年。由於幽禁地係普希金童年故鄉，那裡樸實的鄉村生活，促使他的心境趨於沉穩並專於寫作。他開始接近勞動人民，也搜集民歌、格言、諺語，開啟了研究俄國歷史的機遇。這期間他留下許多豐富成果。包括抒情詩、童話詩、敘事詩及 1825 年寫下著名的歷史劇《鮑里斯·戈杜諾夫》（俄語：Борис Годунов），它取材於十六世紀末至十七世紀初俄國歷史上的真實事件。還有長篇詩體小說《葉甫蓋尼·奧涅金》是普希金整整用了八年時間完成的重要作品，其筆下的奧涅金厭惡上流社會的虛偽生活，可又無自己的生活目標，這個形象恰好表現了當時俄國進步的貴族青年思想上的鬱悶；因詩體音韻輕巧、優美，被名作曲家柴可夫斯基（1840-1893）譜為歌劇，致使此詩廣為流傳。

此外，十餘篇敘事詩，多為 1820 至 1830 年間所作，取材包括俄羅斯民間故事、神異傳說及特殊的民族習俗、自然景致等。1831 年 2 月，普希金與 19 歲的奧斯科第一美少女娜塔莉亞結婚。1833 年秋，詩人再度回到其父親領地波爾金諾，在那裡完成了敘事詩〈青銅騎士〉，童話《漁夫和金魚的故事》，小說《黑桃皇后》等。其間，由於其妻美貌驚動彼得堡，甚至引起沙皇尼古拉一世注意，宮廷邀宴不斷的生活令普希金深感痛苦。普希金最後的重要作品是歷史小說《上尉的女兒》，在這小說裡，普希金又成功地塑造出一個自信又酷愛自由，深受人民擁戴的農民起義領袖普加喬夫的形象，同時，也譴責了沙皇的專制和殘暴；這在當時是極大膽的行徑。1837 年 1 月 27 日，普希金因妻子緋聞與流亡到俄國的法國保王黨人丹特士決鬥，兩天後，因傷重去世，年僅 38 歲。據說這是沙皇精心策劃的一個陰謀，為此，使全體俄羅斯人哀痛萬分，憤懣之士紛紛抗議，為之沸騰。

普希金一生的創作富有崇高的思想，他深信光明必勝黑暗，人類的博愛必能戰勝奴役和壓迫,因而在世界文壇引起許多共鳴。1829 至 1836 年，是普希金創作的巔峰期；其間創作了 12 部敘事長詩，其中，最主要的是〈魯斯蘭和柳德米拉〉、〈高加索的俘虜〉（1822）、〈青銅騎士〉（1833）等。普希金劇作並不多，最重要的是歷史劇《鮑里斯‧戈杜諾夫》（1825）。去世前數年，其寫作重心已漸由韻文轉向非韻文。包括 1831 年《貝爾金小說集》裡有五篇散文故事，1834 年《黑桃皇后》，1836 年《上尉的女兒》等；內容人物真實親切，並以客觀的描寫取代主觀表述。他真是俄羅斯浪漫主義文學的傑出代表、現代文學的始祖；因而獲「偉大的俄國人民詩人」、「俄羅斯詩歌的太陽」等稱號。

二、賞析

想認識俄國的詩，想了解俄國現代文學抒情的傳統，研究普希金是最好的入門；其詩歌語言洋溢著浪漫主義的繽紛色彩，讀來餘韻十足，也反映了詩人對自由的熱烈追求。如 1815 年寫下的〈我的墓誌銘〉，這首詩是年僅 16 歲的普希金作品，竟預言了自己流星般燦爛卻短暫的一生：

> 這裡埋著普希金；他畢生快樂，
> 結交年輕的繆思、愛神和懶散，
> 未曾有什麼善行，但蒼天為證，
> 是個好人。

從看似短小、簡潔的句中，彷彿看見了一個聰穎而充滿抱負的詩人在自我形象的塑造上,企圖要將心的夢田植入更多的意念，包含足以與繆思為友、追求愛情與自由、顛覆黑暗世界並嚮往光明的想法。而情感和願望是普希金經過痛苦的蛻變後，一切努力和創作的背後動力。需要明確的是，現實主義作為普希金的精神內核仍有其極大影響。在這兒，我們不妨欣賞一下這首 1818 年寫下的詩〈致查阿達耶夫〉，這可以說是帶有某些浪漫主義色彩的現實主義作品。詩人用諷刺、犀利的筆法描述出心中對沙皇制度的憤懣，以正義的界線去界開黑暗與光明，突出昂揚的激情：

> 愛、希望和虛名的
> 欺騙短暫愉悅了我們，

年少的歡樂已經消失,
如夢、如晨霧;
我們心中仍燃燒希望,
致命勢力的壓迫下,
我們以焦灼的心情
傾聽祖國的召喚。
我們懷著期待的折磨,
等候神聖的自由時刻,
如年輕的戀人
等候已訂的約會。
當我們為自由燃燒,
當心靈為榮譽活躍,
朋友,奉獻給祖國
我們至高的熱情吧!
同志,相信吧:將升起
一顆醉人的幸福之星,
俄羅斯將自夢中驚醒,
在專制制度的廢墟上,
一一鏤刻我們的姓名!

　　詩裡的查阿達耶夫(1794-1856)是歷史哲學家及出版家,1816年在沙皇村與普希金相識成為摯友。查阿達耶夫有強烈愛國意識,政治思想傾向激進。1836年因寫文批判當局而遭沙皇尼古拉一世以精神病罪名入監拘禁。普希金既能滿懷深深的同情去揭示俄羅斯被壓迫的知識青年遭受沙皇專制的苦難,又能以無限的信心為光明的未來而高歌。因而,人們,不能不為詩中的強烈情緒而感動。詩人在南俄的坎坷歲月,使他同勞動人民的心靠得更緊了,而愛情也給他提供了取之不盡的創作素材和詩的感受。如 1825 年寫下的〈假如生命欺騙了你〉,詩中有著這樣感情炙人的句子:

假如生命欺騙了你,
莫悲傷,別生氣!
憂愁之日要克己,
要相信快樂會降臨。

心靈憧憬著未來,
眼前的總令人沮喪:

一切將轉眼不在，
逝去的常令人懷想。

　　面對著瞬息變幻的現實，普希金必須說出自己的心裡話。在這兒，詩人沒有直接抨擊和批評被沙皇遠調南俄的惡行，而是攫取一段關於愛遭遇了無法克服之障礙，揭露自己苦心尋找思想和以強烈的火樣的熱情去擁抱生活的心情。然而，在他捕捉生活，創作的同時，不僅僅局限於視覺或聽覺的感受，而是通過全心靈的觀照。像詩人在1828年寫下的〈冷風依然吹颳〉一詩那樣，把詩美體現出來：

冷風依舊吹颳，
送來凌晨的寒。
春雪初融的地上，
冒出早生的小花。
彷彿來自蠟世界，
從芳香的蜜室
飛出第一隻蜂，
飛向初開的花
探問春的訊息：
貴客是否就要駕臨，
草地是否就要轉綠，
白樺是否就要茂密，
嫩葉是否就要綻放，
稠李是否就要開花？

　　此詩情象的流動，雖帶有一點淒涼的色彩，但其多彩的形象和那有意的重複，增添了對愛情無限的惆悵和懷舊的情緒，這都是在詩人感情的催動下展現的。再試看這首在1828年標誌著詩人感情生活的〈回憶〉，很有神韻：

當喧囂的白晝如死者靜默，
　　　　城市無聲的街道
覆蓋半透明的夜影
　　　　與睡夢，日間辛勤的酬報，
痛苦的失眠在
　　　　靜寂中牽曳，

寂寥的夜裡燃燒我的心，
　　　　彷彿蛇在嚙咬；
幻想沸騰，憂思壓抑的智慧
　　　　擠迫過剩的沉重思維；
回憶在我眼前默默
　　　　伸展長長的畫卷；
我厭惡地閱讀自己的生命，
　　　　我顫抖，我詛咒，
流著熱淚，痛苦抱怨，
　　　　洗不去悲哀的詩行。

　　其實，普希金短暫的人生是複雜的。他在詩中歌詠過窮苦的勞動大眾，詛咒過沙皇給人民帶來的苦難和專政的罪行，還悼念過為批評專政而犧牲的友人，為人民立下了一個勇敢嘗試的榜樣。可是，在感情上，詩人也是一種癡鳥，是一個以自己的感情慨然高歌著大自然的美與人類的希望之鳥。如同印度詩人泰戈爾（1861-1941）所說一般：「生命從世界得到資產，愛情使它得到價值。」[2]，普希金在 1829 年的另一首名詩〈愛過妳〉，亦從另一段愛情體驗受著痛苦的煎熬，這當然有些絕望之感，但也表明了愛情的到來是要勇於付出代價的：

愛過妳：也許，愛火
在我心裡未完全隕熄；
但它不再煩擾妳，
不願再惹妳憂傷。
絕望無言地愛妳，
有時羞澀，有時妒忌。
懇切溫存地愛妳，
願他對妳一樣珍惜。

　　此詩是普希金獻給愛人安娜・阿列克謝耶夫娜・奧列尼娜（1808-1888）的。奧列尼娜（乳名安涅塔）是彼得堡公共圖書館館長、考古學家奧列寧的千金小姐。奧列尼娜和普希金接觸之後，

---

[2] 《泰戈爾經典詩選：生如夏花》，譯者：鄭振鐸，臺灣，遠足文化，2011.12，頁 84。

隨即墜入愛情，普希金對她也充滿了情意。1828年夏，普希金很想和奧列尼娜結為夫妻，但卻遭到了她的父親的拒絕；因而傷心地離開了彼得堡。後來，普希金與奧列尼娜一家關係大大疏遠的另一原因，是她的父親越來越靠近沙皇，且對普希金的諷刺短詩極為不滿。這期間，普希金在1828年左右寫下許多愛情詩，如〈她的眼睛〉、〈你和您〉、〈美人兒啊，不要在我面前唱起〉、〈豪華的京城，可憐的京城〉、〈唉，愛情的絮絮談心〉等，應該是由奧列尼娜引發出來的，這不能不說是詩人在表達詩情上的苦心經營。

　　詩人他一生追求理想，追求愛情，也追求藝術上的創新。但時時遇到挫折，使他感到迷惘與苦悶。失去愛後，1829年普希金又認識娜塔莉亞·岡察洛娃，這是詩人在一次旅途中寫下對她的思念的詩〈夜霧瀰漫在格魯吉亞山崗上〉，節奏和韻律都是和詩相吻合的，這就增加了此詩的音律美：

　　　夜霧瀰漫在格魯吉亞山崗上，
　　　阿拉戈河在我眼前喧響。
　　　我憂鬱輕快，我的哀思發亮；
　　　妳的麗影充塞我的愁腸。
　　　妳，只有妳……沒有什麼
　　　能驚動我的悲傷。
　　　心再度燃燒再要愛——因為
　　　不能不把妳愛上。

　　小小的一首八行詩，便把讀者的心抓住了。詩人借景抒情，他站在格魯吉亞山崗上，從夜霧瀰漫的畫面中，使人看到了詩人悲喜交感又期盼的心；這就使他的愛情詩更為絢麗多姿。在那個年代，普希金如果對人民的痛苦漠不關心，只關在象牙塔裡自我吟醉，就算不上是個真正的詩人；同樣，在沙皇處心積慮的重壓下，只有悲苦地呻吟或憤恨，而無法向人民昭示出光明的前途，或為祖國人民爭取自由和幸福而奮鬥，也不會成為偉大的文學家。普希金的可貴之處，恰恰在於：他對人民苦難的同情和對光明的渴求是他鮮明的思想傾向。如詩人在1834年寫下的〈是時候了，朋友，是時候了！〉一詩，他對愛情帶來的痛苦與渴望心的平靜，他的正義與犧牲的精神，正代表了他悲苦而璀璨的命運，給人們寄予了無限的同情：

是時候了，朋友，是時候了！心要求平靜，
歲月一天天飛去，每一片刻帶走
一部分生命，我倆
準備共同生活……一看，已將死去，
世間沒有幸福，但有安寧與自由。
我曾夢想令人欣羨的命運——
我，疲倦的奴隸，早已盼望逃去
辛勤勞作與真正安逸的遙遠居所。

　　詩人雖抒發了一種又恨又愛的複雜感情，並表達了一種要使勞動人民新生的渴望。這表面上寫的是朋友，但實際上卻都是在象徵處於反抗俄皇鬥爭中的俄國人民的互相團結；正是靠了這種在心靈深處的互相共鳴與攜手，才能讓普希金向他所熱愛的祖國和人民捧出了許多堅實的、閃耀著灼人的光芒的文學作品。

三、浪漫與睿哲的肖像：普希金

　　記得唐代詩人劉禹錫的《秋詞》裡寫道：「晴空一鶴排雲上，便引詩情到碧霄。」夜讀普希金詩，思索之後，心情也像是看到：秋天晴朗的天空中一隻仙鶴排開雲層，不停不息地在微光中飛翔；而我的詩興也隨它到了蔚藍的天上，愛上了它一樣，也可感覺到他離開塵世的自由了。這位曾舉著「火把」，迎向「太陽」的歌手，他雖不怨天，在沙皇專政時期又經過種種挫折和磨難中；卻奇蹟地活出極強的藝術生命力。其藝術的主要使命，在於將情致深摯而見於文字的意象保持一種高貴的情操及純真的美。他在大量地寫下抒情詩的同時，也雙寫了十四首長篇敘事詩，這是他詩歌創作中最豐盛的階段。這些詩歌是普希金的本真，是靜默的沉思；大致洋溢著浪漫主義的繽紛色彩，也反映了詩人對自由的熱烈追求。

　　再者，普希金詩的語言精練程度也很高，尤以其中的〈高加索俘虜〉等詩作，更可視為詩體長篇小說《葉甫蓋尼·奧涅金》的補充。確實，他是俄羅斯近代文學的奠基者和俄羅斯文學語言的創建者。他促使俄羅斯文學走上了現實主義的道路，給詩歌以血液和呼吸！其詩歌不但體現了詩人的一種胸襟，一種浩然之氣的人格；而所要表達的主題思想，又造成了一個完整的藝術境界，有如黎前的黑暗——是偉大的，這就與西方的一些純意象派詩大不同。它總是通過人民群眾最熟悉的事物，或敘事，或抒情，或描寫，或比興；給讀者打下深刻的印象。詩人把理想和愛寄託於無際的星空，就像隻靈鳥不停地鳴唱，早已贏取天國之永恆；其不朽的一生，也傳聞於世，對世界文學的繁榮是有極大促進作用的。

—2013.03.04

【刊登臺灣《新原人》季刊，2013 春季號，第 81 期，頁 164-173。】

I. Biography

Pushkin (Aleksandr Pushkin, 1799-1837) is a world-renowned Russian poet and the greatest literary giant. Born in 1799 in Moscow into a noble family with rich poetic culture, he was able to write poetry in French at the age of eight, and wrote the poem "Memories of Tsarskoye Selo" at the age of fifteen. The poem is fresh and timeless, showing his extraordinary talent, and was praised by the old poet Gavriil Romanovic Derzavin (1743-1816). After graduating in 1817, he joined the Ministry of Foreign Affairs and began to get close to the literary circle of the Decembrists.[3] At that time, due to the rise of Russian national consciousness, he wrote many political lyric poems, such as "To Zaadyev" (1818) and "Ode to Freedom" (1817), which reflected the aristocratic revolutionary movement in literature. Unexpectedly, in 1820, he was transferred to southern Russia. However, the beautiful and peaceful landscapes and heroic customs of the Caucasus and Crimea aroused Pushkin's admiration for freedom. He lived there for four years and completed many long narrative poems, dramas, and poems praising pure love and beautiful nature.

In 1824, while in the south, Pushkin fell in love with Elizabeth, the beautiful wife of the Governor of Odessa, Vorontsov. He had a

---

[3] In 1825, Russian noble revolutionaries launched an armed uprising against the serfdom and the Tsarist autocracy. Because the uprising took place in December of the Russian calendar, the Russian noble revolutionaries who led the uprising were called "Decembrists" in Russian history.

conflict with the Governor and was dismissed by the Tsar. He was imprisoned in the village of Mihavst, his father's territory, for two years. Since the place of imprisonment was Pushkin's childhood hometown, the simple rural life there made him calm and focused on writing. He began to get close to the working people and collected folk songs, aphorisms, and proverbs, which opened up the opportunity to study Russian history. During this period, he left many fruitful results. Including lyric poems, fairy tale poems, narrative poems and the famous historical drama *Boris Godunov* (Russian: Борис Годунов) written in 1825, which is based on real events in Russian history from the late 16th century to the early 17th century. There is also the long poetic novel "Eugene Onegin", which is an important work that Pushkin spent eight years to complete. Onegin in his writing hates the hypocritical life of the upper class, but has no goals in life. This image just reflects the ideological depression of the progressive Russian aristocratic youth at that time; because the poetic rhythm is light and beautiful, it was composed into an opera by the famous composer Tchaikovsky (1840-1893), making this poem widely circulated.

In addition, more than ten narrative poems were written between 1820 and 1830, and were based on Russian folk tales, myths and legends, special national customs, natural scenery, etc. In February 1831, Pushkin married Natalia, the 19-year-old most beautiful girl in Oskov. In the autumn of 1833, the poet returned to his father's territory, Bolkino, where he completed the narrative poem "The Bronze Knight", the fairy tale *The Story of the Fisherman and the Goldfish*, and the novel *The Queen of Spades*. During this period, because his wife's beauty shocked St. Petersburg and even attracted the attention of Tsar Nicholas I, Pushkin felt deeply distressed by the constant invitations to court banquets. Pushkin's last important work was the historical novel *The Captain's Daughter*, in which Pushkin successfully created the image of Pugachev, a confident and freedom-loving leader of the peasant uprising who was deeply loved by the people. At the same time, he also condemned the tsar's autocracy and cruelty. This was a very bold act at the time. On January 27, 1837, Pushkin dueled with Dantes, a French royalist who had fled to Russia, because of his wife's scandal. Two days later, he died of his injuries at the age of 38. It is said that this was a conspiracy carefully planned by the tsar, which made all Russians extremely sad, and the angry people protested and boiled over it.

Pushkin's works throughout his life were full of lofty ideas. He firmly believed that light would triumph over darkness and that human fraternity would triumph over slavery and oppression, which resonated with many people in the world literary world. 1829 to 1836 was the peak period of Pushkin's creation; during this period, he created 12 narrative poems, among which the most important ones were "Ruslan and Lyudmila", "The Prisoner of the Caucasus" (1822), and "The Bronze Knight" (1833). Pushkin did not write many plays, the most important of which was the historical play *Boris Godunov* (1825). A few years before his death, the focus of his writing had gradually shifted from rhymed to non-rhymed. Including five prose stories in the 1831 *Belkin Fiction Collection*, *The Queen of Spades* in 1834, *The Captain's Daughter* in 1836, etc.; the content and characters are real and intimate, and objective description replaces subjective expression. He is truly an outstanding representative of Russian romantic literature and the ancestor of modern literature; therefore, he was named "the great Russian people's poet" and "the sun of Russian poetry".

II. Appreciation

If you want to know Russian poetry and want to understand the lyrical tradition of modern Russian literature, studying Pushkin is the best way to get started; his poetic language is full of the colorful colors of romanticism, which is full of lingering aftertaste and also reflects the poet's passionate pursuit of freedom. For example, "My Epitaph" written in 1815, a poem written by Pushkin when he was only 16 years old, predicted his life which was brilliant but short like a meteor:

> Here lies Pushkin; he lived a happy life,
> made friends with young Muse, Eros and Laziness,
> did not do any good deeds, but the heavens are his witness,
> he was a good man.

From these seemingly short and concise sentences, we can see that a smart and ambitious poet tried to implant more ideas in his dream field in the shaping of his self-image, including the idea of being friends with Muse, pursuing love and freedom, subverting the dark world and yearning for light. Emotion and desire are the driving force behind all Pushkin's efforts and creations after his painful transformation. It should be made clear that realism, as the spiritual core of Pushkin, still has a great influence. Here, we might as well appreciate the poem "To Zacharias Ataev" written in 1818, which can be said to be a realist work with some romantic colors. The poet used irony and sharp writing to describe his resentment towards the Tsarist system, using the boundary of justice to separate darkness and light, highlighting the high-spirited passion:

> Love, hope and false reputation
> The deception briefly delighted us,
> The joy of youth has disappeared,
> Like a dream, like morning mist;
> Hope still burns in our hearts,
> Under the pressure of fatal forces,
> We listen to the call of the motherland with anxious hearts.
> We are tortured by expectation,
> Waiting for the sacred moment of freedom,
> Like young lovers
> Waiting for an already scheduled date.
> When we burn for freedom,
> When our hearts are active for honor,
> Friends, dedicate our highest enthusiasm to the motherland!
> Comrade, believe it: a star of intoxicating happiness will rise,
> Russia will wake up from its dream, and on the ruins of the autocratic system, our names will be engraved one by one!

The Zahadayev in the poem (1794-1856) was a historian, philosopher and publisher. He met Pushkin in Tsarskoye Selo in 1816 and became a close friend. Zahadayev had a strong sense of patriotism and his political thoughts tended to be radical. In 1836, he was imprisoned by Tsar Nicholas I on charges of mental illness for writing articles criticizing the authorities. Pushkin could reveal the sufferings of oppressed Russian intellectuals under the Tsarist autocracy with deep sympathy, and sing for a bright future with infinite confidence. Therefore, people cannot help but be moved by the strong emotions in the poem. The poet's rough years in southern Russia made him closer to the working people, and love also provided him with inexhaustible creative materials and poetic feelings. For example, in "If Life Deceives You" written in 1825, there are such emotional sentences:

> If life deceives you,
> Don't be sad, don't be angry!
> On the day of sorrow, you must restrain yourself,
> Believe that happiness will come.
>
> The mind looks forward to the future,
> The present is always frustrating:
> Everything will be gone in the blink of an eye,
> The past is often missed.

Faced with the ever-changing reality, Pushkin must speak his mind. Here, the poet did not directly attack and criticize the evil deeds of being exiled to southern Russia by the Tsar, but captured a story about love encountering insurmountable obstacles, revealing his painstaking search for ideas and his intense passion to embrace life. However, when he captured life and created, he was not limited to visual or auditory feelings, but observed with his whole heart. Like the poem "The Cold Wind Still Blows" written by the poet in 1828, the poetic beauty is embodied:

> The cold wind still blows,
> Bringing the cold of the early morning.
> On the ground where the spring snow has just melted,
> Early flowers emerge.
> As if from the wax world,
> from the fragrant honey house
> flew the first bee,
> flew to the newly opened flowers
> to inquire about the message of spring:
> Will the distinguished guest come soon,
> Will the grass turn green soon,
> Will the birch grow lush,
> Will the young leaves bloom,
> Will the bird cherry blossom?

Although the flow of the imagery in this poem has a bit of sad color, its colorful images and the intentional repetition add to the infinite melancholy and nostalgic feelings of love, which are all displayed under the impetus of the poet's emotions. Let's take a look at the poem "Recollections" written in 1828, which marked the poet's emotional life. It is very poetic:

> When the noisy day is as silent as the dead,
> The silent streets of the city
> Covered with translucent night shadows
> And dreams, the reward for hard work during the day,
> Painful insomnia drags in
> Silence,
> The lonely night burns my heart,
> Like a snake biting;
> Fantasy is boiling, and the wisdom suppressed by worries
> Crowds the excessive heavy thoughts;
> Memories silently stretch out a long scroll in front of my eyes;
> I read my life with disgust,
> I tremble, I curse,
> Shedding hot tears, complaining in pain,
> The lines of poetry that cannot wash away the sorrow.

In fact, Pushkin's short life was complicated. In his poems, he sang praises to the poor working masses, cursed the suffering brought to the people by the Tsar and the crimes of dictatorship, and mourned his friends who died for criticizing dictatorship, setting a brave example for the people. However, in terms of emotions, the poet is also a fool, a bird that sings the beauty of nature and the hope of mankind with his own emotions. As the Indian poet Rabindranath Tagore (1861-1941) said: "Life gets assets from the world, and love gives it value."[4] Pushkin's other famous poem "I Loved You" in 1829 also suffered from the pain of another love experience. This is of course a bit of despair, but it also shows that the arrival of love requires the courage to pay the price:

---

[4] *Selected Classic Poems of Tagore: Life is Like Summer Flowers*, Translated by Zheng Zhenduo, Taiwan, Yuanzu Culture, 2011.12, p. 84.

一隻慨然高歌的靈鳥——讀普希金詩

>   I have loved you: perhaps, the fire of love
>   is not completely extinguished in my heart;
>   but it no longer bothers you,
>   I don't want to make you sad again.
>   I love you desperately and silently,
>   sometimes shy, sometimes jealous.
>   I love you with sincerity and tenderness,
>   I hope he will cherish you as much as you do.

This poem was dedicated by Pushkin to his lover Anna Alexeevna Olenina (1808-1888). Olenina (nicknamed Annetta) was the daughter of Olenin, the director of the Petersburg Public Library and an archaeologist. After Olenina and Pushkin met, they immediately fell in love, and Pushkin was also full of affection for her. In the summer of 1828, Pushkin wanted to marry Olenina, but was rejected by her father, so he left Petersburg sadly. Later, another reason why Pushkin's relationship with Olenina's family became greatly alienated was that her father became closer and closer to the Tsar and was extremely dissatisfied with Pushkin's satirical short poems. During this period, Pushkin wrote many love poems around 1828, such as "Her Eyes", "You and You", "Beauty, Don't Sing in Front of Me", "Luxury Capital, Poor Capital", "Alas, Love's Chatter", etc., which should be inspired by Olenina. This can be said to be the poet's painstaking efforts in expressing poetry.

The poet pursued ideals, love, and artistic innovation throughout his life. But he encountered setbacks from time to time, which made him feel confused and depressed. After losing his love, Pushkin met Natalia Gontcharova again in 1829. This is the poem "Night Mist Diffuses on the Georgian Hills" written by the poet during a journey to express his longing for her. The rhythm and rhyme are consistent with the poem, which increases the rhythmic beauty of the poem:

>   Night mist diffuses on the Georgian hills,
>   The Arago River roars before my eyes.
>   I am melancholy and light, my sorrow shines;
>   Your beautiful shadow fills my sorrow.
>   You, only you....nothing
>   can stir my sorrow.

My heart burns again to love again — because
I can't help but fall in love with you.

This small eight-line poem captures the reader's heart. The poet uses the scenery to express his emotions. He stands on the hills of Georgia. From the night mist, people can see the poet's mixed feelings of joy and sorrow and expectation. This makes his love poems more colorful. In that era, if Pushkin was indifferent to the suffering of the people and only stayed in the ivory tower to indulge in self-recitation, he would not be considered a real poet; similarly, under the heavy pressure of the Tsar's conspiracy, he could only moan or resent miserably, but could not show the people a bright future, or fight for the freedom and happiness of the people of the motherland, and he would not become a great writer. The preciousness of Pushkin lies precisely in: his sympathy for the suffering of the people and his desire for light are his distinct ideological tendencies. As the poet wrote in 1834, "It's time, my friend, it's time!", his pain brought by love and his desire for peace of mind, his justice and spirit of sacrifice, represent his tragic and brilliant fate, giving people infinite sympathy:

> It's time, my friend, it's time! The heart demands peace,
> The years fly by day by day, each moment takes away
> a part of life, we are ready to live together... and look, we are about to die,
> There is no happiness in the world, but there is peace and freedom.
> I once dreamed of an enviable fate —
> I, a tired slave, have long hoped to escape
> to the distant home of hard work and true comfort.

Although the poet expressed a complex emotion of hatred and love, and expressed a desire to give the working people a new life. On the surface, this is about friends, but in fact it symbolizes the mutual solidarity of the Russian people in the struggle against the Russian emperor; it is precisely because of this mutual resonance and cooperation in the depths of the heart that Pushkin was able to present many solid and shining literary works to his beloved motherland and people.

III. Romantic and wise portrait: Pushkin

I remember the poem *Autumn Poem* by Tang Dynasty poet Liu Yuxi: "A crane flies above the clouds in the clear sky, and the poetic sentiment reaches the blue sky." When I read Pushkin's poems at night and pondered, I felt as if I saw a crane flying above the clouds in the clear autumn sky, flying non-stop in the dim light. My poetic sentiment followed it to the blue sky, and I fell in love with it. I could also feel his freedom from the world. This singer who once held a "torch" to welcome the "sun" did not blame the heavens, and he experienced many setbacks and hardships during the Tsarist dictatorship, but he miraculously lived out a strong artistic vitality. The main mission of his art is to maintain a noble sentiment and pure beauty in the images that are deeply emotional and reflected in the text. While he wrote a large number of lyric poems, he also wrote fourteen long narrative poems, which was the most prosperous period of his poetry creation. These poems are Pushkin's true nature and silent meditation, they are generally full of romantic colors and also reflect the poet's passionate pursuit of freedom.

Furthermore, the language of Pushkin's poems is also very refined, especially poems such as "The Caucasian Captive", which can be regarded as a supplement to the poetic novel *Eugene Onegin*. Indeed, he is the founder of modern Russian literature and the creator of Russian literary language. He pushed Russian literature onto the path of realism and gave poetry blood and breath! His poems not only embody the poet's broad mind and a personality of great spirit; the theme and thought he wanted to express also created a complete artistic realm, like the darkness before dawn — it is great, which is very different from some pure imagist poems in the West. It always uses the things that the people are most familiar with, whether narrative, lyrical, descriptive, or metaphorical. It leaves a deep impression on readers. The poet placed his ideals and love in the infinite starry sky, just like a spiritual bird that keeps singing, and has already won the eternity of heaven. His immortal life is also known to the world, which has greatly promoted the prosperity of world literature.

—March 4, 2013.

〔Published in Taiwan's *New Original Man* Quarterly, 2013 Spring Issue, No. 81, pp. 164-173.〕

19 杜國清詩歌的意象節奏
The Image Rhythm of Du Guoqing's Poems

一、其人其詩

　　杜國清（1941- ），台中豐原人，臺灣大學外文系畢業，日本關西學院大學日本文學碩士、美國史坦福大學中國文學博士。曾任加州大學聖塔芭芭拉東亞語言文化研究系教授等職，為《笠》詩刊創辦人之一。著有詩集、評論、翻譯等多種，獲中興文藝獎、詩笠社翻譯獎、文建會翻譯成就獎等殊榮。

　　杜國清的早期詩作側重表現在主觀情志的具象表現的含義，它強調形象的真實性，有時是受到某一物象的啟示和觸動，而引起詩意的湧發，把生活和人性的題材上發揮出來；更擅長將一組在意義上有密切關聯的圖象排列在一起，淋漓盡致地表達出或輕柔、或激昂，或重濁、或悠揚，或暗諷或洪大等情狀的藝術手法，從而使意象節奏變得新奇，愈見詩人之心手之妙。中年後，尋幽探勝，寄情於山水，寫下許多景物詩、感懷詩或文化省思，都能體現著詩人的奇思妙想。

二、佳作細析

　　所謂意象節奏是意象與意象之間的節奏關係，它依分行排列的文學樣式，可分為力度節奏（即意象本身的運動節奏）、轉換節奏（即由此意象到彼意象所構成的轉換關係）及密度節奏（指一首詩或一句詩中意象數量的多少）。誠然，詩歌是節奏性最強的語言藝術；透過詩人想像將視覺的意象予以節奏化，藉以情感取得與自然的和諧，那麼，所有難以言語的感覺都將瞬間觸動讀者的心靈。杜國清從小在臺灣長大，血液裡有著鄉土的歷史積澱。大學畢業後，再到日本和美國留學；因而他的詩歌具有「學院派的知性手法」。從本質上來說，其詩歌有抒情的藝術，也有空間性的藝術，都靠內在的節奏反映出空間的主體性變遷，來傳達詩人瞬間永恆的生命感知。可以說，節奏和韻律是其詩歌的生命，能喚醒讀者相應感慨的各種意象（imagery）。也正是這種客觀意象的暗示，才能喚起空間畫面感及對審美的聯想。如這首早期之作〈勿忘草〉：

她從遠方寄來一根勿忘草
　　藍色的小花捲藏著蕊蕊的
　　祝福
　　我將她僅能給我的祝福
　　珍種在心的深處
　　每當新月掛在幽谷的山巔
　　那把銀勺子就澆醒山旅的回憶
　　每當晚風輕拂著垂柳
　　她那多韵的嬌姿就在我思念的
　　長河裡　浮漾著
　　如此　那根勿忘草在我心上生根
　　我以夕陽下哀思的淚釀血
　　以血　供養這棵異卉
　　它那嗜血的根鬚不久竟蔓成
　　紅藍的細網　撈住我的心
　　朵朵小花隨著我心的喜憂而變色
　　婷婷枝葉隨著我心的悸動而生姿
　　當我心肌上長滿了日子的蘚苔
　　啊啊　我心變成誰也觀賞不到的
　　愛之幽園裡的一缽美麗的　盆景
　　如此　懷著她僅能給我的祝福
　　當我躺在荒草間　血淚斷流
　　心已朽　這棵勿忘草啊
　　是否仍在晚風中獨自搖曳
　　向這世界宣示我的告別辭
　　是否替她哀悼我那空虛的幸福
　　然後　懊——枯——萎——

　　這裡，意象的轉換，已表現出時空的跳躍性，詩歌節奏迅捷，情感卻如同柔美的慢版，音韻極為優美。其中，勿忘草化作祝福，思念變為長河，歲月匆逝，彷彿只一瞬間。再如1969年寫的圖象詩〈祭〉，其意象力的指向是向下的，往往伴隨著悲傷、消沉的情感：

　　雜草山上

　　　　誰願驚醒這荒涼的寂靜
　　來奉獻花束紀念愛

　　　　　的青春　　以及
　　　　焚枯的
　　　古之偶像
　　　　的圖讖
　　　　穿黑衣　　　以及
　　　　暗自低泣的未亡人
　　　　　竟以手絹輕拭淚水的臉

　　　　　　　　引駐過客

　　首先,「雜草山上」引出的悲淒、愁苦、不堪回首的心境與追悼儀式的蒼涼、無可奈何的情感色調相契合。接著,排列的文字宛如喪儀中隆起的草墓前,左右各有對明燭,沿邊站立的親友也啞默地對著亡靈、無限哀思。那暗自低泣的未亡人,輕拭著淚更傳達出一種痛苦的悲劇氣氛。讀著這首詩,我們的頭也會不由自主地黯然垂落。

　　〈鄉愁〉全詩二十句,句句意象如連環,節節相生:

　　　　大甲溪邊那遼闊的黃色土原
　　　　自古鼎立著三個葫蘆形土墩
　　　　傳說中那三個葫蘆墩的口裡
　　　　經常冒著白煙從日出到黃昏

　　　　太陽光傾注在這三個葫蘆裡
　　　　附近村落因此經常發生火災
　　　　於是前人開一條河從中穿繞
　　　　葫蘆的乾土上才長出花草來

　　　　為了求神保佑這一片好風水
　　　　前人又在墩下建造了土地廟
　　　　廟前常有老人在拉琴或清唱
　　　　公雞母雞也常來拉屎或撒尿

　　　　在廟前抑壓哀憂的古琴聲中
　　　　幾個小孩搗著彩色的紙牌玩
　　　　長扇公主的眼睛裡沾滿雞屎
　　　　卻將諸葛的八陣圖一手搗翻

童年貼滿了多彩多樣的牌面
在回憶的輪盤上一再旋轉著
少年的心葫蘆滿懷鄉土的熱
鄉愁從中穿繞像故鄉那條河。

從總體上看,這首詩的意象密度大,其節奏轉換也快。詩中描寫童年生活的閒適與自得、諧趣、自然的情感很一致;在回憶的探尋中發著光。而詩人把古琴聲轉換成視覺意象,然後與廟前拉琴的老人、玩紙牌、看故事書的小孩等情景疊印在一起,給人思古幽懷的感受。這些意象用「回憶的輪盤」、「旋轉」緊緊疊合在一起,加強了詩裡的詩間因素,使鄉愁的凝結更為突出。

接著這首〈鼠〉,則給人急速、迅猛的節奏,他通過「齒爪」這樣疊字建行形式將「鼠輩橫行」視覺化,呈現出詩人心靈遊盪的過程、淨化的過程:

　　齒爪齒爪齒爪齒爪齒爪齒爪齒爪齒爪齒爪
只要樹有皮,穀有殼,屍體有棺材
只要人類有食物
　　齒爪齒爪齒爪齒爪齒爪齒爪齒爪齒爪齒爪
只要地下有莖,倉裡有糧,腐屍還有骨頭
只要咱們還活著
　　在這地球上,咱們抗議
人類誣告我輩是人類的賊
　　在這地球上,咱們控訴
人類妨礙我輩過街的自由
影響咱們繁殖的快樂
　　在這地球上,假如還有德先生的話
我輩願意在白天出來
和所有哺乳類動物競選

某種意義上,詩人如一位玄思的智者,此詩在旋轉運動之中,力度大,傳達出底層百姓的一種壓迫和困窘的境遇和思想。暗旨:某些政府官員們貪污腐敗、商業上假貨橫行,社會上造假欺詐事件,鋪天蓋地,使得治安與環境變得惡劣不堪;但惡了却不知如何防禁;法紀敗壞了却不知如何修治;徒然耗費許多資源。詩人以站在弱勢族群立場來表達其「不平而鳴」及嘲諷之聲。最後推介這首圖象詩〈蜘蛛〉，蜘蛛在詩中的運動是緩慢的，如「穿著緇黑袈裟　盤坐著」，是無聲地「蜷伏著」、「等待著」，反映出蜘蛛蓄勢而發的一種力量而又從容不迫的形影：

　　　撐著一瓣薔薇花　　等待著的　　蜘蛛
　　　　穿著緇黑袈裟　　盤坐著的　　蜘蛛
　　　　　寂寥的背影　　蜷伏著的　　蜘蛛

　　　　　以生癩且僵化的肢腳　霸守著
　　　　　一座方城觸霉的口腹擺出
　　　　　旁若無人的態勢自囚在陰
　　　　　暗的小天地咀嚼城垣下
　　　　　眾多蚊子的屍體戴黑眼鏡
　　　　　以自我為中心的獨裁者啊
　　　　　以沾血且痺麻的肢腳　霸守著

　　　蜘蛛　蜷伏著的　　偽裝的德性
　　　蜘蛛　等待著的　　織善誘的謊言
　　　蜘蛛　盤坐著的　　默想虛偽的價值

　　雖然在藝術與神話中，蜘蛛常成了一種象徵－代表耐心、殘忍和創造力的各種組合。但是，詩人把蜘蛛的意象由文字排列的圖象貫穿下來，利用蜘蛛的自然形態和特徵，展現的是牠們機警、狡猾甚至孤傲的多樣性的形像，使人覺得新奇而趣味。其實，外界萬花筒般飛速變化的世界，只是更加劇了牠們內心的寂寥。句中，最中間低凹部份即蜘蛛的口器，旁有二隻短短的觸肢；而其盤坐的冷酷，繪出了蜘蛛痛苦與征服時矛盾的線條。整個畫面視覺刺激的鋒利性極強，使人過目難忘。

三、杜國清：詩苑的時空哲人

　　杜國清是位十分積極推動臺灣文學的學者，畢生致力於對文學的價值認知，以及詩歌創作；並計劃主持「臺灣文學英譯叢刊」的出版，在海外的詩人中是鮮見的。這也許是身為知識份子共有的心靈體現，還表現出一位學者不倦的學術追求。他的詩歌取材廣泛，既歌吟文化古蹟、奇山異水、也歌吟風物，抒發鄉土情懷。大致上，都很有立意，能呈現出鮮明的時代色彩，啟人遐思。他是位站在中西文化匯合處的詩人,卻始終不忘本;其圖象詩在詩歌研究論著中也帶有開創性,也是具有世界特色的時空哲人。這時空可以是現實的不同時空,也可以是心理的不同時空,還可以是現實與心理交叉的時空;而杜國清的能力就體現在這些時空中所取得的自由運行的藝術表現上。哲人說:「我思故我在。」他對人生的哲思往往用意象語言呈現出來,句中的節奏如江水般綿延不斷,細細品讀,就能體味到他對失去的純真的追求、對文學的反思與關懷臺灣的視野。

—2011.11.01 作

【刊臺灣《笠》詩刊,第 290 期,2012.08.15.】

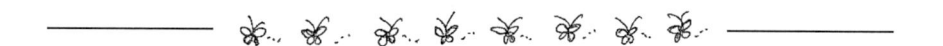

I. The Man and His Poems

Du Guoqing (1941-), born in Fengyuan, Taichung, graduated from the Department of Foreign Languages and Literature of National Taiwan University, received a Master's degree in Japanese Literature from Kansai Gakuin University, Japan, and a doctorate in Chinese Literature from Stanford University. He was a professor in the Department of East Asian Languages and Cultures at the University of California, Santa Barbara, and was one of the founders of the journal *Li Poetry*. He has written many poetry collections, reviews, translations, etc., and has won many honors, including the Zhongxing Literature and Art Award, the Shili Society Translation Award, and the Council for Cultural Affairs Translation Achievement Award.

Du Guoqing's early poems focused on the concrete expression of subjective emotions. They emphasized the authenticity of images. Sometimes he was inspired and touched by a certain image, which caused the outpouring of poetic ideas and brought them into play on the themes of life and human nature. He was also good at arranging a group of images that were closely related in meaning, and vividly expressed the artistic techniques of gentle, passionate, heavy, lingering, ironic or grand situations, thereby making the rhythm of images novel while showing the poet's mind and hand. After his middle age, he began to explore secluded places and expressed his feelings in mountains and rivers. He wrote many landscape poems, poems of feelings or cultural reflections, all of which reflected the poet's wonderful ideas.

II. Analysis of excellent works

The so-called image rhythm is the rhythmic relationship between images. It can be divided into dynamic rhythm (i.e. the rhythm of the movement of the image itself), transition rhythm (i.e. the transition relationship from one image to another) and density rhythm (referring to the number of images in a poem or a sentence) according to the literary style of line arrangement. Indeed, poetry is the most rhythmic language art. Through the poet's imagination, the visual image is rhythmic, and the emotion is used to achieve harmony with nature. Then, all the unspeakable feelings will instantly touch the reader's heart. Du Guoqing grew up in Taiwan, and the history of his hometown is in his blood. After graduating from university, he went to Japan and the United States to study. Therefore, his poetry has the "academic intellectual approach". In essence, his poetry is both lyrical art and spatial art, and both rely on the inner rhythm to reflect the subjective changes of space to convey the poet's instantaneous and eternal life perception. It can be said that rhythm and rhyme are the life of his poetry, which can awaken the reader's corresponding imagery. It is precisely the suggestion of this objective image that can evoke the sense of spatial picture and the association of aesthetics. Like this early work "Forget-me-not":

> She sent me a forget-me-not from afar.
> The blue flower curls contain
> Ruirui's blessings.
> I planted the only blessing she could give me
> in the depths of my heart.
> Every time the new moon hangs on the mountain peak in the valley,
> the silver spoon awakens the memories of the mountain journey.
> Every night when the wind blows the weeping willows,
> her graceful and charming figure floats
> in the long river of my thoughts.

In this way, the forget-me-not took root in my heart.
I brewed blood with my tears of sorrow under the sunset,
and used blood to nourish this exotic flower.
Its bloodthirsty roots soon spread into
a fine red and blue net, catching my heart.
The small flowers change color with the joy and sorrow in my heart.
The graceful branches and leaves grow with the throbbing of my heart.
When my heart is covered with the moss of days
Ah, my heart has become a beautiful bonsai in the garden of love that no one can see
So, holding the blessing that she can only give me
When I lie among the weeds, tears and blood flow
My heart has decayed, this forget-me-not
Is it still swaying alone in the evening breeze
Declaring my farewell words to the world
Is it mourning for my empty happiness for her
Then, regretfully — withered — withered —

Here, the transformation of images has shown the leap of time and space. The rhythm of the poem is fast, but the emotion is like a soft slow version, and the melody is extremely beautiful. Among them, forget-me-nots become blessings, thoughts become long rivers, and the years pass by in a flash. Another example is the image poem "Sacrifice" written in 1969, whose imagery is directed downward, often accompanied by sadness and depression:

On the Weedy Hill

Who wants to awaken this desolate silence
To offer a bouquet of flowers to commemorate love
Youth and
The burnt
Ancient idol
The illustration
Wearing black clothes and
The widow who weeps in secret
Takes her hand to wipe her tearful face
Attracting passers-by

First, the sadness, sorrow, and unbearable mood evoked by "On the Weedy Hill" is consistent with the bleak and helpless emotional tone of the memorial ceremony. Then, the arranged words are like a raised grass tomb in a funeral ceremony, with a pair of candles on each side, and the relatives and friends standing along the side are also silently facing the dead soul, infinitely mourning. The widow who is crying quietly and wiping away her tears conveys a painful tragic atmosphere. Reading this poem, our heads will involuntarily droop sadly.

The poem "Homesickness" consists of 20 sentences, each sentence is linked with imagery, and each sentence is like a chain, one section after another: "The vast yellow earth field beside Dajia River / Since ancient times, there have been three gourd-shaped earth mounds / Legend has it that the mouths of the three gourd mounds / often emit white smoke from sunrise to sunset / / The sun shines into these three gourds / Therefore, nearby villages often have fires / So the ancients dug a river through it / Flowers and plants grew on the dry soil of the gourds / In order to pray to God to bless this good feng shui / The ancients People built a land temple under the pier. / Old people often played the violin or sang in front of the temple. / Roosters and hens often came to defecate or urinate. // In front of the temple, the suppressed and sad sound of the guqin was heard. / Several children played with colorful cards. / Princess Changfan's eyes were covered with chicken shit, / but she turned over Zhuge's eight formations with one hand. // Childhood was covered with colorful cards, / spinning again and again on the wheel of memories. / The heart of the young man was filled with the warmth of his hometown. / Nostalgia was flowing through it like a river in his hometown."

Overall, the image density of this poem is large and its rhythm changes quickly. The poem describes the leisurely and contented, harmonious and natural emotions of childhood life, which are very consistent; it shines in the exploration of memories. The poet transforms the sound of the guqin into visual images, and then superimposes them with scenes such as an old man playing the guqin in front of the temple, playing cards, and children reading storybooks, giving people a feeling of nostalgia. These images are tightly superimposed with "the wheel of memories" and "rotation", which strengthens the poetic factors in the poem and makes the condensation of nostalgia more prominent.

Next, the poem "Rat" gives people a fast and fierce rhythm. He visualizes the "rats walking rampant" by overlapping the characters "teeth and claws" to present the poet's wandering and purification process:

> Teeth and claws teeth claws teeth claws teeth claws teeth claws teeth claws teeth claws teeth claws teeth claws
> As long as the tree has bark, the grain has shell, and the body has a coffin
> As long as humans have food
> Teeth and claws teeth claws teeth claws teeth claws teeth claws teeth claws teeth claws teeth claws teeth claws
> As long as there are stems underground, there is food in the warehouse, and the rotting corpse still has bones
> As long as we are still alive
> On this earth, we protest
> Humanity accuses us of being the thieves of humanity
> On this earth, we accuse
> Humanity hinders our freedom to cross the street
> Affecting our joy of reproduction
> On this earth, if there is still Mr. De
> We are willing to come out in the daytime
> and compete with all mammals

In a sense, the poet is like a wise man who is thinking in a mysterious way. This poem is in a rotating motion with great power, conveying the oppressive and embarrassing situation and thoughts of the lower-class people. The hidden meaning is: some government officials are corrupt, counterfeit goods are rampant in business, and fraud cases are everywhere in society, making the public security and environment extremely bad. But no one knows how to prevent and prohibit it. The law and order are corrupted but no one knows how to repair it, and a lot of resources are wasted in vain. The poet expresses his "injustice" and ridicule by standing on the side of the disadvantaged group. Finally, I recommend the image poem "Spider". The spider's movement in the poem is slow, such as "wearing a black robe and sitting cross-legged", "crouching" and "waiting" silently, reflecting the spider's calm and unhurried figure:

> The spider holding a rose petal and waiting
> The spider wearing a black robe and sitting cross-legged
> The lonely back of the crouching spider

> Guarding with shriveled and rigid limbs
> A square city with a moldy stomach
> Imprisoned in the dark world, chewing under the city wall
> The corpses of many mosquitoes wearing black glasses
> A self-centered dictator
> With blood-stained and numb limbs Guarding

> Spider Crouching Pretending to be virtuous
> Spider Waiting Weaving seductive lies
> Spider Sitting cross-legged Contemplating the value of hypocrisy

Although spiders are often used as a symbol in art and mythology, representing various combinations of patience, cruelty and creativity, the poet uses the image of spiders through the images arranged by words, and uses the natural form and characteristics of spiders to show their alert, cunning and even arrogant diversity, which makes people feel novel and interesting. In fact, the fast-changing world outside, like a kaleidoscope, only exacerbates their inner loneliness. In the sentence, the most concave part in the middle is the spider's mouthparts, with two short tentacles next to it; and its cold sitting cross-legged draws the contradictory lines of the spider's pain and conquest. The visual stimulation of the whole picture is so sharp that it is unforgettable.

III. Du Guoqing: The time and space philosopher of the poetry garden

Du Guoqing is a scholar who actively promotes Taiwanese literature. He has devoted his life to the recognition of the value of literature and poetry creation. He also plans to host the publication of the "Taiwanese Literature English Translation Series", which is rare among overseas poets. This may be a spiritual manifestation shared by intellectuals, and it also shows the tireless academic pursuit of a scholar. His poems are widely drawn from cultural relics, strange mountains and rivers, and scenery, expressing local feelings. Generally speaking, they are very intentional, can present a vivid color of the times, and inspire people's reverie. He is a poet who stands at the intersection of Chinese and Western cultures, but he never forgets his roots; his image poems are also groundbreaking in poetry research papers, and he is also a time-space philosopher with world characteristics. This time-space can be different time-spaces in reality, different time-spaces in psychology, or time-spaces where reality and psychology intersect; and Du Guoqing's ability is reflected in the free artistic expression achieved in these time-spaces. The philosopher said: "I think, therefore I am." His philosophical thoughts on life are often presented in image language, and the rhythm of the sentence is as continuous as the river. If you read it carefully, you can appreciate his pursuit of lost innocence, his reflection on literature, and his perspective on Taiwan.

— Written on November 1, 2011.

【Published in Taiwan's *Li Poetry*, Issue 290, August 15, 2012.】

20 時空的哲人——淺析林亨泰的詩歌藝術
Space-time Philosopher: Brief Analysis of Lin Hengtai's Poetic Art

一、傳略

　　林亨泰（1924- ），彰化縣北斗鎮人，國立臺灣師範大學教育系畢業，退休教師。日據時代就開始創作，戰後用中文寫詩；崇尚言簡而意賅，詩風有音樂性、繪畫和思想性，以及政治批判等性質。此外，他的詩論，中鋒重筆，獨具見解。著有詩集《靈魂の產生》（日文詩集，中文《靈魂的啼聲》）、《長的咽喉》、《林亨泰詩集》、《爪痕集》、《跨不過的歷史》；詩論集《現代詩的基本精神：論真摯性》，教育論著《JS 布魯那的教育理論》，譯有法國馬洛所著的《保羅‧梵樂希的方法序說》等多種。詩作及評論對台灣現代詩史影響深遠，從中反映出文學探索前進的鮮明足跡，也是記錄其思想感情的真實寫照。曾獲得「國家文藝獎」等殊榮。

　　在臺灣詩壇上，林亨泰是位有風骨又特兀的重要詩人，詩齡已超過 60 年。早年白色恐怖時期，有過熱血青年的執著追求與悲哀；後來在民主意識普遍抬頭的推動下，他昂然奮起，善用巧思和擬人法來暗諷時政。於 1948 年加入「銀鈴會」、1955 年加入台灣詩壇「現代派」成員，1964 年為笠詩社發起人之一，也是《笠》詩社首任主編。晚年，年逾八旬中風後，記憶開始退化，但仍熱切地夢想把臺灣的奮鬥史透過自傳式文體記錄成書。這是林亨泰對臺灣文學發展的終極關懷，相應地增加了作品的社會意義；如彈響心靈的琴師，發揮著最高的效能和生命，因而贏得了許多讀者的掌聲。

二、詩選賞析

　　林亨泰性穎神澈，見識卓越；詩歌音調和諧，語言冷靜。其詩歌藝術的思想內容，大致有三方面：

　　其一，是在國民黨一黨專政時期的歷史關頭，他以詩的號角，挺身入世，向人民發出呼喚，寫下一段又一段跨時代的故事，如〈群眾〉中的句子，正是時代的強音：

青苔　看透一切地
坐在石頭上　久矣
從雨滴
吸吮營養之後　久矣

在陽光不到的陰影裡
綠色的圖案從暗秘的生活中　偷偷製造著
成千上萬無窮無盡

把護城河著色
把城門包圍把牆壁攀登
把兵營甍瓦覆沒
青苔　終於燃燒了起來[1]

　　228事件，曾伏下了社會與國家對立的狀態；詩人處在危急關頭，切身的感受到，詩的神聖職責即是為真理正義而吶喊。於是在悲憤下，描摹出官兵以強壓對抗民變，終導致臺灣人民心中燃起反抗的怒火。林亨泰的詩，之所以能跨越時空的界限，晚年仍有堅強的意志力；其原因就在於他是詩人真情實感的迸發，對人民的苦難感同身受，這樣的現實書寫，自然能喚起讀者情感上的強烈共鳴。而過去苦澀的回憶，終能迎接光明的未來。再如〈一黨制〉中寫道：「桌子上／玩具鋼琴／／白鍵／黑鍵／／只有／一音」。內裡以調侃的語氣，卻蘊藏著勇於批判國民黨的一黨專政。林亨泰的潛意識裡有著改造社會的熱情和知識份子的良知。他反對強權，冀望把自由、民主的理念傳遞給社會；他散播詩的種子，期待公義得以發揚。詩人對白色恐怖時期的青年學生的思想生活是比較瞭解的，因而，他的一些詩作是針對突發性的社會事件而激發。如〈賴皮狗〉，是以現實主義的筆觸，暗諷當時某些中央民意代表老而不退的行徑。這首詩一出現，震動了整個詩壇，由於詩人是和廣大人民共同著呼吸，因而引起了迴響，具深刻的現實意義：

---

[1] 〈群眾〉寫於1947年228事件發生後不久的日文詩，當時並沒有立即發表，是連同其他三首同期所寫成的詩作〈黎明〉、〈想法〉、〈溶化的風景〉，一起刊登在1979年由日本北原政吉所編的《台灣現代詩集》當中，後來由呂興昌教授以中文與台語進行翻譯。林斤力著，福爾摩沙詩哲林亨泰，〈臺北：印刻，2007〉，頁78。

樓梯的邏輯
只有
要上，就上去
要下，就下來

邏輯的樓梯
只能
不上，就該下
不下，就該上

可是這隻獸
只想一直在那裡
不上，也不下

　　林亨泰歷經 1948 年台師大四六事件[2]後，他的詩作彷彿經過雷電轟出而更堅韌；詩作也隱藏著抗議之聲，更流露出一種逐漸成熟的睿哲。詩，是藝術。他曾說：「不論什麼時代，走過怎樣的歷史，『現實』並不是在無意義的時間中，漫無目標地飛蕩，任自漂流。『現實』是那內化成為自己的呼吸、感覺以及認識的總和。而詩，是透過這些現實的諸多事件，融會於自己的身體感官，而逐漸化形、成長。」[3]由此而知，林亨泰早期的詩藝概括出了臺灣人民充滿流汗的辛勤與韌性、或痛苦的蛻變，能展現出對社會現實的沉重憂患。

　　其二，以現代派思想為主流的林亨泰，善用西方美學的審美觀和用詩的語言突出表達現代性。詩中常夾帶著對人與土地的鄉土情懷，崇尚從細微中著墨，從自然界引發出對人生或社會的感悟。如 35 歲寫下這首有價值的小詩〈風景之二〉，理意暢流，所寓情趣甚多，自有一家的韻味：

---

[2] 四六事件起於以師大為主體，串聯臺大所發起要求提高公費待遇的「反飢餓鬥爭」為主題的學生運動，校園戒嚴也正式啟動。1995 年，臺大與師大的八個改革派社團共同發起四六事件平反運動。直到 2000 年 12 月 25 日，《戒嚴時期不當叛亂暨匪諜審判案件補償條例》進行修正，將四六事件受難者列入適用此條例的對象，並由教育部向受難者家屬道歉。

[3] 林斤力著，福爾摩沙詩哲林亨泰，臺北：印刻，2007，頁 123。

防風林　的
外邊　還有
防風林　的
外邊　還有
防風林　的
外邊　還有

然而海　以及波的羅列
然而海　以及波的羅列

　　詩的創作背景是詩人在溪湖到二林的途中坐在巴士上完成的。這裡，林亨泰運用了強烈的現代意識以及現代主義的一些藝術手法相結合，為隱喻、通感和幻覺。而驚奇、意外也是詩的動力之一；不但體現了一種空靈的寂靜，隱約可聞車窗外的陣陣風聲。韵節也給人一種音樂美，呈現出中西文化合璧的風貌。其中，詩人以一種超現實的藝術觸覺使防風林的物象得以變形而有層叠復沓的林相景致；而後兩行海浪的空間叠景得既真切又有層次感。此詩從防風林引起一系列心靈的變異感覺，旨在揭示戒嚴年代臺灣人民渴求突破心靈禁錮和詩人內心深處那種對廣闊的馳騁天地的一種隱祕的願望。另一首〈進香團〉，恰恰表現了林亨泰的創作觀裡具符號詩、圖象詩等多姿的風格美的一個側面，詩情澎湃，且形象性強，給人一種清新悅目的審美感受：

旗——
▼　黃
▼　紅
▼　青

善男 1　拿著三角形
善男 2　拿著四角形

香束
燭臺
~~~~■
~~~~■

信女 1　拿著三角形
信女 2　拿著四角形

在臺灣諸多的民間信仰中，最主要的是媽祖文化，尤以大甲媽祖節慶文化對臺海兩岸居民生活、文化與精神層面上的影響相當的根深蒂固。從詩的全意看，詩人把對於信仰活動和祭儀的形象組成了雄渾的詩音，使人從視覺上的感受轉化為聽覺的意象。彷彿看到了繞境進香的一支支令旗的黃色方形旗幟，還有各種旗幟於長長的隊伍中，街道兩旁夾雜的當地民眾也擺設香案，恭迎神明的熱鬧。那哨角鑼鼓陣的壯容，充沛淋漓地再現了宗教信仰的威力，然而這威力或是詩人對於兩岸政治對峙、文化交流熱絡的反思；不僅象徵意味濃厚，畫面的藝術魅力，使景象的流動也叫人感動。

　　其三，林亨泰於笠詩社擔任首任主編之際，已走過現代派影響，並大量發表中文詩。由於詩人在中學以前完全接受日本教育，於臺灣師範學院教育系〈今校名改稱臺師大〉就讀時才開始接觸國語；故而，早期的詩都是以日文書寫。在銀鈴會《潮流》復刊後，他開始嘗試以中文寫詩。此階段詩人保持著心態的青春，更重視心靈的感受和意象的創造。他開始走向社會寫實、關懷本土路線，成為跨越語言的一代中，一個推展臺灣詩學的鐵軍。如〈日入而息〉，就洋溢著詩人以悲憫的眼光觀察當時的社會現實；它標誌著詩人的鄉土意識的新發展：

　　　　與工作等長的
　　　　太陽的時間
　　　　收拾在牛車上

　　　　杓柄與杓柄
　　　　在水肥桶裡
　　　　交叉著手
　　　　咯登　嘩啦嘩啦
　　　　嘩啦　咯登咯登
　　　　穿過　黃昏
　　　　回來
　　　　了

　　將早期的農業社會耕農辛勤的背影與忙於水肥糞便的桶子的村農單純簡樸的生活形象，成功地表現出本土化的詩歌特色。林亨泰對鄉土詩的藝術主張是在土地的依托與哺育下，而對農民的質樸善良有了較深切的情感。他一方面肯定了鄉土精神的閃光面，唱出了一曲曲對土地的戀歌；一方面他的鄉土詩見證著早期臺灣農村生活多保留樸真、寂靜的歌頌。其對人生的感悟，也在抒情與敘事的結合上力求融合為一的境界。藝術上由寫實到寫意的聚變，也即是說，詩人從現實性描寫轉向一種永恆性追求。如〈小溪〉，寫得那樣深邃又空濛，深具哲思：

    寂靜的日子
    水清澄
    河底砂上
    水靜止

    魚
    和
    魚

    寂靜的日子
    風透明
    河畔堤上
    風凝固

    草
    和
    草

    詩人以腳代筆向小溪步行而去⋯若雲水飄逸，尋求心靈的靜音。詩中第二、四段，在韻律上音樂感是很強的；不僅是意象的跳躍，證明詩人思路和視野的開闊，而且是感覺挪移的好例證，它把詩人在自然的靜穆中，對時事的慨嘆等心理活動串在一起，造成一種神秘的美感。正如希臘詩人挨利蒂斯（Odysseas Elytis，1911-1996）曾說：「我們所指的美，甚至在光明大放中也能只保持其神秘，只有它有這種惑人的光彩。」[4]回顧林亨泰詩創作的歷程，他從大學時代便與詩結下了不解之緣；教書後，讀詩寫詩、寫詩論或譯作，都升騰出一種火一般的熱情，也閃爍著藝術個性的光

---

[4] 楊匡漢、劉福春編，《西方現代詩論》，廣州市：花城出版社，1988年，頁 650 頁。

彩。做為一個時空間的哲人與以現實主義思想為中心的林亨泰，晚年病中的他，仍為喜愛他的詩的許多讀者提供了可貴的啟示。

三、小結：林亨泰詩藝的美學價值

　　林亨泰才氣豪邁，詩尤敏捷，落筆立就，堪稱為才子。50年代是林亨泰創作的成名期，他的詩具有豐富的歷史內涵，其早期之作中著重於現實批判是其詩歌的重要指向；然而，由於加入現代詩社後，時空的差異，使他對人民思想及文化有了更透徹的瞭解，以語言的機智和巧妙組合，造成獨特的藝術效果。後來又加入《笠》詩人的階段，決定以對本土文化的認同，寫出時代的滄桑變化。詩人的生命律動，是對土地與人民的愛，絕大部份也反映了他個人生活美學的哲思，這是對其人品詩品比較客觀的評價。筆者以為，林亨泰詩藝風格美的成因有二：

（一）審美價值。詩歌意象是詩人主觀情志的具象載體，一首好的現實主義詩歌能通過意象引讀者進入詩所描寫的客觀環境中，讓人感受到當時的情況。林亨泰的諸多佳作，恰恰具備了語言美、音樂美、建築美及符號美的審美內涵；也正因有這些原素的有機組合才能打動讀者的心弦。

（二）歷史價值。林亨泰的部份詩作既是詩也是歷史的縮影或對社會現實的真實寫照。但他詩中的意象具有創新性，不用陳言，能把感覺化成鮮活的具象。不僅以詩言志抒懷，還善以暗諷手法記錄下事件的真相，無形中也提供了研究史學者有力的依據，詩行間隱含著對臺灣人民悲憫的感慨。

　　如上所述，從美學的角度加以分析，林亨泰的詩，有些是縱手而成的即興詩，有些是觸物興懷的「苦吟」，有些是對現實社會的控訴……公平地說，其詩絕大部份是精闢而獨到的，才能卓然自成一家，有極高的參考價值。詩人的本性把詩藝的一切魅力和對臺灣人民的政治智慧及尊嚴結合起來，既能發人深思，又深具力量。細嚼其詩，同樣也是一種美的吹拂；其詩作受到文壇的高度肯定，這是毋庸置疑的。

－2011.9.2 作

【刊於臺灣台北的《全國新書資訊月刊》，2012年9月，第165期，頁30-35。】

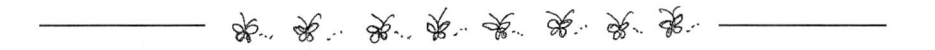

I. Biography

　　Lin Hengtai (1924-), a native of Beidou Town, Changhua County, graduated from the Department of Education at National Taiwan Normal University, and is a retired teacher. He began to create during the Japanese occupation and wrote poetry in Chinese after the war. He advocates simplicity and richness of meaning, and his poetry style has musical, pictorial, ideological, and politically critical characteristics. In addition, his poetry theory is sharp and has unique insights. He has written poetry collections such as *The Birth of the Soul* (Japanese poetry collection, *The Cry of the Soul* in Chinese), *The Long Throat*, *Lin Hengtai Poetry Collection*, *Claw Marks Collection*, and *History That Cannot Be Crossed*; poetry theory collection *The Basic Spirit of Modern Poetry: On Authenticity*, educational theory *The Educational Theory of JS Bruner*, and translated *Preface to Paul Van Lech's Method* by French Malot. His poems and reviews have had a profound impact on the history of modern poetry in Taiwan, reflecting the clear footprints of literary exploration and progress, and are also a true portrayal of his thoughts and feelings. He has won the "National Arts Award" and other honors.

　　In the Taiwanese poetry circle, Lin Hengtai is an important poet with style and uniqueness, and he has been a poet for more than 60 years. In the early years of the White Terror, he had the persistent pursuit and sorrow of a passionate young man; later, driven by the general rise of democratic consciousness, he rose up and used ingenuity and personification to satirize current affairs. He joined the "Silver Bell Association" in 1948 and the "Modern School" of Taiwanese poetry in 1955. In 1964, he was one of the founders of the Li Poetry Society and the first editor-in-chief of the Li Poetry Society. In his later years, after a stroke in his 80s, his memory began to deteriorate, but he still ardently dreamed of recording Taiwan's struggle history in an autobiographical style. This is Lin Hengtai's ultimate concern for the development of Taiwanese literature, which correspondingly increases the social significance of his works; like a musician who plays the zither that resonates with the soul, he exerts the highest efficiency and vitality, thus winning the applause of many readers.

II. Poetry Appreciation

Lin Hengtai has a clear mind and outstanding insight; his poems have harmonious tones and calm language. The ideological content of his poetry art can be roughly divided into three aspects:

First, at the historical juncture of the Kuomintang's one-party dictatorship, he stepped into the world with the trumpet of poetry, called on the people, and wrote one cross-era story after another, such as the sentence in "The Crowd"[5], which is the strong voice of the times:

> Moss sees through everything
> Sitting on the stone for a long time
> From the raindrops
> After sucking nutrients for a long time
> In the shadows where the sun cannot reach
> Green patterns are secretly created from the secret life
> Thousands and thousands of endless
> Coloring the moat
> Surrounding the city gates and climbing the walls
> Covering the roof tiles of the barracks
> Moss finally burned up

The 228 Incident had laid the foundation for the confrontation between society and the country. The poet was in a critical moment and felt that the sacred duty of poetry was to cry out for truth and

---

[5] "The Crowd" was written in Japanese shortly after the February 28 Incident in 1947. It was not published immediately at the time. It was published together with three other poems written at the same time, "Dawn", "Thoughts", and "Melting Scenery", in the *Taiwan Modern Poetry Collection* edited by Japanese Kitahara Masayoshi in 1979. Later, Professor Lu Xingchang translated it into Chinese and Taiwanese. Lin Jinli, Formosa Poet and Philosopher Lin Hengtai, Taipei: Yinke, 2007, p. 78.

justice. So in grief and anger, he depicted the officers and soldiers using coercion to resist the civil unrest, which eventually led to the anger of resistance in the hearts of the Taiwanese people. The reason why Lin Hengtai's poetry can transcend the boundaries of time and space and still have strong willpower in his later years is that it is an outburst of the poet's true feelings and empathy for the suffering of the people. Such realistic writing can naturally arouse strong emotional resonance in readers. And the bitter memories of the past can finally usher in a bright future. For example, in "One-Party System", it is written: "On the table/toy piano//white keys//black keys//only/one note." The tone of his poems is ironic, but it contains the courage to criticize the KMT's one-party dictatorship. Lin Hengtai's subconscious mind has the passion to reform society and the conscience of an intellectual. He opposes power and hopes to pass on the ideas of freedom and democracy to society; he spreads the seeds of poetry and hopes that justice can be promoted. The poet has a better understanding of the ideological life of young students during the White Terror period, so some of his poems are inspired by sudden social events. For example, "Lazy Dog" is written in a realistic style, secretly satirizing the behavior of some central representatives of public opinion who are old but still unwilling to retire. As soon as this poem appeared, it shook the entire poetry world. Since the poet was breathing together with the masses, it caused an echo and had a profound realistic meaning:

> The logic of the stairs
> Only
> To go up, go up
> To go down, go down
> The logical stairs
> Can only
> If you don't go up, you should go down
> If you don't go down, you should go up
> But this beast
> Just wants to stay there
> Neither go up, nor go down

After Lin Hengtai experienced the April 6th Incident at National Taiwan Normal University in 1948[6], his poems seemed to be more resilient after being struck by thunder and lightning; his poems also concealed the voice of protest and revealed a kind of gradually mature wisdom. Poetry is art. He once said: "No matter what era or what history we have gone through, 'reality' is not flying aimlessly in meaningless time. 'Reality' is the sum of breathing, feeling and cognition that is internalized into oneself. Poetry is gradually formed and grown through the many events of these realities and the integration into one's own body senses."[7] From this, we can know that Lin Hengtai's early poetry art summarizes the hard work and resilience of the Taiwanese people, or the painful metamorphosis, and can show the heavy worries about social reality.

Second, Lin Hengtai, who takes modernist thought as the mainstream, is good at using the aesthetics of Western aesthetics and poetic language to highlight the expression of modernity. Poems often carry a nostalgic feeling for people and land, advocating to write from the details, and to draw insights into life or society from nature. For example, this valuable little poem "Landscape No. 2" written at the age of 35, with a smooth flow of ideas and a lot of interest, has its own charm:

> Outside of the windbreak forest
> Outside of the windbreak forest
> Outside of the windbreak forest
> Outside of the windbreak forest

---

[6] The April 6 Incident started with a student movement led by National Taiwan Normal University, which was linked to the National Taiwan University and demanded an increase in public funding. The campus martial law was officially launched. In 1995, eight reformist societies from National Taiwan University and National Taiwan Normal University jointly launched the April 6 Incident Redress Movement. It was not until December 25, 2000 that the "Regulations on Compensation for Improper Rebellion and Espionage Trials during the Martial Law Period" was amended to include the victims of the April 6 Incident in the applicable scope of this regulation, and the Ministry of Education apologized to the victims' families.

[7] Lin Jinli, *Formosa Poet Lin Hengtai*, Taipei: Ink, 2007, p. 123.

However, the sea and the waves are listed
However, the sea and the waves are listed

The background of the poem was that the poet was sitting on the bus on the way from Xihu to Erlin. Here, Lin Hengtai used a strong modern consciousness and some modernist artistic techniques to combine metaphors, synaesthesia and hallucinations. Surprise and surprise are also one of the driving forces of the poem. It not only reflects a kind of ethereal silence, but also the sound of wind can be heard faintly outside the car window. The rhythm also gives people a kind of musical beauty, presenting a combination of Chinese and Western cultures. Among them, the poet uses a surreal artistic touch to transform the image of the windbreak forest into a layered and repeated forest landscape; and then the spatial superposition of the two lines of waves is both real and layered. This poem evokes a series of spiritual changes from the windbreak forest, aiming to reveal the Taiwanese people's desire to break through the spiritual confinement during the martial law era and the poet's secret desire for a vast world of galloping deep in his heart. Another poem, "The Pilgrimage Group", precisely shows the beauty of Lin Hengtai's creation concept, which has a variety of styles such as symbolic poetry and image poetry. It is full of poetic emotion and strong image, giving people a refreshing and pleasing aesthetic feeling:

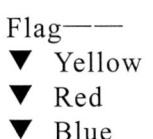

Flag——
▼ Yellow
▼ Red
▼ Blue

Good man 1　　Holding a triangle
Good man 2　　Holding a quadrilateral

Incense bundle
Candle stand
~~~~■
~~~~■

Believers 1　　Holding a triangle
Believers 2　　Holding a quadrilateral

Among the many folk beliefs in Taiwan, the most important one is Mazu culture, especially the Dajia Mazu Festival culture, which has a deep-rooted influence on the lives, culture and spiritual levels of residents on both sides of the Taiwan Strait. From the overall meaning of the poem, the poet has combined the images of religious activities and rituals into a majestic poetic sound, which transforms people's visual feelings into auditory images. It seems that you can see the yellow square flags of the pilgrims, and various flags in the long procession. The local people on both sides of the street also set up incense tables to welcome the gods. The magnificent appearance of the whistle, horn, gong and drum array fully reproduces the power of religious belief. However, this power may be the poet's reflection on the political confrontation and cultural exchanges between the two sides of the Taiwan Strait; not only is the symbolism strong, but the artistic charm of the picture also makes the flow of the scene touching.

Third, when Lin Hengtai served as the first editor-in-chief of Lishishe, he had already gone beyond the influence of modernism and published a large number of Chinese poems. Since the poet received a complete Japanese education before junior high school, he only began to come into contact with Mandarin when he was studying in the Department of Education of Taiwan Normal College (now renamed National Taiwan Normal University); therefore, his early poems were all written in Japanese. After the resumption of publication of Ginlinghui's "Chaoliu", he began to try to write poems in Chinese. During this period, the poet maintained a youthful state of mind and paid more attention to the feelings of the mind and the creation of images. He began to move towards social realism and caring about the local line, becoming a strong soldier in promoting Taiwanese poetry in a generation that transcends languages. For example, "Rest at Sunset" is full of the poet's observation of the social reality of the time with a sad eye; it marks the new development of the poet's rural consciousness:

> The time of the sun, which is as long as the work, is collected on the ox cart
>
> The handle of the scoop and the handle of the scoop
> In the bucket of water and fertilizer,
> Crossing hands,

Rumble, clatter, clatter
Rumble, clatter, clatter
Through the dusk,
Come back

The hard-working backs of the farmers in the early agricultural society and the simple and plain life images of the peasants busy with buckets of water, fertilizer and feces successfully express the localized poetic characteristics. Lin Hengtai's artistic proposition for rural poetry is that he has a deeper feeling for the simplicity and kindness of the farmers under the support and nourishment of the land. On the one hand, he affirmed the shining side of the rural spirit and sang a love song for the land; on the other hand, his rural poetry witnessed that early Taiwanese rural life mostly retained simple and quiet praises. His perception of life also strives to merge lyricism and narrative into one. The fusion from realism to impressionism in art, that is, the poet turned from realistic description to a pursuit of eternity. For example, "The Stream" is written so profoundly and ethereal, full of philosophical thoughts:

Silent Days
Water is clear
On the riverbed sand
Water is still

Fish
and
Fish

Silent Days
Wind is transparent
On the riverbank
Wind is frozen

Grass
and
Grass

The poet walks towards the stream with his feet as a pen...like clouds and water floating, seeking the silence of the soul. The second and fourth paragraphs of the poem have a strong sense of musicality in terms of rhythm; not only do the leaps in imagery demonstrate the poet's broad thinking and vision, but they are also a good example of the transfer of feelings. They string together the poet's psychological activities such as his lamentations about current affairs in the tranquility of nature, creating a mysterious sense of beauty. As the Greek poet Odysseas Elytis (1911-1996) once said, "The beauty we refer to can remain mysterious even in the midst of the bright light, and only it has this enchanting brilliance."[8] Looking back on the course of Lin Hengtai's poetry creation, he has had an indissoluble bond with poetry since his college days; after teaching, he has been reading and writing poetry, writing poetry theory or translating, all of which have risen with a fiery passion and shone with the brilliance of artistic personality. As a philosopher of time and space and centered on realism, Lin Hengtai, in his later years of illness, still provided valuable inspiration to many readers who loved his poetry.

III. Summary: The aesthetic value of Lin Hengtai's poetry

Lin Hengtai is a man of great talent, and his poems are particularly agile. He can write poems as soon as he puts pen to paper, and he can be called a talented person. The 1950s was the period when Lin Hengtai became famous. His poems have rich historical connotations. His early works focused on the criticism of reality, which was an important direction of his poems. However, after joining the Modern Poetry Society, the difference in time and space gave him a more thorough understanding of people's thoughts and culture, and he created unique artistic effects with the wit and clever combination of language. Later, he joined the stage of the poets of *Li*, and decided to write about the vicissitudes of the times with his recognition of local culture. The rhythm of the poet's life is the love for the land and the people, and most of it also reflects his personal philosophy of life aesthetics, which is a relatively objective evaluation of his character and poetry. The author believes that there are two reasons for the beauty of Lin Hengtai's poetry style:

---

[8] Yang Kuanghan and Liu Fuchun, eds., *Western Modern Poetry*, Guangzhou: Huacheng Publishing House, 1988, p. 650.

1. Aesthetic value. Poetic imagery is a concrete carrier of the poet's subjective emotions. A good realist poem can lead readers into the objective environment described in the poem through imagery, allowing people to feel the situation at that time. Many of Lin Hengtai's masterpieces have the aesthetic connotations of linguistic beauty, musical beauty, architectural beauty and symbolic beauty; it is precisely because of the organic combination of these elements that they can touch the heartstrings of readers.

2. Historical value. Some of Lin Hengtai's poems are both poems and microcosms of history or true portrayals of social reality. However, the imagery in his poems is innovative, and without exposition, he can turn feelings into vivid concrete images. Not only does he express his feelings through poetry, but he also records the truth of events with irony, which invisibly provides a strong basis for historians. The lines of poetry contain a feeling of sadness for the Taiwanese people.

As mentioned above, from an aesthetic perspective, some of Lin Hengtai's poems are impromptu poems, some are "painstaking poems" inspired by things, and some are complaints about the real society... To be fair, most of his poems are insightful and unique, which makes him stand out and have a high reference value. The poet's nature combines all the charm of poetry with the political wisdom and dignity of the Taiwanese people, which is both thought-provoking and powerful. Chewing on his poems is also a kind of beautiful breeze; there is no doubt that his poems are highly recognized by the literary world.

—Written on September 2, 2011.

21 崇高的樸素——讀《高準游踪散紀》
Sublime Simplicity: Reading *Gao Zhun's Travel Notes*

一、孤松的風範

高準（1938- ），上海金山張堰人，23歲畢業於國立臺灣大學，中國文化研究所碩士。赴美國、澳大利亞悉尼大學進修，悉尼大學東方學系博士班結業。獲選為英國劍橋大學副院士，曾任悉尼大學高級講師、美國柏克萊加州大學研究員、美國愛荷華大學國際榮譽作家，曾任中國文化大學教授，詩潮詩社社長兼主編等，詩作入選《百年中國文學經典》等數十種選集，現自行寫作。高準一生樸實無華，目光堅定無私。雖然他的孤高性格使他很孤立，但這反而使他把精力都用在學養上；除了寫詩、散文，也從事教授及出版過文學批評與繪畫史研究等著作。

《高準游踪散紀》是部兼備美學和文史價值的散文著作，能真正從中汲取出思想的寶藏，精湛的文字涵蓋著作者旅遊的意趣及對有關人物的印象；能強調愛國的熱情，對自然現象的多變之美也十分敏感。認真細致地品味其作品，我們便會感受到一個思想者對於人生的體驗與思考；彷彿融入一種抒情的、象徵的優雅風景畫，這也正是作者內心情感的一種幅射，更忠實地表現現實。本書在內涵方面，無論愛國、憂世、愛情、親情、友情，或對動物與生態的關懷與悲憫、對人類前途的感歎、對暴政的抗議、對歷史人物的敬仰、對歷史滄桑的緬懷、以及對山水自然的寫照…，莫不有優美的篇章，使讀者有如臨其境。

二、理性的明晰　似畫的文采

高準的散文題材可謂豐富多樣。如卷一「少年遊」〈春的腳步〉末段所述：「心靈與心靈攜手，飛向無盡的藍天，飛向綿綿的草原，……啊，心靈與心靈擁舞。春日的陽光呀，灑遍了每一片自由的土壤。」其歌詠大自然愉快清新的表現，可以說是高準取之不盡的靈感源泉,也使得詩人的青春姿態躍然紙上!〈霧社廬山記〉是詩人從心靈深處自然迸發出巨大的熱情讚美了廬山:「…這是一面不須拭擦的鏡子,將照澈你疲倦的靈魂;是一個不識榮利的少女,帶給你絢麗而永不破滅的幻想。」在這樣的境界中,我們清晰地看到了一個滿懷浪漫豪情的詩人形象。〈史克蘭溪畔一夜〉的作者進行生動形象的描寫:「…人怎能征服自然呢?征服了自然,就失去了自然。失去了自然的人是什麼呢?怕只是一塊塊污濁的有機體罷了。」文中感情真摯、激昂,他是以一個默默的探索者的姿態進行著與自然的對話,然而又是深沉有力的,也只有這樣的思考才有審美價值。

在卷二的「畫廊散步」裡,高準於旅美期間先後參觀了美國國家美術館、紐約博物館、古根漢博物館,對館內畫展的考察或畫家的評介,以詩性的筆觸標示出對中西藝術論述的一種高度。除瞭解到法國高更(Paul Gauguin)是他心愛的畫家外,作者對畫家何懷碩、劉國松及一起習畫的友人文霽的畫評,均憑借著敏銳的藝術直覺與豐厚的美學底蘊,寫出了具有前瞻性的觀點,文字中可以寫表出空間的形相與色彩。在形式方面,高準則作了更多的嘗試,新詩外也有近體詩,比如卷三的大陸紀遊詠史詩十三題裡,包括五言古體〈訪伯牙台〉等、五言律詩〈登泰山吟〉、七言律詩〈謁大禹陵〉等、七言絕句〈重到西湖二首〉,另還有自創詞體、民歌體、商籟體、雙行體等,亦有多種不同字數的齊言體,可見他是怎樣充分運用了形象思維來表達。

〈燕京散記〉裡,高準走訪北京天安門、北京大學、故宮,登上了長城,情不自禁地想起自己寫過的一首《夢登長城吟》:

千山萬水此登臨,獵獵天風金鐵鳴。
北瞻瀚漠峰如海,南望中原氣象森。
塞草黃沙千載意,振衣長嘯老龍吟。
秦皇莫道功名烈,直欲揮鞭下庫倫!

他的深邃目光抽象地揭示了思古幽情的人生內涵。此外,高準也走向泰山、訪問了山東農學院和泰安師專。然後他朗誦了一首 1969 年底之作〈念故鄉〉,這首詩我在《高準詩集全編》找到了,詩是如此純淨,如此寬廣,使讀者能深入地體認其情感熱度。高準詩歌藝術的淵源是豐富複雜的,這與他所處的時代環境及求學經歷都有密切的關係。出身於書香門第的高準，受過民族傳統文化的薰陶，對童年居住的中國自然有著深厚的情感。那如母親般溫柔的故鄉，直讓作者張開臂膀，直想雀躍奔跑其間了。在最後一段詩裡，他吶喊道：

> 故鄉呀　我喊您的名字　寫你的名字
> 而你是聽不到的　你也看不到我的詩
> 但終究我只有愛你呀愛你
> 因為我血管裡呀也只有你的血液

　　作者將思鄉之情壓抑在心靈深處，忍受著痛苦的情感煎熬。由於他博采古今中西藝術文化，因而融合創造了一個豐富多彩的散文天地。其中，〈念故鄉〉、〈中國萬歲交響曲〉二十多年來為大陸詩壇所歌頌，並於1979-2001年間，由第一版《葵心集》歷經增版及改編四次而成《高準詩集全編》，讚美的呼聲不歇。再如1983年，高準於加州柏克萊寫下〈長江行腳〉末段：「莽莽山河，蒼蒼煙靄，似乎在沉默的等待著，等待著一個新的希望……。」作者將一種愛國的憂思貫穿於浩瀚的宇宙，既抒寫了情感，同時又滲透了理性的認識。

　　另外，卷四裡，高準對先妣事略等文中人物的形象極為用心；其母親擔任前聖瑪利亞女校〈今改名聖約翰技術學院〉董事33年，父親高啟明為著名都市計劃學家，祖父高平子為中國現代天文學的開創者，而外祖父姚光〈或稱石子先生〉，是清末民初的詩人。作者對其撰述都作一番認真的梳理，這是高準對文壇作出的新貢獻。晚年的他，不論生活如何艱辛，創作與閱讀成了能表現崇高和精神自由的手段，如〈悼念一隻小野貓〉：「一隻小野貓，這樣可憐的生存著，卻仍不能久活。…」此文包含著豐富的含義，並將人與自然、死亡與永恆，個人的孤獨與哲思，成功營造出他哀悼野貓之死的哀傷氣氛。其他作品有文學論集、詩集、繪畫史等多種。其散文能表現出浩然開闊的襟懷和清高德操，情感濃郁，總能讓讀者獲得藝術的美感享受或感悟出某種人生哲思。

三、散文之精蘊　敲擊人心

　　《高準游踪散紀》所要傳達的是個人情志的抒發和感情體驗，主要以追緬及行走各地藝文、山水景物，表達出知識份子的覺知，

崇高的樸素——讀《高準游踪散紀》

或蘊涵著情思和感慨；其中穿插於文的舊詩，其藝術性也是作者的匠心所在。如〈讀耶律楚材傳二首〉〈七絕〉之一：

> 治國安邦代有臣，勝殘止殺始難倫；
> 行仁去暴千秋業，青史悠悠唯此人！

高準對蒙古帝國時期隨成吉思汗從軍參政，官至中書令（宰相）的大臣耶律楚材十分崇敬。因耶律楚材對蒙古族的漢化做出了突出貢獻，他數度以仁心勇略化除暴行，使蒙古不再實行屠城之舉，令高準於大陸遊歷其間，特前往謁見耶律公之墓。由此足見高準對歷史人物的理解是具有遠見卓識的。

高準的祖父是國際著名天文學家高平子，1982 年，國際天文學聯合會決議以月球上的一座環形山命名為高平子山。當作者 50 歲返鄉參加高平子百年紀念會於上海、青島兩地舉行後，他順便走訪曲阜，翌年寫下〈謁孔子墓〉，收錄於此書大陸紀遊詠史詩十三題中。詩語氣壯情逸，有智性和藝術性的哲思，在第三段裡寫道：「文化的爝火啊由您而燃亮／代代呵輝耀着是禮樂詩書／您教導著什麼是仁心仁術／惟不憂與不惑能不懼險阻」。作者把孔子悲天憫人的仁者風範及孜孜不倦的精神，盡入詩中，而延續中華文化任務才是高準博大精深的思想內涵。雖然今年已 73 歲的高準，但筆耕不輟，年初傳來正欲出版的《高準游踪散記》裡的一篇〈悼念一隻小野貓〉。在文中，我看到了他生活困窘的一面、與小貓間真情相依偎、人性的光輝與靈魂痛苦的呼喊。今年文藝節收到此書後，在唐山出版社陳隆昊社長的協助下舉辦了發表會於文協，實踐了高準自己的這一理想。

左起：司馬中原、高準、林明理、綠蒂、鍾鼎文、向陽〈陳隆昊攝影於中國文藝協會〉，台北市，2011.6.12，林明理講評於高準新書發表會。
From left: Sima Zhongyuan, Gao Zhun, Lin Mingli, Lu Di, Zhong Dingwen, Xiang Yang (Photographed by Chen Longhao at the Chinese Literature and Art Association), Taipei, 2011.6.12, Lin Mingli's commentary at Gao Zhun's new book launch.

高準一生曾放射過燦爛奪目的光輝，45 歲時，大陸出版過他的詩集，聲噪一時，因為是大陸所出第一本當代臺灣的個人詩集。51 歲時還親赴大陸要求釋放被拘捕的臺灣民歌手侯德健，獲得成功。後以簡樸方式數次隻身到大陸漫遊，足跡遠抵帕米爾高原。他在 39 歲時曾創辦過《詩潮》詩刊，第一集遭人誣陷被查禁，後繼續出版，共出七集，由武漢中國當代作家代表作陳列館所收藏。43 歲訪遊大陸後，他以詩抒發情志，以散文寫出現實人生的真善美及瞻仰中國山河的感慨。這本《高準游踪散記》充分展出他的特殊才學，舊詩或古文皆有音外之韻，象外之旨；文字雅潔，耐人尋味。閱讀時，也有一種靜謐的喜悅、一種敲擊人心的力量。他對愛情期盼著「永恆、純一」，是如此的純粹、堅持，對民族之愛的熱忱，讓人看到了他直想創造光明的內心世界的一面，也看到了文章裡煉意成象的藝術功夫。這種努力飛翔的孤影，恰恰也給了我很深刻的印象。

―2011.6.21 晨

【刊臺灣臺北的《全國新書資訊月刊》，2011 年 7 月，第 151 期，頁 54-57，合照 1 張。】

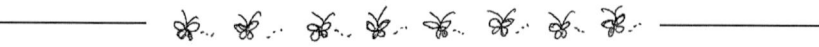

I. The integrity of a lone pine

　　Gao Zhun (1938-), born in Zhangyan, Jinshan, Shanghai, graduated from National Taiwan University at the age of 23 with a master's degree from the Institute of Chinese Culture. He went to the United States and the University of Sydney, Australia for further studies and completed the doctoral program of the Department of Oriental Studies at the University of Sydney. He was elected as an associate academician of the University of Cambridge in the United Kingdom. He was a senior lecturer at the University of Sydney, a researcher at the University of California, Berkeley, and an international honorary writer at the University of Iowa. He was a professor of the Chinese Culture University, the president and editor-in-chief of the Shichao Poetry Society, etc. His poems were selected for dozens of anthologies such as *A Century of Chinese Literary Classics*. He now writes his own poems.

崇高的樸素——讀《高準游踪散紀》

Gao Zhun was simple and unpretentious throughout his life, with a firm and selfless vision. Although his aloof personality made him very isolated, it made him devote all his energy to learning. In addition to writing poems and essays, he also taught and published works such as literary criticism and painting history research.

Gao Zhun's Travel Notes is a prose work with both aesthetic and literary and historical values. It can truly draw out the treasure of thought. The exquisite text covers the author's interest in travel and his impression of related people. It can emphasize patriotic enthusiasm and is very sensitive to the changing beauty of natural phenomena. Carefully and meticulously appreciating his works, we will feel a thinker's experience and thinking about life; as if integrated into a lyrical, symbolic and elegant landscape painting, this is also a radiation of the author's inner emotions, and more faithfully expresses reality. In terms of content, this book contains beautiful chapters, whether about patriotism, worldly concerns, love, family affection, friendship, or concern and sadness for animals and ecology, sighs for the future of mankind, protests against tyranny, admiration for historical figures, nostalgia for the vicissitudes of history, and descriptions of mountains, rivers and nature..., making readers feel as if they are there.

II. Rational clarity and artistic talent

The themes of Gaozhen's prose are rich and diverse. As stated in the last paragraph of "Footsteps of Spring" in Volume 1 "Youthful Travels": "Soul and soul join hands and fly towards the endless blue sky, towards the soft grassland...ah, soul and soul dance. The spring sunshine shines on every piece of free soil." The song's expression of the joy and freshness of nature can be said to be an inexhaustible source of inspiration for Gao Jun, and it also makes the poet's youthful demeanor leap off the paper! In "Records of Lushan in Wushe", the poet praised Lushan with great enthusiasm from the depths of his heart: "...This is a mirror that does not need to be wiped, which will illuminate your tired soul; it is a girl who knows no glory, bringing you gorgeous and everlasting fantasy." In such a state, we clearly see the image of a poet full of romantic passion. The author of "A Night by the Skland River" vividly describes: "...How can people conquer nature? If you conquer nature, you lose nature. What is a person who loses nature? I am afraid he is just a piece of dirty organism." The emotions in the text are sincere and passionate. He is talking to nature in the posture of a silent explorer, but it is deep and powerful. Only such thinking has aesthetic value.

In the second volume, "Walking in the Gallery", Gao Jun visited the National Gallery of Art, the New York Museum, and the Guggenheim Museum during his stay in the United States. His inspection of the exhibitions in the museums and his comments on the painters marked a high level of discussion on Chinese and Western art with poetic strokes. In addition to knowing that Paul Gauguin of France was his favorite painter, the author's comments on the painters He Huaishuo, Liu Guosong, and his friend Wen Ji, who studied painting with him, all relied on his keen artistic intuition and rich aesthetic background to write forward-looking views, and the text can express the shape and color of the space. In terms of form, Gao Junze made more attempts. In addition to new poems, there are also modern poems. For example, in Volume 3, the thirteen topics of mainland travel poems include five-character ancient style "Visiting Boya Terrace", five-character regulated verse "Song of Mount Tai", seven-character regulated verse "Visiting Dayu's Mausoleum", seven-character quatrain "Two Poems on Revisiting West Lake", and self-created lyrics, folk songs, Shangluo, couplets, etc. There are also various types of regular verses with different word counts, which shows how he fully utilized figurative thinking to express himself.

In "Yanjing Notes", Gao Jun visited Tiananmen Square, Peking University, and the Forbidden City in Beijing, and climbed the Great Wall. He couldn't help but think of a poem he wrote, "Dream of Climbing the Great Wall": "I have climbed thousands of mountains and rivers, hunting for the sound of the wind and iron in the sky. / Looking north, the vast desert peaks are like the sea, and looking south, the Central Plains are majestic. / The grass and yellow sands of the frontier have a thousand years of meaning, and I shake my clothes and listen to the old dragon's roar. / The Qin Emperor should not say that his achievements were great, he just wanted to whip Kulun!" His deep eyes abstractly revealed the life connotation of nostalgia. In addition, Gao Jun also went to Mount Tai and visited Shandong Agricultural University and Tai'an Teachers College. Then he recited a poem he wrote in late 1969, "Thinking of My Hometown". I found this poem in *The Complete Poetry of Gao Zhun*. The poem is so pure and so broad that readers can deeply appreciate its emotional intensity. The origins of Gao Jun's poetry are rich and complex, which are closely related to the era and environment he lived in and his experience in studying. Born into a scholarly family, Gao Jun was influenced by the traditional culture of the nation and naturally had deep feelings for China, where he lived in his childhood. The hometown, as gentle as a mother, made the author open his arms and want to run there with joy. In the last verse, he cried out: "Homeland, I call your name and write your name / But you can't hear it and you can't see my poems / But in the end, I only love you, love you / Because there is only your blood in my veins", the author suppressed his homesickness deep in his heart and endured the painful emotional torment. Because he has learned from ancient and modern Chinese and Western art and culture, he has created a rich and colorful world of prose. Among them, "Homeland" and "Long Live China Symphony" have been praised by the mainland poetry circle for more than 20 years. From 1979 to 2001, the first edition of *Kui Xin Collection* was expanded and revised four times to become *The Complete Poetry of Gao Zhun*, and the praises have never stopped. For example, in 1983, Gao Jun wrote the last paragraph of "Traveling Along the Yangtze River" in Berkeley, California: "The vast mountains and rivers, the misty clouds, seem to be waiting silently, waiting for a new hope..." The author permeates a patriotic thought into the vast universe, expressing emotions while permeating rational cognition.

In addition, in Volume 4, Gao Jun is very careful about the image of the characters in the text, such as the biography of his late mother; his mother served as the director of the former St. Mary's Girls' School (now renamed St. John's Institute of Technology) for 33 years, his father Gao Qiming is a famous urban planner, his grandfather Gao Pingzi is the founder of modern Chinese astronomy, and his maternal grandfather Yao Guang (also known as Mr. Shizi) is a poet in the late Qing Dynasty and early Republic of China. The author carefully sorted out his writings, which is Gao Zhun's new contribution to the literary world. In his later years, no matter how hard his life was, writing and reading became a means to express the sublime and spiritual freedom, such as "Mourning a Little Wild Cat": "A little wild cat, living so pitifully, but still can't live long...." This article contains rich meanings, and successfully creates a sad atmosphere of mourning the death of the wild cat by combining man and nature, death and eternity, personal loneliness and philosophy. Other works include literary collections, poetry collections, painting history, etc. His prose can express a broad mind and noble moral character, and rich emotions, which can always make readers enjoy the beauty of art or feel a certain philosophy of life.

III. The essence of prose touches people's hearts

The purpose of *Gao Zhun's Travel Notes* is to express personal emotions and emotional experiences. It mainly expresses the perception of intellectuals, or contains emotions and feelings, by tracing and traveling to various places to see art and landscapes. The old poems interspersed in the text are also the author's ingenuity. For example, one of the seven quatrains in "Two Poems on Reading the Biography of Yelu Chucai" reads: "There are ministers who govern the country and keep the country safe. It is difficult to stop killing and win. Only this person can practice benevolence and eliminate violence for thousands of years. History will record this person!" Gao Zhun has great respect for Yelu Chucai, a minister who served as a military officer and participated in politics with Genghis Khan during the Mongol Empire and served as the Minister of the Central Secretariat (Prime Minister). Because Yelu Chucai made outstanding contributions to the sinicization of the Mongolian people, he eliminated atrocities with his benevolence and courage several times, so that Mongolia no longer carried out massacres. Gao Zhun traveled to the mainland and went to visit Yelu Gong's tomb. This shows that Gao Zhun's understanding of historical figures is far-sighted.

Gao Zhun's grandfather is the internationally renowned astronomer Gao Pingzi. In 1982, the International Astronomical Union decided to name a ring-shaped mountain on the moon as Gaopingzi Mountain. When the author returned home at the age of 50 to attend the Gao Pingzi Centennial Memorial held in Shanghai and Qingdao, he visited Qufu by the way. The following year, he wrote "Visiting Confucius' Tomb", which is included in the thirteen poems of the book's mainland travel and historical poems. The poem is full of vigor and emotion, with intellectual and artistic philosophical thoughts. In the third paragraph, it says: "The cultural torch is lit by you / It shines for generations with rituals, music, poetry and books / You teach what is benevolence and benevolence / Only when you are not worried and not confused can you not be afraid of dangers and obstacles." The author put Confucius's benevolent demeanor and tireless spirit into the poem, and continuing the mission of Chinese culture is the profound connotation of Gao Zhun's thoughts. Although Gao Zhun is 73 years old this year, he has not stopped writing. At the beginning of the year, I received an article "Mourning a Little Wild Cat" from "Gao Zhun's Travel Notes" which is about to be published. In the article, I saw the difficult side of his life, the true love between him and the little cat, the glory of humanity and the painful cry of the soul. After receiving the book at this year's Arts Festival, with the help of President Chen Longhao of Tangshan Publishing House, a press conference was held at the Cultural Association, realizing Gao Jun's own ideal.

Gao Jun had radiated brilliant brilliance throughout his life. When he was 45 years old, his poetry collection was published in mainland China, which made a sensation because it was the first contemporary Taiwanese personal poetry collection published in mainland China. At the age of 51, he went to mainland China in person to demand the release of the arrested Taiwanese folk singer Hou Dejian, and was successful. Later, he traveled alone to mainland China several times in a simple way, and his footsteps reached as far as the Pamir Plateau. At the age of 39, he founded the poetry magazine "Shichao". The first volume was banned due to false accusations. He continued to publish it, and a total of seven volumes were collected by the Wuhan Museum of Contemporary Chinese Writers. After visiting the mainland at the age of 43, he expressed his emotions in poetry and wrote about the truth, goodness and beauty of real life and his feelings of admiring the mountains and rivers of China in prose. This book "Gao Zhun's Travel Notes" fully demonstrates his special talent. The old poems or ancient texts have a rhythm beyond the sound and a purpose beyond the image; the words are elegant and thought-provoking. When reading, there is also a kind of quiet joy and a power that strikes the heart. His expectation for love to be "eternal and pure" is so pure and persistent. His passion for love for the nation shows his inner world that he always wants to create a bright world, and also shows his artistic skill in refining ideas into images in his articles. This lonely figure trying to fly also left a deep impression on me.

—On the morning of June 21, 2011.

〔Published in *National New Book Information Monthly* in Taipei, Taiwan, July 2011, Issue 151, Pages 54-57, 1 group photo.〕

22 陳義海詩歌的思想藝術成就
The Ideological and Artistic Achievements of Chen Yihai's Poetry

摘要 Abstract

陳義海，作為雙語詩人已走過了三十年的創作歷程，現為鹽城師範學院文學院院長。他的詩歌曾經獲得沃里克大學 40 周年校慶英文詩歌競賽第二名。三十年來，他以浪漫、纖細的詩思為表現出他所理想的美而歌唱，並以清麗多彩的筆墨，描繪出了各具其態的藝術形象，也翻譯出版過世界名著與文學著作等多種，為中國當代詩壇做出了實質的貢獻。本文以其詩集《狄奧尼索斯在中國》為基礎，嘗試對其詩歌的思想藝術做一探討。

Chen Yihai, a bilingual poet, has gone through thirty years of creative experience and is currently the dean of the School of Literature at Yancheng Normal University. His poetry once won the second place in the English poetry competition held in the 40th anniversary celebration of the University of Warwick. Over the past thirty years, he has sung with romantic and delicate poetic thoughts to express his ideal beauty, and has used clear and colorful writing to depict artistic images with their own unique styles. He has also translated and published many world classics and literary works, making substantial contributions to China's contemporary poetry scene. This article is based on his collection of poems *Dionysus in China* and attempts to explore the ideological art of his poetry.

關鍵詞： 陳義海、詩歌、藝術、唯美主義。
Keywords: Chen Yihai, poetry, art, aestheticism.

　　在陳義海接受中西合璧的正規教育，並吸收、轉化為自己的現代詩歌書寫之餘，我們可以從這本《狄奧尼索斯在中國》詩集中窺見、感受陳義海身影與豐采的藝術形象，甚至發現被後期象徵主義詩壇的領袖古爾蒙（R.de, 1858-1915）詩人隔世繼承、並重新發揚了抒情的形式；而意象主義甚或唯美主義的精神情懷，也在作者的創新承續中，鎔鑄為全新詩作與不凡的神采內涵。

陳義海詩歌的思想藝術成就

　　在閱讀此詩集的各種表現手法，由「象」而「意」地凸出主旨、風格的創造的過程中；該如何經由對藝術形象的解剖，以體會隱於詞外之「情」或鑑別其詩歌藝術之美？關於此，作者在自序裡已提及，他始終堅持，詩歌不能少掉兩樣東西：一是美，二是崇高。作者也將此詩集與過去的詩集做了比較，稱這裡的詩歌，似乎多了些許蒼涼，他稱說，這種蒼涼是「跨文化語境中的秋風辭」。其實，陳義海的可貴之處，恰恰在於：他既是「用生命和詩歌結合」的學者詩人，深邃而憂傷，寫實又似幻影，又善以在平凡中鋪陳出不凡的聯想與想像。當然，他的詩篇裡的孤獨與愛情、痛苦與期盼……時而冷凝時而溫馨，忠於生命又追尋詩歌永恆。因而，不論其描寫生活中的感觸或是異域題材的詩，都可看出作者並非只關在象牙塔裡自我吟咏和悲吟，而是其風格能呈現出淨化後靈魂之音這一鮮明的思想傾向。如這首〈希爾頓酒店〉詩中這樣感情炙人的句子：

　　我數了數
　　我是第二十七個

　　我在燈光無力的一角坐下
　　我看不見鋼琴
　　所以鋼琴也看不見我

　　但我聽見她

　　音樂用二十七雙細膩的手
　　撫摸著二十七顆粗糙的心

　　當 whiskey 把我的血染成咖啡色
　　我的血管裡奔騰著多惱河的咖啡因

　　雖然淚水朦朧了我的雙眼
　　但我依然看見
　　隔著窗紗
　　空中的月光是用一種象形文字寫的

　　全詩在酒店琴聲中寄託深摯的情感，他的預感、思慮和深深的憂愁，不僅是愛情磨難的見證者，而且也是想鏟除這不幸的思

想者。也許有人稱呼他為「唯美主義者」，雖不無道理，但畢竟不夠全面。陳義海，還有昂然勤奮的一面。確實如此！他在完成這部詩集的寒假裡，每天埋首於辦公室工作 10 至 12 個小時。他說，我一直在努力，但不知努力的結果如何。從中，可以看出，有不少詩就是寫酒神，也寫出了詩人對未來的憧憬與孤獨的探索。如這首小詩〈酒〉，陳義海在進行詩歌創作的同時，還致力於翻譯詩歌的探究。他在 2009 年出版的第一本個人詩集《被翻譯了的意象》後，沒想到，不到半年，2010 年 8 月又出版了中英雙語詩集《迷失英倫》；接著，又立即出版了這本詩集，並在書後寫下一篇後記，陳述「詩人怎樣翻譯自己的詩歌」。其中研究了詩歌與英譯之間的一些問題，對學術研究是有裨益的。而此詩是詩人一面形象地理解世界，一面又借助於形象向人解說世界的深度：

　　我自以為世界上只有我一個人醒著
　　其實，醒著的還有酒
　　不管夜有多深
　　它總圓睜著它的眼睛

　　我自以為世界上只有酒醒著
　　其實，醒著的還有我
　　請不要說我的淚已乾
　　杯沿上依然掛著一滴露珠，苦的

　　在這部詩集裡所創造的酒神狄奧尼索斯[1]形象的明確度上，似乎已將酒神的想像、聯想等透過形象思維規律的延伸，透徹出詩人孤獨的本質的描繪。可見，形象思維確是陳義海詩歌創作的生命；而浪漫觀念在其心底孕育，終結成粒粒真珠。在這裡，詩人抒發了一種五味雜陳的複雜感情，並表達了一種想要新生的欲望。如同法國著名詩人古爾蒙，R.de 的代表作《西茉納》般，這首〈十

---

[1] 書名的狄奧尼索斯（Dionysus）是古希臘的藝術之神，也是葡萄酒與狂歡之神。據傳說，他是宙斯（Zeus）和西姆萊公主（Semele）所生的兒子。在希臘國家博物館的古幣館中陳列著一枚鑄有狄奧尼索斯頭像的古希臘錢幣，他面帶希臘眾神所共有的平靜表情，頭髮是用葡萄蔓結成髮髻，並有葡萄葉裝飾著他的前額，猶如頭戴王冠，這是酒神狄奧尼索斯的象徵。

陳義海詩歌的思想藝術成就

四行的春天〉裡，作者也延續了古爾蒙鮮明塑造出翹首企盼的情人形象來。此詩裡的西茉納，很可能也是陳義海所愛好的名字；以見譬喻之精巧，予人溫婉輕靈之感：

　　生命之偶然如同一朵紅玫瑰
　　死亡之必然如同一朵紅紅的玫瑰
　　西茉納，請你從草葉上輕輕滴下
　　像絕望一樣完美，像完美一樣絕望
　　只有梨樹，站在絕望的那一頭
　　一邊盛開一邊朗誦下一段：

　　死亡之必然如同一朵紅玫瑰
　　生命之偶然如同一朵紅紅的玫瑰
　　西茉納，太陽在緩緩升起
　　露珠在溫柔地死去
　　只有最後的桃花
　　在水邊一邊凋零一邊朗誦上一段

　　西茉納，春天如一只頹廢的小羊
　　在我的憂鬱上快活地蹦著，唱著

　　此詩所用的藝術手法自然是擬人，其中，「愛情」自也是「憂鬱的」；在舊有的意象中又派生出新的意象，加上又有美麗繽紛的色彩反覆地點綴其間，令思念之情若現若隱，更增添了美感力。詩行至最後一段，在一種迷離幽隱的意緒中，忽然連結成不息的愛的節奏，反而帶來赫然有力的情感。陳義海在這本集子共收錄詩歌 120 首，其中，有 20 首是出自二十多歲時的詩作。雖自認是生澀，難免有「為賦新詞強說愁」之嫌；但卻不失為清俊逸麗，又浪漫、奔放，洋溢著想像的筆調。當詩人中年後，詩性更具有時間上的伸展性，又具有空間上的廣闊性。如這首〈夜晚應該有一個自己的名字〉，當詩人以濃重的色彩描繪了夜，交織著人們的希望，憂傷和想像之後，又發出了深沉的嘆息：

　　千萬年來，夜晚沒有一個自己的名字
　　夜晚應該有一個屬於自己的名字
　　而不是借用我的筆名

夜晚應該有自己的國籍
夜晚應該有自己的故鄉
夜晚應該有自己的母親

夜晚應該有自己的語法
夜晚應該有自己的衣服
夜晚應該有自己的情人

夜晚應該有自己的詩歌
夜晚應該有自己的酒杯
而不是固執地附著在我的杯子上

夜，這戴著神秘面紗的姑娘，在作者筆下形成了紛呈凝煉的「意象群」，以凸出「孤獨」之意。此詩比之於陳義海過去的作品，思想更為深邃，精神境界更為宏闊。作者自己強調，生命短暫，詩歌永恆。寫詩應該通過自己的心寫，陳義海的詩歌常與花草的舞動情狀或動物、四季的表情等，自然地連結在一起，想像與取譬俱美。如這首〈寂寞的城〉，就是作者誠摯情懷的抒發：

我總是在夜深人靜的時候上路
只有在夜深人靜的時候
耳朵才開始傾聽，只有
在夜深人靜的時候
沿街的房子才開始長出大大小小的耳朵

美麗的鮮花因為有了欣賞才格外嫵媚
清脆的馬蹄聲因為有了傾聽才格外美麗
夜色中的背影因為有了注視才格外孤寂
是啊，因為有了風
我的斗篷更像一面絕望的旗

夜深了，馬蹄聲激勵著我的孤寂
如果我的心是一座寂寞的城
我希望有你來居住
如果你的城是一顆寂寞的心
我希望你的心中有一座寂寞的城

抒真情，乃是詩生命。在中國北宋畫家郭熙的《林泉高致‧畫意》書中，曾提出著名的「詩是無形畫，畫是有形詩」[2]的論斷。其論點，就是從藝術的目的——美上來要求。陳義海也指出，正是狄奧尼索斯讓他找到了這本詩集的靈魂；換言之，他的這部詩集洋溢著他對酒神崇高美的想像與愛。他以一個中國詩人試圖突破時空的界限，循著藝術之神的光輝去描繪出心中每一感動之美。如這首〈孤獨有一張美麗的面孔〉，雖呈現出偏於調和性的陰柔風格，但情味綿渺，有著「孤獨」本然面貌的懷想：

孤獨有一張美麗的面孔
倒映在水中
像一朵水仙花
呢喃著水中的天空

天空流經之處
皆有河岸鉗制
致使天空不能自由散漫

孤獨有條不紊地流淌著

她的臉上刻著蒼老的年輕
她的皺紋青翠欲滴
她流淌在陽光下面

橋樑交流著此岸和彼岸的絕望
一葉輕舟
像個失敗的勸說者
航行在美麗的面孔上

也只有痛苦的美才能蠶食遠方

作者在追隨狄奧尼索斯的遨遊想像的宇宙之際，不免也會想像到自己孤獨的愁味。他認為，酒神精神在生活中，也是一種短暫的超脫，在文學中，卻能把情感、美感、性情的「狂喜」（Ectasy），更符合生命本體地表現出來。幾乎和狄奧尼索斯一樣，作為雕塑

---

[2] 沈子丞，《歷代論畫名著匯編》，第 72 頁，文物出版社。

的酒神狄奧尼索斯的表情是平和的，但有著時間藝術所獨有的美感力；陳義海的詩歌也同樣有同繪畫相通的那種繪畫美。然而，這種以感情注入物象的繪畫美，不僅體現在對多種畫面的描繪上，而且也從人物肖像的描繪上表現出來。如這首〈一個把憂傷描繪得無限美麗的人〉，或許是勾勒了詩人自己的外部形象：

> 一個把憂傷描繪得無限美麗的人
> 上帝一定會寬恕他
>
> 每當我走過考文垂郊外的紀念公園
> 我的腳步總會被那無名的小花喚住
> 是的，電台裡說，已經是春天了
> 他們告訴我說，我的憂傷青翠欲滴漫山遍野
> 一直伸展到艾汶河的那一邊
> 終於被沃里克城堡擋住去路
>
> 一個把憂傷描繪得無限美麗的人
> 可以飛行在天使的行列中
> 當我墜落
> 軌跡潔白如憂傷
> 憂傷如梨花在東方的一聲嘆息

沃里克城堡是一座位於英國中世紀風格的古堡，而艾汶河（AVON），是取自名詩人莎士比亞故鄉的河，兩岸綠柳成行，景致典雅。據作者自序，當「悲」和「憂傷」被藝術地表達時，其實，那也應該是一種符合酒神精神的「狂喜」。其實，詩人對他的內心是非常理解的，那孤獨絕塵的身影、不求名利的心情，以及對昔日自然美景的緬懷，透過詩人的懷想，形象鮮明的表現在文字裡；這使得整首詩中所欲塑造的詩人本然面貌，有更晰的展現。

總的說，陳義海詩歌的思想藝術，曾有多種評論，但最確切的恐怕是「深邃、絕塵」四字。儘管他在近些年來寫了不少翻譯詩歌，這恐怕更得力於他對外國詩歌的研究和借鑑。深邃和深沉是兩個不同的概念。深沉的詩，一般也較為含蓄；但含蓄的詩，有的可能是深沉的，有的也可能不是深沉的。陳義海詩歌的可貴之處，恰恰是把「深邃」和「絕塵」兩者結合起來了。他在藝術手法的運用及語言的音韻上，都有自己的特點，這就構成其藝術風

格不可少的因素；而詩人總是自覺不自覺地把自己的孤獨情緒及想像糅入詩作中。

—2013.05.17

【刊內蒙古《集寧師範學院學報》，2014年第3期，第36卷，總第126期，頁7-10，以及刊登於(封二)林明理新詩一首〈葛根塔拉草原之戀〉。】

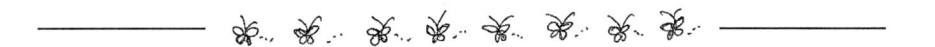

While Chen Yihai received a formal education that combined Chinese and Western elements, and absorbed and transformed them into his own modern poetry writing, we can also glimpse and feel Chen Yihai's artistic image and style from this collection of poems *Dionysus in China*. We can even find that the lyrical form was inherited and re-developed by the poet R. de (1858-1915), the leader of the late Symbolist poetry world, Gourmont. The spiritual feelings of imagism and even aestheticism were also melted into new poems and extraordinary connotations in the author's innovative inheritance.

While reading the various techniques of expression used in this poetry collection, in the process of highlighting the theme and style from "image" to "meaning", how can we appreciate the "emotion" hidden beyond the words or identify the beauty of its poetic art through the dissection of the artistic images? Regarding this, the author has mentioned in the preface that he always insists that poetry cannot lack two things: one is beauty, and the other is sublimity. The author also compared this collection of poems with his past collections, saying that the poems here seemed to have a bit more desolation. He said that this desolation was "the autumn wind in a cross-cultural context". In fact, the valuable thing about Chen Yihai is that he is a scholar-poet who "combines life and poetry". He is profound and sad, realistic and illusory, and is good at laying out extraordinary associations and imaginations in the ordinary. Of course, the loneliness and love, pain and expectation in his poems... are sometimes cold and sometimes warm, loyal to life and pursuing the eternity of poetry. Therefore, whether his poems describe his feelings in life or are about exotic themes, it can be seen that the author is not just shut up in an ivory tower chanting and lamenting to himself, but his style can present a distinct ideological tendency of the sound of a purified soul. Take the poem "Hilton Hotel" for example:

> I counted
> I am the twenty-seventh
>
> I sat down in a corner where the light was dim.
> I can't see the piano
> So the piano can't see me either
>
> But I heard her
>
> Music with twenty-seven pairs of delicate hands
> Caressing twenty-seven rough hearts
>
> When whiskey turns my blood into coffee color
> There's a river of caffeine running through my veins
>
> Although tears blurred my eyes
> But I still see
> Through the window screen
> The moonlight in the sky is written in a kind of hieroglyphics

The whole poem expresses deep emotions in the music of the piano in the hotel. His premonition, thoughts and deep sorrow are not only witnesses of the suffering of love, but also the thinker who wants to eradicate this misfortune. Some people may call him an "aestheticist", which is not without reason, but it is not comprehensive enough. Chen Yihai also has a proud and hardworking side. That's right! During the winter vacation when he was completing this collection of poems, he worked 10 to 12 hours a day in the office. He said, I have been working hard, but I don't know what the result of my efforts will be. From this, we can see that many poems are about the god of wine, and also about the poet's longing for the future and exploration of loneliness. For example, in this short poem "Wine", Chen Yihai, while writing poetry, was also committed to the exploration of poetry translation. After he published his first personal poetry collection *Translated Images* in 2009, he unexpectedly published a bilingual Chinese-English poetry collection *Lost in*

England in August 2010 within less than half a year. Then, he immediately published this poetry collection and wrote an afterword at the end of the book, stating "How a poet translates his own poetry". It studies some issues between poetry and English translation, which is beneficial to academic research. This poem is about the poet understanding the world in images and using images to explain the depth of the world to people:

> I thought I was the only one awake in the world
> In fact, there is still wine in the room.
> No matter how deep the night is
> It always keeps its eyes wide open
>
> I thought that the only person in the world who was awake was alcohol
> In fact, I am also awake
> Please don't say my tears have dried
> There is still a drop of dew on the edge of the cup, bitter

The clarity of the image of Dionysus[3] created in this collection of poems seems to have extended the imagination and association of Dionysus through the laws of figurative thinking, and thoroughly depicted the essence of the poet's loneliness. It can be seen that figurative thinking is indeed the lifeblood of Chen Yihai's poetry creation; and romantic ideas are nurtured in his heart and eventually become pearls. Here, the poet expresses a complex mixture of emotions and a desire for rebirth. Just like the representative work "Simona" by the famous French poet R.de, in this poem "Sonnets of Spring", the author also continues R.de's vivid creation of the image of the eagerly awaited lover. The Ximona in this poem is probably also the name that Chen Yihai likes; it shows the exquisiteness of the metaphor, giving people a gentle and light feeling:

---

[3] Dionysus in the title is the ancient Greek god of art, wine and revelry. According to legend, he was the son of Zeus and Princess Semele. In the Coin Hall of the National Museum of Greece, there is an ancient Greek coin with the head of Dionysus on it. He has the calm expression shared by all Greek gods, his hair is tied into a bun with grape vines, and his forehead is decorated with grape leaves, as if he is wearing a crown. This is the symbol of Dionysus, the god of wine.

> The accident of life is like a red rose
> Death is as inevitable as a red rose
> Simona, please drop gently from the grass
> Perfect as despair, desperate as perfection
> Only the pear tree stands at the end of despair
> As it blooms, I recite the next paragraph:
>
> Death is as inevitable as a red rose
> The accident of life is like a red rose
> Simona, the sun is rising slowly
> The dewdrops are dying gently
> Only the last peach blossom
> Withering by the water while reciting the previous paragraph
>
> Ximena, spring is like a decadent lamb
> Leaping merrily on my melancholy, singing

The artistic technique used in this poem is naturally personification, among which "love" is naturally "melancholy"; new images are derived from the old images, and beautiful and colorful colors are repeatedly dotted in between, making the feeling of longing appear and disappear, adding to the beauty. At the last paragraph of the poem, in a hazy and obscure mood, it suddenly connects into an endless rhythm of love, which brings about a surprisingly powerful emotion. Chen Yihai included a total of 120 poems in this collection, 20 of which were written when he was in his twenties. Although he admits that his writing is somewhat awkward and inevitably seems to be "forcing sadness in order to compose new words", his writing style is still clear, elegant, romantic, unrestrained and overflowing with imagination. When a poet reaches middle age, his poetry becomes more extended in time and more vast in space. For example, in the poem "Night Should Have Its Own Name", after the poet described the night with rich colors, interweaving people's hopes, sorrows and imaginations, he sighed deeply:

> For millions of years, the night has not had a name of its own
> The night should have a name of its own
> Instead of using my pen name

Night should have its own nationality
The night should have its own hometown
The night should have its own mother

The night should have its own grammar
You should have your own clothes at night
You should have your own lover at night

The night should have its own poetry
You should have your own wine glass at night
Instead of stubbornly clinging to my cup

  Night, this girl wearing a mysterious veil, forms a colorful and concise "group of images" in the author's writing to highlight the meaning of "loneliness". Compared with Chen Yihai's previous works, this poem has deeper thoughts and a broader spiritual realm. The author himself emphasized that life is short, but poetry is eternal. Poetry should be written from one's heart. Chen Yihai's poems are often naturally connected with the dancing of flowers and plants or the expressions of animals and the four seasons, with beautiful imagination and metaphors. For example, this poem "Lonely City" expresses the author's sincere feelings:

I always hit the road in the dead of night
Only in the dead of night
The ears begin to listen, only
In the dead of night
The houses along the street began to grow ears of different sizes

Beautiful flowers are especially charming because they are appreciated
The crisp sound of horse hooves is especially beautiful because we listen
The back figure in the night is particularly lonely because of being watched

Yes, because of the wind.
My cape is more like a flag of despair

It's late at night, the sound of horse hooves inspires my loneliness
If my heart is a lonely city
I hope you come live here
If your city is a lonely heart
I hope there is a lonely city in your heart

Expressing true feelings is the life of poetry. In his book *Linquan Gaozhi·Huayi*, Guo Xi, a painter from the Northern Song Dynasty in China, made the famous statement that "poetry is invisible painting, and painting is visible poetry"[4]. Its argument is to demand it from the purpose of art-beauty. Chen Yihai also pointed out that it was Dionysus that made him find the soul of this collection of poems; in other words, his collection of poems is filled with his imagination and love for the sublime beauty of Dionysus. As a Chinese poet, he tried to break through the boundaries of time and space, and followed the glory of the god of art to depict every touching beauty in his heart. For example, the song "Loneliness Has a Beautiful Face" has a more harmonious and feminine style, but it is still full of lingering emotions and contains the nostalgia of the true nature of "loneliness":

Loneliness has a beautiful face
Reflected in the water
Like a daffodil
Whispering the sky in the water

Where the sky flows
All have river bank clamps
So that the sky cannot be free

Loneliness flows in an orderly manner

Her face is engraved with old and young
Her wrinkles are green and lush
She flows under the sunshine

The bridge communicates the despair of this side and the other side

---

[4] Shen Zicheng, Collection of Famous Works on Painting Throughout the Ages, page 72, Cultural Relics Publishing House.

A light boat
Like a failed persuader
Sailing on beautiful faces

Only the beauty of pain can erode the distance

　　While following Dionysus's journey through the imaginary universe, the author cannot help but imagine his own loneliness and sorrow. He believes that the Dionysian spirit is also a kind of brief transcendence in life, but in literature, it can express the "ecstasy" of emotion, beauty, and temperament in a more life-oriented way. Almost like Dionysus, the expression of Dionysus as a sculpture is peaceful, but it has the aesthetic power unique to the art of time. Chen Yihai's poetry also has the same kind of pictorial beauty as painting. However, this kind of painting beauty that injects emotion into objects is not only reflected in the depiction of various pictures, but also in the depiction of character portraits. For example, this poem, "A Person Who Depicts Sorrow as Infinitely Beautiful", perhaps outlines the poet's own external image:

　　　　A person who depicts sadness in an infinitely beautiful way
　　　　God will forgive him.

　　　　Whenever I walk through Memorial Park outside Coventry
　　　　My steps are always stopped by the nameless little flower
　　　　Yes, the radio said it's spring
　　　　They told me that my sorrow was green and dripping all over the mountains
　　　　Stretching all the way to the other side of the Avon River
　　　　Finally, we were blocked by Warwick Castle.

　　　　A person who depicts sadness in an infinitely beautiful way
　　　　Can fly among the angels
　　　　When I fall
　　　　The track is as white as sadness
　　　　Sadness is like a sigh of pear blossoms in the east

　　Warwick Castle is a medieval castle in England. The River Avon is named after the hometown of the famous poet Shakespeare. The banks are lined with green willows, and the scenery is elegant. According to the author's preface, when "sorrow" and "sorrow" are expressed artistically; in fact, it should also be a kind of "ecstasy" that conforms to the Dionysian spirit. In fact, the poet understands his inner world very well. His lonely figure, his indifference to fame and fortune, and his remembrance of the natural beauty of the past are vividly expressed in the text through the poet's memories. This makes the poet's true appearance that he wants to portray in the whole poem more clearly presented.

Generally speaking, there have been many comments on the ideological and artistic conception of Chen Yihai's poetry, but the most accurate one is probably the four words "profound and extraordinary". Although he has written a lot of translated poems in recent years, this is probably more due to his research and reference to foreign poetry. Profundity and deepness are two different concepts. Profound poems are generally more implicit; but some implicit poems may be profound, while others may not be profound. The value of Chen Yihai's poetry lies precisely in the combination of "profundity" and "uniqueness". He has his own characteristics in the use of artistic techniques and the rhyme of language, which constitute an indispensable element of his artistic style; and the poet always consciously or unconsciously incorporates his lonely emotions and imagination into his poems.

— May 17, 2013.

〔Published in the *Journal of Jining Normal College*, Inner Mongolia, Issue 3, 2014, Volume 36, Issue 126, Pages 7-10, and Lin Mingli's new poem "Love on the Gegentala Grassland" published on the second cover.〕

23 尋找恬淡中的感性——以《魯迅圖傳》為視角
Seeking Sensibility in Tranquility: From the Perspective of *Lu Xun's Illustrated Biography*

摘要 Abstract

《魯迅圖傳》熠熠閃爍著魯迅思想的光輝,本文嘗試從文本中尋找「恬淡中的感性」的魯迅,並提出一些新的學術見解。

The Biography of Lu Xun is shining with the brilliance of Lu Xun's thoughts. This article attempts to find Lu Xun who is "the sensibility in calmness" from the text, and proposes some new academic insights.

關鍵詞:魯迅、詩歌、思想感情。
Keywords: Lu Xun, poetry, thoughts and feelings.

一、前言

一九三六年十月十九日,魯迅病逝於上海,他生前所存留的手稿等珍貴的史料,在經過一百四十年後,由上海魯迅紀念館負責編撰並結集成《魯迅圖傳》問世;不僅形式講究,也傳達著一代大文豪魯迅獨特的思想感情。除了保留魯迅一生經歷的傳奇,生動精美的插圖、史實的趣味詞源知識及經典的文學語錄穿插全書,使其編撰的文本也熠熠閃爍著魯迅思想的光輝。

二、從《魯迅圖傳》看魯迅

作為一位集結文學創作、翻譯研究及思想的大家,魯迅的作品中,歷來注重詩意充沛的文字、兼容許多新鮮活潑的思想,表現出其冷靜而有理性,卻又起於感性的悲憫的風格。因此,與同時期的世界文豪或過往的文學家相比,此書不僅記錄了魯迅生於顛沛流離的亂世中種種苦痛或生命的律動,在他以冷靜與熱情之間的真摯抒寫與憂國憂民的情懷中,其精神內涵或咀嚼、回味的強度上,更給讀者一種迴腸盪氣、思古看今的強烈感動。

若從最初魯迅決計要中斷學醫，轉學文藝的心路歷程看，當時的他有兩種面貌，一個是就此走向改造中國社會的新征途，另一個是決心利用文藝力量，把心中對文學應傳達其思想情感的理想境界實現。這兩種面貌的差別，前一個面貌，構築了魯迅的人文主義理想圖景，促使他一步步勇敢地張揚自己悲憫社會、追求精神自由，與為勞動者發聲的愛國精神。後一個面貌，則根據他的思想，把創作與翻譯世界文學，和推展中國文藝的發展當己任，終其一生，勤奮不懈，像個無畏風雨的引航者，把希望帶給每個人，讓光明驅走黑暗。

　　如果我們追溯魯迅文學的發展，比較他各個時期的著作，也可以從求學的側面解開為何魯迅文學能吸引國際學界研究及興趣的原因。他在最早的留日時期，就接觸到世界文學，並把日本現代文學代表作家夏目漱石（1867-1916）列為心中最愛的四個外國作家之一。或許是夏目漱石精擅書法、漢詩及英文研究，其小說也擅長對人物心理的細微描摹，讓魯迅很快地走進作家創作的心靈深處，並開啟了自己心中的一扇窗子；因而，當魯迅返回祖國後，陸續也出版多種小說等文學著作及譯書。

　　在留學期間這一時間點上，他的文學創作雖然尚未「崛起」，但大量閱讀英、日、俄語與課業學習仍在相當程度上影響著魯迅的閱讀文學慣性，在其精神上與文學的世界觀，實際上是一致的。這也影響了返國後的魯迅，不管是從事教學、創刊、翻譯及創作詩歌、小說或論述，寫下大量的文學作品，都應與這個時期的他滿懷激情和救國的信心有關。

　　而魯迅也一直抱著積極的人生態度，以文字的力量，實現其愛國的決心；在書畫等作品中，有的流露出悲憤或批判，反對封建的傾向或撰寫傳奇色彩的人物，也有歌詠友情或愛情等，為社會主義的發展開闢了新的道路，也大多成了文學不朽之作。甚至到了晚年，還翻譯了日本藥學家劉米達夫的《藥用植物》一書[1]，

---

[1] 上海魯迅紀念館編著：《魯迅圖傳》，上海文化出版社，2021年版，第99頁。

由此可見，他的知識廣泛地涉及醫學、植物學、美學、歷史與文學，他的作品，就像一棵松樹在陽光雨露下漸漸參天，長成大樹，讓世人瞻仰。

美國詩人愛默生（1803-1882）曾說，在一切偉大的詩人身上，都有一種人性的智慧，這種智慧要比他們所用的任何才能都更為優越。而魯迅在 1933 年為慘遭暗殺的好友寫下《悼楊銓》的詩中說：「豈有豪情似舊時，花開花落兩由之。何期淚灑江南雨，又為斯民哭健兒。」[2]（Gone was the noble spirit of the past: / So what if blossoms open but to fall? / I never thought my tears, like southern rain, Would flow for one more of our finest sons.）他寫出其中的憂患艱難之想，內心的悲慟，寫時代風雲的激蕩，與友人的溫情相遇，也寫出孤獨而勇毅的靈魂，一切都在他筆下自然地流出，以臻藝術的極致「真情」，無疑愈發令人動容。其心琴上彈出來的詩音，有別於其他詩人把激憤的豪情、赤裸裸的諷喻之情融入情景和詩語之中，透過其翻譯中的英文，「I never thought my tears, like southern rain」，不難感受到瀰散在空中的哀傷氣息，這些恰恰是魯迅顯露出感性的一面。

閱覽魯迅作品或書畫能明顯感覺到其中蘊含的質感與力度，能感覺到他像個勇者的形象永遠矗立在那裡，在他和許廣平之間的鰜鰈情深，何止是一種文字裡的涵括。簡略地說，魯迅除了是個強者的形象，其實是個愛家庭的人，只是他將熱烈濃郁的深情隱於平和寧靜之中。就像兩人相互扶持，他們在文學上都有著兀立不羈的共同追求，他們從相遇到相知，也是因對社會人生的思考，以及對深深根植於中國土地的關懷有了同樣的志向，才能譜出一段感人的戀曲。這樣的相互依存的經歷，直到魯迅死後，大批群眾瞻仰其遺容，靈堂的遺像下面，放著許廣平的輓詞《魯迅夫子》，不只意味著兩人愛情的堅貞，也有著許廣平內心強度的激情。

在魯迅晚年，仍堅強地面對病痛，直到生命的最後一刻，仍抱持以文學救中國的信心。最終在後世的瞻仰與閱讀中，從他憂鬱的沉思傾吐胸懷到對中國文學的巨大貢獻的體悟；他開闊的胸懷，與深愛鄉土及文學藝術，是可以讓人感受到的。

---

[2] 上海魯迅紀念館編著：《魯迅圖傳》，上海文化出版社，2021 年版，第 259-260 頁。

三、結語

　　身為一個時代的巨人，魯迅總是在自己所在的地方完成許多不容易卻令人讚賞的作品，作為喜歡他的文學的讀者，我始終相信，他的精神猶在，令人尊崇。至於魯迅的感性一面，誠如他在 1934 年題贈一首中英詩給愛人許廣平的詩中所言：「十年攜手共艱危，以沫相濡亦可哀。聊借畫圖怡倦眼，此中甘苦兩心知。」（After ten hard years of danger faced hand in hand, / Keeping each other alive like fish out of water, / I hope that this album will freshen your eyes: / We both know the joys and the sorrows we have seen.）借此，一種看似樸實無華的語言，其實詩裡已表現了一種自由意志的詩性力量。這首情詩，主觀感覺印象並不刻意追求與其小說形式技巧的花樣百出，反而更能呈現出其感性的真摯情懷，也使人感受到一種崇高的樸素之美。

　　最後，我想簡單談一下，魯迅既是一個偉大的作家，又是詩人、翻譯家，他筆下的書畫及文學作品像他一樣，是「說不盡」的。此書編選的目的，就是為了品茗其不可言傳的書畫神韻及留下的著述、書信之類的語言精華，甚至是其收藏的自製植物標本，也妙不可言。他的感性主要是反映在他的生活和文藝創作中，其中有許多外國的作家、詩人，也有畫家、藝術家等朋友，正因他具有鮮明的性格、豐富的想像力、和深厚的思想內蘊，才能使其作品具有更高的審美價值，並與世界文學寶庫中，相提並論。

　　德國詩人里爾克（Rainer Maria Rilke, 1875-1926）曾寫下這樣一句名言：「讓人變得更公正，並能預知未來，是每個深刻的愛情之特質。」[3]在魯迅最純粹的感情中，由此書也可以看出，他與許廣平兩人之間真誠的愛情與友情，其高貴之處，是他們一起攜手走過風雨的心境與精神，彼此詮釋愛情，蔚為中國文史上最深邃、推動時代巨輪下的擎手，互補共生，直到晚年，他們倆都不曾在文學的努力上稍懈，彷若濁世中一股清流，讓讀者初次感受到研究魯迅的思想感情及其論著的迫切意義。

　　該書的主要特點是：一、選取魯迅手稿與照片中存在的背景深入分析。二、充分考慮魯迅一生與時代背景的關係。三、重視

---

[3] 里爾克，《慢讀里爾克》，臺北，商周出版，2015 年版，第 113 頁。

尋找恬淡中的感性——以《魯迅圖傳》為視角

魯迅家庭背景、求學過程及其文學思想源流的考察，都是依據時地兩方面著眼的。

筆者以為，魯迅之所以能成為偉大的思想家，是因他洞悉了時代環境脆弱的黃土地上，只有以民族命運當作考察的視角，在審美觀照（aesthetic contemplation）與審悲的甘美之中，轉而將思考力集中於描摹人生苦難的一面，並注重在細節部分的突顯，其小說才有喜劇的意味。他總是帶著溫暖的悲憫，在筆下的許多文本中往往流露出一種反諷的思維和崇高性的英雄色彩；同時，也專注於翻譯文學的創作與研究上。

但細讀其中，他心中最偉大的情感，包括愛情和友情以外，魯迅真正的快樂，就是讓中國人民勇敢地走在陽光底下，從而其創作的精神內涵，有著一種道德的崇高性。雖然，至今仍有少數論者對其文學批評的判斷有所誤解，但都如曇花一現；因為，他既是中國新文化運動的領袖之一，其作品更影響到許多現代文學創作，而其翻譯文學也在世界上引起學界的深度認同與強烈共鳴。

這是在拜讀此書後，對於魯迅一生的成就，生活恬淡、簡樸，留下的深刻印象；我始終認為，魯迅的為人處世，最引人尊敬的，「悲憫」是其精神，「恬淡中的感性」才是其本質；而魯迅的寫作精神也永久烙印在文人的心中。

—2021.11.13 完稿

【刊中國，《上海魯迅研究》，總第 93 輯，上海魯迅紀念館編，2022.08，頁 245-249。】

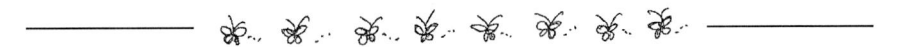

I. Introduction

On October 19, 1936, Lu Xun died of illness in Shanghai. After 140 years, the precious historical materials such as his manuscripts left behind by him were compiled and compiled into *Lu Xun Pictorial*

Biography by Shanghai Lu Xun Memorial Hall. Not only is the form exquisite, but it also conveys the unique thoughts and feelings of a great writer Lu Xun. In addition to preserving the legend of Lu Xun's life experience, the vivid and exquisite illustrations, interesting etymological knowledge of historical facts and classic literary quotations are interspersed throughout the book, making the text compiled by him also shine with the brilliance of Lu Xun's thoughts.

II. Looking at Lu Xun from *Lu Xun Illustrated Biography*

As a master who combines literary creation, translation research and thoughts, Lu Xun's works have always focused on poetic words and many fresh and lively thoughts, showing his calm and rational, yet emotional and tragic style. Therefore, compared with the world's literary giants or past writers of the same period, this book not only records the various pains or rhythms of life that Lu Xun experienced in the turbulent times of wandering, but also gives readers a strong feeling of nostalgia and thinking about the present through his sincere expression of his feelings between calmness and enthusiasm, and the intensity of his spiritual connotation or chewing and aftertaste.

If we look at the mental journey of Lu Xun's initial decision to interrupt his medical studies and switch to literature, he had two faces at that time. One was to embark on a new journey of transforming Chinese society, and the other was to use the power of literature to realize the ideal realm in his heart that literature should convey his thoughts and emotions. The difference between these two aspects is that the former aspect constructed Lu Xun's humanistic ideal picture, prompting him to step by step bravely promote his patriotic spirit of pity for society, pursuit of spiritual freedom, and voice for workers. The latter aspect, based on his thoughts, took the creation and translation of world literature and the promotion of the development of Chinese literature and art as his own responsibility. Throughout his life, he worked hard and tirelessly, like a fearless pilot, bringing hope to everyone and letting light drive away darkness.

If we trace the development of Lu Xun's literature and compare his works in different periods, we can also understand from the perspective of studying why Lu Xun's literature can attract research and interest from the international academic community. During his earliest stay in Japan, he was exposed to world literature and listed Natsume Soseki (1867-1916), a representative writer of modern Japanese literature, as one of his four favorite foreign writers. Perhaps it was because Natsume Soseki was proficient in calligraphy, Chinese poetry and English studies, and his novels were also good at depicting the subtle psychology of characters, which allowed Lu Xun to quickly enter the depths of the writer's creation and opened a window in his heart; therefore, when Lu Xun returned to his motherland, he also published a variety of novels and other literary works and translations.

Although his literary creations had not yet "emerged" during his study abroad, his extensive reading of English, Japanese, and Russian and his academic studies still had a considerable impact on Lu Xun's literary reading habits, which were actually consistent with his spiritual and literary worldview. This also affected Lu Xun after he returned to China. Whether he was engaged in teaching, founding a magazine, translating, or writing poetry, novels, or essays, he wrote a large number of literary works, which should be related to his passion and confidence in saving the country during this period.

Lu Xun also always held a positive attitude towards life, and realized his patriotic determination with the power of words; in his calligraphy and painting works, some of them revealed sadness or criticism, opposed feudal tendencies or wrote legendary characters, and some sang praises of friendship or love, etc., which opened up a new path for the development of socialism, and most of them became immortal literary works. Even in his later years, he translated the book *Medicinal Plants* by Japanese pharmacist Liu Midao[4], which shows that his knowledge widely involved medicine, botany, aesthetics, history and literature. His works are like a pine tree that gradually grows into a big tree under the sun and rain, and let the world admire it.

American poet Emerson (1803-1882) once said that all great poets have a human wisdom that is superior to any talent they use. In 1933, Lu Xun wrote in his poem "Mourning Yang Quan" for his friend

---

[4] Shanghai Lu Xun Memorial Hall, *Lu Xun Pictorial Biography*, Shanghai Culture Publishing House, 2021 edition, page 99.

who was tragically assassinated, "Gone was the noble spirit of the past: / So what if blossoms open but to fall? / I never thought my tears, like southern rain, would flow for one more of our finest sons." [5] He wrote about the worries and hardships, the sorrow in his heart, the turbulence of the times, the warm encounters with friends, and the lonely but courageous soul. Everything flowed out naturally from his pen, achieving the ultimate "sincerity" in art, which is undoubtedly more moving. The poetry played on his heart harp is different from other poets who integrate fiery passion and naked irony into the scene and poetry. Through the English translation, I never thought my tears, like southern rain, it is not difficult to feel the sad atmosphere in the air, which is exactly the emotional side of Lu Xun.

Reading Lu Xun's works or calligraphy and paintings, you can clearly feel the texture and strength contained in them, and you can feel that he is always standing there like a brave man. The deep love between him and Xu Guangping is more than just a kind of text. In short, Lu Xun is not only a strong man, but also a family-loving person. It is just that he hides his passionate and deep affection in peace and tranquility. Just like the two people supporting each other, they both have a common pursuit of literature. They met and got to know each other because they had the same aspirations for thinking about social life and caring deeply rooted in the land of China, which made them compose a touching love song. This interdependent experience lasted until Lu Xun's death. A large number of people came to pay their respects to his remains. Under the portrait in the mourning hall, Xu Guangping's eulogy *Master Lu Xun* was placed, which not only meant the loyalty of the two people's love, but also the strong passion of Xu Guangping.

In Lu Xun's later years, he still faced the pain firmly, and until the last moment of his life, he still held the confidence to save China with literature. Finally, in the admiration and reading of later generations, from his melancholy meditation to his great contribution to Chinese literature, his broad mind and deep love for his hometown and literature and art can be felt.

---

[5] Shanghai Lu Xun Memorial Hall, *Lu Xun Pictorial Biography*, Shanghai Culture Publishing House, 2021 edition, pages 259-260.

III. Conclusion

As a giant of his time, Lu Xun always completed many difficult but admirable works in his own place. As a reader who likes his literature, I always believe that his spirit is still there and worthy of respect. As for Lu Xun's sentimental side, as he wrote in a Chinese-English poem dedicated to his lover Xu Guangping in 1934: "After ten hard years of danger faced hand in hand, / Keeping each other alive like fish out of water, / I hope that this album will freshen your eyes: / We both know the joys and the sorrows we have seen." (After ten hard years of danger faced hand in hand, / Keeping each other alive like fish out of water, / I hope that this album will freshen your eyes: / We both know the joys and the sorrows we have seen.) Through this, a seemingly plain language actually expresses a poetic power of free will. This love poem, in its subjective impression, does not deliberately pursue the variety of formal techniques of its novels, but instead can better present its true sentimental feelings and make people feel a kind of noble and simple beauty.

Finally, I would like to briefly talk about Lu Xun. He is not only a great writer, but also a poet and translator. His calligraphy, painting and literary works are like him, "inexhaustible". The purpose of compiling this book is to appreciate his inexpressible charm of calligraphy and painting, as well as the language essence of his writings, letters and other works, and even his collection of self-made plant specimens, which are also wonderful. His sensibility is mainly reflected in his life and literary creations, among which there are many foreign writers, poets, painters, artists and other friends. It is precisely because of his distinctive personality, rich imagination and profound ideological connotation that his works have higher aesthetic value and can be compared with the world's literary treasure house.

German poet Rainer Maria Rilke (1875-1926) once wrote a famous saying: "It is the characteristic of every deep love that it makes people more just and predict the future."[6] In Lu Xun's purest feelings, this book also shows that he and Xu Guangping had a sincere love and

---

[6] Rilke, *Slow Reading of Rilke*, Taipei, Business Weekly Publishing, 2015 edition, page 113.

friendship. The nobleness of their relationship lies in the state of mind and spirit of walking through the storm together, interpreting love to each other, and becoming the most profound hand in the history of Chinese literature, pushing the wheel of the times, complementing each other and coexisting. Until their later years, they never slackened in their literary efforts, like a clear stream in the turbid world, allowing readers to feel for the first time the urgent significance of studying Lu Xun's thoughts and feelings and his works.

The main features of this book are: 1. Select the background existing in Lu Xun's manuscripts and photos for in-depth analysis. Second, fully consider the relationship between Lu Xun's life and the background of the times. Third, pay attention to the investigation of Lu Xun's family background, the process of studying, and the source of his literary thoughts, all of which are based on the time and place.

The author believes that the reason why Lu Xun can become a great thinker is that he has a deep understanding of the fragile environment of the times on the loess land. Only by taking the fate of the nation as the perspective of investigation, in the aesthetic contemplation and the sweetness of juxtaposition, can he focus his thinking on depicting the suffering of life and pay attention to highlighting the details, so that his novels have a comedic meaning. He always carries a warm sadness, and in many of his texts, he often reveals an ironic thinking and a noble heroic color; at the same time, he also focuses on the creation and research of translated literature.

But if you read it carefully, you will find that the greatest emotion in his heart, including love and friendship, is that Lu Xun's real happiness is to let the Chinese people walk bravely under the sunshine, so the spiritual connotation of his creation has a kind of moral sublimity. Although there are still a few theorists who have misunderstood his literary criticism, they are all like a flash in the pan; because he is one of the leaders of China's New Culture Movement, his works have also influenced many modern literary creations, and his translated literature has also aroused deep recognition and strong resonance in the academic community around the world.

This is the deep impression I got after reading this book about Lu Xun's life achievements, his quiet and simple life. I always think that the most respectable thing about Lu Xun's way of dealing with people is that "sadness" is his spirit, and "sensibility in tranquility" is his essence; and Lu Xun's writing spirit is also permanently imprinted in the hearts of literati.

——Manuscript completed on November 13, 2021.

【Published in China, *Shanghai Lu Xun Research*, Volume 93, edited by Shanghai Lu Xun Memorial Hall, August 2022, pages 245-249.】

24 評吳鈞的《魯迅詩歌翻譯傳播研究》
Comments on Wu Jun's *A Study of the Translation and Communication of Lu Xun's Poems*

摘要 Abstract

吳鈞是魯迅詩歌翻譯傳播研究的開創者。魯迅詩歌英譯由於在世界傳播語言中占有獨特地位,被研究者普遍認為是有待進一步開掘的富礦。隨吳鈞論述的藝術探究,有益於拓寬魯迅詩歌英譯研究的視野以及對詩學的認識。

Wu Jun is an inaugurator of the study of translation and communication of Lu Xun's poems. Because of the unique position of the translation of Lu Xun's poems in the communication of the world, it is regarded generally as the rich mineral resources for further research by the scholars. Following Wu Jun's explanation of her artistic research, the readers will be benefited to widen the visual field of poem translation and deepen the understanding of poetics.

關鍵詞:魯迅、詩歌、英譯、藝術、吳鈞。
Keywords: Lu Xun, poems, English translation, art, Wu Jun.

　　魯迅(1881-1936)詩歌英譯由於在世界傳播語言中占有獨特地位,被研究者普遍認為是有待進一步開掘的富礦。印象中的吳鈞教授,文才橫溢;而這本《魯迅詩歌翻譯傳播研究》,章節中的翻譯理論探討與英譯的藝術研究,使人印象鮮明。書裡涵蓋魯迅詩歌英譯的許多優點,也借由傳譯到國際上,提供了海外譯者許多借鑒與思考。本書譯詩包括魯迅全部的詩作 66 題 81 首,包括了魯迅的格律詩、新體詩及民歌體詩,是國內第一本魯迅詩歌全英譯本。

一、魯迅詩歌英譯的表現價值

　　魯迅一生共創作了 81 首詩歌,包括舊體詩約 68 首,現代詩約 13 首。他的詩歌內容大多涉及中國現代史上重要時事與滄桑變化的反映,他以自己的幽默諷刺和針泛時弊等創作方法,將真理與詩藝統一在一起，激情謳歌出充滿新奇的比喻與想像，不平凡的人生與青春，真誠的愛情與友情。吳鈞將魯迅作品中的詩歌創作分為早期（1900－1912）即南京求學至辛亥革命前後，中期（1918－1926）即「五四」前夕至「五四」退潮期，後期（1928-1935），即大革命失敗至 30 年代國民黨抗戰時期。縱觀魯迅的全部詩作，可以看出，抒發民族豪情與對親友的懷思是其重要主題。他以「揭露社會黑暗」為中心，構築著自己的人文主義理想願景；其充沛的感情，也彰顯出時代和個人的獻身精神為其特徵。

儘管魯迅詩歌表現價值取向廣為學界推崇與研究已久，然而，魯迅詩歌全英譯，目前國際間並沒有全面完整地分析過。吳鈞是魯迅詩歌全譯的開啟者，除了精益求精地英譯魯迅詩歌，也在續推的修訂本中針對為詩歌翻譯再確證，且將魯迅詩歌翻譯進行了韻律的再推敲和優化。因為魯迅詩歌大多是舊體詩並且是押韻的，而此前的幾個魯迅詩歌英譯本不僅譯詩數量不足，而且還存在著研究分析與學理性不足的缺失。基於此，吳鈞將英譯的問題探討以正確理解魯迅詩歌的真義為至關的重要性，並對英美著名學者及中國學者的譯文中，作一比較。最後，她提出可信的論點，只有依民族習慣的表達及反覆推敲至傳神易懂，才能將魯迅詩歌譯出原詩的神韻和精彩，因而引起學界的注目。

二、魯迅詩歌翻譯理論的探究

魯迅晚期作品是詩歌創作的高峰期，基調是反映對時代的艱難與黨政間鬥爭的悲憤。所以，在精神上與憂思是一致的。在《魯迅詩歌翻譯傳播研究》一書中，吳鈞將魯迅詩歌英譯價值取向概括為獨特的風骨美、真摯的情感美、高雅的文采美等三方面逐一分析後，她認同，魯迅詩歌創作的來源於生活的論述。因為，魯迅曾說：「詩人者，攖人心者也」[1]，又說，「詩人感物，發為歌吟，吟已感漓，其事隨訖」[2]，由此，可體會魯迅對詩歌要求的心靈表現及審美感悟是早已萌生的事實。

吳鈞探究魯迅詩歌英譯，比較研究國內外學者翻譯的優點及缺失，從新的「譯即易」的翻譯觀點出發，提出以「譯即易」詩歌翻譯理論的創見，她將魯迅詩歌翻譯理論與中國「易經」的精神相

---

[1] 魯迅：《魯迅全集》第一卷，北京人民文學出版社，2005 年版，頁 70。
[2] 魯迅：《魯迅全集》第九卷，北京人民文學出版社，2005 年版，頁 353。

通性作一考究。探究魯迅《摩羅詩力說》的「不易」的詩學思想，強調詩產生於詩人的心靈又打動讀者心靈的觀點，評價魯迅的新詩創作對中國 20 世紀的新詩發展實具有精神啟蒙的現實意義。

三、吳鈞：魯迅詩歌英譯研究的開拓者

吳鈞在她書裡，從魯迅詩歌的創作本體的角度出發，來要求自己英譯魯迅詩歌首要的標準就是神似。她透過魯迅詩歌英譯的不同版本，就形美與句似作一比較，指出只有恰當地把握住詩歌的風格與格式整齊的美感，才能達到傳神翻譯的預期效果。她還就詩歌的音美與韻似上，將魯迅詩歌英譯成音韻和諧，對偶連貫的技巧在翻譯中進行借鑒和運用，期將魯迅精彩詩歌在世界範圍內廣為傳播的借鑒，這種具有打動人心的審美感染力，更是作為汲取對魯迅詩歌英譯有益的經驗。

接著，吳鈞又從十九世紀末英國著名的漢學家及傳教士理雅各（1815-1897）的《易經》英譯與傳播中探究魯迅詩歌翻譯和傳播的可資借鑒的經驗，這是具有啟迪作用的；她還對德國傳教士兼漢學家的衛禮賢的譯介中國典籍的翻譯傳播汲取了借鑒。最後，匯總魯迅的文學創作中存有大量的文化典故或民間俚語，用心推敲出最貼近魯迅的心靈表現中的那份特殊的「領會感動」。在她的英譯魯迅詩歌中，我們看到了，魯迅對文藝的心靈表現性質，也彷彿看到了他滿懷抑鬱憂憤的心情。特別是通過一系列詩歌英譯，表現出的更廣闊、更深刻的翻譯傳播研究內容。總的說，此書在魯迅詩歌英譯論界應會影響深重；而吳鈞的才華智慧，也因而產生有益的成果。可以相信，魯迅重視精神的涵養和豐富的思想內容是最值得稱道的；其詩歌語言藝術也像他筆下的人物一樣，是有其不可言傳的神韻的。

而吳鈞對詩歌的英語翻譯及其研究更可以將魯迅詩歌所表現的深刻內涵向世界廣為傳播。

—2012.12.19 作

【刊中國《上海魯迅研究》，2013 春，上海社會科學院出版社，頁 199-201。】

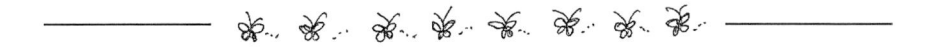

The English translation of Lu Xun's poems (1881-1936) occupies a unique position in the world's communication language and is generally considered by researchers to be a rich mine to be further explored. My impression of Professor Wu Jun is that he is a man of great literary talent; and this book, "Research on the Translation and Dissemination of Lu Xun's Poetry", is very impressive with its chapters that explore translation theories and study the art of English translation. The book covers many advantages of the English translation of Lu Xun's poems, and through its international translation, it provides a lot of reference and thinking for overseas translators. The translated poems in this book include all 81 poems of Lu Xun, including 66 titles, metrical poems, modern poems and folk poems. It is the first complete English translation of Lu Xun's poems in China.

I. The expressive value of English translation of Lu Xun's poems

Lu Xun created a total of 81 poems in his lifetime, including about 68 classical poems and about 13 modern poems. The contents of his poems mostly involve reflections of important current events and changes in modern Chinese history. With his own creative methods such as humor, satire and criticism of current ills, he unified truth and poetic art, and passionately eulogized novel metaphors and imagination, extraordinary life and youth, and sincere love and friendship. Wu Jun divides the poetry creation in Lu Xun's works into the early period (1900-1912), which is from his study in Nanjing to around the Revolution of 1911, the middle period (1918-1926), which is from the eve of the May Fourth Movement to the ebb tide of the May Fourth Movement, and the late period (1928-1935), which is from the failure of the Great Revolution to the Kuomintang's anti-Japanese war in the 1930s. Looking through all of Lu Xun's poems, we can see that expressing national pride and longing for relatives and friends are important themes. He built his own vision of humanistic ideals centered on "exposing social darkness", and his rich emotions also demonstrated his dedication to the times and himself.

Although the value orientation expressed in Lu Xun's poems has long been widely praised and studied by the academic community, there has been no comprehensive and complete analysis of the English translation of Lu Xun's poems internationally. Wu Jun is the initiator of the complete translation of Lu Xun's poems. In addition to translating Lu Xun's poems into English with great care, he also reconfirmed the translation of poems in the revised editions he continued to promote, and re-examined and optimized the rhythm of his translation of Lu Xun's poems. Because most of Lu Xun's poems are classical and rhymed, the previous English translations of Lu Xun's poems not only lacked the number of translated poems, but also lacked research, analysis and academic rationality. Based on this, Wu Jun explores the importance of English translation in order to correctly understand the true meaning of Lu Xun's poetry, and makes a comparison between the translations of famous British and American scholars and Chinese scholars. Finally, she put forward a credible argument that only by expressing according to national customs and repeatedly polishing the text until it is vivid and easy to understand can Lu Xun's poems be translated with the charm and splendor of the original poems, thus attracting the attention of the academic community.

II. Research on Lu Xun's poetry translation theory

Lu Xun's late works marked the peak of his poetry creation, and the basic tone was to reflect his grief and indignation at the difficulties of the times and the struggle between the party and the government. So, spiritually it is consistent with worry. In the book *Research on the Translation and Dissemination of Lu Xun's Poetry*, Wu Jun summarized the value orientation of the English translation of Lu Xun's poetry into three aspects: unique beauty of style, sincere beauty of emotion, and elegant beauty of literature. After analyzing them one by one, she agreed that Lu Xun's poetry creation originated from his discussion of life. Because Lu Xun once said, "A poet is one who touches people's hearts"[3], and "A poet is moved by things and expresses them in songs. Once the songs are full of emotion, the work

---

[3] Lu Xun, *The Complete Works of Lu Xun*, Volume 1, Beijing People's Literature Publishing House, 2005, p. 70.

is done"[4]. From this, we can understand that the spiritual expression and aesthetic perception that Lu Xun required in poetry had already sprouted a long time ago.

Wu Jun explored the English translation of Lu Xun's poems, and made a comparative study of the advantages and disadvantages of the translations by scholars at home and abroad. Starting from the new translation perspective of "translation is easy", she proposed the innovative theory of poetry translation based on "translation is easy". She examined the spiritual connection between Lu Xun's poetry translation theory and China's "Book of Changes". This paper explores the "unchangeable" poetic thought in Lu Xun's *On the Power of Mara Poetry*, emphasizes the view that poetry originates from the poet's soul and touches the reader's soul, and evaluates that Lu Xun's new poetry creation has practical significance of spiritual enlightenment for the development of new poetry in China in the 20th century.

III. Wu Jun: a pioneer in the study of English translation of Lu Xun's poems

In her book, Wu Jun takes the perspective of the creative essence of Lu Xun's poetry as the starting point and requires that the primary criterion for translating Lu Xun's poetry into English is similarity in spirit. She compared the beauty of form and similarity of sentences through different English translations of Lu Xun's poems, and pointed out that only by properly grasping the style and neat format of the poem can the expected effect of vivid translation be achieved. She also borrowed and applied the techniques of Lu Xun's poems in English translation, including harmonious rhyme and parallelism, in terms of the beauty of sound and rhyme of poetry, hoping to spread Lu Xun's wonderful poems around the world. This kind of touching aesthetic appeal can serve as a useful experience for the English translation of Lu Xun's poems.

Then, Wu Jun explored the experience that could be learned from the English translation and dissemination of the *Book of Changes* by James Legge (1815-1897), a famous British sinologist and missionary in

---

[4] Lu Xun, *The Complete Works of Lu Xun*, Volume 9, Beijing People's Literature Publishing House, 2005 edition, page 353.

the late 19th century, which was enlightening; she also drew lessons from the translation and dissemination of Chinese classics by the German missionary and sinologist Richard Wilhelm. Finally, we summarize the large number of cultural allusions or folk slang in Lu Xun's literary works, and carefully ponder the special "understanding and emotion" that is closest to Lu Xun's spiritual expression. In her English translation of Lu Xun's poems, we see the spiritual expression of Lu Xun's literature and art, and we also seem to see his depressed and indignant mood. In particular, through a series of English translations of poetry, it demonstrates a broader and deeper content of translation and communication research. In general, this book should have a profound impact on the English translation of Lu Xun's poems, and Wu Jun's talent and wisdom will also produce beneficial results. It can be believed that Lu Xun's emphasis on spiritual cultivation and rich ideological content is most commendable; his poetic language art, like the characters he wrote about, has its inexpressible charm.

Wu Jun's English translation and research on poetry can further spread the profound connotations expressed in Lu Xun's poetry to the world.

— Created on December 19, 2012.

〖Published in China's *Shanghai Lu Xun Studies*, Spring 2013, Shanghai Academy of Social Sciences Press, pp. 199-201〗

25 簡論許達然詩的通感
On the Synaesthesia in Xu Daran's Poems

一、貼進現實的底層關懷

　　許達然（1940- ），本名許文雄，臺南市人，是歷史學者、散文家。美國哈佛大學碩士、芝加哥大學博士、西北大學退休教授。2005年冬天，他回到臺灣東海大學擔任講座教授。從事台灣史研究，著有學術用書、散文、詩集等多種。獲青年文藝獎、金筆獎、府城文學特殊貢獻獎、吳三連文學獎等殊榮。

　　為了探索許達然詩的魅力所在，我們不妨先瞭解其詩的語言具有哪些共同特徵，以及哪些特有的素質？

　　（一）豐沛的學養與鄉土文學的特徵：許達然詩風質樸，語言不深隱曲折、意象繁複；重在言志，而言志又離不開對現實的關懷與價值認同的思索上，有詩人自覺的「入世」態度。他在自序裡說過：「在我想念的版圖裡，臺灣占據著很大的面積。」他的詩歌創作，並非直接敘事寫史，而是用歷史的眼

1983年夏天在芝加哥，左起：許達然、陳映真、杜國清、非馬（照片提供：林明理）
In the summer of 1983 in Chicago, from left: Xu Daran, Chen Yingzhen, Du Guoqing, William Marr. (Photo provided by: Lin Ming-Li)

光審視臺灣的風土文化、庶民生活的變遷或生態環境更迭的細節，用歷史的責任承載情感；藉以體現出其深悲或感慨，成為「警醒」的特殊風格。他在成名作《含淚的微笑》中已初露端倪。他說：「悲哀的不是痛苦，而是表達不出痛苦」。如果說，許達然擅於用現實中一個不起眼的變化來寫民心、民情，常落筆於貼進現實的底層關懷，收筆於內在痛苦的回憶，且抒寫兼具哲理和人道精神；從這個特徵上來說，他對百姓簡苦生活的敘寫是最具社會現實性，也最有鄉土意識的歷史意義。

　　（二）深受現代主義文學的影響與獨特的視域：許達然不主張用作品去再現生活，而是提倡從人的心理感受出發，表現「底

層文學」的關照。他注重表現人物的意識活動本身，從作品中力求有所突破，確是事實。自 1979 年起，他相繼出版了《土》、《吐》、《遠方》、《水邊》、《人行道》、《防風林》、《同情的理解》等散文集，其新詩〈叠羅漢〉亦獲得吳濁流文學獎項。詩創作的特點是，強烈的時代意識與對鄉土變遷中的社會給予無聲的質疑。以通感、對比、烘托等藝術手法，在意象的營造中隱現著對底層社會的深刻描摹，從而形成獨特的鄉土現代性。主題則注重人生觀察和社會批評，這種把底層社會寫得真實而樸素，不是將醜惡本質化，而是介入自己的鄉土經歷和情感去體察民間，這種介入式的思索無疑提升了詩歌具理性與感性交融的品味，使得評論家南方朔以「碎片書寫」（Writing Fragmentarily）來形容他的文字具有很大的聯想性和跳躍度。同時，也顯示了身為一個詩人學者的思想高度以及「文學是社會事業」的寬廣視域。

二、詩的通感表現

關於通感，德國著名美學家費歇爾曾說過：「人的各個感官本不是孤立的，它們是一個感官的分支，多少能夠互相代替，一個感覺覺響了，另一個感官作為回憶、作為和聲、作為看見的象徵，也就起了共鳴。」[1]簡言之，通感就是五官感覺的相通，把不同感官的感覺溝通起來，借聯想引起感覺轉移的心理現象。

也可以說，是一種物我兩忘的內心體驗。運用通感，可以使詩的意象更具體，此外，也可突破人的思維定勢，深化藝術。許達然常以詩記錄現實人生的種種真貌，情意貫徹，無需旁敲側擊，頗有哲人的意味。如 1991 年寫下的〈焦灼〉，著眼於通感意象之表現：

> 森林劈拍火了就燻熄唒啾
> 穿戴著火的鹿悚然發現樹
> 反了，都敢探成灰
> 撇下逃不走的天
> 滿臉塗抹著灰的
> 氣色

---

[1] 轉引自《西方美學家論美和美感》，商務印書館，1980 年版，第 236 頁。

這是以聽覺寫視覺，彷彿使我們聽到了森林劈拍著火時傳來燋熄的啁啾聲。全詩洋溢著想像的筆調，有邏輯性的關連在心靈上再生或記憶的心靈影像。詩人以通感、擬人等手法，描摹出大自然留給我們的寶貴資源——森林遭殃的情景；而「滿臉塗抹著灰的氣色」，取譬俱美，也鮮明塑造出十分焦急的形象來。在義旨探究之間，如何維護生態環境的社會責任。歸根到底，這才是詩人的深情想望。

接著，在 1994 年詩人寫下的〈海天〉，是一個寓意深刻的比喻，感發而然：

　　天闊得好無聊
　　凭空潛入海聊天
　　一翻臉就把湛藍煮沸
　　爭吵的聲音濺起
　　花朵蕩漾
　　泱泱不平的情敘

此詩明顯的以「天闊」氣勢為貫穿，特別是輔以連海，以證臺灣政黨分立、批鬥，也寓褒貶於詩語之中。結語作「泱泱不平的情敘」，沉默中寄托詩人的反諷之情；使讀者不僅了解當前政治的歷史真相，且能具體感受到詩人對社會歷史氣圍。這是以視覺寫聽覺，傳神地表現出「爭吵的聲音濺起」，彷彿是泱泱不平的浪花正蕩漾著；而其創造性的審美想像，就是通感生成的根本所在。其實，許達然風格穩重的文藝思維裡，也有些穿插諧趣性的語言文字，比如在 1995 年寫下的〈動物園〉，可算中期詩歌創作過程中具有標誌意義的事件之一：

　　都是無端無期徒刑的居住
　　還有不被收養的鼠老是自助來吃
　　飽著不被收養的蚤活著咬
　　給應邀來觀賞的揉死
　　還動的物都拒絕活著相看絕種

此詩靠的是暗示、譬況和象徵。語言冷雋，形式新穎，也有批判性諧趣。最後一句「還動的物都拒絕活著相看絕種」這就表現了在特定情境中，詩人對那些瀕臨絕種的動物們失去自由或盜獵者把牠們製成標本的惡行與生存物資也簡陋不堪之痛的體驗。但許達然對情感的抒發、渲洩以及體驗過程都是此詩詩性存活的關鍵。許達然詩裡通感哲學的基礎就是客觀事物都不是孤立存在的，它們之間有著千絲萬縷的聯繫。這或許，正因為詩人認真地想擔負起深入研究臺灣社會人文的責任，也為詩的審美生成預留了想像空間。詩生於情，情生於境。可以說，「詩以緣情」的美學特徵也是許達然詩性的本來面目。比如他在 2004 年寫下的這首〈失業〉，是近些年失業者或邊緣人的痛苦寫真：

家是公家高架橋下
路踏著我走
地址是流浪
收集破爛的
饑餓聲音

第一句是視覺意象，大概是表現流浪者四處為家的窘境。接下去是用視像來表達聽象，有通感的手法在：「路踏著我走／地址是流浪」，給人痛感。這裡喻示著：面對當下全球不景氣的襲擊，許多失業的流浪漢族群，處於這樣一種無可逆轉的事實下，我們的社會是否該認真探詢，怎樣開始一種適合或安頓於他們的生活和生存意識。在某種精神上，這是詩人最最深沉動人的想法。這種隱藏於小市民故事，當中的理性思考的力度，似乎遠比寫出某些城市的萎靡面更為深刻和沉重。而最後「收集破爛的饑餓聲音」，表現了許達然潛意識對失業問題嚴重的複雜心情，一下子把讀者帶到無限美妙的通感世界。再如 1996 年寫下的〈豐收〉，許達然對於部落族民應具了解之同情，方可下筆，讓讀者留下了深刻的烙印：

再破落都要守住閃鑠的碎片
還有菖蒲揮劍也挽不住鄉人

走不掉的菠菜臭了
茭白筍還老實長著斑點
想念牛，草都老了
鼠吃不慣素食紛紛私奔
眾虫矜持繼續咬苦瓜
日頭吞不下，蕃薯葉謝了

> 金針花在地都等乾了
> 菜頭在地還寧做脯也不爛的

　　德國哲學家黑格爾（Hegel, 1770-1831）曾提出，顏色的和諧、聲音的和諧、形象的和諧具有同等意義。在這裡，許達然對於理解原住民生活艱苦的現實語境，應該是有一定意義的。就算菖蒲插於門戶上，夜夜祈求離鄉打拼的族人平安，也一樣是令人心酸的畫面。每當一遇天災，災區運不出外的蔬果，連老天都發愁的情景，與期待豐收的視覺造成情感上的反差；然而，在此表述中我們不難看到許達然的人道精神依然強烈存在。它不僅昭示了渴望改變底層生活的歷史性要求，也凸顯了這種要求難以實現的焦慮。接著，在詩人 41 歲時發表的〈黑面媽祖〉中，一樣是許達然極力為漁民爭取的自由，依然還是必須從政治的無形束縛中才得以解脫：

> 阿公去天后宮燒香保庇阿爸討海，
> 媽祖靜看海，看不到阿爸回來；
> 不是魚，木魚硬縮著頭。
>
> 阿姊去福安宮拜拜保庇姊夫行船，
> 媽祖靜聽海，聽不見姊夫叫喊；
> 不是魚，船躲不開風颱。
>
> 阿母去慈生宮跪求保庇我換頭路，
> 媽祖靜看海，看不到我傷發膿，痛：
>
> 我拒絕再抓魚後被抓，
> 不如無國籍的魚。

　　這些台語的語素應是蓄意的創作，他以詩積極地介入社會政治，以文學確立了自己的現代性追求，也正是這種追求使得許達然找到了自己的精神歸宿和生存支點。如同他曾說：「我相信文藝力，所以才也寫作，不然就專心做學者研究歷史與社會了。文學、歷史、社會應溶和在一起；文學在歷史與社會情況下產生，也可影響社會與歷史。」就是這種憂民的悲憫，使此詩裡的故事與人物共存於詩人的視覺凝視當中，其價值核心仍然是許達然詩歌所傳遞的「希望我寫的都與社會及人民關聯」的理想。在台灣，黑面媽祖是百姓所熟悉的神祇形象。詩裡引申的是，討海人生活的辛酸,且隱含著臺灣因國家定位尚未被多數國家認同,間接道出了因無國籍而出海捕魚者,連魚都不如的悲哀。詩的語調是低沉的,且不斷震盪擴散。最後,介紹這首〈新村〉,在敘述效果上,再次確認了許達然對於「歷史是一種解釋,從這裡看,文學和歷史便可以連在一起。」這段自白的依附與追隨:

　　天。雲廢耕後,日頭蹲下來親視
　　無田的牛低頭咀嚼自己的影子

　　疏忽
　　春天那年攜雨來約我外出
　　我竟不領情躲起來讀柏拉圖

　　詩人用「日頭蹲下來親視」〈視覺〉、「無田的牛低頭咀嚼自己的影子」〈觸覺〉來描寫現代化的新村,「春天那年攜雨來約我外出」〈聽覺〉,最後一句,讓讀者的思維隨著種種感覺的轉換不斷跳躍,跟著進入詩人閱讀的審美世界。此詩藝術的手段,似乎是許達然為了表達「反農田廢耕」後各地農事普遍蕭條的感知;毋寧把關注的重心,轉移到詩本身所透露出來對農民的憂思情緒。

　　以上這些詩歌著力於許達然的思想傾向,詩的結構謹嚴,條理清晰;且透過通感技巧的運用,藉以突破語言的局限,也豐富了審美情趣。就選題而言,許達然向來喜歡有哲學深度的思想家。如能細讀其詩,較之其它散文作品,視野應更為開闊。他以探尋臺灣文化史發展的基本走向,尤其是對歷史的研究時段、主題範圍,是很有學術意義的。許達然主張,「寫作,不能失去創造力和格調。」晚年的他,詩風更趨於內斂、反諷或抒寫寓言風格。他是位熟諳英、法、日語,曾獲美國傅爾博萊特等研究獎金的學者;在臺灣社會史這一研究領域上也充分運用其學術資源,並以詩文予以拓展與深化文學中加以多重層面實踐應用。

三、崇高美的追求與臺灣史研究的學者

　　許達然寫詩文時,能引出自覺批判的透射,以及對臺灣社會本身的關注。他曾明確表示,忍耐孤獨,是必要的修養。以及「到底我們不是政客,只能用文章關心社會。文學能影響人的心靈,但要改變社會是不容易的」。然而,身為一個有覺悟的詩人學者,

他要在文學作品中去追求罕見的崇高美；因此，在其深刻的思維下，透過樸拙的文字，在在說明許達然的詩在表現崇高美時正是從底層文學去表現生命的偉大、心靈的堅強與崇高的。

　　比如他寫東門城下的攤販、被綁赴刑場的豬隻、被強制拆屋的住戶、廢氣污染下的木麻黃、垃圾堆中的人生故事等等，均能展現出巧妙而準確的喻象，能把他生命的熱力與對文學寫作的堅持突顯出來。我認為對其文學的正確評價應涵括四個層面：第一是詩歌，第二是歷史，第三是散文，第四是文化史。這四個層面就像四個同心圓，光明清瑩；他靜觀萬象，萬象如在鏡中。其空明的覺心，映照許達然澹泊的一生，在臺灣史研究也產生了深遠的影響。有評家甚至認為，他的散文含蓄蘊藉，似乎比詩更好。對此，我認為，許達然出身於台南一個貧困的家庭，勤學刻苦以致弱視重聽。他用生命書寫的詩歌，我們應可以感受得到其語言的情趣，而能給人以深刻的啟示的。

－2011.10.12 作

【刊於臺灣台北的《全國新書資訊月刊》，2013 年 7 月，第 175 期，頁 36-40，以及照片 1 張。】

I. Based on the reality of the bottom line

　　Xu Daran (1940-), real name Xu Wenxiong, is a native of Tainan City. He is a historian and essayist, with master of Harvard University, PhD of University of Chicago, and retired professor of Northwestern University. In the winter of 2005, he returned to Tunghai University in Taiwan as a professor. He is engaged in the research of Taiwan history and has written many academic books, essays, poetry collections, etc. He has won the Youth Litcrature Award, the Golden Pen Award, the Fucheng Literature Special Contribution Award, the Wu Sanlian Literature Award and other honors.

　　In order to explore the charm of Xu Daran's poems, we might as well first understand the common characteristics and unique qualities of the language of his poems.

1. Abundant learning and characteristics of local literature: Xu Daran's poetry style is simple, the language is not profound and tortuous, and the imagery is comple. The emphasis is on expressing one's aspirations, and expressing one's aspirations is inseparable from the concern for reality and the thinking about value identification, and the poet has a conscious "worldly" attitude. He said in his preface: "In the territory I miss, Taiwan occupies a large area." His poetry creation is not a direct narrative or historical writing, but rather uses a historical perspective to examine Taiwan's local culture, the changes in the lives of ordinary people, or the details of the changing ecological environment, and uses historical responsibility to carry emotions, thereby to reflect his deep sorrow or emotion and become a special style of "alertness". He had already shown his potential in his famous work *Smile with Tears*. He said: "What is sad is not the pain, but the inability to express the pain." If we say that Xu Daran is good at using an inconspicuous change in reality to write about people's hearts and sentiments. He often starts with the grassroots concerns that are close to reality and ends with the memories of inner pain, and his writing is both philosophical and humanitarian. From this feature, his narration of the simple and hard life of the people is the most socially realistic and has the most local-conscious historical significance.

2. Deeply influenced by modernist literature and with a unique perspective: Xu Daran does not advocate using his works to reproduce life, but advocates starting from people's psychological feelings and expressing the care of "grassroots literature". It is true that he focuses on expressing the characters' conscious activities themselves and strives to make breakthroughs in his works. Since 1979, he has published a series of essay collections including *Soil, Spit, Distance, Waterside, Sidewalk, Windbreak,* and *Sympathetic Understanding*. His new poem "Stacked Monks" also won the Wu Zhuoliu Literature Award. The characteristics of poetry creation are a strong sense of the times and silent questioning of the changing society in the countryside. Through the use of artistic techniques such as synaesthesia, contrast, and embellishment, a profound depiction of the lower class society is implicit in the creation of images, thus forming a unique rural modernity. The themes focus on life observation and social criticism.

This kind of writing about the lower class society is realistic and simple. It does not essentialize ugliness, but involves one's own rural experience and emotions to understand the people. This kind of interventionist thinking undoubtedly enhances the taste of poetry that blends rationality and sensibility, which makes critic Nan Fangshuo describe his writing as "Writing Fragmentarily" with great associative and jumpy nature. At the same time, it also shows the height of his thoughts as a poet and scholar and his broad vision that "literature is a social cause".

II. Synesthesia in poetry

Regarding synaesthesia, the famous German aesthetician Fischer once said: "Human senses are not isolated, they are branches of a sense organ and can replace each other to a certain extent. When one sense rings, another sense organ resonates as a memory, as a harmony, as a symbol of sight."[2] In short, synaesthesia is the communication of the five senses, which connects the sensations of different senses and causes the psychological phenomenon of sensory transfer through association.

It can also be said that it is an inner experience of forgetting both oneself and the world. The use of synaesthesia can make the imagery of poetry more specific. In addition, it can also break through people's fixed thinking and deep art. Xu Daran often uses poetry to record the true aspects of real life. His emotions are consistent without any indirect remarks, which is quite philosophical. For example, in "Anxiety" written in 1991, the focus is on the expression of synaesthesia images:

> The forest is on fire and it will burn out.
> The deer wearing fire found the tree with horror
> On the contrary, they all dare to explore into ashes
> Leaving behind the sky that cannot escape
> His face was covered with ash
> Complexion

---

[2] Quoted from *Western Aestheticians on Beauty and Aesthetic Sense*, Commercial Press, 1980 edition, page 236.

This is a visual description based on hearing, as if we can hear the chirping sound of the forest burning when it is on fire. The whole poem is full of imaginative writing, with logical connections to the mental images that are reproduced or remembered in the mind. The poet uses synaesthesia and personification to describe the disaster of the forest, a precious resource left to us by nature; and "his face is covered with gray complexion" is a beautiful metaphor, which also vividly creates a very anxious image. While exploring the meaning, how to maintain the social responsibility of the ecological environment. In the final analysis, this is the poet's deepest desire.

Then, in 1994, the poet wrote "Sea and Sky", which is a metaphor with profound meaning and inspiration:

> The sky is so boring
> Dive into the sea and chat
> Once you turn against me, the blue sky will boil
> The sound of quarreling splashed
> Flowers swaying
> A huge and unfair narrative

This poem is clearly permeated with the momentum of "the vastness of the sky", especially with the addition of the sea, to prove the division and criticism of political parties in Taiwan, and also to imply praise and criticism in the language of the poem. The conclusion is a "vast narration of injustice", expressing the poet's irony in silence. It enables readers not only to understand the historical truth of current politics, but also to feel the poet's concrete attitude towards social history. This is a description of hearing through vision, vividly showing the "splashing sounds of quarreling", as if huge and uneven waves are rippling. Its creative aesthetic imagination is the root of the generation of synaesthesia. In fact, Xu Daran's steady literary thinking is also interspersed with some humorous language and words, such as "Zoo" written in 1995, which can be regarded as one of the landmark events in his mid-term poetry creation process:

> All of them are residents of life imprisonment without reason.
> And the rats that are not adopted always come to eat by themselves
> Full of unadopted fleas, biting alive

Kneel to death those who were invited to watch
All living things refuse to live and watch each other become extinct

This poem relies on suggestion, simile and symbol. The language is witty, the form is novel, and it also has critical humor. The last sentence "Those that are still alive refuse to live and watch each other become extinct" expresses the poet's painful experience of the endangered animals losing their freedom or being made into specimens by poachers and having to live on with their meager supplies in a specific situation. But Xu Daran's expression, venting and experience of emotions are the key to the poetic survival of this poem. The basis of the synaesthesia philosophy in Xu Daran's poems is that objective things do not exist in isolation, but are inextricably linked with each other. Perhaps, it is precisely because the poet seriously wants to take on the responsibility of conducting in-depth research on Taiwan's society and humanities that he reserves room for imagination for the aesthetic generation of poetry. Poetry is born from emotion, and emotion is born from environment. It can be said that the aesthetic feature of "poetry is about emotion" is also the true nature of Xu Daran's poetic nature. For example, the song "Unemployment" he wrote in 2004 is a painful portrait of the unemployed or marginalized people in recent years:

Home is under the public viaduct
The road is walking on me
The address is wandering
Collecting junk
Hunger Sounds

The first sentence is a visual image, probably expressing the plight of wanderers who have no home anywhere. The next step is to use visuals to express auditory images, with the technique of synaesthesia: "The road walks on me / The address is wandering", giving people a sense of pain. This implies that in the face of the current global recession, many unemployed homeless people are facing such an irreversible fact. Should our society seriously explore how to start a life and survival consciousness that is suitable or settled for them? In a certain spirit, this is the poet's most profound and moving thought. The power of rational thinking hidden in the stories of the petty bourgeoisie seems to be far more profound and heavy than writing about the decadent side of certain cities. The final "collection of tattered hungry sounds" expresses Xu Daran's subconscious and complex feelings about the seriousness of the unemployment problem, and immediately brings readers to an infinitely wonderful world of synaesthesia. For example, in Harvest, written in 1996, Xu Daran wrote with sympathy for the tribesmen, which left a deep impression on the readers:

> No matter how dilapidated we are, we must hold on to the fragments of the shining
> Even if Acorus calamus waved his sword, he couldn't stop the villagers.
>
> The spinach that can't be removed is smelly
> The wild rice shoots still have spots on them
> I miss the cows, the grass has grown old
> Rats can't get used to vegetarian food and run away
> The insects continued to bite the bitter melon
> The sun can't swallow it, the sweet potato leaves are withered
> The golden needle flowers are all dried up on the ground
> The turnips on the ground are better to be dried than rotten.

The German philosopher Hegel (1770-1831) once proposed that harmony of colors, harmony of sounds, and harmony of images have the same meaning. Here, Xu Daran's contribution to understanding the difficult real-life context of the indigenous people should be of some significance. Even if calamus is inserted on the door and people pray every night for the safety of their fellow villagers who have left their hometown to work hard, it is still a sad scene. Whenever a natural disaster occurs, the fruits and vegetables from the disaster area cannot be transported out, and even God is worried, which creates an emotional contrast with the visual expectation of a good harvest; however, in this expression, it is not difficult for us to see that Xu Daran's humanitarian spirit is still strong. It not only reveals the historical desire to change the lives of the lower classes, but also highlights the anxiety that such a demand is difficult to achieve. Then, in the poem "Black-Faced Mazu" published when the poet was 41 years old, Xu Daran also tried hard to fight for the freedom of fishermen, but he still had to break free from the invisible constraints of politics:

Grandpa went to the Tianhou Temple to burn incense and pray for his father to ask for the sea.
Mazu quietly looked at the sea, and could not see her father coming back;
It's not a fish, the wooden fish has its head shrunk.

My sister went to Fu'an Temple to pray for her brother-in-law's journey.
Mazu listened to the sea quietly, and could not hear her brother-in-law shouting;
If you are not a fish, the boat cannot avoid the wind typhoon.

My mother went to Cisheng Temple to kneel and beg for protection so that I could change my way.
Mazu quietly looks at the sea, but cannot see my wound festering and pain:

I was caught after I refused to catch any more fish,
Not as good as a stateless fish.

These Taiwanese morphemes should be deliberate creations. He actively intervened in social politics through poetry and established his pursuit of modernity through literature. It was this pursuit that enabled Xu Daran to find his spiritual home and fulcrum for survival. As he once said, "I believe in the power of literature and art, so I write. Otherwise, I would concentrate on being a scholar studying history and society. Literature, history, and society should be integrated together. Literature is produced in historical and social contexts, and can also influence society and history." It is this compassion for the people that makes the stories and characters in this poem coexist in the poet's visual gaze. The core value of this poem is still the ideal conveyed by Xu Daran's poetry: "I hope that everything I write is related to society and the people." In Taiwan, the Black-Faced Mazu is a deity familiar to the people. The poem alludes to the bitterness of the lives of fishermen, and implies that Taiwan's national status has not yet been recognized by most countries. It indirectly expresses the sadness of those who go out to sea to fish because they are stateless and are not even as good as the fish. The tone of the poem is low and constantly oscillates and spreads. Finally, I would like to introduce this poem "New Village". In terms of narrative effect, it once again confirms Xu

Daran's attachment to and following of this confession: "History is a kind of interpretation. From this point of view, literature and history can be connected together."

> The sky. After the clouds stopped farming, the sun squatted down to look
> The landless cow lowers its head to chew its own shadow
> Negligence
> That spring, the rain came to ask me for an outing
> I didn't appreciate it and hid away to read Plato

The poet uses "the sun squats down to see with its own eyes" (vision), "the fieldless cow lowers its head to chew its own shadow" (touch) to describe the modern new village, and "that year in spring, the rain came to ask me out" (hearing). The last sentence allows the reader's thinking to jump continuously with the transformation of various senses, and follow into the poet's aesthetic world of reading. The artistic means of this poem seems to be that Xu Daran wants to express his perception of the general depression of agricultural affairs in various places after the "anti-farmland abandonment". Rather, he shifts the focus of attention to the worried emotions about farmers revealed in the poem itself.

The above poems focus on Xu Daran's ideological tendencies. The structure of the poems is rigorous and the logic is clear. Through the use of synaesthesia techniques, they break through the limitations of language and enrich the aesthetic taste. As far as topic selection is concerned, Xu Daran has always liked thinkers with philosophical depth. If you can read his poems carefully, your horizons will be broader than those of his other prose works. His exploration of the basic direction of the development of Taiwan's cultural history, especially the research period and subject scope of history, is of great academic significance. Xu Daran advocates that "writing should not lose creativity and style." In his later years, his poetry style tended to be more restrained, ironic, or allegorical. He is a scholar who is fluent in English, French and Japanese, and has won the Fulbright Research Fellowship in the United States. He also fully utilizes his academic resources in the research field of Taiwan's social history, and expands and deepens it through poetry and prose, and applies it in literature on multiple levels.

III. The pursuit of sublime beauty and scholars studying Taiwan history

When Xu Daran writes poetry and prose, he is able to bring out conscious critical reflections and concern for Taiwanese society itself.

It has been clearly stated that tolerating loneliness is a necessary quality. And "After all, we are not politicians. We can only express our concern for society through writing. Literature can influence people's minds, but it is not easy to change society." However, as a conscious poet and scholar, he pursues rare sublime beauty in literary works; therefore, with his profound thinking, through simple and clumsy words, it is explained that Xu Daran's poems, when expressing sublime beauty, are precisely expressing the greatness of life, the strength and sublimity of the soul from the grassroots literature.

For example, when he wrote about the vendors under the East Gate of the city, the pigs tied to the execution ground, the residents whose houses were forcibly demolished, the Casuarinas polluted by exhaust gas, the life stories in the garbage dump, etc. He was able to use clever and accurate metaphors to highlight the passion of his life and his persistence in literary writing. I believe that a correct evaluation of his literature should cover four levels: first, poetry, second, history, third, prose, and fourth, cultural history. These four levels are like four concentric circles, bright and clear. He observes everything quietly, and everything seems to be reflected in a mirror. His clear and enlightened mind reflects Xu Daran's simple and unpretentious life and has also had a profound impact on the study of Taiwan history. Some critics even believe that his prose is subtle and profound, and seems better than poetry. In this regard, I believe that Xu Daran was born into a poor family in Tainan and studied so hard that he became blind and hard of hearing. The poems he wrote with his life should enable us to feel the charm of the language and give people profound inspiration.

—Written on October 12, 2011.

〔Published in the *National New Book Information Monthly* in Taipei, Taiwan, July 2013, Issue 175, Pages 36-40, and 1 photo.〕

26 簡論非馬的散文創作——讀《不為死貓寫悼歌》有感[1]

A Brief Analysis of William Marr's Creative Essay Writing: On reading *I Will Never Write a Dirge for a Dead Cat*

摘要 Abstract

美詩人非馬博士在讀書時即開始發表作品,他的詩文題材多樣、蘊涵豐富、諧趣盎然,內容多為抒發個人悲憫情懷、旅遊點滴、對社會民生的反映、對生態環保的關注和對寫詩與簡樸生活的記敘。非馬工作之餘,致力於寫詩、譯詩、散文、繪畫雕刻的創作,終於成為國際知名的詩人與藝術家。本文以《不為死貓寫悼歌》為路標,循著時光隧道,探尋非馬獨特的夾詩散文創作的精神之旅。

Dr. William Marr (Fei Ma), a Chinese-American poet, started publishing his works while he was still in school. His poems and essays are humorous and full of imagination. Their subjects range from his personal thoughts and feelings to what he saw and heard during his many world tours, from his observation and reflection on today's society to his concern with the environment, and from the experience of his creative activities to his simple everyday life. As a professional engineering researcher, he has devoted most of his spare time to writing, translating, painting and sculpting, and has established himself as an internationally known poet and artist. This article uses his book of essays, *I Will Never Write a Dirge for a Dead Cat*, as a guide to trace the course of his unique essay writing — embedding his short poems in his essays.

關鍵詞: 散文、詩歌、藝術、寫實性、現代性。
Keywords: Essay, poetry, art, realism, modernism.

---

[1] 非馬(1936-),本名馬為義,生於台中市,1961年到美國留學,獲威斯康辛大學核工博士,阿岡國家研究所退休後,致力於詩藝創作。曾獲吳濁流文學獎等殊榮。

一、非馬：自然渾樸的詩人

　　非馬的一生，充滿著神奇、朝氣，純真、樸實和希望。他是縱橫半世紀新詩創作的先鋒，也是科學家兼藝術家。最近由秀威出版的散文集《不為死貓寫悼歌》，涵蓋著他畢生對生活的哲思和自身精神深處的叩問，也間接描繪出二十世紀末期的歷史文化語境下時代的、社會的、與其卓越詩藝的共同印記。

　　關於非馬的創作力，到了晚年仍是文思泉湧。他在〈不知老之已至〉這樣敘述：「說實話，不是我不服老，而是我一直不知道也不認為自己老。」這可能跟他二十多年如一日的有恆鍛煉身體，加上安定平靜的生活、恬淡樂觀的心情有關。非馬自阿岡國家研究所退休後，將寫作及繪畫雕刻作為自己生命的皈依和寄託，期待能與自然進一步進行精神和情感的交流。

　　然而，在這些詩藝的創作中，隱藏在他溫婉的個性下是對生命的簡單理解及生活美學。面對自我的超越與救贖的使命感，他開始在追求自然的夢裡尋求提昇靈魂的方法。於是，出版一本優秀的散文集成為他的夢想與嶄新的創作泉源。他在《不為死貓寫悼歌》一書中，讓散文裡藏著詩的靈魂，並穿插一些自己的畫作。這種詩藝共融的夢幻基調，讓此書的情感底色更明亮，是當今散文界前所未有的。作者以純淨活潑的的筆觸，寫下許多對自然的歌詠、求學歷程的甘苦、社會觀察的營造等題材，沒有半點矯揉，赤誠地抒繪出自己的人生。他一面積極樂觀地道出自己對人生的理解，一面記述自己的詩路歷程，全書充滿了厚實感和思想性。

二、散文中見風骨

　　《不為死貓寫悼歌》書中以讀者熟悉的視覺語言，表達個人主觀經驗上的內涵意義。他曾自白：「有詩的日子，充實而美滿，陽光都分外明亮，使我覺得這一天沒白活。通常一首好詩能為我們喚回生命中快樂的時光，或一個記憶中的美景。它告訴我們，這世界仍充滿了有趣及令人興奮的東西。它使我們覺得能活著真好。」這是說，詩就是非馬生命的存在形態，雖然藝術是由非馬所創造出來，但一旦完成，它本身即具有自足的生命。因此，非馬的散文所彰顯出來的，也不管它是寫實的、意趣的、緬懷的，我們不能以文學的單一性眼光來看待文本的對象。因為，在藝術的思考中，作品從來不只是純粹概念的，而是具體且由詩藝伴生的靈感得到的。

比如寫於1994年的〈永恆的泥土〉，便是他的真情流露：

> 從十三歲離開廣東鄉下，先到台灣，後到美國，這幾十年當中，很少有機會接觸到泥土，但泥土似乎早已滲入了我的血液。即使身處鋼筋水泥高樓大廈的都市，仍有許多東西能引起我對泥土的記憶。我隨時可聞到泥土芳香的氣息。

此篇生動地描寫非馬的父母對子女無私的奉獻與犧牲，深深地影響了他的一生。但他同樣是一個富有使命感和抒情的作家，他對台灣早期農村生活的刻劃，描述得入木三分，夾附的詩也感人肺腑。另一篇寫於1998年的〈學鳥叫的人〉，顯示了人與自然的密切關係，有深厚的韻味：

> ……從停車場到辦公大樓，他一路吹著口哨。輕快、流利，有如一隻飲足了露水的小鳥。我緊跟在他後面，靜靜地分享著他的愉悅，沒出聲同他打招呼。…那段時間，我正為妻的病奔忙，多少有點心力交瘁，各種小毛病也乘虛而入。雖然還沒到髮蒼蒼視茫茫的地步，卻真的有點齒搖搖了。是這聲口哨把我叫醒。是它告訴我，振作起來呀！秋天是忙碌的季節，飽滿多汁的果實，沒有空暇呼痛叫苦。一個禮拜後，我滿心感激地寫下了這首題為〈入秋以後〉的詩：

> 入秋以後
> 蟲咬鳥啄的
> 小小病害
> 在所難免
> 但他不可能呻吟
> 每個裂開的傷口
> 都頃刻間溢滿了
> 蜜汁

這是非馬自己對真實人生的最佳告白，作者用詩活潑了他的散文，語言真誠而自然。其實，此書的許多作品都能帶給讀者舒緩心情及淨化心靈的作用。

非馬在〈不為死貓寫悼歌〉一文中曾提到「而我們如何能期望，一個沽名釣譽甚至趨炎附勢想分得一點政治利益的人，能替大眾發言，為時代做見證，寫下震撼人心的偉大作品？充其量，他只能或只配替死貓寫寫悼歌。」他的散文以寫實性、社會性見長，對社會歪風的諷刺，常一針見血。比如 2001 年寫的〈外賓〉：

> 在中國，作為外賓似乎理所當然地享有特權。而這種特權並非外賓們自己要求或爭取得來的。從好的方面看，它是中國人一向好客的表現。但它更可能是一種根深蒂固、不可救藥的媚外行為。

諸如此類的寫作手法，常讓讀者眼睛應接不暇，最能激發及滿足讀者的想像力，非馬儼然成為人民心聲的詮釋者。此外，比如〈看電視過年〉，也抒發了海外遊子的赤子鄉懷：

> 在海外，觀看國內傳過來的春節聯歡節目，近年來似乎也已成了許多人過年的儀式。在電視的鞭炮與賀年聲中，飄泊海外的遊子，彷彿也置身故鄉，分享著家人過年的歡樂。

在這裡，非馬捨棄了迂迴、重疊的手法，呈現出一種平舖直述的清純。他的散文沒有凝重莊嚴的神秘氛圍，也沒有敏感纖細的浪漫思維；反倒是有一種「一目了然」的簡單趣味，卻能激起讀者感情共鳴及閱讀情緒上的愉悅。在〈有詩為證〉文中，他說：「如果有人問我，我生平的「本行」是什麼，我一定會毫不猶豫地說：『詩！』但我自己心裡明白，科技只是我賴以謀生的工具，詩才是我夢寐以求全力以赴的生活內涵。或者用時髦的說法，科技是冷冰冰的硬體，詩才是溫暖並活潑我生命的軟體。」這大概是非馬把詩伸展到散文領域的動機與動力。

三、非馬：藝術光環普耀文壇

我們常說，一個成功的詩人，少不了天時、地利、人和中的任何一個條件。我認為，定居於芝加哥的詩人非馬，能傲視華文文壇的原因在於：

（一）是從創作的數量和質量看，他迄今已出版了 20 餘冊書。他的詩文廣受讀者的喜愛與評者的肯定。

（二）是從文體創新看，非馬的散文，展現了現代風貌，讓讀者不得不佩服其構思的奇妙和想像力的豐富。

（三）是散文結合詩畫於文的表現方面作出了示範。他既是一位優秀的科學家，同時也是個傑出的詩畫家。在散文的用字、意蘊以及題材選擇的安排上，都與傳統的抒情文本有所區別。

令人印象深刻的是，書中有篇 2007 年寫的〈雪花與煤灰齊飛的日子〉，呈現出簡單、感性誠實的生活記趣：

> 不久前同兩個兒子談起當年在密爾瓦基城所過的雪花與煤灰齊飛的日子，他們都笑我又在那裡編造憶苦思甜的故事。我說我這可是在憶甘思甜。在那些年輕且充滿對未來憧憬的歲月裡，許多本來是苦的東西，現在咀嚼起來，竟都帶點甘味，如青澀的橄欖。

本質上，非馬的藝術追求是一種圓融的生命境界。堅毅的精神及刻苦的生活回憶，常在他的筆下浮現，顯得分外親切動人。他的純情恰可彌補現代都市人的失落感。對人生、藝術或現實的社會，都存有一種深情、一種關注的悲憫。《不為死貓寫悼歌》讀起來既不像是對於夢幻光影的捕捉，也不像是在聆聽一首浪漫的純粹音樂；反倒像是一種鄉思的吐露與生活心情的自我抒發，是歡笑與汗水交織過程的記述，老少咸宜，百讀不厭。最值得推崇的是，他始終胸懷一種怡然自在的生命觀照，其思想之淵博、新詩創作之超越，無疑是使此書邁向成功的最大原因。最後引用書中一段名言，作為推介此書以及衷心的祝福：

> 英國作家福特（Ford Maddox Ford, 1873-1939）說：「偉大詩歌是它無需注釋且毫不費勁地用意象攪動你的感情；你因而成為一個較好的人；你軟化了，心腸更加柔和，對同類的困苦及需要也更慷慨同情。

—寫於 2010.11.12

【刊於美國《亞特蘭大新聞》*Atlanta Chinese News*，2011.01.14。】

簡論非馬的散文創作──讀《不為死貓寫悼歌》有感

I. William Marr[2]: A natural and simple poet

William Marr's life was full of magic, vigor, innocence, simplicity and hope. He was a pioneer in modern poetry creation for half a century, and was also a scientist and artist. The essay collection *No Elegy for a Dead Cat*, recently published by Xiu Wei, covers his lifelong philosophy of life and his deep spiritual questioning. It also indirectly depicts the common imprint of the times, society, and his outstanding poetic art in the historical and cultural context of the late twentieth century.

As for William Marr's creativity, he was still full of ideas even in his later years. In "Not Knowing That I'm Old", he recounted: "To be honest, it's not that I don't accept my old age, but I have never known or considered myself old." This may be related to his consistent physical exercise for more than 20 years, as well as his stable and peaceful life and calm and optimistic mood. After retiring from the Argonne National Research Institute, William Marr has taken writing, painting and sculpture as his refuge and sustenance in life, hoping to further communicate spiritually and emotionally with nature.

However, hidden in these poetic works, beneath his gentle personality, is a simple understanding of life and the aesthetics of living. Faced with the mission of self-transcendence and redemption, he began to seek ways to elevate his soul in his dream of pursuing nature. Therefore, publishing an excellent collection of essays became his dream and a new source of inspiration. In his book *No Elegy for a Dead Cat*, he hides the soul of poetry in his prose and intersperses some of his own paintings. This dreamy tone of poetry and art makes the emotional background of the book brighter, which is unprecedented in the prose world today. The author uses pure and lively brushstrokes to write about many themes such as the praises of nature, the joys and sorrows of studying, and the creation of social observations. Without any affectation, he sincerely depicts his own life. On the one hand, he

---

[2] William Marr (1936-), whose real name is Ma Weiyi, was born in Taichung City. He went to the United States to study in 1961 and received a Ph.D. in nuclear engineering from the University of Wisconsin. After retiring from the Argonne National Research Laboratory, he devoted himself to poetry creation. He has won the Wu Zhuoliu Literature Award and other honors.

expresses his understanding of life in a positive and optimistic manner, on the other hand, he records his own poetic journey. The whole book is full of substance and thoughtfulness.

II. Character is reflected in prose

The book *No Elegy for a Dead Cat* uses visual language familiar to readers to express the connotation of personal subjective experience. He once confessed: "The days with poetry are full and happy, the sun is especially bright, making me feel that the day is not lived in vain. Usually a good poem can bring back happy moments in our lives or a beautiful scene in our memories. It tells us that the world is still full of interesting and exciting things. It makes us feel great to be alive." This means that poetry is the form of existence of William Marr. Although art is created by William Marr, once it is completed, it has a self-sufficient life in itself. Therefore, no matter what William Marr's prose shows, whether it is realistic, interesting, or nostalgic, we cannot view the object of the text from a single literary perspective. Because, in artistic thinking, the work is never purely conceptual, but concrete and inspired by poetry.

For example, "Eternal Soil", written in 1994, is a true expression of his feelings:

> Since I left the countryside of Guangdong at the age of thirteen, I first went to Taiwan and then to the United States. In the past few decades, I have rarely had the opportunity to come into contact with soil, but soil seems to have already seeped into my blood. Even though I live in a city full of steel and concrete skyscrapers, there are still many things that evoke my memories of the earth. I can smell the fragrance of the earth at all times.

This article vividly describes William Marr's parents' selfless devotion and sacrifice for their children, which deeply influenced his life. But he is also a writer with a strong sense of mission and lyricism. His depiction of early rural life in Taiwan is extremely vivid, and the accompanying poems are also very touching. Another article written in 1998, "The Man Who Learned to Sing Birds", shows the close relationship between man and nature, and has a profound charm:

簡論非馬的散文創作——讀《不為死貓寫悼歌》有感

...He whistled all the way from the parking lot to the office building. Light and fluent, like a bird that has drunk enough dew. I followed closely behind him, quietly sharing his joy, without saying a word to greet him. ...During that time, I was busy taking care of my wife's illness, and I was somewhat exhausted, so various minor ailments took advantage of the situation and crept in. Although he is not yet at the stage of gray hair and blurred vision, his teeth are indeed a little loose. It was the whistle that woke me up. It tells me to cheer up! Autumn is a busy season, with plump and juicy fruits, leaving no time for complaining. A week later, I wrote this poem titled "After Autumn" with a grateful heart:

After autumn
Insect bites and bird pecks
Minor disease
Inevitable
But he couldn't moan
Every open wound
All of a sudden it was filled
Honey

This is William Marr's best confession of real life. The author uses poetry to liven up his prose, and the language is sincere and natural. In fact, many works in this book can soothe readers and purify their souls.

William Marr once mentioned in his article "Don't Write an Elegy for a Dead Cat" that "How can we expect a person who seeks fame and reputation or even curries favor with the powerful to get a share of political benefits to speak for the masses, bear witness to the times, and write great works that shock people? At best, he can only or is only qualified to write a eulogy for a dead cat." His essays are known for their realism and social nature, and his satire on social malpractices is often incisive. For example, "Foreign Guests" written in 2001:

Being a foreign guest in China seems to be a privilege that is taken for granted. This privilege was not requested or fought for by the foreign guests themselves. On the positive side, it is a reflection of the traditional hospitality of the Chinese people. But it is more likely a deep-rooted and incurable form of fawning on foreigners.

Writing techniques like these often leave readers overwhelmed and are most able to stimulate and satisfy readers' imagination. William Marr has become the interpreter of the people's voice. In addition, for example, "Watching TV during the New Year" also expresses the homesickness of overseas wanderers:

> Overseas, watching the Spring Festival Gala programs transmitted from China seems to have become a New Year ritual for many people in recent years. Amid the sounds of firecrackers and New Year greetings on TV, those who are living overseas seem to be back home, sharing the joy of the New Year with their family.

Here, William Marr abandoned the roundabout and overlapping techniques and presented a pure and straightforward statement. His prose does not have a solemn and mysterious atmosphere, nor does it have sensitive and delicate romantic thinking; instead, it has a simple interest that is "clear at a glance" and can arouse readers' emotional resonance and emotional pleasure in reading. In the article "Poetry as Evidence", he said: "If someone asked me what my main profession in life was, I would answer without hesitation: poetry! But I know in my heart that technology is just a tool for me to make a living, and poetry is the content of life that I dream of and devote all my energy to. Or to put it in a trendy way, technology is the cold hardware, and poetry is the software that warms and enlivens my life." This is probably William Marr's motivation and driving force for extending poetry into the field of prose.

III. William Marr: His artistic halo shines on the literary world

We often say that to be a successful poet, one must have any one of the following conditions: the right time, the right place, and the right people. I think the reason why William Marr, a poet who lives in Chicago, can dominate the Chinese literary world is that:

Firstly, judging from the quantity and quality of his works, he has published more than 20 books so far. His poems and essays are widely loved by readers and recognized by critics.

Secondly, from the perspective of stylistic innovation, William Marr's prose displays a modern style, which makes readers admire his wonderful conception and rich imagination.

Thirdly, it sets an example in the expression of combining poetry and painting in prose. He is an excellent scientist, as well as an outstanding poet and painter. The words used, implications, and subject matter chosen in prose are different from traditional lyrical texts.

What is particularly impressive is that there is an article in the book written in 2007, "The Days When Snowflakes and Coal Ash Fly Together", which presents a simple, emotionally honest account of life:

> Not long ago, I talked to my two sons about the days when snowflakes and coal dust were flying together in Milwaukee. They laughed at me and said I was making up stories about reminiscing about the good old days. I said I was recalling the bitter days. In those young full of longing for the future, many things that were originally bitter now taste sweet when chewed, like green olives.

In essence, William Marr's artistic pursuit is a harmonious state of life. The spirit of perseverance and memories of hard life often emerge in his writing, appearing particularly intimate and moving. His innocence can just make up for the sense of loss of modern urbanites. There is a deep affection and a compassion for life, art, and real society. Reading "No Elegy for a Dead Cat" does not feel like capturing a dreamy light and shadow, nor does it feel like listening to a pure romantic music; instead, it feels like an expression of homesickness and a self-expression of life moods, a record of the interweaving process of laughter and sweat, suitable for all ages and never tire of reading. What is most admirable is that he always maintains a carefree outlook on life. The profoundness of his thoughts and the transcendence of his new poetry creation are undoubtedly the biggest reasons for the success of this book. Finally, I would like to quote a famous quote from the book as a recommendation for this book and a heartfelt blessing:

> Ford Maddox Ford (1873-1939), an English writer, once said: "Great poetry is that which stirs your emotions with images without comment and effortlessly. You become a better person; you are softened, your heart becomes softer, and you become more generous and sympathetic to the sufferings and needs of your fellow men."

—Written on November 12, 2010.

【Published in *Atlanta Chinese News*, USA, January 14, 2011】

27 讀東行詩集《水果之詩》
Reading Dong Xing's Poetry Collection *Poems of Fruits*

　　這是一部特殊的詩集。說它特殊，是因為目前詩壇上無人這樣寫過。

　　東行，本名張月環，屏東潮州鎮人，日本國立岡山大學博士，目前任教於屏東商業技術學院。著有《家鄉的雨》隨筆集、《我與巴爾克》短篇小說集、《風鈴季歌》詩集及《川端康成の美の性格》論文集等多種。這本《水果之詩》涵蓋五十種水果為主題，集合1980年代至2011年創作所出版的中日對照詩集，是留日十年的東行，揮筆留下了對家鄉深愛而熱情的歌唱，以及對日本俳句加以研究，再昇華為藝術形象的體驗，也是她用心血釀製成的甜美果實。書裡穿插的水果圖片絕大部份由日本大阪的虎谷知彥拍攝，在視覺藝術方面的造詣很高，加以國際俳句作家黃靈芝（1928-　）對本詩集的監修及日本岡山大學名譽教授赤羽學、吉備國際大學教授岡崎郁子、高雄師範大學退休教授李若鶯等三位學者為序，可謂是其詩作的精品，也代表了東行總體的藝術追求和語言風格。

　　細細品味，可以得出這樣一個認識，即東行詩作的內涵就是在其詩歌中蘊含的細膩感覺，尤其是她用心靈體察各種水果，似有神來之筆創造出多彩的藝術形象，而所夾雜的情思和餘韻常常被讀者所稱道。這也許是嚴羽《滄浪詩話》中說的「大抵禪道唯在妙語，詩道亦在妙語。」當然，對東行這本詩集來說，時而會有這種妙悟後聯想出新奇景象的感受。如〈椰子〉一詩，是深厚的鄉情必然，她懷念故鄉屏東，寫來自然情真意切，很感人的：

　　　風揚起帆
　　　船盪漾在綠林原野中
　　　一彎弓月伴隨婆娑
　　　以南臺灣獨特舞步
　　　掃蕩群海　赫赫頂天於大地
　　　款款風情
　　　淡淡地　淡淡底汁色
　　　清中帶乳白　沒有喧染唇齒的芬芳

　　　　　　　也讀不出任何酸辣心機
　卻一點一滴　　滴滴融入夏季
　　因而可口

　　「一灣弓月伴隨婆娑」是全詩之魂，或是眼睛。東行大半生的時光一直和故鄉生活在一起，她熱愛故鄉，懷有理想。留日返國教學之餘，也投入到詩歌的創作中，且大多採用托物言志和即物生情等手法。故鄉的椰子樹雖然常為南臺灣的天空增添一份旖旎的風情，東行却以審美理念為切入點，借此盡展在對大千世界的觀察與感情中的思緒和微妙的心理變化，是富有創造性的。

　　東行返鄉後，隨著年齡的增長，對無常世界也有了新的頓悟。或許是日本的和歌、連歌、茶道等文化的審美觀，為她詩歌創作開闢了一些管道，而莊子的消遙遊使她找到了審美的致高點。加以禪學的妙悟為她創造俳句藝術和情趣提供了最佳的手法表現。其中，臺灣的俳句大師黃靈芝作家的監修，也讓東行的這本詩集不只是借物抒情，還體現自己的生存價值。讓詩集不但有了生命，還有了個性。總的風格則在於它的幽默、苦澀和情趣性。再如〈芭樂〉一詩：

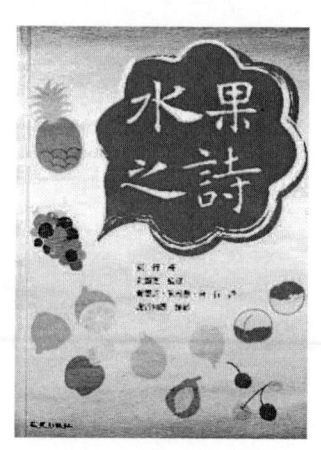

　　我總是在
　　枝椏低垂的彼端
　　偷偷地望著
　　陽光自葉間掠過
　　麻雀從一株跳躍到另一株
　　精確又專注地尋找我
　　老去的弟兄
　　我偷偷地望著
　　偷偷地長大……

　　青春　已化為灰燼
　　沒有火　我依舊燃燒
　　只是
　　不適合消化
　　留著紅子
　　只想證明
　　曾經是存在的

> 曾經年輕過
> 也曾美麗過

　　東行以無心的心境,深刻剖析了自己純粹心懷之所在。這種表達感情的藝術方式,在寫對愛的思念時,更增加了詩的內在力度。是啊,即便等待的日子很長很長,也無悔地耐心等待,因為作者和它曾經擁有過燦爛的過去。哪怕只是一瞬,也已足夠。詩裡最後則回歸於對童真年華,有一種返璞歸真的哲思在內,也充滿了對愛的堅持,令人激賞。且看另一首〈櫻桃〉,這當然是東行的力作之一:

> 五月的彩虹
> 泡在香檳裡

　　詩好就好在一開頭就把讀者帶入境界。作者不但把櫻桃比喻成五月的彩虹,而且「泡在香檳裡」給人一種新鮮的出奇制勝之感,尤以第二行起頭以「泡」一字,正是詩中的審美源泉。這都起到了以象蘊情、情景交融的境地,詩中也體現出的禪意的趣味性。〈木瓜〉一詩,則是另一份真情:

> 夢中常見
> 一排排一列列
> 纍纍木瓜樹
> 台北高雄一只相思
> 木瓜牛奶
> 如泉似乳溫潤溫潤
> 是冬之井
> 　夏之鶯
> 天下一品如今兄弟有誰嚐
> 當憶我　遠在東洋
> 遍尋芳草問瓜棚

　　寫得清純,樸素恬淡,內裡溶聚著對故鄉強烈的思情。詩,是情、象、理的有機結合,而「情」是詩魂所在。詩的可貴處,正在於東行也從古典詩詞中汲取了營養。敘事與抒情間,又把作者對故鄉的想念,對木瓜牛奶的渴望顯露於意象之中。特別是把木瓜牛奶喻為「是冬之井／夏之鶯」一句，更是難得，頗有通感之妙。再如〈桑葚〉一詩，語言極富概括力和質感：

　　串串紫瑪瑙
　　論食論補兩相宜
　　鳥也饞　人也饞
　　蘊藏風味一番贊

　　寥寥幾筆，就把桑葚的形象和特色生動地展現出來。據《本草備要》中記載：桑椹甘涼，利五臟關節，安魂鎮神，聰耳明目，生津止渴，利水消腫。而這種意境的開拓，又常常借助於俳句的某些典故。俳句是日本古典短詩，最早出現於《古今和歌集》，至江戶時代（1600年－1867年）則有從「俳諧連歌」產生的俳句、連句、俳文等。東行在此詩集中，也有其他詩作內裡有著類似俳句的文化氣息。如〈鳳梨〉、〈無花果〉、〈紅毛丹〉等。但我認為，此詩集最突出的特徵還在於東行對現代詩和古老的東方美學內在神韻方面的繼承與創新。從中可看出東行在學習古典詩詞與日語等方面所下功夫之深。當然，東行非專業詩人，對一個學者來說，創作上能達到這般境地及自我要求，已是難能可貴。此外，篇末還附有一些彩色的臺灣水果郵票，篇前也有自序的中日翻譯，亦對讀者會有更深的啟示。相信東行會有更多佳作問世。

　　　　　　　　　　　－2016.5.23 作者為詩評家寫於台東

【刊臺灣臺南市《鹽分地帶文學》のコンテンツをもっと見よう雙月刊，第64期，2016年6月，頁177-182及李若鶯教授攝影林明理照。】

　　This is a special collection of poems, and it is special because no one in the poetry world has written like this.

　　Dong Xing, whose real name is Zhang Yuehuan, is from Chaozhou Town, Pingtung. He holds a doctorate from Okayama University, Japan, and currently teaches at Pingtung University of Commerce and Technology. He has written many books, including the essay collection *Rain in Hometown*, the short story collection *Me and Bark*, the poetry

讀東行詩集《水果之詩》

collection *Wind Bell Season Song* and the essay collection *The Beautiful Character of Kawabata Yasunari*. This book, *Poems of Fruits*, covers fifty kinds of fruits as the theme. It is a collection of Chinese and Japanese poems created and published from the 1980s to 2011. It is the result of her ten years of studying in Japan, leaving behind a passionate song of love for her hometown, as well as her experience of studying Japanese haiku and sublimating it into an artistic image. It is also the sweet fruit brewed with her hard work. Most of the fruit pictures in the book were taken by Tomohiko Toraya in Osaka, Japan, who has a high level of achievement in visual art. In addition, the international haiku writer Huang Lingzhi (1928-) supervised the collection of poems, and three scholars, including Emeritus Professor Akabane Manabu of Okayama University, Professor Okazaki Ikuko of Kibi International University, and Retired Professor Li Ruoying of Kaohsiung Normal University, wrote the prefaces. This can be regarded as a masterpiece of his poems, and also represents the overall artistic pursuit and language style of Toyoko.

If you savor it carefully, you can come to the conclusion that the connotation of Dong Xing's poems is the delicate feeling contained in her poems, especially her use of her mind to perceive various fruits, creating colorful artistic images as if inspired by a stroke of genius, and the mixed emotions and aftertaste are often praised by readers. This may be what Yan Yu said in *Canglang Poetry Talk*: "Mostly, Zen is only about wonderful words, and poetry is also about wonderful words." Of course, for Dong Xing's collection of poems, sometimes there will be such a feeling of associating new scenes after wonderful enlightenment. The poem "Coconut" is a natural expression of deep nostalgia. She misses her hometown Pingtung, and writes with natural feelings and is very touching:

> The wind raises the sails
> The boat ripples in the green forest and wilderness
> A crescent moon accompanies the dancing
> With the unique dance steps of southern Taiwan
> Sweeping the seas and towering over the earth
> A graceful style
> Lightly, lightly colored
> Clear with milky white, there is no fragrance that stains the

> lips and teeth
> No sour and spicy thoughts can be read
> But it blends into the summer bit by bit
> So it is delicious

"A crescent moon accompanies the dancing" is the soul of the whole poem, or the eyes. Dong Xing has lived in her hometown for most of her life. She loves her hometown and has ideals. After returning to Japan to teach, she also devoted herself to poetry creation, and most of her poems used methods such as expressing her thoughts through objects and expressing her feelings through objects. Although the coconut trees in her hometown often add a beautiful scenery to the sky of southern Taiwan, Dong Xing used aesthetic concepts as a starting point to fully display her thoughts and subtle psychological changes in her observation and feelings of the world, which is creative.

After returning to her hometown, as she grew older, she also had a new epiphany about the impermanent world. Perhaps it was the aesthetics of Japanese culture such as waka, renga, and tea ceremony that opened up some channels for her poetry creation, and Zhuangzi's travels helped her find the pinnacle of aesthetics. In addition, the wonderful enlightenment of Zen provided her with the best method to express her creation of haiku art and interest. Among them, the supervision of Taiwan's haiku master Huang Lingzhi also makes Dong Xing's poetry collection not only express emotions through objects, but also reflects his own survival value. It makes the poetry collection not only alive, but also has personality. The overall style lies in its humor, bitterness and interest. Another example is the poem "Guava":

> I am always
> at the other side of the drooping branches
> looking secretly
> at the sunlight passing through the leaves
> at the sparrows jumping from one plant to another
> looking for
> my old brother
> accurately and attentively
> I look secretly
> growing up secretly...

讀東行詩集《水果之詩》

> Youth
> has turned to ashes
> without fire
> I still burn
> just
> unsuitable for digestion
> leaving the red seeds
> just to prove
> that
> I once existed
> I was young
> and beautiful

  Dong Xing deeply analyzes his pure heart with a carefree state of mind. This artistic way of expressing emotions adds to the inner strength of the poem when writing about the longing for love. Yes, even if the days of waiting are very long, I will wait patiently without regrets, because the author and it once had a brilliant past. Even if it is just a moment, it is enough. The poem finally returns to the innocent years, with a philosophical thought of returning to the basics, and is full of persistence in love, which is admirable. Let's look at another poem "Cherry", which is certainly one of Dong Xing's masterpieces:

> May's Rainbow
> Soaked in Champagne

  The good thing about poetry is that it brings readers into the realm at the beginning. The author not only compares cherry to the rainbow in May, but also "soaked in champagne" gives people a sense of freshness and surprise, especially the word "soak" at the beginning of the second line, which is the source of the aesthetics in the poem. This has played a role in the realm of blending emotions with images and scenes, and the poem also reflects the interest of Zen. "Papaya", this poem is about another true feeling:

> I often see it in my dreams
> Rows and rows of papaya trees
> A tree in Taipei and Kaohsiung

> Papaya milk
> Like a spring and milk, warm and moist
> It is a well in winter
> An oriole in summer
> The best in the world, who will taste it now
> Remember me, far away in the East
> Searching for fragrant grass and melon sheds

It is written in a pure, simple and tranquil style, and it contains a strong feeling for the hometown. Poetry is an organic combination of emotion, image and reason, and "emotion" is the soul of poetry. The value of poetry is that the journey to the east also draws nourishment from classical poetry. Between narration and lyricism, the author's longing for his hometown and his desire for papaya milk are revealed in the imagery. In particular, the sentence comparing papaya milk to "a well in winter and an oriole in summer" is rare and has a sense of synaesthesia. Another example is the poem "Mulberry", which is very comprehensive and textured:

> Strings of purple agate
> Both food and tonic
> Birds are greedy and people are greedy
> The hidden flavor is praised

In just a few words, the image and characteristics of mulberry are vividly displayed. According to the *Compendium of Materia Medica*, mulberry is sweet and cool, beneficial to the five internal organs and joints, soothing the soul and calming the mind, sharpening the ears and eyes, promoting the production of body fluids and quenching thirst, and promoting diuresis and reducing swelling. And the development of this artistic conception often relies on certain allusions in haiku. Haiku is a classical Japanese short poem that first appeared in the Kokin Wakashu. In the Edo period (1600-1867), there were haiku, renga, and haiwen that were derived from haikyō renga. In this collection of poems, Togyuki also has other poems with a cultural atmosphere similar to haiku. For example, "Pineapple", "Fig", "Rambutan", etc. But I think the most outstanding feature of this collection of poems is Togyuki's inheritance and innovation of the inner charm of modern poetry and ancient oriental aesthetics. From this, we can see how much effort Togyuki put into learning classical poetry and Japanese. Of course, Togyuki is not a professional poet. For a scholar, it is rare to reach such a state and self-requirement in creation. In addition, there are some colorful Taiwanese fruit stamps at the end of the article, and there is also a Chinese-Japanese translation of the preface at the beginning of the article, which will also give readers a deeper enlightenment. I believe that there will be more excellent works in the East.

— May 23, 2016,
the author wrote it in Taitung for the poetry critic

【Published in the bimonthly のコンテンツをもっと見よう in Tainan City, Taiwan, No. 64, June 2016, pages 177-182; Professor Li Ruoying took photos of Lin Ming-Li.】

28 生命風景的畫冊——讀李若鶯詩集《謎・事件簿》
A Picture Album of the Scenery of Life: Reading Li Ruoying's Poetry Collection *Mystery Incident Book*

　　為人清透而處世寬容的李若鶯（1950-　），生於高雄，是南台灣的學者作家。她是高雄師範大學國文系退休教授，現任《鹽分地帶文學》主編，曾獲高雄市文學獎。著有《花落蓮成—唐宋詞散論》、《唐宋詞鑑賞通論》、《現代詩修辭運用析探》、《寫生》等。近作詩集《謎・事件簿》內涵豐富，收錄作者詩作七十餘首，記錄其生活和情感中快樂的、悲傷的心曲，處處注滿真情。品讀之下，使人可以真切地看到和聽到她借自己的筆觸，將那些觸使她心動的「也許是靜物，也許是風景，也許是一朵鹿角花，也許是紅樓的燈，也許是森巴搖擺的舞步，也許是美麗邂逅中感動的笑聲，也許是為父親送別的呼喚⋯」都勾起了她的充沛的感情。

　　若鶯在詩集自序裡說：「詩如果不能照見詩人的靈魂，觸動讀著心弦，將只是一朵隨開隨落的花，它的綻放，也就是它的死亡。」在生命之重面前，若鶯自高中起便打工，一路苦讀至博士，她努力駕馭命運、超越痛苦。心性清澄而愛靜思的她，退休幾年後，便與林佛兒喬遷到西港鄉居享受優閒、專於戶外攝影及創作；寫詩以外，若鶯也是女性散文創作的旗手。善用意象的創造，筆墨細膩，文采溫婉，將女性對世事的感悟和對自然的觀察和重要社會事件的深刻認知，在書中表現其情感的內斂和文字的詩性確是若鶯詩歌的一大特點。

　　正如若鶯在1987年，毅然選擇結束婚姻，做了二個孩子的單親家長。十年後歲暮，旅居日本朋友某回台探親，特來相訪後，在這首詩〈我依然在流浪〉裡，我們可以清晰地感受到她不平靜的靈魂：

　　　　從十年前的櫻花中你走來
　　　　港口沉默蹲踞
　　　　春帆帶雨消逝在海霧裡
　　　　行囊沉甸甸是提不動的滄桑

生命風景的畫冊──讀李若鶯詩集《謎·事件簿》

眸光交鎖
往事被點醒如暗夜煙火
白駒躍過肋骨的牆籬匆匆來去
揚起的蹄塵有老檜的陳香新柿的青澀

起出封藏石頭下那瓮花雕
翻閱 3x5 或 4x6 的記憶
唉　不過一些被鏡頭切割的黛綠
在穿梭的唱歎中
努力尋找遺失的圖籍
好在酒後循著原路回去
明天你會重返久違的故里
如果窗下那株桃花問起
你就　你就
請就這樣告訴她
我依然天涯浪跡

　　從最後一句「我依然天涯浪跡」，我們感受了「悲從中來」，也看到了詩人的內心。她認為：「我的詩是我的生命圖景，而我的生命體驗反映了時代風潮和社會現象。」若鶯經過離別動盪的社會環境及教學生涯後，她冀望能過安寧的日子，回歸簡靜的寫作與編輯生活，於是在 2004 年五月，決定辭去教職，同年月底，詩人邀女同事在御書房餐廳為退休前道別而作的詩〈夏季的邀約〉，閱讀此詩彷彿是秋風輕拂楊樹的舞動：

這是夏天
風鈴　紫檀　紫薇　鳳凰　阿勃樂　陸續登場
有些花開　綻開　離開
有些花謝　披謝　道謝
小小一片指甲似的黃槐
辭謝枝葉隨風遠颺

像演完戲的演員清空舞台的道具
謝幕下場
吹著口哨走開
下一齣戲
如果還有腳力

將在未知的遠方
　　劇本還在上帝手上

　　生命的時序已臨秋
　　秋天的封面
　　金黃的色彩
　　被風掀開的某一頁
　　隱約繽紛自己童年的
　　癡騃

　　還留戀著的就是大家了
　　我將在六月十日星期四
　　白天遜讓給夜晚美麗將點燃的六點鐘
　　在御書房和大家話別

　　這只是一場
　　雲的邀約
　　請妳
　　就順著風的方向吹

　　如上的詩意描寫，充斥在這本詩集之中。再如2011年夏，若鶯與林佛兒隨同畫家陳志良初訪鰲鼓濕地而作的〈沉靜的鰲鼓〉，有較濃的文學氣息，文字和情感配合，使詩之觀照的生活心靈化，大大拓寬了讀者對濕地的深刻體認：

　　沉靜　以巨大的
　　森林的綠蔭般的色彩
　　籠罩濕地
　　鷺鷥
　　盟鷗
　　鸕鶿
　　鳥的美無聲
　　夕陽無聲

　　漁船滑過
　　三個躡足的訪客
　　一種有重量的安靜

生命風景的畫冊——讀李若鶯詩集《謎·事件簿》

不知名的相忘於江湖
夕照隱去後退潮的海棚
閃熾無法調繪的顏彩

湖水
菱荇
木麻黃
紅樹林
馬鞍藤
黃槿稞葉樹
血桐木
白千層
瘠查某

眾生去來
鰲鼓無聲
我亦無聲
巨美無聲
讚美無聲

　　這首詩的節奏感鮮明，其「巨美無聲」的意境就是詩。這也正是這一時期若鶯詩歌增加了對觀察自然的視角的基本面貌。此外，有關懷九二一集集大地震、女童被凌虐事件、八掌溪事件等描寫，也確實蘊藏著某種力量。詩人跨過傳統，其所突出的是自我的主體意識抬高。她站在臺灣，看著歷史及社會的變遷，關注著臺灣的人民。除了頗具現代詩的詩作之外，若鶯的詩也不乏對於重大時事的關懷和社會情態進行深度的審視。這本詩集表現出的主體精神和對自我生命流程的深刻體認，顯示出李若鶯女性詩歌的潛力。如果我們細讀若李鶯情詩的發展，比較她各個時期的情詩，也可以從中解開一些謎題。總之，詩是若鶯心靈之歌，無論是詩中洋溢的悲傷或幸福之感，在我收到她寄贈來的詩集及特別遠從台南來台東探訪我，我表示由衷的謝意，也感謝她與林佛兒攜手合作編輯《臺灣風土》所付出的辛勤與汗水。

　　　　　　　　　　　　　　　　　　　　　　　—2016.5.20

【刊臺灣《海星》詩刊，2016.09，第 21 期秋季號，頁 16-19。】

文評集粹讀本
Selected Readings in Literary Reviews

Li Ruoying (1950-), clear-headed and tolerant, was born in Kaohsiung and is a scholar and writer in southern Taiwan. She is a retired professor of the Department of Chinese Literature at Kaohsiung Normal University and is currently the editor-in-chief of *Salt Zone Literature*. She has won the Kaohsiung City Literature Award. She has written *Flowers Falling and Lotuses Growing: Essays on Tang and Song Ci*, *General Theory of Appreciation of Tang and Song Ci-poetry*, *Analysis of the Use of Rhetoric in Modern Poetry*, *Sketch*, etc. The recent poetry collection *Mystery Incident Book* is rich in content, including more than 70 poems by the author, recording the happy and sad songs in her life and emotions, and is full of true feelings everywhere. Reading the poems, one can truly see and hear that she used her pen to describe the things that moved her heart, "maybe still life, maybe scenery, maybe a stag horn flower, maybe the lights of the Red Mansion, maybe the swinging steps of samba, maybe the moving laughter in a beautiful encounter, maybe the call to bid farewell to her father..." All of them evoked her abundant emotions.

Ruo Ying said in the preface to her poetry collection: "If poetry cannot illuminate the poet's soul and touch the heartstrings, it will only be a flower that blooms and falls. Its blooming is also its death." Faced with the weight of life, Ruo Ying has been working since high school and studied hard all the way to a doctorate. She strives to control her fate and transcend pain. She is a person of pure mind and loves meditation. After retiring for a few years, she moved to the countryside of Xigang with Lin Fuerqiao to enjoy leisure, focus on outdoor photography and creation. In addition to writing poetry, Ruoying is also a standard-bearer of female prose creation. She is good at creating images, delicate and gentle in writing, and expresses women's perception of the world, observation of nature and profound understanding of important social events in the book. The restraint of emotions and the poetic nature of words are indeed a major feature of Ruoying's poetry.

Just as Ruoying resolutely chose to end her marriage in 1987 and became a single parent of two children. Ten years later, a friend who lives in Japan came back to Taiwan to visit her family. After visiting her, we can clearly feel her restless soul in this poem "I am still wandering":

> You came from the cherry blossoms ten years ago
> The harbor crouched in silence
> The spring sails disappeared in the sea mist with rain
> The bag was heavy with the vicissitudes of life that could not be lifted
> The eyes were locked
> The past was awakened like fireworks in the dark night
> The white horse jumped over the wall of ribs and came and went in a hurry
> The hoof dust raised had the old fragrance of old cypress and the greenness of new persimmon
>
> Take out the urn of Huadiao hidden under the stone
> Read the memory of 3x5 or 4x6
> Alas However, some dark green cut by the lens
> In the sigh of shuttle
> Trying to find the lost books
> Fortunately, after drinking, I went back along the original route
> Tomorrow you will return to your long-lost hometown
> If the peach blossom under the window asks
> You just you just
> Please tell her like this
> I am still wandering around the world

From the last sentence "I am still wandering around the world", we feel the "sorrow from it" and see the poet's heart. She believes: "My poems are the pictures of my life, and my life experience reflects the trend of the times and social phenomena." After leaving the turbulent social environment and teaching career, Ruo Ying hoped to live a peaceful life and return to a simple writing and editing life. So in May 2004, she decided to resign from her teaching position. At the end of the same year, the poet invited a female colleague to the Yu Shufang Restaurant to write a poem for her farewell before retirement "Summer Invitation". Reading this poem is like the autumn wind blowing the dance of the poplar trees:

This is summer
Wind chimes, red sandalwood, crape myrtle, phoenix, and apollo appear one after another
Some flowers bloom, bloom, and leave
Some flowers wither, and thank you Thank you
A small piece of yellow acacia as small as a fingernail
Thank you for the branches and leaves swaying in the wind

Like actors who have finished a play and clear the stage props
Walk away with a whistle
The next play
If I still have the strength
Will be in an unknown distance
The script is still in God's hands

The time sequence of life has come to autumn
The cover of autumn
The golden color
A certain page opened by the wind
Vaguely colorful
The foolishness of my childhood
The ones who still miss it are you

I will say goodbye to everyone in the imperial study on Thursday, June 10
When the day gives way to the beauty of the night and will be lit at six o'clock.

This is just an invitation from the clouds
Please blow in the direction of the wind

  The above poetic description is filled in this collection of poems. Another example is the poem "Silent Aogu" written by Ruo Ying and Lin Fuer in the summer of 2011 when they accompanied painter Chen Zhiliang on their first visit to Aogu Wetland. It has a strong literary flavor, and the combination of words and emotions makes the life observed in the poem spiritualized, greatly broadening the reader's profound understanding of the wetland:

Silent With huge
The green shade-like colors of the forest

Enveloping the wetland
Heron
Gull
Corpse
The beauty of birds is silent
The sunset is silent

The fishing boat glides by
Three treading visitors
A kind of weighty silence
Anonymous forgetfulness in the world
The sea shelf at low tide after the sunset disappears
Flashing colors that cannot be painted

Lake water
Water chestnuts
Casuarinas
Mangroves
Saddle vines
Yellow hibiscus tree
Tung tree
Mealela
Land of the dead

The coming and going of people
The drum is silent
I am also silent
The great beauty is silent
Praise is silent

  The rhythm of this poem is distinct, and its artistic conception of "great beauty and silence" is poetry. This is also the basic aspect of Ruoying's poems during this period that added a new perspective on observing nature. In addition, the descriptions of the 921 earthquake, the abuse of girls, and the Bazhang River incident do contain a certain power. The poet transcends tradition, and what she highlights is the elevation of her own subjective consciousness. She stands in Taiwan, watching the changes in history and society, and paying attention to the people of Taiwan. In addition to poems that are quite modern, Ruoying's poems also show concern for major current events and in-depth examinations of social conditions. The subjective spirit and deep understanding of the process of one's own life expressed in this collection of poems show the potential of Li Ruoying's female poetry. If we carefully read the development of Li Ying's love poems and compare her love poems of different periods, we can also solve some puzzles. In short, poetry is the song of Li Ying's soul. Whether it is the sadness or happiness in the poems, I expressed my sincere gratitude when I received the collection of poems she sent me and came to Taitung from Tainan to visit me. I also thank her for her hard work and sweat in co-editing *Taiwan Customs* with Lin Fu'er.

— May 20, 2016.

【Published in Taiwan *Starfish* Poetry Magazine; September 21, 2016, Autumn Issue, pages 16-19.】

29 讀《廣域圖書館》——兼述顧敏與圖書館管理的理論與實務
Reading *Wide Area Library*: Discussing Karl Ku and the Theory and Practice of Library Management

一、顧敏其人

顧敏（Karl Min Ku），生於 1945 年，畢業於美國芝加哥多明尼克大學圖書館暨資訊科學研究所碩士，為著名的國際圖書館及中文資訊應用專家，現任臺灣臺北市「國圖」館長兼漢學研究中心主任。他在國會圖書館長任內，曾首創「新聞知識管理系統」，將各種異質數位媒體，整合匯入系統，產生多元功能的客戶需求服務。顧敏也規劃「網站圖書館」，完成第一代中文全文法律資料庫及資訊系統，榮獲北美地區華美圖書館協會頒發 1990 年傑出貢獻獎。曾任「立法院」秘書處處長、「立法院國會圖書館館長」、聯合國圖書館協會聯盟常務委員會委員、亞太地區國會圖書館協會會長等，並執教於輔仁大學、世新大學多年。講授：媒體識讀、西文參考、中文分類編目、傳播與社會、資訊科學導論、圖書館國際組織、圖書館採訪學。自 2008 年 8 月 1 日接任台灣的「國圖」第 12 任館長以來，致力推動國際圖書資訊合作及文化交流，讓世界文化資源共享之目標臻於完善。

顧敏對於創作，有奮鬥的恆心，也隱含著某種崇高的理想，能從多重角度探討圖書館在不同歷史階段中的變化與前瞻。比如顧敏的書《從傳統到數位圖書館》，內容詳細介紹國會圖書館，如何從一個傳統的小型圖書閱覽室與資料室，在顧敏與館員協力下，促成國會圖書館的立法誕生，也將該館蛻變成為國際公認具有服務活力的現代化數位圖書館。而《圖書館向前行—21 世紀的思維》為顧敏擔任亞太地區國會圖書館協會會長等職務期間，受邀參加各項重要性會議，發表對於數位化時代圖書館經營問題的經驗作法或心得、側記。其涵蓋主題有廣域圖書館、館際合作、圖書館與知識管理、圖書館員的資訊素養和圖書館國際組織活動等；此書的另一特色是，提供 5 個會議報告之簡報檔供讀者參考。

2009 年 12 月，顧敏的第八本專書《廣域圖書館－數位圖書館時代的知識文明》，全書涵蓋 8 章，就廣域圖書館論述、網路數位圖書館的註解、圖書館變換化管理、圖書館知識管理、現代化知識領航、圖書館館際合作等方面提出可行的方案及建言。企圖以「廣域圖書館」為新世紀的圖書館命名，為圖書館界與讀者勾勒新世紀的圖書館發展樣貌。由上而知，顧敏的創作及論述在圖書館管理範疇中是無可爭辯的價值核心。他冀望藉由理論與實務的配合，落實新世紀大媒體圖書館的實現，這也是帶引國圖走向世界這一現代性目標中的一環。同樣，他對教學也具有強烈的使命感。對圖書館管理與發展的理想的追求，構成了他創作的潛在的核心主題，這一點在他的著作中表現得極為清晰。

二、創作的精神歷程及重要論述

（一）、推動有特色的「國圖」願景

顧敏曾說，一個民族的存在，文明與文化的高度是非常重要的。他身上深具書卷氣質，誠懇、認真，除了積極於專業研究著述及發表外，也熱心參與圖資領域專業團體的事務。雖然台灣是從 1970 年代開始發展館際合作服務，但一直到 1995 年教育部圖書館事業委員會委託學者研訂「全國圖書館館際合作綱領」，才開始推動圖書館館際合作，以達全台各圖書館能資訊互助的目的。在顧敏眼中，國家圖書館是「陪伴」各行各業的圖書館，他希望把最具珍藏價值的「古籍」、「經典」等，以複製品或真品方式展出，在館內規劃參觀動線，讓國圖能創造觀光的價值及新的精神面貌。

唯「國圖」館藏空間有限，如何將資訊有效數位化，藉以儲存更多資訊、強化檢索效率、空間動線規範等，都是重要議題。他開始著手導入「電子商務」概念，讓民眾計量付費，但仍必須要有免費使用的空間，鼓勵民眾使用。顧敏也勾勒出心中的藍圖，比如提出 1.提升圖書館社會價值、培養高素質圖書館員；2.普及知識消費概念，提供分級化服務；3.推動知識管理、打造廣域圖書

館（Metalibrary）等措施。而在他的領隊下,「國圖」不僅僅是服務某一部份人,提供資訊傳遞轉換的服務功能,它更是在文化、教育、觀光與休閒等方面,成為一種跨文化交流的珍貴寶庫。

(二)、《廣域圖書館》論述的交相互應：

誠然,在過去十多年來,數位革命最成功的地方,在於統合數位資料、聲音、影像、動畫等原本分立的載體於一種全新的多重載體之上。而網路革命則由原本透過資料庫或資料庫供應系統的體現,所建構成的連線知識服務；不但帶給人類通訊方面的鉅大利益,包括各種的通訊功能,都能應用在不同頻寬的網路之上,而且網路革命也進一步促進了資訊數位化的腳步。

廣域圖書館的理念與實踐這一主題,在精神向度上,仍然是新世紀以來圖書館管理者的現代性夢想的延續。顧敏所關切的是,渴望台灣國圖與世界同步的歷史性要求,在國際舞台上,發揮更加重要的作用。因此,在他這本《廣域圖書館》的新書裡,已描繪出新世紀的圖書館景象,這也是顧敏於圖書館實務領域中推行的重要理念。他為自己製訂了一些計劃與目標,幾乎包含了下述研究的全部,其重要論點,可作為圖書館管理思潮在研究中的具體表現：

1. 數位圖書館的意義：從一個圖書館員的角度而言,應包括數位典藏與數位服務兩項圖書館的職能,缺一不可。因此,圖書館應積極設法將網站圖書館組建成一個多度空間的圖書館服務網,並導入系統化的「圖書館知識管理」模式,完美符合使用者之所需,發揮比以往傳統圖書館更大的服務能量。

2. 圖書館的變換化管理：新世紀的圖書館必須面對一連串來自數位革命後,大環境快速轉換所衍生複雜的挑戰性管理,包括：E化的科學、學習、工作環境、政府部門、以及整個社會的邁向E化。因此,顧敏提出「變換化圖書館管理」和「超越傳統圖書館服務」兩項主張,認為這是解決當前文獻處理、圖書館事業、和資訊服務專業所面對的許多核心問題時的兩條新路線。

3. 「虛擬實境複合圖書館」及「現代化知識領航」議題：因慮及目前大多數的圖書館都將面臨「複合圖書館」的情境與挑

戰，亦即新興的電子圖書館與所謂的傳統圖書館之間的複合。顧敏提出發展「虛擬實境複合圖書館」的新思維，強調將「資訊」、「傳播」、「儲存」結合，就能產生完美的「虛擬實境複合圖書館」。至於「現代化知識領航」方面。顧敏則強調知識領航是知識管理的後端工程，隨著新世紀的來臨，知識領航工作的系統化、智慧化與全面化，將促使龐大而複雜的人類各種知識系統，在多元多重的運用下仍能精確被使用者立即檢索獲取。

4. 圖書館知識管理的變換途徑：就圖書館學門而言，知識管理的實際績效在於知識領航工作的績效。知識領航的功能在擴大——不再只是如傳統圖書館中替讀者找到他們所需要的資訊而已，而是直接對於知識創新、知識組織、知識擴散這三個知識管理的核心層面。因此，新世紀的圖書館知識管理則是能量型的知識管理，必須以數學模式的方式，精算出知識的能量，包括：知識的互動性、知識的散佈性、知識的交叉影響性、以及知識的成長或退化曲線等等。

5. 新世紀知識管理與知識領航：二十一世紀開始，知識管理變成一種直接的具有生命力的驅動力量，知識管理與知識領航在新世紀中將更為密切。知識領航工作的系統化、智慧化與全面化，將促使龐大而複雜的人類各種知識系統，在多元多重的運作下，仍然可以有條不紊的尋求出確為所需，而及時取得的知識及信息。唯有兩者相互配合，才能順利解決資訊暴脹的問題。這也是圖書館學門所面臨的跨世紀挑戰與使命。

綜上概述，顧敏對「廣域圖書館」的研究，在充分的學理基礎上，從外國的知識中攝取精華，在圖書館管理思想交流中，激發了顧敏的創作靈感。沒有顧敏工作與教學的辛勞，就沒有顧敏創作的輝煌。由此，我們可以深刻地感受到顧敏創作的研究精神和向著圖書館管理的現代化與國際化奮進的決心。

三、結語：顧敏—「廣域圖書館」學理的先驅者

顧敏在圖書館管理工作與創作上的成就，既是他個人勤奮所學的案例，也是先進國家圖書館學與資訊時代潮流的必然。透過對「廣域圖書館」論述的要點，有利於從新的角度來加深對顧敏創作圖書館學理價值的認識。

讀《廣域圖書館》——兼述顧敏與圖書館管理的理論與實務

在信息領域中，知識創新不只是新世紀高端技術得以迅速發展的源頭，也是讓社會信息暢通的重要關鍵。而如何促使「廣域圖書館」理念的實現？個人提出以下淺見：

（一）、學科館員制度的有效實施：記得此書裡提及，20世紀圖書館學大師雪拉 Jesse Shera，針對第一次資訊革命後曾指出：「優秀圖書館員的動機，並非通常所說的愛好圖書，而是愛好真理－無論它在何處，以何種方式出現。知識的終極及於智慧，智慧是全面理解真理的力量－圖書館員專業精神即基於此。」因此，學科館員制度的建立是知識經濟時代知識創新的要求，在知識管理的積極推動下，或可加快「廣域圖書館」願景的實現。（二）、以讀者用戶為中心的價值取向：必須由方便讀者出發的服務取向，加以圖書館管理的人本取向，建立能反映信息的有效管道，依需求性建立舒適親切的圖書館空間。可喜的是，今年2月23日國家圖書館「漫畫屋」已正式啟用。漫畫屋的空間規劃更是能夠牽引各圖書館在文化創意及數位內容產業上的啟迪指導作用。未來圖書館管理者須將長期以來把數位圖書館的創建、管理、傳遞、和利用等建構，打破其原固有封閉狀態的保守思想；讓用戶可以通過大型的檢索系統來發現信息，以有效地增加其實用性。

作者參加 2009.6.19 臺北市「國圖」會上與顧敏館長合影
The author took a group photo with Director Gu Min at the National Library of China meeting in Taipei on June 19, 2009

就資料的蒐尋而言，速度可以解決「量」的問題，這是肯定的；但是所帶來的成果是利弊各半的。顧敏認為，速度解決了「量」的問題，卻也製造了另一個「量」的更大問題。知識成長或是學術研究，絕不是單單的「數量問題」，「質的問題」更為重要，實為至理名言。筆者以為，蒐尋速度策略是科技業界追求表現目標之一，在圖書館資訊化發展的表現上越快速，可能因越加偏重求主觀上解決資料蒐尋上「量」的問題，而忽略了追求資料本身具有的那種非物質的、非描述性的、純粹是美的特性，也應被當成是圖書館資訊發展未來應該追求的理想。我們無須在質與量上進行過嚴格的比較，但這些經驗仍將激發感情的要素，在圖書館資訊化的大躍進間，應找得到與其相對應之平衡點。比如將如何呈現美的影像或美的典範，以提供資料穩定與安全性、隱私性或智慧財產權保障等因素為策略之考量。

　　目前台灣圖書館學科相關研究正處於形而上學階段，譬如圖書資訊學系前稱圖書館學系，發展方向由圖書服務轉向圖書資訊服務，所學習的課程內容包括了圖書資訊服務、知識管理、數位典藏、數位學習、Web2.0 等。相較於具有獨立學科意義的科學，尚有許多努力開拓的空間；其根本原因是對於此學科大多缺乏認知價值及方法理性，去構建參考文獻。依我看來，在全球化的新世紀信息時代，像顧館長那樣積極研究圖書館學領域的學者，常能帶給讀者啟迪促生新的創作或啟示。他擁有豐富的國際視野、充分的資訊管理經驗、和溫儒的素養，常以數位時代的高度，提出卓越的觀點。而《廣域圖書館》內容的真知灼見，這就更加堅定了他在館長期間與學界的獨特地位。

—2010.4.29 作

【刊登臺灣臺北的《全國新書資訊月刊》，2010 年 6 月，第 138 期，頁 41-44。】

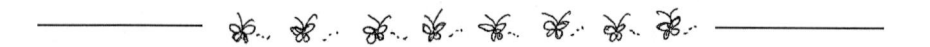

I. Karl Ku

　　Karl Ku, born in 1945, graduated from the Library and Information Science Institute of Dominican University in Chicago, USA. He is a well-known international library and Chinese information application expert. He is currently the director of the National Library of China and the director of the Sinology Research Center in Taipei City, Taiwan. During his tenure as the director of the Library of Congress, he pioneered the "News Knowledge Management System", integrating various heterogeneous digital media into the system to generate multi-functional customer demand services. Gu Min also planned the "Website Library" and completed the first generation of Chinese full-text legal database and information system, and was awarded the 1990 Outstanding Contribution Award by the Chinese American Library

Association of North America. He has served as the Director of the Secretariat of the Legislative Yuan, the Director of the Congressional Library of the Legislative Yuan, a member of the Standing Committee of the United Nations Alliance of Library Associations, and the President of the Congressional Library Association of the Asia-Pacific Region. He has also taught at Fu Jen Catholic University and Shih Hsin University for many years. He teaches: media literacy, Western reference, Chinese classification and cataloging, communication and society, introduction to information science, international library organizations, and library interviews. Since taking over as the 12th director of the National Library of Taiwan on August 1, 2008, he has been committed to promoting international library information cooperation and cultural exchanges, so as to achieve the goal of sharing world cultural resources.

Gu Min has a persistent spirit of struggle for creation, and also has a certain lofty ideal. He can explore the changes and prospects of libraries in different historical stages from multiple perspectives. For example, Gu Min's book *From Traditional to Digital Library* introduces the Library of Congress in detail, how it was transformed from a traditional small library reading room and data room to the legislative birth of the Library of Congress under the cooperation of Gu Min and the librarians, and also transformed the library into a modern digital library recognized internationally for its service vitality. The book *Libraries Moving Forward: Thinking in the 21st Century* is a collection of Gu Min's experiences, thoughts, and profiles on library management issues in the digital era during his tenure as president of the Asia-Pacific Congressional Library Association. The book covers topics such as wide-area libraries, interlibrary cooperation, libraries and knowledge management, information literacy of librarians, and international library organization activities. Another feature of the book is that it provides 5 conference report presentations for readers' reference.

In December 2009, Gu Min published his eighth book, *Wide Area Library: Knowledge Civilization in the Digital Library Era*. The book covers 8 chapters, proposing feasible solutions and suggestions on wide area library discussion, annotation of online digital library, library transformation management, library knowledge management, modern knowledge navigation, and inter-library cooperation. It attempts to name the library of the new century as "wide area library" and outline the development of the library of the new century for the library industry and readers. As can be seen from the above, Gu Min's creations and discussions are the indisputable value core in the field of library management. He hopes to realize the new century big media library through the combination of theory and practice, which is also part of the modern goal of leading the National Library to the world. Similarly, he also has a strong sense of mission for teaching. The pursuit of the ideal of library management and development constitutes the potential core theme of his creation, which is very clear in his works.

II. The spiritual process and important discussions of creation

1. Promote the distinctive vision of "National Library".

Gu Min once said that the existence of a nation is very important for the height of civilization and culture. He has a deep bookish temperament, is sincere and serious. In addition to actively researching and publishing professional works, he is also enthusiastic about participating in the affairs of professional groups in the field of library resources. Although Taiwan began to develop interlibrary cooperation services in the 1970s, it was not until 1995 that the Ministry of Education's Library Affairs Committee commissioned scholars to develop the "National Library Interlibrary Cooperation Guidelines" and began to promote interlibrary cooperation to achieve the goal of information mutual assistance among libraries across Taiwan. In Gu Min's eyes, the National Library is a library that "accompanies" all walks of life. He hopes to exhibit the most valuable "ancient books" and "classics" in the form of replicas or authentic ones, and plan the visiting routes in the library so that the National Library can create tourism value and a new spiritual outlook.

However, the collection space of the "National Library" is limited. How to effectively digitize information to store more information, enhance retrieval efficiency, and standardize spatial routes are all important issues. He began to introduce the concept of "e-commerce" to allow people to pay by the meter, but there must still be space for free use to encourage people to use it. Gu Min also outlined the blueprint in his mind, such as (a) Improving the social value of libraries and cultivating high-quality librarians. (b) Popularizing the concept of knowledge consumption and providing graded services. (c) Promoting knowledge management and building a wide-area library (Metalibrary) and other measures. Under his leadership, the "National Library" not only serves a certain group of people and provides information transmission and conversion service functions. It has also become a precious treasure house of cross-cultural exchanges in terms of culture, education, tourism and leisure.

2. The mutual correspondence discussed in *Wide Area Library*:

Indeed, the most successful aspect of the digital revolution over the past decade is the integration of digital data, sound, image, animation and other originally separate carriers on a new multi-carrier. The Internet revolution is the connection knowledge service constructed by the original embodiment of database or database supply system; it not only brings great benefits to human communication, including various communication functions, which can be applied on networks of different bandwidths, but also further promotes the pace of information digitization.

The concept and practice of the wide area library is still a continuation of the modern dream of library managers since the new century in terms of spiritual dimension. What Gu Min is concerned about is the historical demand for the National Library of Taiwan to keep pace with the world and play a more important role on the international stage. Therefore, in his new book "Wide Area Library", he has described the library scene of the new century, which is also an important concept that Gu Min promotes in the field of library practice. He has made some plans and goals for himself, which almost include all of the following research. Its important arguments can be used as a specific manifestation of library management trends in research:

(1) The meaning of digital library: from the perspective of a librarian, it should include the two functions of the library: digital collection and digital service, neither of which can be missing. Therefore, libraries should actively try to build a multi-dimensional library service network from the web library and introduce a systematic "library knowledge management" model to perfectly meet the needs of users and exert greater service capabilities than traditional libraries in the past.

(2) Transformation Management of Libraries: Libraries in the new century must face a series of complex and challenging

management derived from the rapid transformation of the macro environment after the digital revolution, including: e-science, learning, work environment, government departments, and the entire society's move towards e-commerce. Therefore, Gu Min proposed two propositions: "transformative library management" and "transcending traditional library services", believing that these are two new routes to solve many core problems currently faced by document processing, library business, and information service professionals.

(3) "Virtual reality hybrid library" and "modern knowledge navigation" issues: Considering that most libraries will face the situation and challenges of "hybrid library", that is, the combination of emerging electronic libraries and so-called traditional libraries. Gu Min proposed a new idea of developing "virtual reality hybrid library", emphasizing that the combination of "information", "communication" and "storage" can produce a perfect "virtual reality hybrid library". As for "modernized knowledge navigation", Gu Min emphasized that knowledge navigation is the back-end project of knowledge management. With the advent of the new century, the systematization, intelligence and comprehensiveness of knowledge navigation will enable the vast and complex human knowledge systems to be accurately retrieved and obtained by users in multiple applications.

(4) The transformation path of library knowledge management: As far as library science is concerned, the actual performance of knowledge management lies in the performance of knowledge navigation. The function of knowledge navigation is expanding — it is no longer just to help readers find the information they need as in traditional libraries, but directly affects the three core aspects of knowledge management: knowledge innovation, knowledge organization, and knowledge diffusion. Therefore, library knowledge management in the new century is energy-based knowledge management, which must use mathematical models to accurately calculate the energy of knowledge, including: the interactivity of knowledge, the dissemination of knowledge, the cross-influence of knowledge, and the growth or degeneration curve of knowledge, etc.

(5) Knowledge Management and Knowledge Navigation in the New Century: At the beginning of the 21st century, knowledge management has become a direct and vital driving force. Knowledge management and knowledge navigation will be even closer in the new century. The systematization, intelligence and comprehensiveness of knowledge navigation work will enable the vast and complex human knowledge systems to seek out the knowledge and information that are needed and obtained in a timely manner under multiple and multiple operations. Only when the two cooperate with each other can the problem of information explosion be successfully solved. This is also the cross-century challenge and mission faced by library science.

In summary, Gu Min's research on "Wide Area Library" has absorbed the essence from foreign knowledge on a sufficient theoretical basis, and inspired Gu Min's creative inspiration in the exchange of ideas on library management. Without Gu Min's hard work and teaching, there would be no brilliance of Gu Min's creation. From this, we can deeply feel Gu Min's creative research spirit and his determination to strive for the modernization and internationalization of library management.

III. Conclusion: Gu Min: Pioneer of *Wide Area Library* Theory

Gu Min's achievements in library management work and creation are not only a case of his personal hard work and learning, but also a necessity of the trend of advanced national library science and information age. Through the key points of the discussion on "Wide Area Library", it is helpful to deepen the understanding of the theoretical value of Gu Min's creative library from a new perspective.

In the information field, knowledge innovation is not only the source of the rapid development of high-end technology in the new century, but also an important key to the smooth flow of social information. How to promote the realization of the concept of "Wide Area Library"? I would like to offer the following suggestions:

(1) Effective implementation of the subject librarian system: I remember that the book mentioned that Jesse Shera, a master of 20th century librarianship, once pointed out after the first information revolution: "The motivation of an excellent librarian

is not the love of books as commonly said, but the love of truth - no matter where and in what form it appears. The ultimate goal of knowledge is wisdom, and wisdom is the power to fully understand the truth — the professionalism of librarians is based on this." Therefore, the establishment of a subject librarian system is a requirement for knowledge innovation in the knowledge economy era. With the active promotion of knowledge management, it may accelerate the realization of the vision of a "wide-area library".

(2) The value orientation centered on readers and users: the service orientation must be based on the convenience of readers, and the humanistic orientation of library management must be added to establish an effective channel that can reflect information, and establish a comfortable and friendly library space based on demand. Fortunately, the "Comic House" of the National Library was officially opened on February 23 this year. The space planning of the comic house can also guide the enlightenment and guidance of various libraries in the cultural creativity and digital content industry. In the future, library managers must break the conservative thinking of the original closed state of the creation, management, delivery, and utilization of digital libraries for a long time; let users find information through large-scale search systems to effectively increase its practicality.

As far as data collection is concerned, speed can solve the problem of "quantity", this is certain; but the results it brings are half good and half bad. Gu Min believes that speed solves the problem of "quantity", but also creates another bigger problem of "quantity". Knowledge growth or academic research is by no means a simple "quantity problem", "qualitative problem" is more important, which is indeed a wise saying. The author believes that the search speed strategy is one of the performance goals pursued by the technology industry. The faster the performance of library informatization development, the more likely it is that it will focus more on subjectively solving the problem of "quantity" in data collection, while ignoring the pursuit of the non-material, non-descriptive, and purely beautiful characteristics of the data itself, which should also be regarded as the ideal that library information development should pursue in the future. We do not need to make a strict comparison between quality and quantity, but these experiences will still inspire emotional elements. In the great leap forward of library informatization, we should find a corresponding balance point. For example, how to present beautiful images or models of beauty, to provide data stability and security, privacy or intellectual property protection and other factors as strategic considerations.

Currently, library-related research in Taiwan is in the metaphysical stage. For example, the Department of Library and Information Studies was formerly known as the Department of Library Studies. The development direction has shifted from library services to library information services. The courses studied include library information services, knowledge management, digital collections, digital learning, Web2.0, etc. Compared with science, which has independent academic significance, there is still a lot of room for development; the fundamental reason is that most of this discipline lacks cognitive value and methodological rationality to construct reference literature. In my opinion, in the new century of globalization and information age, scholars like Director Gu who actively study in the field of librarianship can often inspire readers and promote new creations or enlightenment. He has a rich international vision, sufficient information management experience, and gentle qualities, and often puts forward outstanding views from the height of the digital age. The insightful content of *Wide Area Library* further consolidates his unique position in the academic community during his tenure as director.

— Written on April 29, 2010

〔Published in the *National New Book Information Monthly* in Taipei, Taiwan, June 2010, Issue 138, Pages 41-44.〕

30 一隻勇毅的飛鷹——讀楊宗翰《隱於詩》
A Courageous Eagle: Reading Yang Zonghan's *Hidden in Poetry*

一、其人其詩

　　現任臺北教育大學教授、詩人學者楊宗翰（1976-　），在今年四月最新出版的詩集《隱於詩》的同時，也一直保留著寫詩的堅持與熱情，一如他曾說的：「寫詩就是在面對真實、書寫現實、曲筆誠實。」而這個強烈的意念，如同鷹在高空中翱翔於時間和速度裡，明亮的眸子迄今仍朝前方勇敢地戰鬥，也正是有這份勤奮的精神，才能把詩人引向其筆下具有詩性心靈的特質。書裡的內涵包括了愛以及對自我的誠實，或者說，這也是詩人內心世界的感悟，以及如何以詩實現「自我救贖」的過程。

　　生長於臺北市的楊宗翰，天秤座的他，為人謙遜、平易近人，有邏輯的分析力，一生追求寧靜和諧與堅強的個性鮮明。年輕時，他所經歷的社會挫折與心靈苦惱也不少，但也因而促使他苦學有成，並力圖在詩歌創作中尋找一塊淨土。在學界，他專注於當代新詩史與教學；如今，四十六歲的他，教書之餘，不僅懂得享受安靜帶來的平和，還在《聯合文學》出版此詩集，勇登詩歌創作的巔峰。

　　《隱於詩》是菁英詩人出版的一部傑作；其表達的形式中，沒有晦澀難以理解的詞彙，沒有對想像力的限制，並在作品中保持「以象蘊情、情景交融」的抒情感，也是他血液裡流淌的詩行。

　　全書著力於對詩美理想的追求，沿著詩人感覺的經緯度伸向更廣闊的空間探索，以無數的意象從而組成了一部優美獨特的協奏曲；時而帶有較強的思辨色彩和厚重感，時而沉鬱抒情，如天空之鷹優雅旋舞，亦如夜星與青松吟詠般動人。

　　他把生命中最好的青春時光奉獻給文學，其詩歌的偉大在於融合韻律與大自然之音的和諧，它賦予詩歌崇高的重要性，又能維持各自的特色高度，讓我除了讚嘆，實在無法多加形容。

二、應時而變的抒情詩基調

在楊宗翰寫抒情題材的詩作中,〈夜有所思〉,是我喜愛的一首小詩。其感情的基調雖然是痛苦的,但詩人直面這種痛苦卻沒有任何粉飾,反而運用想像之花,結出愛情的形象之果,給讀者心靈的搖撼是持久的。詩人寫道:

> 有雷隱隱
> 響在醒與夢的邊緣
> 有小雨落下
> 落在行人閤上的雙眼
>
> 有妳出現
> 只是距離好遠、好遠
>
> 有我無助
> 正像這首蹩腳的詩
> 毫無技巧可言

同一題材,詩人的〈贈妳以風景〉則體現了對愛情具有更深刻的體會:

> 電纜上的鳥卻是稀落底逗點
> 株株檳榔滴落自天空
> 像細頸的驚嘆
> 三兩開苞的花朵句號一個冬季
> 湖畔以倒影默問山巒的硬度
>
> 羽毛雲朵搖拍思維
> 努力把自己寫成一封情書
> 待你細讀卻發現:
> 字字皆錯,句句是淚

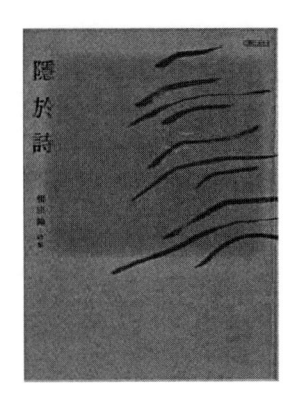

這首詩不是為寫景而寫景,而是詩人靈魂的全部傾入,使人轉向對愛情的深思。雖然,面對悲傷的感情在掩卷之後,更教人覺得感傷,然而,詩人用全心靈的觀照,藉以懷念著那遠方的人,以獨具的藝術概括力,蘊聚著其深深的詩情。另一首〈夏蟬〉,詩的思想是重抒情的藝術，心境上卻有一種禪道意蘊，且具有詩人敏銳的穿透力：

> 蟬聲在咖啡上遊走
> 冷了的瓷杯燥熱泛紅
>
> 一些些禪也溢了出來
>
> 無法遏止
> 滾燙字跡沿嘴角滴落

　　從藝術講，這是詩人以心靈體驗所促成的獨特韻味的意境。更可貴的是他對愛情的那份癡情，已轉化為一種生活中的謐靜。看來詩人的悟性，無論是寫大自然，或在生活中揭示某些偶得的哲思，已將應時而變的抒情詩基調，達到了更高層次的境界，但仍不失詩人的純真。

三、結語

　　如果說，宗翰的詩只抒寫自己心底的一些感觸，那是不可能成為在臺灣學界備受矚目的詩人的。因為他在語言運用上的創新是明顯的，且為臺灣新詩史做出過積極的貢獻。記得法國象徵派詩歌先驅波特萊爾（Charles Pierre Baudelaire）有句名言：「英雄就是對任何事都全力以赴，自始至終，心無旁騖的人」。正如波特萊爾所說，楊宗翰教授對詩歌的熱愛始終如一，他亦如一位勇於探索詩歌聖殿的英雄，而我深信，今後他必然會寫出更多優美感人的詩歌。

—2023.04.26 寫於臺東

【刊臺灣《金門日報》*Kenmen Daily News* 副刊，2023.06.10，以及林明理畫作一幅。】

I. The Person and His Poems

Yang Zonghan (1976-), currently a professor at Taipei University of Education and a poet and scholar, has maintained his persistence and passion for writing poetry while publishing his latest collection of poems, *Hidden in Poetry*, in April this year. As he once said, "writing poetry is about facing the truth, writing about reality, and being honest in a roundabout way." This strong idea is like an eagle soaring in the sky in time and speed, with its bright eyes still fighting courageously forward. It is precisely this diligent spirit that can lead the poet to the characteristics of a poetic soul in his writing. The content of the book includes love and honesty to oneself, or in other words, it is also the poet's perception of his inner world and the process of how to achieve "self-salvation" through poetry.

Yang Zonghan, who grew up in Taipei City, is a Libra. He is humble, approachable, logical, and has a distinct personality of pursuing tranquility, harmony, and strength throughout his life. When he was young, he experienced a lot of social setbacks and spiritual distress, but this also prompted him to study hard and try to find a pure land in poetry creation. In academia, he focused on the history and teaching of contemporary new poetry; now, at the age of 46, in addition to teaching, he not only knows how to enjoy the peace brought by quietness, but also published this collection of poems in *United Literature*, bravely reaching the pinnacle of poetry creation.

Hidden in Poetry is a masterpiece published by an elite poet. In its form of expression, there are no obscure words or restrictions on imagination, and the lyrical feeling of "using images to express emotions and blending scenes" is maintained in the work, which is also the poetry flowing in his blood.

The whole book focuses on the pursuit of the ideal of poetic beauty, extending to a broader space exploration along the longitude and latitude of the poet's feelings, and forming a beautiful and unique concerto with countless images. Sometimes it has a strong speculative color and heaviness, and sometimes it is melancholy and lyrical, like the graceful dance of an eagle in the sky, and as moving as the chanting of night stars and green pines.

He devoted the best years of his youth to literature. The greatness of his poetry lies in the harmonious fusion of rhythm and the sounds of nature. It gives poetry a lofty importance while maintaining its own unique height. I can't describe it in words except admiration.

II. The Tone of Lyric Poetry Changing with the Times

Among Yang Zonghan's lyrical poems, "Thoughts at Night" is one of my favorites. Although the basic tone of his emotion is painful, the poet faces this pain without any embellishment. Instead, he uses the flower of imagination to produce the image of love, which has a lasting impact on the reader's soul. The poet wrote:

> There is thunder
> Ringing on the edge of waking and dreaming
> A little rain is falling
> Falling on the closed eyes of passers-by
>
> You show up
> It's just so far, so far away
>
> I am helpless
> Just like this crappy poem
> No skills at all

On the same subject, the poet's "Giving You the Landscape" reflects a deeper understanding of love:

> The birds on the cables are sparse commas
> Betel nut drops from the sky
> Like the exclamation of a thin neck
> A few flowers blooming in full bloom end a winter
> The lakeside reflects the hardness of the mountains
>
> Feather Cloud Panning Thinking
> Try to write yourself into a love letter
> When you read carefully, you will find:
> Every word is wrong, every sentence is tearful

This poem is not written for the sake of describing the scenery, but is the poet's entire soul poured into it, leading people to deep contemplation on love. Although facing the sad feelings makes people feel even more sad after closing the book, the poet uses his whole heart to miss the person far away, and his unique artistic generalization ability contains his deep poetic sentiment. Another poem "Summer Cicada" is about the art of lyricism, but the state of mind has a Zen connotation and the poet's keen penetrating power:

> The sound of cicadas wandering over the coffee
> The cold porcelain cup is hot and red
>
> Some Zen also overflowed
>
> Unstoppable
> Hot words dripping from the corners of the mouth

From an artistic point of view, this is a unique artistic conception created by the poet's spiritual experience. What is even more valuable is that his infatuation with love has been transformed into a kind of tranquility in life. It seems that the poet's insight, whether he is writing about nature or revealing some occasional philosophical thoughts in life, has brought the tone of lyrical poetry that changes with the times to a higher level, but the poet still retains his innocence.

III. Conclusion

If Zong Han's poems only expressed some of his inner feelings, he would not have become a poet that attracted much attention in Taiwan's academic circles. Because his innovation in language use is obvious and he has made positive contributions to the history of modern Taiwanese poetry. I remember a famous quote by Charles Pierre Baudelaire, the pioneer of French symbolist poetry: "A hero is someone who gives his all to everything he does, from beginning to end, without distraction." As Baudelaire said, Professor Yang Zonghan's love for poetry has always been consistent. He is like a hero who dares to explore the temple of poetry. I firmly believe that he will write more beautiful and touching poems in the future.

— Written in Taitung on April 26, 2023.

【Published in the supplement of Taiwan's *Kenmen Daily News*, June 10, 2023, together with a painting.】

31《華痕碎影》中蘊含的魯迅審美思維
Lu Xun's Aesthetic Thoughts in *Bits & Pieces of Memories*

一、前言

《華痕碎影 上海魯迅紀念館藏魯迅先生手跡、藏品擷珍》一書令人耳目一新的魯迅書藝等珍藏作品和觀點，從宏觀層面來說，魯迅，這個如此熱愛祖國、為大地而為奮鬥而生的賢者，他為無數的千萬人民點燃那盞希望之燈，深耕文學土壤。他的手跡、版畫、明信片、藏書、箋紙、書法等六大類的藏品擷珍，成為

林明理畫作：〈山水之間〉

稀世的寶藏。他將整個生命投入，無論是創作或翻譯，詩書畫或評論，都在近代文學史中成為不朽。這些永恆的珍寶，如今收編成書，對魯迅研究的美學內涵作了重要的補充，也是一種知識或魯迅美學價值觀的傳承的一種方式，已變成令人陶醉的讚頌。

二、魯迅審美思維面面觀

該書涉及魯迅博古通今的美學觀及橫跨中西美學思想的不同範式之間的共同規律，在在表現了魯迅對蒐藏品的愛好及其反思性的思考。茲舉幾例：首先，魯迅對美的感知是其與生俱有的能力，也是其文學涵養的潛在反映；一方面在珍藏作品中體認審美對象的藝術價值、風格及其創作的寓意，一方面在審美欣賞中領悟文化或人文精神等不同層面的影響。

例如，在魯迅精心編印十二種版畫圖冊中，不僅主張打破中西藝術思維的隔閡，擇取中國的美學思想，也要採用西方藝術的良規，中西合璧，促使將來的作品有藝術內涵的豐富性。此外，他在1934年間，精選五十八幅青年木刻家的作品，赴法國巴黎展覽，使萌芽期的中國新興木刻藝術水平得到提高。書裡的一幅木刻畫《失業者》，精雕細琢、維妙維肖地表現出失業者的共同遭遇，

也映射著當年中國木刻版畫的技巧發展與藝術風格演化的軌跡。再如《出路》，畫中的男子面臨貧困中生死抉擇的痛苦，當然也有魯迅運用悲憫底層人物的文化視角來觀照。

而木刻家陳煙橋的《耕耘》，著實表現出勞動者在土地上努力求生存的意象，與成為永恆經典的法國畫家弗朗索瓦・米勒筆下的《拾穗者》，都有著反映貧苦人以求溫飽的寓意。凡此等等，收藏的版畫內容都不乏有著魯迅的現實主義美學思想的核心，主要是為悲憫底層勞動者的心聲為出發，而這一個深心，是從對人生與中國文藝發展的反思而發出的；原來，「用藝術涵養魯迅的靈魂」，才是其獨特的審美思維，引領讀者對其珍藏的木刻畫產生精神上的愉悅感受，也就跟著產生了美的聯想，及現實世界中各種覺醒或隨機的社會命題思考。

在魯迅生前，明信片也曾作為一種回禮品，有許多珍藏品可能來源於友人或委託收集後真實的收藏體驗。在微觀內容上，也不乏有著魯迅眉批的獨特價值。或許，魯迅將每一種西方人物的繪圖視為無比精彩的文化傳承，運用藝術的思維和文化多元性驅動未來，逐漸形成普遍而共同的中西藝術交流。

其他諸如魯迅酷愛收藏中外文學書籍的癖好，尤以日本譯本小說等書、文學期刊，或學刊讀物、藝術月刊等，不難看出魯迅對文學藝術的感知都十分出色。而在箋紙的題款、遺存的詩書畫作品中，或花卉，或植物、昆蟲，或人物、山水，都頗有雅趣，有一種禪的「歡喜自在」，讓人不覺莞爾。

在魯迅親筆書寫的全部文字，就規模而言，已經出版的魯迅手跡，尚稱可觀，並且涵蓋其主要創作年代；除了書稿稿件、題字、日記、信札等墨跡中，可窺視其書法行書優美生動、典雅清麗的特殊風格，也帶有將其所思所想，力注於筆端。除此之外，魯迅縱橫中西藝術的獨特眼光、通古博今的美學觀，亦是將西方文藝引入中國的先驅者之一。

三、結語

該書成功之處，大致歸功於編委精選圖文，加以分類和對資料採擷內容的深度，有一定的美感度，致使該書在魯迅研究中成為重要的一個成果。誠如俄國學者羅素諾索夫在他的《修辭學》

書中所述，聯想是「那種和一件已有概念的事物一起能夠想像出和它有關的其它事物來的稟賦。」[1]當我心中想到魯迅的書畫及其美學思想，想到他對審美文藝所提供的獨特情感，想到他超脫了名利得失的生活美學，想到在他細緻觀察景物後得出的書畫作品。儘管這些聯想是對觀賞魯迅書畫等手稿或珍藏事物的聯想所引起的審美體驗，而該書的確能夠進行更充分地闡述，使其存在的魯迅美學內涵再獲得重要的補充。

　　書中的圖解，與審美聯想相契合的，含有三個方向，推動魯迅美學研究的發展、預示魯迅成為了推動中國對西方美學交流的重要推手身份、暗示魯迅的非凡經歷跟其審美思維的豐富性。這是因魯迅重視精神、捨棄物質，也崇尚美學，故而，研究書裡的魯迅的手跡、藏品，總能伴隨著愉悅，確有其意義的。

—2024.03.28 作

【刊登臺灣《中華日報》China Daily News，副刊，2024.05.21，及林明理畫作〈山水之間〉一幅。】

I. Introduction

　　Bits & Pieces of Memories: Collection of Mr. Lu Xun's Handwriting and Collections in Shanghai Lu Xun Memorial Hall is a refreshing collection of Lu Xun's calligraphy and other treasures and views. From a macro perspective, Lu Xun, a wise man who loves his motherland so much and lives for the earth, has lit the lamp of hope for countless millions of people and cultivated the soil of literature. His collections of six categories, including handwriting, prints, postcards, books, paper, and calligraphy, have become rare treasures. He devoted his entire life to writing or translation, poetry, calligraphy, painting or commentary, and has become immortal in the history of modern literature. These timeless treasures, now collected into a book, have

---

[1] 童慶炳著，《中國古代心理詩學與美學》，台北，萬卷樓出版，1994 年初版，頁 138。

made an important supplement to the aesthetic connotation of Lu Xun's research. It is also a way of passing on knowledge or Lu Xun's aesthetic values, and has become an intoxicating praise.

II. A comprehensive view of Lu Xun's aesthetic thinking

The book involves Lu Xun's extensive aesthetics and the common laws between different paradigms of Chinese and Western aesthetic thinking, which shows Lu Xun's love for collecting and his reflective thinking. Here are a few examples: First, Lu Xun's perception of beauty is his innate ability and a potential reflection of his literary cultivation; on the one hand, he recognizes the artistic value, style and implication of the aesthetic objects in the collected works, and on the other hand, he comprehends the influence of different levels such as culture or humanistic spirit in aesthetic appreciation.

For example, in the twelve print albums carefully compiled by Lu Xun, he not only advocates breaking the barriers between Chinese and Western artistic thinking and choosing Chinese aesthetic ideas, but also adopting the good rules of Western art, combining Chinese and Western, and promoting the richness of artistic connotations in future works. In addition, in 1934, he selected 58 works by young woodcut artists and exhibited them in Paris, France, which improved the level of China's emerging woodcut art in its infancy. A woodcut painting in the book, *The Unemployed*, is meticulously carved and vividly depicts the common experience of the unemployed, and also reflects the development of Chinese woodcut techniques and the evolution of artistic styles at that time. Another example is *The Way Out*, in which the man in the painting faces the pain of life and death in poverty, and of course Lu Xun also uses the cultural perspective of the tragic underclass to observe.

And the woodcut artist Chen Yanqiao's *Tillage* truly expresses the image of workers struggling to survive on the land, and the *Gleaners* by the French painter François Millet, which has become an eternal classic, both have the meaning of reflecting the poor people's struggle for food and shelter. All of these, the contents of the prints collected are full of the core of Lu Xun's realistic aesthetic thought, mainly for the voice of the sad bottom workers, and this deep heart is from the reflection on life and the development of Chinese literature and art. It turns out that "using art to cultivate Lu Xun's soul" is his unique aesthetic thinking, leading readers to have a spiritual pleasure in his collection of woodcuts, and then to have aesthetic associations, and various awakening or random social propositions in the real world.

During Lu Xun's lifetime, postcards were also used as a kind of return gift. Many of the collections may come from friends or commissioned collections after real collection experiences. In terms of micro content, there is also the unique value of Lu Xun's marginal notes. Perhaps, Lu Xun regarded every drawing of Western figures as an incomparable cultural heritage, using artistic thinking and cultural diversity to drive the future, and gradually formed a universal and common exchange of Chinese and Western art.

Other things, such as Lu Xun's hobby of collecting Chinese and foreign literary books, especially Japanese translated novels, literary journals, or academic journals, art monthly magazines, etc. It is not difficult to see that Lu Xun's perception of literature and art is very outstanding. In the inscriptions on paper, the surviving poems, calligraphy and paintings, whether flowers, plants, insects, or figures, landscapes, they are all quite elegant, with a kind of Zen "joy and freedom" that makes people smile.

Among all the texts written by Lu Xun, the published Lu Xun handwriting is still considerable in terms of scale, and covers the main years of his creation; in addition to the manuscripts, inscriptions, diaries, letters and other ink marks, one can see the unique style of his calligraphy, which is beautiful and vivid, elegant and beautiful, and also has the power to put his thoughts and ideas into the tip of the pen. In addition, Lu Xun's unique vision of Chinese and Western art and his aesthetics of ancient and modern times also made him one of the pioneers in introducing Western literature and art to China.

III. Conclusion

The success of this book is largely attributed to the editorial committee's selection of pictures and texts, classification, and depth of data collection, which has a certain aesthetic appeal, making this book an important achievement in Lu Xun research. As Russian scholar Russo-Nosov said in his book *Rhetoric*, association is "the gift of being able to imagine other things related to a thing that already has a concept."² When I think of Lu Xun's calligraphy and painting and his aesthetic thoughts, his unique emotions for aesthetic literature, his life aesthetics that transcend fame and fortune, and his calligraphy and painting works derived from his careful observation of the scenery. Although these associations are aesthetic experiences caused by the association of viewing Lu Xun's calligraphy and painting manuscripts or treasures, this book can indeed provide a more comprehensive explanation, so that the existing Lu Xun aesthetic connotation is further supplemented.

The illustrations in the book are consistent with the aesthetic association, and contain three directions: promoting the development of Lu Xun's aesthetic research, foreshadowing that Lu Xun has become an important promoter of China's exchange with Western aesthetics, and hinting at Lu Xun's extraordinary experience and the richness of his aesthetic thinking. This is because Lu Xun attaches importance to spirit, abandons material things, and advocates aesthetics. Therefore, studying Lu Xun's handwriting and collections in the book is always accompanied by pleasure and is indeed meaningful.

— Written on March 28, 2024

〔Published in *Taiwan's China Daily News*, supplement, May 21, 2024, and a painting by Lin Mingli, "Between Mountains and Rivers".〕

---

[2] Tong Qingbing, *Ancient Chinese Psychological Poetry and Aesthetics*, Taipei, Wanjuanlou Publishing, first edition in 1994, page 138.

32 評黃淑貞《以石傳情——談廟宇石雕意象及其美感》[1]
Comments on Huang Shuzhen's *Using Stone to Express Emotions: On the Imagery and Aesthetics of Temple Stone Sculptures*

摘要 Abstract

黃淑貞對石雕很有感情，也是當代對廟宇石雕美學的建築美學家。《以石傳情》內容豐富，以艋舺龍山寺為例，生動地反映了石雕意象的美學義涵，極具文化與歷史價值。

Huang Shuzhen has a deep affection for stone carvings and is also a contemporary architectural aesthetician who is interested in the aesthetics of temple stone carvings. *Expressing Emotions through Stone* is rich in content. Taking the Longshan Temple in Monga as an example, it vividly reflects the aesthetic connotation of stone carving imagery and is of great cultural and historical value.

關鍵詞：石雕、意象、艋舺龍山寺、藝術。
Keywords: stone carving, image, Longshan Temple in Mengjia, art.

一、石雕意象的文化內涵與美學觀點

石雕是指以石為材料雕制而成的中國傳統工藝品。作者親身感受到廟宇石雕的古樸之情，內心顯得充實而喜悅。她以文字和視覺語言細緻地觀察石雕意象的文化內涵，引發建築等學界對此題材所隱藏的美學底色進行探索和深思。

首先，什麼是美學？希臘語翻譯為 aisthetikos。簡言之，是「以藝術作為主要物件的一種感觀的感受」。它根源於人對現實的審美

---

[1] 黃淑貞（Shu-Cheng Huang, 1967- ），台灣師範大學文學博士，著有《辭章章法四大律研究》、《以石傳情・談廟宇石雕意象及其美感》、《篇章對比與調和結構論》、《遇見天籟・國語文創新教學設計》、《發現，校園空間・臺北市明德國中公共藝術教學》、《國中國文章法教學》等書。現任慈濟大學助理教授。

關係,經由創造,從而發展出對美或崇高的一種規律的科學。而美學意識是形而上的藝術直覺,是以人的靈性去體驗到的本原的、悠遠的美感經驗。

本論文以不偏離石雕特有的文化內涵和審美特點,而是提高愛好者和讀者的鑒賞水準為重點。如何凸顯美學觀點是石雕藝術需要反思其深度與義涵的一項創新的視域,藉以反映出作者的精神本性,以期對其著作的研究有所裨益。

從文獻記載略悉,「艋舺」是台北市萬華區的舊名,是日據前台北市開發最早的地方。所謂「一府二鹿三艋舺」,說明著萬華地區昔日的風華,也代表早期開發與台南、鹿港並駕齊驅,極具歷史的意義。寺廟是先民精神生活的寄託所在,石雕不僅具裝飾作用,且反應先民心理需求及象徵的歷史意義。

艋舺龍山寺係創建於清乾隆三年(西元 1738 年),迄今有二百七十二年歷史,於 1985 年被內政部定為國家二級古蹟,前後歷經嘉慶年大修、同治年小修、日據大正年間的大改修,以及台灣光復後的數度修築。據文獻考究,於一九二〇大修時,遠從中國惠安聘請了莊德發、蔣金輝等石匠師傅;至一九五五年又重修大殿時,由張木成、蔣按水、蔣銀牆等師傅負責龍柱。全寺總面積一千八百餘坪,坐北朝南,面呈「日」字形,為傳統三進四合院宮殿式建築,融儒、釋、道三教於一堂。其中,以石雕藝術表現最為凸出。殿內有銅鑄蟠龍檐柱一對,花鳥柱及牆堵等石雕,精工細緻。所採用的石材,主要有泉州白石、青斗石、礱石及觀音山石的交互運用,石雕牆堵,紋理極雅緻細膩。

正殿屋頂採歇山重簷式,四面走馬廊,共四十二根柱子構成。全寺屋頂螺旋藻井全斗拱築構而成,不用一釘一鐵,神龕雕工極為精細。脊帶和飛簷由龍、鳳、麒麟等吉祥動物造形,裝飾以彩色玻璃瓷片剪粘和色彩瑰麗的交趾陶。後殿則以山牆分隔為三組屋頂,中間為歇山重簷式,兩翼為單簷硬山式[2]。作者就廟宇石雕

---

[2] 歇山重簷式屋頂結構圖(如附圖 1),歇山式屋頂,四面斜坡的屋面上部轉折成垂直的三角形牆面。由一條正脊、四條垂脊、四條依脊組成,所以又稱九脊頂。歇山頂分單簷和重簷兩種,所謂重簷,就是在基本歇山頂的下方,再加上一層屋簷,和廡殿頂第二簷大致相同。這種重疊觀念,通常上簷為歇山頂,騎在一座硬山式屋頂上方,形式挺拔華麗。其

看歷史小說中的英雄人物及其所表達的意象與美學義涵，整體而言，廟宇是移民精神生活的重心，它保存了許多的傳統文化及歷史典故，故事內容多取材於《三國演義》、《封神榜》等民間故事，三川殿外牆堵上有多幅書法家的拓印石刻，也是石雕技藝的寶庫。

取自台灣古建築圖解事典 李乾朗著
（附圖一）Figure 1

《以石傳情》的論述是以「多、二、一〈0〉」結構的學理，探索石雕意象所形成的各種紋理風情。作者認為，藝術是一個有機體，在內是「力」的迴旋，對外是一個獨立的「統一」形式；統合了「多」與「二」後，所形成的風格、韻味、氣象、境界等，屬於「一〈0〉」。它可形成「統一美」、「意境美」與「渾沌美」等各種美感效果。在研究中確有清晰的脈絡可尋，如同她投入石雕藝術所傳達的意象和樸素的建築學，皆可提升讀者藝術與文化融合的素養。

取自台灣古建築圖解事典 李乾朗著
（附圖二）Figure 2

次，上下簷縫間露出木結構斗拱，亦為裝飾的焦點，此結構可解決通風透氣及部份採光的問題；一般佛教寺院中的大雄寶殿的頂就是重簷歇山頂。例如中國的天安門、故宮的太和門、保和殿、幹清宮等就是重簷歇山頂。而臺灣的艋舺龍山寺也有歇山重簷式屋頂結構，但臺北府城北門則為單簷歇山頂。在中國古代，建築屋頂的樣式有嚴格的等級限制。其中重簷歇山頂等級高於單簷廡殿頂，僅低於重簷廡殿頂，而單簷歇山頂低於單簷廡殿頂，只有五品以上官吏的住宅正堂才能使用，後來也有些民宅開始使用歇山頂。

單簷硬山式屋頂結構圖（如附圖 2），硬山頂，即硬山式屋頂，是兩坡出水的五脊二坡式，由一條正脊和四條垂脊組成。其最大的特點就是其兩側山牆把檁頭全部包封住，由於其屋簷不出山牆，故名硬山。屋頂在山牆牆頭處與山牆齊平，沒有伸出部分，簡單樸素。在等級最低，低於廡殿頂、歇山頂、懸山頂。根據清朝規定，六品以下官吏及平民住宅的正堂只能用懸山頂或硬山頂。而宮牆中兩廡殿房也多有硬山頂。硬山頂文載方面出現較晚，在宋朝的《營造法式》中未見記載。可能隨著明、清時期廣泛使用磚石構建房屋，硬山頂才得以大量採用。硬山頂的特點是有利於防風火，而懸山頂則有利於防雨。

評黃淑貞《以石傳情——談廟宇石雕意象及其美感》

二、從偶發思維到石雕意象的聯想

廟宇石雕歷來被認為是我們中華民族的國粹藝術，雖然有的歷經千餘年歲月，但從它們身上煥發出的光彩仍熠熠生輝。我們從這些凝固的生命裡不僅看到了我們偉大民族的歷史，更能深刻體悟到石雕藝術創作的真諦。

臺灣廟宇石雕藝術的表現方式，因受了傳統建築的空間觀念、禮制上的次序關係及視覺的感受力等因素影響，而有其特定的規制與原則。《以石傳情》主要探討石雕意象歷史的聯想性、象徵性以及建築美學的思維。

廟宇石雕是中國最具有象徵性的建築美學，也兼具裝飾性及潛移默化的教育功能。由書中，我觀察到艋舺龍山寺的具體象徵有三：（一）、除了是附近大多數居民的精神信仰中心外，其石材厚實的質感及師傅們精湛的雕工，刻劃出一幅幅浮雕的建築美，從而達到教化及敬畏的作用。（二）、龍山寺內石雕的草葉類圖紋，以靈芝最為常見。據研究，靈芝具有延年益壽的功效，也是德仁的象徵。在這裡，意象的聯想也可表現廟宇石雕師從精神到自然的宇宙所有，都著眼於對觀者最細微的心靈角落刻劃到廣闊無垠的宇宙天際，他們通過石雕藝術的博大的審美內涵和崇高的精神，為後人留下珍貴的歷史記錄。（三）、石雕藝術之最的「龍柱」，其審美認識和審美價值在於它是雕花柱的一種。龍柱的圖案雖因時代而有所不同，越是早期常見的龍柱造形，越是單純而很有力感；一如艋舺龍山寺的龍柱也刻有一條長龍盤繞再微刻一些雲彩和水波的花樣。

但咸豐之後，有許多廟宇龍柱身上，都增加了人物帶騎，或搭配吉獸、仙人之類做裝飾。然而，我以為，越是呈現繁複而華麗的雕工，反而失去樸素的建築感。值得慶幸的是，艋舺龍山寺對歷史故事的傳遞，有著極大的包容力與趣味性；對石材或圖案形體的使用與組合，也有很大的自由度，可以觸發觀者現代審美主體不同的情緒和聯想，油然而生不同的美感。

據我所知，過去國內的相關文獻，光在廟宇石雕圖案的撰述方面並未有突出的表現，特別是建築界忽略對歷史文化理論的文學研究更是事實。此書綜合作者的知識對廟宇石雕的有意識運用，改變和拓寬了讀者以往熟悉的建築藝術視角，不僅給台灣建築學界及文界帶來了新的審美內容，而且對華人以後研究廟宇石雕的發展奠定了基礎。

從意識和審美的角度來看，體現為是一種精神的存在。作者是台灣傑出的學者作家，她不迎合大眾審美趣味，反而敢於創新，挑選看是冷門的廟宇石雕為主題範圍，用心拍攝下許多詩意盎然的圖案，如花瓶上的八卦，劉備甘露寺赴約的故事、各種花卉、葫蘆、拂塵、香爐、文房器物等等的象徵記號，都賦予新的詮釋與生命。其孜孜不倦的精神，刻苦有成。然而也就是這種個性成就了她獨特的風格，她在石雕藝術審美上的新追求，從作品的精神內涵到文字表現形式都超越了時代，也彰顯了她不同凡響的藝術審美品位。比如她敘述了一段：「龍山寺後殿壁堵上刻有『紅毛番騎象吹法螺』石雕，兩旁配以花瓶堵，雕工生動，表示有請洋人看守廟堂，以反映出中西接觸初期，民間對外不滿的心情，也寓有「吉祥有聲報平安」之意。」這樣的詮釋手法，對教學上，具有畫龍點睛的功效；而透過出版與論述，台灣讀者得以追尋艋舺龍山寺的建築美學思維與文學踪跡。

三、結語：觀《以石傳情》之感懷

綜上所述，黃淑貞的學術淵博，而其筆處思深意遠。文本無一贅言，嶄新耐讀。這些無不顯示其清雅素淨的本色。我粗粗一讀，《以石傳情》史料豐富，由參考文獻中，可以想見，她是翻閱了許多鮮為人知的古書、中外檔案的，論述也客觀直言。作者在台師大意象學專家陳滿銘教授的指導下，用盡心血創作了新穎的意象學題材。全書分七章，經由文學、美學與哲學的詮釋角度，滲透著她對廟宇石雕的熱情和文化的思索。其中，不乏描繪石雕的讚頌，作者懷著純真的心靈和對艋舺龍山寺石雕探索的青春理想，與建築藝術進行精神和情感的交流，直接表露對廟宇石雕藝術的摯愛。

黃淑貞的文學道路正如她的人生道路一樣起伏，既有十餘年任教於國中經歷，又有峰迴路轉之勢。然而，多次獲得全國創新教學活動設計特優獎，與中學生一起努力於公共藝術等教學活動，正是她生命中最為快樂的時期。此後，她所塑造的堅毅形象也一步步向

評黃淑貞《以石傳情──談廟宇石雕意象及其美感》

光明靠攏。博士畢業後,再度投身教職,投入最愛的文學研究,專研文章章法、中國語文教學、建築美學領域。在我眼底,淑貞是滿懷信心、有理想能堅持到底的人;有快樂、有煩憂,敏感又聰慧的性格。此書很榮幸地由台灣「國立臺灣藝術教育館」評選中脫穎而出,贊助成書;而這似乎恰好說明了作者論文的優越性,在這個意義上,此書拓展了石雕的意境,也豐富了其表現力。

—2010.10.22 作

【福建省《莆田學院學報》,第 17 卷,第 6 期,總第 71 期,2010.12,頁〈封三〉。】

I. Cultural Connotation and Aesthetic Viewpoint of Stone Carving Imagery

Stone carving refers to traditional Chinese handicrafts carved from stone. The author personally felt the simplicity of the temple's stone carvings, and his heart felt fulfilled and joyful. She carefully observes the cultural connotations of stone carving imagery with text and visual language, prompting academic circles such as architecture to explore and reflect on the aesthetic background hidden in this subject matter.

First of all, what is aesthetics? The Greek translation is aisthetikos. In short, it is "a sensory experience with art as the main object." It is rooted in people's aesthetic relationship to reality, and through creation, it develops into a scientific law of beauty or the sublime. Aesthetic consciousness is a metaphysical artistic intuition, an original and profound aesthetic experience experienced through human spirituality.

This paper does not deviate from the unique cultural connotation and aesthetic characteristics of stone carving, but focuses on improving the appreciation level of enthusiasts and readers. How to highlight aesthetic viewpoints is an innovative perspective that stone carving art needs to reflect on its depth and connotation, so as to reflect the author's spiritual nature in order to benefit the study of his works.

文評集粹讀本
-Selected Readings in Literary Reviews-

According to historical records, "Monga" is the old name of Wanhua District in Taipei City, and it was the earliest developed place in Taipei City after the Japanese occupation. The saying "One Fu, two Lukang, and three Mengjia" illustrates the former glory of the Wanhua area. It also represents that its early development was on par with Tainan and Lukang, which is of great historical significance. Temples are the place where our ancestors placed their spiritual lives. Stone carvings not only serve as decorations, but also reflect the psychological needs of our ancestors and have symbolic historical significance.

The Longshan Temple in Monga was founded in the third year of Emperor Qianlong's reign in the Qing Dynasty (1738 AD), and has a history of 272 years. It was designated as a national second-class historical site by the Ministry of the Interior in 1985. It has undergone major renovations during the Jiaqing period, minor renovations during the Tongzhi period, major renovations during the Taisho period under Japanese rule, and several renovations after Taiwan's restoration. According to historical records, during the major renovation in 1920, stonemasons such as Zhuang Defa and Jiang Jinhui were hired from Hui'an, China; when the main hall was rebuilt again in 1955, masters such as Zhang Mucheng, Jiang Anshui and Jiang Yinqiang were responsible for the dragon pillars. The temple has a total area of over 1,800 square meters. It faces south and is shaped like a "sun". It is a traditional three-courtyard palace-style building that integrates Confucianism, Buddhism and Taoism. Among them, stone carving art is the most prominent. Inside the hall, there is a pair of bronze coiled dragon eaves columns, flower and bird columns, and stone carvings on the wall buttresses, all of which are exquisitely crafted. The stones used mainly include Quanzhou white stone, Qingdou stone, Long stone and Guanyinshan stone. The stone carvings and wall blocks have extremely elegant and delicate textures.

The main hall has a double-eaved roof with hip roofs and corridors on all four sides, and is made up of forty-two pillars in total. The spiral caisson on the roof of the temple is constructed entirely of brackets without using a single nail or piece of iron, and the carvings on the shrine are extremely delicate. The ridge bands and flying eaves are shaped like auspicious animals such as dragons, phoenixes and unicorns, and are decorated with colored glass and porcelain tiles and colorful pottery. The rear hall is divided into three groups of roofs by gables. The middle one is of the double-eaved hip-and-gable style[3], and the two wings are of the single-eaved hip-and-gable style.[4] The author looks at the heroic characters in historical novels and the images and aesthetic connotations they express through the stone carvings in the

---

[3] The structural diagram of the hip-and-gable roof with double eaves (see Figure 1). The hip-and-gable roof has four sloping roof surfaces that turn into vertical triangular walls. It consists of one main ridge, four vertical ridges and four secondary ridges, so it is also called nine-ridge roof. There are two types of hip roofs: single-eaved and double-eaved. The so-called double-eaved means adding another layer of eaves under the basic hip roof, which is roughly the same as the second eaves of the gable roof. This overlapping concept usually has a hip roof as the upper eaves, riding on top of a hard mountain roof, with a tall and gorgeous form. Secondly, the wooden brackets exposed between the upper and lower eaves are also the focus of decoration. This structure can solve the problems of ventilation and partial lighting. Generally, the roof of the main hall in a Buddhist temple is a double-eaved hip roof. For example, China's Tiananmen Square, the Gate of Supreme Harmony in the Forbidden City, the Hall of Preserving Harmony, and the Palace of Heavenly Purity all have double-eaved hip roofs. The Longshan Temple in Wanhua, Taiwan also has a double-eaved hip roof structure, but the North Gate of Taipei City has a single-eaved hip roof. In ancient China, the styles of building roofs were strictly restricted by class. Among them, the double-eaved hip roof is higher in rank than the single-eaved hip roof and only lower in rank than the double-eaved hip roof, while the single-eaved hip roof is lower than the single-eaved hip roof. It can only be used in the main hall of the residences of officials above the fifth rank. Later, some private houses also began to use the hip roof.

[4] The single-eaved hip roof structure diagram (see Figure 2) shows that the hip roof is a five-ridge, two-slope roof with two slopes, consisting of a main ridge and four vertical ridges. Its biggest feature is that the gables on both sides completely cover the purlins. Since the eaves do not extend beyond the gables, it is called a hard mountain. The roof is flush with the gable at the gable head, with no protruding parts, and is simple and plain. It is the lowest in level, lower than the hip roof, gable roof and hip roof. According to Qing Dynasty regulations, the main hall of the residence of officials below the sixth rank and civilians could only have a hip roof or a gable roof. Many of the rooms on both sides of the palace walls also have gable roofs. The hip roof appeared relatively late in written records and was not found in the "Construction Regulations" of the Song Dynasty. It may be that with the widespread use of brick and stone to construct houses during the Ming and Qing dynasties, gable roofs were widely adopted. The characteristic of the hard top is that it is conducive to preventing wind and fire, while the gable top is conducive to preventing rain.

temple. On the whole, the temple is the focus of the spiritual life of immigrants. It preserves many traditional cultures and historical allusions. The story contents are mostly taken from folk stories such as *Romance of the Three Kingdoms* and *Investiture of the Gods*. There are many stone carvings rubbings by calligraphers on the outer wall of the Sanchuan Hall, which is also a treasure trove of stone carving skills.

The discussion of *Expressing Emotions through Stone* is based on the theory of the "many, two, one (0)" structure, exploring the various textures and styles formed by stone carving images. The author believes that art is an organism, which is the rotation of "force" internally and an independent "unified" form externally. After integrating "many" and "two", the style, charm, atmosphere, realm, etc. formed belong to "one (0)". It can create various aesthetic effects such as "unified beauty", "artistic beauty" and "chaotic beauty". There is indeed a clear thread to be found in her research, just like the imagery and simple architecture she puts into stone carving, both of which can enhance readers' literacy in the integration of art and culture.

II. From accidental thinking to the association of stone carving images

Temple stone carvings have always been regarded as the quintessence of Chinese art. Although some of them have gone through thousands of years, the brilliance radiating from them is still shining. From these solidified lives, we not only see the history of our great nation, but also deeply understand the true meaning of stone carving art creation.

The expression of Taiwan's temple stone carving art has its own specific regulations and principles, influenced by factors such as traditional architectural spatial concepts, ritual order relationships, and visual sensitivity. *Expressing Emotions through Stone* mainly explores the associative and symbolic nature of stone carving imagery history and architectural aesthetic thinking.

Temple stone carvings are the most symbolic architectural aesthetics in China, and they also have both decorative and subtle educational functions. From the book, I observed that there are three specific symbols of the Monga Longshan Temple: (1) In addition to being the spiritual belief center of most residents nearby, the thick texture of its stone and the exquisite carving skills of the masters have carved out the architectural beauty of the reliefs, thus achieving the purpose of education and awe. (2) Among the grass leaf patterns carved in the stone in Longshan Temple, Ganoderma lucidum is the most common. According to research, Ganoderma lucidum has the effect of prolonging life and is also a symbol of Naruhito. Here, the association of images can also express the universe from the spiritual to the natural. The temple stone sculptors focus on depicting the most subtle corners of the viewer's mind to the vast horizon of the universe. Through the broad aesthetic connotation and lofty spirit of stone carving art, they leave precious historical records for future generations. (3) The "Dragon Pillar", the best of stone carving art, has an aesthetic recognition and aesthetic value because it is a kind of carved column. Although the patterns of dragon pillars vary from era to era, the earlier and more common dragon pillar shapes are simpler and more powerful. For example, the dragon pillar of Longshan Temple in Monga is carved with a long coiled dragon and some clouds and water wave patterns.

But after Emperor Xianfeng, many temples added figures and horses to the dragon pillars, or decorated them with auspicious beasts, immortals, etc. However, I think that the more complex and gorgeous the carvings are, the more the simple architectural sense is lost. Fortunately, the transmission of historical stories by the Monga Longshan Temple is extremely tolerant and interesting; there is also a great deal of freedom in the use and combination of stone or pattern forms, which can trigger different emotions and associations of the viewer's modern aesthetic subject, giving rise to different aesthetic feelings.

As far as I know, relevant domestic literature in the past has not made any outstanding achievements in the description of temple stone carvings. It is especially true that the architectural community has neglected literary research on historical and cultural theories. This book integrates the author's knowledge and consciously uses temple stone carvings to change and broaden readers' previously familiar perspectives on architectural art. It not only brings new aesthetic content to Taiwan's architectural and literary circles, but also lays the foundation for the future development of Chinese research on temple stone carvings.

From the perspective of consciousness and aesthetics, it manifests itself as a spiritual existence. The author is an outstanding scholar and writer in Taiwan. She does not cater to the public's aesthetic taste, but dares to innovate. She chooses seemingly unpopular temple stone carvings as the theme, and carefully photographs many poetic patterns, such as the gossip on the vase, the story of Liu Bei's appointment at Ganlu Temple, various symbolic signs of flowers, gourds, whisks, incense burners, stationery, etc., all of which are given new interpretations and life. His tireless spirit and hard work have paid off. However, it is this personality that has made her unique style. Her new pursuit of stone carving art aesthetics, from the spiritual connotation of her works to the textual expression, has surpassed the times and also demonstrated her extraordinary artistic aesthetic taste. For example, she narrated a passage: "On the wall of the rear hall of Longshan Temple, there is a stone carving of 'a red-haired foreigner riding an elephant and blowing a conch shell', with vase blocks on both sides. The carving is vivid, indicating that foreigners were invited to guard the temple, reflecting the people's dissatisfaction with foreign countries in the early days of Sino-Western contact, and also implies 'auspicious sounds herald peace'." This kind of interpretation method has the effect of adding the finishing touch to teaching; and through publication and discussion, Taiwanese readers are able to trace the architectural aesthetic thinking and literary traces of the Longshan Temple in Monga.

III. Conclusion: Thoughts after watching *Stones of Love*

To sum up, Huang Shuzhen is academically knowledgeable and her writing is profound and far-reaching. The text is concise and novel and worth reading. All these show its elegant and simple nature. After a quick reading, I found that *Expressing Emotions through Stone* is rich in historical materials. From the references, I can imagine that she has read many little-known ancient books and Chinese and foreign archives, and her discussion is also objective and straightforward. Under the guidance of Professor Chen Manming, an expert in imagism at National Taiwan Normal University, the author devoted all his efforts to creating novel imagistic themes. The book is divided into seven chapters, which are permeated with her passion for temple stone carvings and cultural thinking through the perspectives of literature, aesthetics and philosophy. Among them, there are many praises for stone carvings.

評黃淑貞《以石傳情──談廟宇石雕意象及其美感》

With a pure heart and youthful ideals of exploring the stone carvings of Longshan Temple in Mengjia, the author has a spiritual and emotional exchange with the architectural art, and directly expresses his love for the temple stone carving art.

  Huang Shuzhen's literary path is as ups and downs as her life path. She has taught in junior high school for more than ten years, and has also experienced twists and turns. However, the happiest period of her life was when she won many National Excellence Awards for Innovative Teaching Activity Design and worked with middle school students on teaching activities such as public art. Since then, the strong image she created has gradually moved towards the light. After graduating with a doctorate, he returned to teaching and devoted himself to his favorite literary research, specializing in article structure, Chinese language teaching, and architectural aesthetics. In my eyes, Shuzhen is a person who is full of confidence, has ideals and can persevere to the end; she has a happy, worried, sensitive and intelligent personality. This book was honored to be selected and sponsored by the National Taiwan Center for Arts Education in Taiwan; this seems to just illustrate the superiority of the author's thesis. In this sense, this book expands the artistic conception of stone carving and enriches its expressiveness.

—Written on October 22, 2010.

〖*Journal of Putian University*, Fujian Province, Vol. 17, No. 6, No. 71, 2010.12, page "Cover 3".〗

來自 2025.04.29 哈佛大學圖書館感謝信

尊敬的林明理博士：

  我謹代表哈佛圖書館，對您於 2025 年 4 月 29 日收到的以下捐贈表示感謝：

  《漢魏六朝接明理》

  自 1638 年以來，哈佛大學一直受益於朋友、教職員工、校友和其他有興趣創建和擴大圖書館藏書的人士的慷慨捐贈。圖書館盡一切努力將捐贈的資料添加到我們的永久收藏中。

  根據美國國稅局的要求和哈佛大學的禮品政策，這封信確認該禮物未提供任何商品或服務，並且大學保留將現有收藏中重複的物品或不屬於我們收藏政策範圍的物品出售給其他機構的權利。

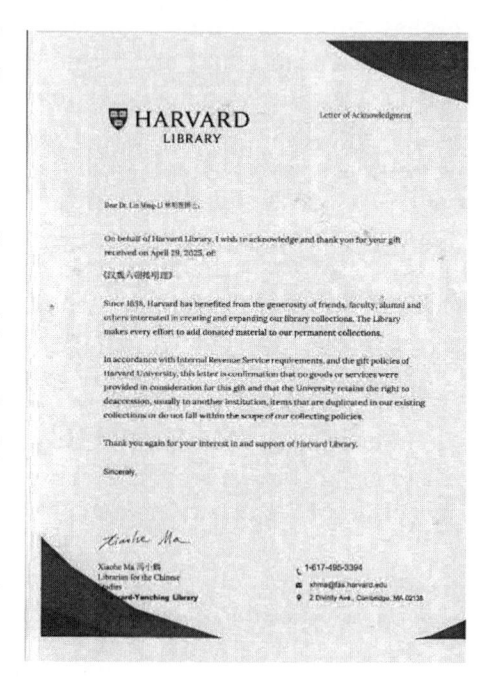

  再次感謝您對哈佛圖書館的關注與支持。

真摯地，
馬小鶴

國家圖書館出版品預行編目資料

文評集粹讀本（漢英對照）／林明理　著、張智中　譯
－初版－
臺中市：天空數位圖書　2025.06
面：17*23 公分
ISBN：978-626-7576-18-2（平裝）
1. CST：詩評
812.18　　　　　　　　　　　　　　　　　　114008406

書　　　名：文評集粹讀本（漢英對照）
發　行　人：蔡輝振
出　版　者：天空數位圖書有限公司
作　　　者：林明理
譯　　　者：張智中
美工設計：設計組
版面編輯：採編組
出版日期：2025 年 6 月（初版）
銀行名稱：合作金庫銀行南台中分行
銀行帳戶：天空數位圖書有限公司
銀行帳號：006—1070717811498
郵政帳戶：天空數位圖書有限公司
劃撥帳號：22670142
定　　　價：新台幣 680 元整
電子書發明專利第　Ｉ　306564　號
※如有缺頁、破損等請寄回更換

版權所有請勿仿製

服務項目：個人著作、學位論文、學報期刊等出版印刷及DVD製作
影片拍攝、網站建置與代管、系統資料庫設計、個人企業形象包裝與行銷
影音教學與技能檢定系統建置、多媒體設計、電子書製作及客製化等
TEL　　：(04)22623893　　　　MOB：0900602919
FAX　　：(04)22623863
E-mail　：familysky@familysky.com.tw
Https　：//www.familysky.com.tw/
地　　址：台中市南區忠明南路 787 號 30 樓國王大樓
No.787-30, Zhongming S. Rd., South District, Taichung City 402, Taiwan (R.O.C.)